D0381992

# DEVIL SAID
# BANG

# DEVIL SAID BANG

## A SANDMAN SLIM NOVEL

### RICHARD KADREY

HARPER Voyager
*An Imprint of HarperCollinsPublishers*

DEVIL SAID BANG. Copyright © 2012 by Richard Kadrey. All rights reserved. Printed in the United States of America. No part of this book may be used or reproduced in any manner whatsoever without written permission except in the case of brief quotations embodied in critical articles and reviews. For information address HarperCollins Publishers, 10 East 53rd Street, New York, NY 10022.

HarperCollins books may be purchased for educational, business, or sales promotional use. For information please write: Special Markets Department, HarperCollins Publishers, 10 East 53rd Street, New York, NY 10022.

FIRST EDITION

*Designed by Paula Russell Szafranski*

Library of Congress Cataloging-in-Publication Data has been applied for.

ISBN 978-0-06-209457-5

12 13 14 15 16 OV/RRD 10 9 8 7 6 5 4 3 2 1

*To Ginger and Diana for making this happen.*

*And to Holly, Sarah, and Dave for the gravy.*

*To descend into Hell is easy; Night and day, the gates*
*of dark Death stand wide; But to climb back again, to*
*retrace one's steps to the upper air—There's the rub,*
*the task.*

—*Aeneid*, BOOK 6

*In this world there's two kinds of people, my friend:*
*those with loaded guns and those who dig. You dig.*

—CLINT EASTWOOD, *The Good, the Bad and the Ugly*

# ACKNOWLEDGMENTS

Thanks to Patty for the art and Wil for being an excellent guy. Thanks to Elsabeth Hermens for anime advice and to Tim Holland for French guidance. Thanks to Dino, Martha, and Lorenzo for letting me tag along. Thanks to Pamela Spengler-Jaffee, Jessie Edwards, Will Hinton, and the rest of the team at HarperCollins. And thanks as well to everyone on Twitter and Facebook who sent in song suggestions. As always, thanks to Nicola for everything else.

# DEVIL SAID BANG

"Me and the Devil Blues"

"Devil's Stompin' Ground"

"Your Pretty Face Is Going to Hell"

"Don't Shake Me, Lucifer"

"Hell Is Around the Corner"

"Hellnation"

"Up Jumped the Devil"

I punch the tunes into the jukebox and make sure it's turned up loud. I've loaded up the juke with a hundred or so devil tunes. The Hellion Council can't stand it when I come to a meeting with a pocketful of change. Wild Bill, the bartender, hates it too, but he's a damned soul I recruited for the job, so he gets why I do it. I head back to the table and nod to him. He shakes his head and goes back to cleaning glasses.

Les Baxter winds down a spooky "Devil Cult" as I sit down with the rest of Hell's ruling council. We've been here in the Bamboo House of Dolls for a couple of hours. My head hurts from reports, revised timetables, and learned opinions. If I didn't have the music to annoy everyone with, I would probably have killed them all by now.

Buer slides a set of blueprints in my direction.

Hellions look sort of like the little demons in that Hieronymus Bosch painting *The Garden of Earthly Delights*. Some look pretty human. Some look like the green devils on old absinthe bottles. Some are like what monsters puke up after a long weekend of eating other monsters. Buer looks like a cuttlefish in a Hugo Boss suit and smells like a pet-store Dumpster.

"What do you think of the colonnades?" he asks.

"The colonnades?"

"Yes. I redesigned the colonnades."

"What the fuck are colonnades?"

General Semyazah, the supreme commander of Hell's legions, sighs and points to a line of pillars at the center of the page. "That is a colonnade."

"Ah."

If the hen scratchings on the blueprints are different from the last bunch of hen scratchings Buer showed me, I sure as hell can't tell. I say the first thing that pops into my head.

"Were those statues there before?"

Buer waves his little cuttlefish tentacles and moves his finger across the paper.

"They're new. A different icon for each of the Seven Noble Virtues."

He's not lying. They're all there. All the personality quirks that give Hellions a massive cultural hard-on. Cunning. Ruthlessness. Ferocity. Deception. Silence. Strength. Joy. They're represented by a collection of demonic marble figures with leathery wings and forked tongues, bent spines and razor dorsal fins, clusters of eyestalks and spider legs. The colonnades look like the most fucked-up miniature golf course in the universe and they're on what's supposed to be the new City Hall.

"I have an idea. How about instead of the Legion of Doom

we put up the Rat Pack and the lyrics to 'Luck Be a Lady'?"

"Excuse me?" says Buer.

"What I mean is, it looks a little fascist."

"Thank you."

"That wasn't a compliment."

I push the blueprints away with the sharpened fingers of my left hand, the ugly prosthetic one on my ugly prosthetic arm.

Buer doesn't know how to react. None of them do.

There's Buer the builder, Semyazah the general, Obyzuth the sorceress, and Marchosias the politician. Old Greek kings used to have councils like this, and since a certain friend hinted I should read up on the Greeks, I have a council too. The last member of the Council is Lucifer. That's me. But I'll get to that part later. The five of us are the big brains supposedly in charge of Hell. Really, we're a bunch of second-rate mechanics trying to keep the wheels from coming off a burning gasoline truck skidding toward a school bus full of orphans and kittens.

The Council is staring at me. I've been down here a hundred days and still, anytime I say anything but yes or no, they look at me like I'm a talking giraffe. Hellions just aren't used to humans giving them back talk. That's okay. I can use that. Let them find me a little strange. A little inexplicable. Playing the Devil is easier if no one has any idea what you're going to do or say next.

They're all still waiting. I let them.

We have these meetings every couple of days. We're rebuilding Hell after it went up in flames like a flash-paper bikini when the original Lucifer, the real Lucifer, blew out of town after sticking me with the job. The trouble for the rest of the Council is that I don't know how fast I want Downtown back in working order.

I say to Buer, "I'm fine with Hellion pride. It's troubled times, the team's in last place, and they need a pep rally. Cool. But I don't want Hell's capital looking like we're about to goose-step into Poland."

Obyzuth turns the blueprints around. I still don't know what she looks like. She wears an ivory mask that covers everything but her eyes, and a curtain of gold beads covers them.

She says, "Buer's designs expand and celebrate many of the classic historical motifs of Hellion design. I like them."

Obyzuth is into the spiritual side of the rebuild and doesn't usually comment on things like this. I've upset her. Good.

I say, "This Nazi Disneyland stuff, it's too cheap and easy. It's like something the Kissi would dream up."

That's hitting below the belt. Calling a Hellion a Kissi is like calling Chuck Norris Joseph Stalin. Buer looks like he wants to stuff the blueprints down my throat with a road flare. Obyzuth and Semyazah look at me like they caught me eating cookies before dinner. Marchosias raises her eyebrows, which is about an inch from her challenging me to a duel at dawn.

The Bad Dad thing usually works. Hellions are big on pecking orders and I have to remind them regularly who's at the top. Now they need a pat on the head from Good Dad before things go all Hansel and Gretel and I end up in the oven.

"You're a talented guy, Buer. You get to redesign all of

Pandemonium for the first time in about a billion years. No one's going to get a chance like that again. Throw out the Albert Speer bullshit and modern up. When God tossed you fallen bastards into Hell the builders were the only ones who saw it as more than a pile of rocks and dust. Do that again."

I can't believe I'm learning how politics and court intrigue work. I feel a little dirty. I miss punching people. It's honest work but I don't get to do it much these days.

Marchosias shakes her head. She's skinny, pale, and birdlike, but her instincts are more like those of a velociraptor.

"I'm not sure. In unstable times people need comfort. They need the familiar."

"No. They don't. They need to see that whoever's in charge has balls and vision. They need to see that we're making a new, bigger, and better Hell than they ever had before."

Obyzuth nods a little to herself.

She says, "I cast the stones this morning, and although I like Buer's work, if things must change, the signs are in an auspicious alignment for it."

"See? We've got auspicious alignments and everything. We're golden. Let's draw up some new plans."

I pick up a handful of little crackers from a bowl on the table and pop them one by one into my mouth. Really, they're fried drytt eggs. Drytts are big, annoying Hellion sand fleas. I know that sounds disgusting, but this is Hell. Besides, if you fry anything long enough, it gets good. The drytt eggs go down like fried popcorn.

Semyazah hardly reacts to anything in these meetings and he chooses his words carefully. He says, "You've been dismissing everyone's ideas for weeks. What ideas do you have?"

"I worry about this place ending up like L.A. All Hellion strip malls, T-shirts, and titty bars. The Pandemonium I remember is more of a Bela Lugosi–and–fog kind of town. When I have to choose between *Dark Shadows* or fanny packs, I'll step over to the dark side every time. Have any of you ever seen a Fritz Lang movie called *Metropolis*?"

They shake their heads.

"You would love it. It's about bigwigs that kick the shit out of proles in a city that's all mile-high skyscrapers, smoke-belching machines, and office towers that look like dragons fucking spaceships. The place is clean, precise, and soul crushing, but with style. Just like you. So that's everyone's homework. Watch *Metropolis*. It's in the On Demand menu."

That's right. Hell steals cable. Call a cop.

The three most popular TV shows Downtown are Lucha Libre, Japanese game shows, and *The Brady Bunch*, which Hellions seem to think is a deep anthropological study of mortal life. I hope watching the Bradys depresses them as much as being trapped here in Creation's shit pipe depresses me.

"Let's take a break. I need a drink."

I walk to the bar and sit down. I make the Council hold its meetings here for a couple of reasons. The first is that Hellions love their rituals, and trying to get anything done is like a Japanese tea ceremony crossed with a High Mass, only even slower. There's enough ritual hand waving down here to put the Dalai Lama to sleep.

Reason two is this place. It's Hell's version of my favorite L.A. bar, the Bamboo House of Dolls. The main difference between this and the other Bamboo House is that Carlos runs the bar in L.A. In Hell, it's my great-great-great-granddad, Wild Bill Hickok.

Wild Bill already has a glass of Aqua Regia ready for me when I sit down.

"What do you think?" I ask.

"About what?"

"About what. About the damn meeting."

"I think you're about to drive them fellers crazy."

"They're not all fellers."

He squints at the Council.

"There's ladies in the bunch?"

"Two."

"Damn. I never did learn to tell the difference with Hellions. 'Course they're all pig-fucking sons of bitches to me, so what do I care if I guess wrong and hurt their feelings?"

I don't think running a bar was ever Bill's dream job and he's not exactly the type to throw around a lot of thank-yous, but I know he likes it better here than in Butcher Valley. Bill died in 1876, was damned, and he's been fighting hand to hand with other killers and shootists in that punishment hellhole ever since. Taking him out was the least I could do for family.

"Is anyone giving you trouble? Do they know who you run the place for?"

"I expect everyone's aware by now. Which don't make me particularly happy. I'm not used to another man fighting my battles for me."

"Think of it this way. This setup isn't just about me having a place to drink. It's about showing the blue bloods who's in charge. If anyone hassles you, it means they're hassling me, and I need to do something loud and messy about it."

He puffs his cigar and sets it on the edge of the bar. There are scorch marks all over the wood.

"Sounds like it's hard work playing Old Nick. I don't envy you."

"I don't envy me either. And you didn't answer my questions."

He's silent for a moment, still annoyed that I'm asking about his well-being.

"No. No one in particular's been causing me grief. These lizardy bastards ain't exactly housebroken, but they don't treat me any worse than they treat each other. And they only get up to that when you and your compadres aren't around. That's when the rowdies come in."

"If you hear anything interesting, you know what to do."

"I might be dead and damned for all eternity but I'm not addle-brained. I remember."

We turn and look at the Council.

He says, "So which one do you figure is going to kill you first?"

"None of them. Semyazah is too disciplined. He saw Hell come apart the last time it didn't have a Lucifer. I don't really get a whiff of murder from any of the others. Do you?"

I finish my drink. He pours me another and one for himself.

"Not them directly. But I figure at least one's scribbling down everything and passing it to whoever's going to do the actual pigsticking."

"That's why I keep the rebuilding slow. Keep the big boys

busy and scattered all over. Makes it harder for them to plan my tragic demise."

"It's funny hearing blood talk like that. I wasn't exactly a planner when I was alive and it never crossed my mind anyone else in the family would ever come by the trait."

"It's new. Since I moved into Lucifer's place, I spend a lot of time in the library. I never read anything longer than the back of a video jacket before. I think it's bent my brain."

"Books and women'll do that. Just don't get to thinking such big thoughts you forget to listen for what's creeping up behind you."

"I never read with my back to the door."

He nods and downs his drink in one gulp.

"All it takes is the one time," Bill says. He looks past my shoulder. "I think your friends are waiting on you."

"Later, Wild Bill."

"Give 'em hell, boy."

The others look impatient when I get back. For a second, I flash on Candy back in L.A. After knowing each other for almost a year, we'd finally gotten together right before I came down here. Managed to squeeze in two good days together. What would she think of Hell's ruling elite hanging on my every word? She'd probably laugh her ass off.

"We did all right today. Knowing what you don't want is about as good as knowing what you do. Let's meet back here at the same time in three days. That enough time for you to sketch out some ideas, Buer?"

He nods.

"I'll watch your *Metropolis* show tonight. And have something for you at the next meeting."

"That's it, then. Anyone have any questions. Any thoughts? Any banana-bread recipes to share with the class?"

Nothing. Hell's a tough room. They gather up papers and notes. Stuff them in leather bags and attaché cases.

"Thanks for coming."

I head back to the bar, where Wild Bill is already pouring me a drink. I need a smoke. I take out a pack of Maledictions and light one up. It might be Hell but at least you can smoke in the bars.

Bill pours a second drink in a different glass and walks away.

Marchosias is behind me. She does this after meetings sometimes. She says she wants to practice her English. I don't mind; after three months of speaking nothing but Hellion, my throat feels like I've been gargling roofing nails.

She says, "What you said to Buer, that was either very rude or very smart."

"The Devil gets to be both at once. It's in the handbook. Look it up."

"You caught everyone off guard. I've never heard you ever mention the Kissi before. Everyone admires how you handled them, you know. Getting others to do your killing is the most elegant way and you did it masterfully."

In another time and place I'd think she was being sarcastic, but I know she's not. She gets off on what I did. Why not? I brought the Kissi down here like we were allies, trapped them between Heaven's armies and Hell's legions, and wiped out most of them in one big royal rumble. That kind of treachery covers pretty much all of the Seven Noble Virtues. Her making goo-goo eyes at me for it makes me want to punch Marchosias very hard and often.

I say, "I'm usually more of a hands-on guy when it comes to killing."

"Of course you are. Sandman Slim has an ocean of blood on his hands. 'The monster who kills monsters,' isn't that what they called you in the arena? Now here you are, Lucifer, the greatest monster of them all. Maybe God really does have a sense of humor."

Her eyes shine when she says it. She loves being this close to the grand marshal of the Underworld parade. She'd like to have Lucifer's power but the thought of it scares her stupid, which makes it that much more exciting. This is why she stays behind. An intimate tête-à-tête with Satan. It's not getting her any brownie points with me and she knows it, but it makes the rest of the Council nervous and that makes it fun for her.

I take a long drag on the Malediction like maybe it'll start a tornado and carry me back home like Dorothy.

"All things considered, I'd rather be in Philadelphia."

She looks at me and then glances at Wild Bill, not getting the joke. Bill ignores her and wipes down another glass.

"While I have you here, you've never told me why you chose me for your council. Or why you decided to create it. Lucifer—"

"The former Lucifer, you mean," I cut her off. "I'm Lucifer now. That other guy goes by Samael these days and he's home crashing with Daddy."

"Pardon me. Samael would never have considered working with anyone but his most trusted generals."

"Maybe if he'd asked more questions, this place wouldn't look like a second-rate Hiroshima. I don't have a problem with getting advice from smart people. And to answer your question, Samael recommended you."

"I'm honored."

She glances over her shoulder. The others are all outside. She's enjoying making them wait.

I say, "Your English is getting better."

"So is your Hellion. You've lost most of your accent."

"Someone told me I sounded like a hick."

"Not that bad. But you've become more dignified, in every way."

"I'll have to watch that. Dignity gives me gas."

Over by the door of the bar someone says, "Are you ready to go, Lucifer?"

It's a military cop named Vetis. He runs my security squad. He's a mother-hen pain in my ass but he's an experienced vet with his shit wired tight. He looks like Eliot Ness if Eliot Ness had a horse skull for a head.

"I'm staying but the lady will be right out."

Vetis goes outside. I nod toward the door.

"Your caravan is waiting."

Marchosias straightens to leave but doesn't move.

"You never come back with us. Why not ride in my limousine with me? It's very comfortable and roomy."

All the councilors travel in individual limos and vans between a dozen guard vehicles. It's like the president, the pope, and Madonna cruising town with a company of demon Wyatt Earps riding shotgun.

"Thanks, but I have my own way back."

"You don't trust me."

"Would you?"

She picks up her bag.

"Probably not."

"Anyway, I like to clear my head after a meeting."

"Of course. I'll see you in three days."

"It's a date."

She slides a leather satchel over her shoulder. Rumor is that the leather is the tanned skin of an old political opponent.

I call after her.

"One more thing. I know one of you is gunning for me. When I find out who it is, I'm going to stuff their skull with skyrockets and set them off like the Fourth of July. Feel free to tell the others. Or keep it to yourself. You're smart. You'll know which is best."

She raises her eyebrows slightly. This time in amusement. She gives me a brief smile and walks out.

Of course she's not going to tell the others. Just like none of them said a word to her when I told them.

"That got her attention," says Bill.

"I already had her attention. She won't tell the others, but I want to see if she tells anyone else."

Bill shakes his head.

"She's not going to tell a soul. She's got a knife tucked up that right sleeve, you know."

"Everyone knows. That's what it's there for."

When Bill starts to pour me another drink, I put my hand over the glass.

"How do you know she's not the one making a play for you?"

"I don't. I don't know about any of them. I'm just stirring the pot and waiting for something interesting to happen."

"That sounds like putting your boot up the ass of fate, and that's a mite dangerous."

I shrug and puff on the Malediction.

"I'm locked in a loony bin with God's worst brats. I have to do something. It's screw with them or get a dog, and I'm not a dog person."

Bill nods. His eyes go soft like they do when he remembers his life before he took a bullet in the back.

"I'm not much for dogs either. I saw an elephant in a tent show once and thought it might be a fine thing to have one of them. Ride up on some Abilene rowdies atop that walking gray mountain and take bets on which of them shits himself first. Yes sir, I'd prefer an elephant to a dog any day."

I push away from the bar and get up.

"Look for a big box and a ton of peanuts on your birthday, Bill."

He hands me the leather jacket and helmet I keep behind the bar during meetings. Let the rest of the Council ride through town like Caesar's army. I'll take my bike down and do a flat-out burn all the way to the palace. Yes, I have a palace. I'm a rich, pampered prince and politician. I'm everything I ever hated.

I slip on the jacket and put on my gloves. Bill watches me out of the corner of his eye, pretending to wipe down the bar. My prosthetic hand and arm are a beautiful horror. A weird combination of organic and inorganic. Like something someone pried off a robot insect. The Terminator meets the Fly. I look at Bill. He nods at my hand.

"Seeing that thing disappear always puts me in a pleasant

mood. No offense, but I keep waiting for it to creep over here and strangle me with my own damn bar rag."

"You have my permission to shoot it if it does."

"Good, 'cause I wasn't going to take the time to ask."

I grab a handful of the drytt-egg crackers, pop a few in my mouth, and put the rest in my jacket pocket.

"Keep your ears open for me."

"I always do," says Wild Bill.

I go out through the rear exit. The motorcycle is parked out back, covered with the dirtiest, shittiest tarp in Hell. No one is ever going to look under it.

They don't exactly have a lot of stock motorcycles Downtown, so I had some of the local engineers build me a 1965 Electra Glide. I'll give the local boys and girls credit. They did their best, but it's a lot more Hellion than Harley. It's built like a mechanical bull covered in plate armor. The handlebars taper to points like they'd be happier on a longhorn's head. The exhaust belches dragon fire and the panhead engine is so hypercharged I can get it glowing cherry red on a long straightaway. There's no speedometer, so I don't know how fast that is, but I'm pretty sure I'm leaving a few land-speed records in the dust.

I swing my leg over the bike and kick it to life. I always put on my helmet last. It's the story of my life that I had to come to Hell to start wearing a helmet. Back in L.A., Saint James, my angel half, hated that I rode bareheaded. All I had to worry about back home was cops. Here it's the paparazzi. I like my solo rides and don't want the rabble to know about them. They give me a chance to blow off steam. Plus, I get to see Pandemonium at street level without flunkies or political suck-ups telling me what they think I want to hear.

I gun the bike and swing into the street. I don't worry about traffic. The streets are still a bombed-out wreck in this part of town, so most of the traffic is trucks hauling soldiers and supplies. Almost everyone else is on foot. I rev the engine, turn, and blast down a side street, taking the long way back to the palace.

Block after block, streets are buckled and houses are knocked off their foundations. But now there's food in the markets and the burning buildings aren't the only lights in the streets. I steer around a panel truck where Hellion soldiers are dragging cuffed and shackled looters. The troops aren't gentle about it. The looters are a bloody limping mess. Fuck 'em.

It wasn't always like this Downtown. I spent eleven years trapped down here, so I got to know the place pretty well. But a mortal named Mason Faim and Lucifer's generals (Semyazah was the lone holdout) tried to start a war with Heaven. Bad idea. The city burned. The sky turned black. Earthquakes opened sinkholes that swallowed whole neighborhoods.

When I look at Hell, I see L.A. It's a funny kind of magic. A Convergence. An image of each place dropped over the other. It's weird but it makes it easier for me to get around. Hellions still see old Hell. They don't need a Fatburger at 2 A.M. If they did maybe they wouldn't be such 24/7 dicks.

I'm going slow putting the place back together, but I can't stall forever. I want to keep these devils, plotters, and knife-in-the-back bastards busy. But sooner or later they're going to finish rebuilding. Until then all I want is to not get assassinated and to figure a way back to the real L.A. and back to Candy, a girl I left behind.

There's a bottleneck up ahead where two collapsed buildings cover most of the street, their roofs almost touching. There's a slight incline between the buildings and smooth road beyond. If I hit it just right, I can get the bike airborne a few yards on the other side. I twist the throttle and I'm doing around fifty when I hit the incline.

They're waiting for me at the top. Two of them.

The one on the right catches me across the chest with a piece of rebar, and instead of a nice smooth flight on the back of the bike, I'm airborne all by myself, doing a backflip onto the asphalt.

I slam down on my gut and look up just as the second attacker gets to work. He runs up a big pile of rubble and launches himself off at me, an armored gorilla in SWAT-team coveralls and hobnail boots. I roll onto my back and try to get up.

Too slow.

He lands feetfirst on me like he thinks if he stomps hard enough he'll get wine. Hobnails isn't finished yet. He kicks me in the side. Long, careful, well-aimed kicks. This guy's had practice. A second later the guy with the rebar joins him in clog-dancing on my ribs. This isn't the quiet ride home I'd hoped for.

If I was a normal mortal, I'd be dead by now or at least a four-way gimp after Hobnails landed on me and snapped my spine. But I'm not a normal mortal and this isn't a normal situation. I'm hard to kill any day of the week and I'm even harder now that I have on Lucifer's armor under my shirt.

One of the goons has gotten bored with kicking and is looking around for something to drop on me. These assholes are having more fun than if they were at Chuck E. Cheese.

I push myself up onto my knees. Going to throw some crazy monkey-style Bruce Lee moves on these guys. Any second now. Soon.

But I just kneel there, letting the two idiots kick me. My mind goes blank. I have the sick, dizzy feeling that I forgot something. There's something I'm supposed to be doing or somewhere else I'm supposed to be. It feels like there's something crawling around behind my eyes. Maybe I'm just supposed to wait until these guys kick the living shit out of me.

Then the feeling is gone. It must have lasted all of ten seconds, but it was long enough for Hobnail and his friend to knock me back on my face. I reach into my pocket, get a handful of the drytt crackers, and throw them. The kicking stops. I push myself back onto my knees.

You know how young vampires without any training can be so twitchy and compulsive they have to organize anything you throw in front of them? The same goes for brain-dead Hellions, and these two don't look like they could run the fryer at McDonald's. When I tossed the crackers, they went for them like zombies after a one-legged blind man.

After all the body shots, I have to crawl a few feet before I can get up. I take off my helmet and set it on the pavement, getting out the black bone blade I always keep hidden in the waistband of my pants.

The Glimmer Twins are crouched on the street, pushing the eggs into neat piles. I wrap my arm around Hobnail's head, pull it back, and drag the blade across his throat. Black

Hellion blood oozes down over my arm like leaking engine oil. His friend is concentrating so hard on stacking eggs that he doesn't see the blade until the last minute. I swing and his head pops off and rolls away, coming to rest against my helmet.

I go over and look at it like maybe I'm going to have the head stuffed and mounted like a big-mouth bass. I'm waiting for a sound. And there it is. The tiniest tick as a boot comes down on a pebble behind me. I spin and toss the head like a scaly bowling ball. Hellion assassination teams usually work in threes. Seeing as how the first two had the combined IQ of waffle batter, whoever is left has to be the squad leader.

He's taller than the other two, with the same not-bright lizard look you see in a lot of the legion's grunts. His SWAT body armor is heavier than the others', so the head just knocks him off balance for a second. He has a Glock strapped to his hip, but he's making flashy fighting moves in the air with a couple of nasty-looking serrated long swords. He could go for the gun, but he wants to make himself a name by slicing up Lucifer old school. Fucking devils and their fucking rituals.

I take a step back like I'm dazzled by his video-game moves. I fought in the arena down here for years. Swords hurt, but after you get cut a few hundred times, they're about as scary as road rash. Meaning they're something to avoid if you can but they're nothing to lose sleep over. Still, they hurt and I'm already hurt. And I lost my snack.

He takes the bait and charges. I step forward and catch his wrist with my forearm, deflecting the blade as it comes down on my head. Now that I'm in striking range, the text-book step two of an attack like this is simple: while your opponent is busy blocking your downward attack, you step in with a forward thrust of your second blade, skewering him like a cocktail wiener. The only problem with it is that every sentient being in the universe knows it and is ready for it. Instead of attacking, I let him plant a powerful shot in my solar plexus. His blade kicks sparks when it hits the armor and snaps in two. It startles him long enough for me to move a couple of steps and plant a foot behind my helmet on the ground.

When he comes back at me, I kick, sending the helmet into his face like a cannonball. I hear bones crunch and he spins around before landing on his face. I stand over him, kick the sword out of his hand, and shove his pistol in my pocket. I grab him by the lapels, spin and slam him headfirst into a pile of rubble. While he's busy trying to breathe through a crushed face, I rifle his dead friends' pockets. Empty. They don't even have dog tags, so I can't tell what part of the legion they're from.

Their boots and body armor are the heavy kind issued to frontline infantry who are basically cannon fodder. But since the war with Heaven is over, clowns like this aren't supposed to have time on their hands. Avoiding this kind of fucking mess is why I'm going slow with the rebuilding. Why aren't these pricks with the rest of the grunts, clearing rubble or rebuilding roads? Did they think if they killed me, one of them would be the new Lucifer? Maybe they were going to share the title—Moe, Larry, and Curly, the Three Infernal Stooges. But not one of this bunch had the imagination or balls to try something like that on their own. Someone put them up to it.

The one I clocked with the helmet is coming around, so I go back to him.

I pick up the unbroken long sword and press it against his throat.

"You awake, sunshine?"

He grunts. Shakes his head, trying to clear it.

"Who sent you?"

"No one. I don't need permission to slaughter mortals."

I lean forward, using my weight to press the tip of the sword into him until he bleeds.

"This mortal signs your paychecks, ugly. Guess who's not getting a Christmas bonus?"

He grimaces and spits.

"A mortal will never be the true Lucifer. Mortals are spirits, good for nothing but torture and chores you could teach an animal. I curse you and the mortal Mason Faim. At least he promised us Heaven. What have you given us?"

"I haven't cut off your arms and legs and made you into a throw pillow. How's that?"

He tenses. Even with the sword at his throat he wants to lunge at me. This guy is the real deal. A true believer. His type built Auschwitz and had lynching parties back home. Who knows what games he and his friends are playing with souls down here?

I take the sword away from his throat and smack his mangled face with the broad side. He groans and doubles over. Lucky bastard. I'd like to be lying down groaning too. My bruised ribs hurt. I toss both of his swords into the nearby sinkhole.

"You still haven't answered my question. Who sent you here?"

He catches his breath and says, "We came on our own to kill the false Lord of Perdition."

I grab his head and press it back into the rubble. I've always been good at telling when people are lying, but Lucifer can see things I can't and the armor gives me bits and pieces of his powers. It's mostly sideshow-level tricks so far but I can tell if someone is wearing a glamour to conceal themselves or if they've been hexed. I look all the way to the back of the assassin's eyes. There's a fluttering inside, like a microscopic strobe light. That's it. He's hexed. Someone sent him and his friends out hunting for me and erased their memories so the fuckwits would think it was their idea. I let go of him and sit above him on the rubble.

"What's your name?"

He looks at me hard. He really hates being questioned by a mortal.

"Ukobach."

I could take Ukobach back to the palace, hand him over to the witches, and let them take his mind apart. They might be able to find something useful inside, but I'm not sure about this guy. Whoever picked these three chose them because they didn't have an overabundance of brain cells. With an intelligent Hellion or human, even after a memory wipe there's usually some residual impressions left. Sometimes you can find it if you dig deep enough and aren't worried about killing them or leaving them a vegetable. But with the power of the hex I saw in Ukobach's eyes, there isn't going to be anything useful inside him. I can't throw him in the asylum or jail. I'm Lucifer, after all. Whoever sent him needs a statement.

"Okay, Ukobach, here's where things stand. You ambushed me and you blew it. Your friends are dead and I don't think you're much use for information. Plus, your goddamn sword ripped my jacket."

He stares at me.

"I'll make it simple. I can kill you now or I can let you live, but it's going to hurt. You choose."

Ukobach shifts his weight. He wants to take one last kamikaze shot at me. I finger the rip in my jacket sleeve. It's not too bad. I can probably get it fixed. I'm kind of hard on clothes. It's all the stabbing and shooting.

"I'd kill you and every mortal in the universe if I could," he rasps. "When your souls reached Hell, I'd spend eternity weaving your guts into tapestries of glorious agony and hang them from every wall and parapet in Pandemonium."

"If wishes were horses we'd all have shit on our boots. Choose, Chuck. A quiet death or a messy life."

"I choose life. Any chance to return and kill you for murdering my comrades is worth whatever feeble punishment a mortal can muster."

I nod.

"I thought so. If I were you, I might have gone the other way."

He kicks low, trying to sweep my ankle. I take his Glock from my pocket and shoot him in the knee. He howls and rolls around, holding his leg. It gives him something to do while I get to work.

I cut six long strips of material from Hobnail's overalls. I

use four around his and his dead friends' wrists. Then I get the Harley on its wheels and roll it back so I can tie the dead men to the rear shocks. I take the last two strips and tie Ukobach too. He kicks at me and swings his fists as I haul him to the bike, but when he moves, it hurts him more than it does me. I loop my arm through the front of the helmet so I can hold it while I ride. There's no sense in hiding who I am now. Before I get on the bike, I look down at Ukobach.

"This isn't the kind of thing I normally do, you understand. Back home I'm a bad person but I'm not this kind of bad. Before he left, Samael told me I was going to have to be ruthless to survive, and he was right. People have to understand that if you dance with the Devil you better not step on his toes."

Ukobach looks up at me. I don't know if it's pain or fear or general boneheadedness but he has no idea what I'm saying. I get on the bike and start the engine.

"And away we go."

The bike creeps forward like it wants to tip over in quicksand. Even a Hellion motorcycle isn't geared to drag three full-grown bodies behind it. I give the bike some throttle. It straightens and moves forward. Slowly at first, but it picks up speed as I twist the throttle. When it feels stable, I kick the bike hard and we shoot down Santa Monica Boulevard to the palace. I don't turn around. I don't want to see what it looks like behind me.

THE CLOSER WE GET to Beverly Hills, the more Hellions there are on the street. They stare and point as I cruise by. I'm tempted to stop and make a joke about how this is how

I always tenderize meat, but I keep rolling without meeting any of their eyes. I don't have to. Seeing their ruler covered in blood and dirt, hauling a few hundred pounds of bleeding bologna behind him, is all they need. The story will be all over town in an hour. By tomorrow there will be rumors that it wasn't three. It'll be a dozen men. Fifty. I killed them with a bitch slap and dragged them with my pinkie.

The guards around the palace see me coming and step out of the way like the Red Sea parting for Charlton Heston. I stop the bike by the palace lawn, heel down the kickstand, and get off. A hundred Hellion soldiers watch me in dead silence.

I say, "This is what happens to assassins."

Soldiers crane their necks or climb onto jeeps and Unimogs for a better look at what I've hauled in.

An officer walks over. I don't know his name and I don't ask. He looks scared.

"I killed two where they jumped me. One was alive when I started back. Gibbet all three. If the live one is still alive after two days, let him go. Alive and skinless, he'll still be an object lesson for others."

"Yes, my lord," says the officer.

I start into the palace but turn after a few steps. I can't tell the condition of the bodies from here. There isn't much of a blood trail behind the bike. That's probably not a good sign for Ukobach. The guards stare at me.

"One of you take my bike into the garage and have it cleaned and polished." Not that I'm ever going to get to ride it again now that everyone knows what it looks like.

I head inside wondering what Candy would think about

what I just did. I'm pretty sure she'd understand. She might even approve. She won't have to, though, because this goes on the long list of things I'm never going to tell her.

IN THIS FUNNY CONVERGENCE HELL, Lucifer's palace is the penthouse of the Beverly Wilshire Hotel. I'm not saying my digs are nice, but I am saying that my rooms make Versailles look like an outhouse.

Palace security guards ring the inside of the lobby. I give them a nod while tracking dirt, road grime, and blood across the carpets. I head straight for my private elevator. Slap my hand over a brass plate on the wall and the elevator doors roll open. Inside I touch another plate and whisper a Hellion hoodoo code. The car starts up, the pulley and wires humming overhead, gently rocking the compartment. It feels good. A Magic Fingers motel massage loosening the tension knots in my shoulders. I move my arms and legs. Rotate my head. The palms of my hands are scraped raw from the fall off the bike, but there's no real damage to anything but my damned jacket.

The car stops at the penthouse. I touch the brass plate again and step out onto the cool polished marble floor. The penthouse is a sight. Like *Architectural Digest* climbed to the top of the hotel roof and shit out a Hollywood movie mogul's château. Windows everywhere. Expensive handmade furniture. Pricey art. And enough bedrooms and bathrooms for all the cowgirls in Montana to stop by for a pillow fight.

I kick off my boots by the elevator. Fuck the lobby carpet. Wash it. Burn it. I don't care. But I don't want blood all over my apartment.

My apartment.

It still feels funny to say, but I have to admit that after the three months the place is starting to feel like home. I used to run a video store in L.A. If I could move the inventory and a wall-size TV in here, I might go totally Howard Hughes and never leave. If I got Candy a day pass, I could definitely get used to the Hellion high life. Up here, surrounded by tinted glass and silk-covered furniture, I'm Sinatra with horns and Pandemonium is my boneyard Vegas.

I go to the bedroom and glance at the peepers I've scattered around the apartment. None are twitching and nothing looks out of place. I can relax. The truth is, I'm less worried about getting into another fight than I am about snoops. I need one place in Hell where I don't have to look over my shoulder 24/7.

In the bedroom I strip off my clothes, dropping them in a heap at the foot of the bed. The ripped jacket I ball up and throw into the closet. I could get it fixed but I'm goddamn Lucifer. I'll tell the tailors to run me off a new one.

I lock the bedroom door and run my hand over the top of the lintel. The protective runes I carved are still there. I get under a hot shower and stay there for a long time.

I might have gotten used to the apartment but I'll never get used to showering in Lucifer's armor. I never take the stuff off. The moment it's gone, I'm vulnerable to any kind of attack. Knife, hoodoo, or a squirrel with a zip gun. I know I look schizo soaping down in this Versace tuna can but I don't have to look at me.

When I'm done I pull on black suit pants, a silk T-shirt, and a hotel robe thick enough to stop bullets. The black blade goes in one pocket and Ukobach's gun in the other. Then over to the dresser for a quick check of the bottom drawer. There's the singularity, Mr. Muninn's secret weapon to restart the universe if Mason or I broke it. There's my na'at, my favorite weapon when I was fighting in the arena. And there's the little snub-nose .38 I brought with me from L.A. One bullet is missing from the cylinder. The one I tricked Mason Faim into blowing through his head three months ago. That's when Saint James, my angel half, took the key I need to leave Hell and left me stranded here. To tell the truth, I'm glad the goody-goody prick is out of my head. But I'd take him back in a second if it would get me the key.

The bedroom doors swing open and Brimborion walks in with a fistful of envelopes and messages. He's something else I never wanted in my life. A personal assistant, which is to say a professional asshole who knows more about me than I do.

"What did I tell you about barging in here without knocking?"

"If I didn't barge in, I'd never find you."

"That's the idea."

Brimborion looks fairly human except he's as skinny as a grasshopper, with limbs and fingers long enough to pluck a quarter from the bottom of a fifth of Jack. He dresses in dark high-collar suits like he fell out of a Dickens story right onto the stick up his ass. He also wears round wire-rim glasses. I think it's those glasses that really make me hate him. What a weird choice for an affectation. I mean, whoever heard of a nearsighted angel?

I say, "How did you even get in here?"

He rolls his eyes heavenward.

"You mean those pretty doodads you scratched above the doors? I'm your personal assistant. I need to be able to follow you anywhere."

He unbuttons his shirt and pulls out a heavy gold talisman hanging from a chain around his neck.

"I have a passkey. It opens any door in the palace no matter how many wards or enchantments are on it."

"Nice. Where can I get one?"

"I'm afraid this is the only one."

"Maybe I should take it."

"Feel free, my lord," he says. "And don't worry. I'll do my best to suppress the scandal."

"What scandal?"

"The one about how the Lord of the Underworld, the Archfiend, the Great Beast is afraid of a glorified secretary. I hate to think what your enemies would make of that."

I want to stack cinder blocks on this four-eyed fuckpop until he explodes. He opens his eyes a tiny bit wider behind the fake glass in his fake glasses and stares.

But the little prick has a point. Until I'm up to Samael's full strength, I don't want ambitious peasants storming the castle with pitchforks and torches.

I reach for the letters and messages, closing my hand around his. I squeeze. Not hard enough to break bone. Just enough to remind him I could if I wanted.

I let up and take my messages. He massages his fingers but doesn't say anything.

"Learn to knock and we can go back to being BFFs. Got it?"

"Of course, my lord."

He does a tiny bow and leaves.

I remember when I was out drinking with Vidocq in L.A. he introduced me to another old-time thief. He said the best way to deal with lock pickers is the simplest. You take all the furniture you can and stack it up so it's perfectly balanced against the top of the door. Anyone who tries to get in will get a dresser or a rocking chair on their head. If you want to fancy things up, you can add a bucket of lye dissolved in water. The real trick is remembering to tell the maid before she comes in the next morning.

I take the na'at out of the dresser and put it under the pillows at the head of the bed. Stacking furniture sounds like too much work.

I toss the messages in the fireplace. Infernal bureaucrats can kiss my ass.

I head down to the library.

THIS IS MY FORT KNOX, my office, and my panic room. I've laid the heaviest protective hoodoo I know around this place. Of all the hideouts I ever thought of running to when things got weird, a library was right behind a leper colony and a burning garbage truck. But here I am.

I haven't paced the place off, but the library looks about a football field long, lined with two floors of books in hundred-foot stretches of ornate dark wood shelves. The ceiling is domed and painted with scenes illustrating the three tenets of the Hellion church. The Thought: God and Lucifer arguing that if humans have free will so should angels. The Act: the war. It's pretty but stiff and trying too hard to look noble, like a Soviet propaganda poster. The New World: Lucifer and his defeated, punch-drunk Bowery boys in Hell. He looks like a tent revival preacher selling snake oil to rubes, but in his own fucked-up way, the slippery son of a bitch is trying to do right by his people.

I've made myself a comfortable squat over by a wall of the Greek wall, the stuff Samael told me to read. In a copy of a half-falling-apart *Reader's Digest*–condensed large-print book on Greek history, I found his notes. (It's embarrassing that he knows me well enough that he left the info in a book written for shut-ins and half-blind grandmas.) He included names of people I could think about for the Council. If *they're* the Hellions I can trust, I'm not ready to meet the ones I can't.

I dragged a plush red sofa trimmed in gold, a big partner's desk, and a few chairs over to my squat. Sometimes I even let people in to use the chairs. Not many and not often, but anyone who comes in is on my turf. I know which carpets cover binding circles. I know which books are hollowed out and stuffed with knives and killing potions.

The desk and nearby shelves are covered with books, paper, pens, and weird little machines. Stuff you can only find at an Office Depot doubling as a night school for amateur torturers. There's a spongy red clamshell that growls when you squeeze it and spits out what I think pass for Hellion staples. They're sharp and thick, like they're designed to punish the paper and not just hold it together. There's something that looks like a set of brass teeth. The teeth chatter sometimes. Sometimes they don't do anything for days. There's a gyroscope that when you spin it talks in a deep monster-movie voice in a language I've never heard before. On one of the bookshelves is a gold armillary sphere. When I touch any of the golden rings, I feel like I've fallen out of myself. Like I'm nowhere and being pushed through empty space by a freezing hurricane. There are stars far away and beyond them a mass of pale boiling vapor streaked with lighting. I think it's the chaos at the edge of the universe and that this is the deep void that separates Hell and Heaven. Wherever and whatever it is, it's a lonely and desolate place.

In L.A., I lived with a dead man named Kasabian who worked for Lucifer and could see into parts of Hell. I don't know if he can see me here, but sometimes I scrawl notes and leave them on the desk for days. Some are to friends. Most are to Candy. We're a lot alike. Neither of us is quite human. And we're both killers. We try to forget about the first as much as possible and try to avoid the second as much as we can, which, the way things are, usually isn't long.

There's a click behind me. I put my hand on my knife and turn.

Two Hellions come in through a false section of bookcase that slides away like Japanese paper doors.

Merihim, the priest, bows. He's in sleeveless black robes. Every inch of his pale face and arms is tattooed with sacred Hellion script. Spells, prayers, and, for all I know, a recipe for chicken vindaloo.

The guy with him, Ipos, is big and blunt. Like a walking fire hydrant in gray rubber overalls. The heavy leather belt around his waist holds tools that range from barbarian crushers to delicate surgical-quality instruments. From a distance you can't tell if he's the palace's maintenance chief or head torturer. His job in the palace makes him a useful agent. No one pays attention to the janitor.

"Did we interrupt playtime with your toys, my lord?" asks Merihim.

"Go harass an altar boy, preacher. I'm working."

On a table near the sofa there's a line of peepers projecting images from around the palace onto an old-fashioned home movie screen I found in a storeroom. I pop out my right eye, drop it into a glass of water, and stick a peeper in the empty socket, rolling back the images the eye picked up like a video rewinding. Like I said, I have a few of Lucifer's powers but mostly Vegas magic-act stuff.

"What are you looking for?" asks Ipos. His voice is a low rumble, like an idling sixteen-wheeler.

"The front of the palace where I dumped the bodies of three bushwhacking assholes. I want to see what happened after I came inside."

Merihim and Ipos are the only two Hellions who can walk in here on their own. They were Samael's confidants and spies and I inherited them with the gig. I don't think Samael would have lasted as long as he did without them. I know I wouldn't still be here.

I roll back to where I came inside and let the peeper play. The officer I talked to barks orders at the troops who are about thirty seconds from a soccer riot trying to get a look at Ukobach and his dead friends. The officer orders most back to their duties and others to take the three bodies to the gibbets. A young officer comes over. They walk along the gory trail where I dragged in the bodies. I try to read their lips but they're too damned far away.

"I see by your hands you were hurt in the attack," says Merihim. "I'll send for a healer from the tabernacle. I daresay they're more discreet than the palace medical staff."

"I'm fine. All the bastards did was murder my jacket. It was a nice one too."

I switch my eyes back, pour myself a shot of Aqua Regia, and hold out the bottle. Merihim shakes his head and walks away. He does that. Prowls the room when we meet. I've never seen the guy sit down. Ipos nods for a drink and picks up a glass with his big bratwurst fingers. When I start to pour, he flinches.

"I'm sorry," he says, and nods in my direction.

"The arm, my lord. Would you mind? It's . . . distracting."

I flex my prosthetic Kissi hand. The Kissi were a race of deformed, half-finished angels that lived in the chaos on the edge of Creation. One of God's first great fuckups while creating the universe. Kissis give Hellions the shakes. I think they see themselves in those other failed angels. It reminds them that even in Hell you can always fall lower.

I dig around in the desk and find a glove. This time he takes a drink. He carries it to the sofa and sits down. I sit on the desk. Merihim prowls.

"Thank you, my lord," says Ipos.

"Stop with the 'my lord' stuff. It bugs me."

"Sorry."

Merihim smiles, leaning over the peepers. Projected images from around the palace flicker on the screen like a silent movie.

"What's up with you?" I ask.

"Nothing. It's always amusing watching you pretend you're not who you really are."

"I'm only interning in Hell for college credit. When I find the right replacement, I'm gone, Daddy, gone."

"Of course you are. Why would you want any influence over the creation of a new Hell? Or care about the welfare of the millions of mortal souls you'll be leaving behind? I wonder if Mr. Hickok will be allowed to keep his tavern or will he be thrown back into Butcher Valley? But what do you care? 'All are equal in the grave.' Isn't that what you living mortals say?"

"Keep talking, smart guy. I'll fake a heart attack and make you Lucifer. Let's see how you like whitewashing this outhouse with a target painted on the back of your bald head."

Ipos glances at the priest.

"It would probably look better than all the scribbling."

Merihim gives him a sharp look, flips through the pages of an ancient Hellion medical book, and sets it down.

"Someone has found out about your habit of riding alone and what routes you take. You can't ever ride like that again."

"I know. There's something else."

I take out the Glock and set it on the desk.

"Where did these pricks get guns? Only officers get to carry weapons these days."

Merihim frowns and crosses his arms.

"We need to find out—very discreetly—if there are any officers who can't account for their weapons."

"There are merchants who sell stolen weapons in the street markets. I can get people on the road repair crews. They might see or hear something," Ipos says.

Merihim nods.

"Good."

"Wait. It gets even better. I checked the attacker who lived. He'd been hexed. He might not have even known what he was doing."

"An enthrallment?" says Merihim. That gets his attention. He comes back to the desk. "That's not a power many in Pandemonium would possess. I doubt that any of the officers could do it."

"Maybe the bastard bribed one of the palace witches," says Ipos.

"I think whoever set up the attack tried to hex me too. After I dumped the bike, I couldn't think or fight or defend myself. I've been in plenty of wrecks and it didn't feel like a concussion. It felt like someone was trying to get inside my head."

Merihim starts wandering again.

"It makes sense. One, Mason Faim created a key that allows him to possess bodies. Two, the key is missing. Three, according to you, it works on mortals. Four, there's no reason to think it wouldn't work on Hellions too. That means whoever arranged your attack either has the key or is in league with whoever does."

Ipos says, "I suppose if any of us would be hard to possess, it would be Lucifer. They probably won't try it on you again."

"This might not be an assassination attempt at all," says Merihim. "An isolated ambush would be a good way to cover up a psychic experiment. If your attackers killed you, all the better. If you killed your attackers, the only evidence would be the corpses of a few rogue soldiers."

"That makes sense. It's one thing to kill Lucifer but another to spellbind him," says Ipos. "You could make him do anything. Something unforgivable."

"Which means I get to live this little drama all over again."

Ipos nods. Merihim picks up the gyroscope from the desk and spins it the wrong way. The ominous voice comes out high and weird. A demonic Alvin and the Chipmunks.

"Definitely," says Ipos.

"And it will be both subtler and more serious. We have access to potion makings in the tabernacle. I'll personally prepare some draughts to protect you from psychic attack."

"What I want to know is why now?" say Ipos. "After all this time, why would someone attack you?"

I shrug.

"Maybe someone caught me counting cards."

Merihim says, "Something has changed. They've discovered something or they're afraid you will, and they need to kill you before you discover it too."

I say, "It's the possession key. Mason wasn't exactly generous with information. He created the key and wouldn't want anyone else using it, so it's not like there's going to be a user manual lying around. Maybe it's taken this long for whoever has it to figure out how it works."

Merihim waves off the comment.

"Perhaps. Speculation is pointless. We need to contact our operatives among the legions and the palace thaumaturgy staff to see what they can find."

"Did anything interesting happen at the Council meeting?" says Ipos.

"Not really. Marchosias wanted to fuck me in her limo to

annoy the others. I called Buer a Nazi and sent them all home to watch a silent movie about good architecture and a mad scientist."

"It sounds charming," says Merihim.

"There's even a robot."

"A masterpiece, then."

Ipos says, "We should get to work."

He sets his glass on the desk, holds it there, and pushes on it. The desk rocks a fraction of an inch up and down.

"I thought so. You wore down one of the legs dragging it over. I'll fix that the next time we meet."

"I can just stick a matchbook under it."

He looks at me.

"No, you can't. You might run the kingdom but I maintain the palace. This is my domain."

"Whatever you say, Mr. Wizard."

After they're gone, I sit down at the desk and light a Malediction. Toss the Glock into the bottom drawer of the desk. I don't like Glocks. They're the gun equivalent of a middle-aged guy buying a Porsche.

From the top drawer I take out a shiny silver Veritas. The coin is a useful little pocket oracle. Another Veritas helped me survive my first few days when I first escaped back to L.A. The Veritas sees the present and the near future and never lies, though sometimes it's a little shit about it.

I flip it and think, What now?

It comes down showing the image of a man pouring money into a woman's hands. I've seen the symbol before. A hooker and her customer. Around the coin's edge, in perfect Hellion script, it reads, *Don't make any long-term investments. Have a good time now.* That's what I mean. The little prick could have just said, *You're doomed,* but it likes showing off.

I toss the Veritas back in the desk, pick up a book, and lie down on the sofa. I'm reading a chapter about a Greek philosopher named Epicurus. The guy was a kind of depressed swinger. Imagine the Playboy Mansion run by Mr. Rogers. Epicurus was all about pleasure but in a stingy eat-your-vegetables-or-you-won't-get-any-dessert kind of way.

A lot of this philosophy stuff puts me right to sleep, but Epicurus must have been able to see into the future when people like me can't read more than a paragraph without checking our e-mail because he spit out the important stuff short and sweet. It's called the Tetrapharmakos and it's a kind of a PowerPoint list to fix whatever ails you. It goes:

> *Don't fear God*
> *Don't worry about death*
> *What is good is easy to get and*
> *What is terrible is easy to endure*

He got it at least half right. That's better than most people.

"Don't fear God." No problem. I met the guy. He had a nervous breakdown and is broken into more pieces than me.

"Don't worry about death." I died a couple of times already. It was boring.

"What is good is easy to get." Here's where Epicurus's head starts disappearing up his own ass. This seems to be a common problem with philosophers.

"What is terrible is easy to endure." Try being born half angel and half human, pal. A nephilim violates all the rules of the universe. I was born an Abomination, the only thing alive hated by Heaven, Hell, and Earth. Try that on for size and tell me how easy it is to endure, you grape-leaf-eating son of a bitch.

I drop the book on the floor. This is all Samael's fault. I should have guessed that part of my torture in Hell would be having to read. L.A. was a lot more fun. Stealing cars, ripping out zombies' spines, and getting shot at. Good times.

I get up and scrawl a note in big block letters and leave it on the desk in case Kasabian can see it.

CANDY. I MISS YOU. STARK.

Lucifer's library has a pretty limited fiction section. I push around the pile of books by the sofa until I find *The Trial* by Franz Kafka. It's about a guy on trial for something he doesn't understand, accused by people he can't find. It's fucking hilarious. It might not be my first choice for how to spend an evening, but it's better than going back to the Greeks. I don't need another morality lecture from a dead guy. I've been getting those half my life.

MY EYES SNAP OPEN a few hours later. I sit up. I don't even remember falling asleep. I get up and check the peepers.

After-hours flunkies sorting and filing endless piles of palace paperwork. Soldiers patrolling the grounds. Cleaners trying to get blood and gravel out of the lobby carpets. All expected. All boring. Good.

In L.A., I used to dream about Hell. In Hell, I dream about L.A., but it doesn't make me any less homesick. Home in my dreams isn't home. I see the city turning soft and sinking into the desert. Whole neighborhoods are swallowed or just wink out of existence. The sky is black and bruised like Hell's, and then turns normal again. Sometimes instead of fighting in the arena, my arena dreams turn into a floodlit Hollywood and Vine.

This time I'm circling a Hellion roughly the size and shape of a locomotive. I have to fight with a rusty junkyard na'at while Casey Jones has a shield and a Vernalis, a kind of steel crab claw the size of your average go-go dancer. A bunch of red leggers, freelance raiders and looters, hoot and cheer for blood.

We drive each other back and forth across the killing floor. I slip one of his attacks and get in close. Just as I'm about to open him up like a can of pork and beans, my na'at jams. It was rigged and the Hellion knew it. The next thing I know, I'm on my knees screaming. There's a wet sound as the Vernalis slices through meat and crunches through bone. When I look down, my left arm is lying in the intersection next to a three-month-old *People* magazine.

And that's not even the worst dream. The worst are when I wake up sweating from nightmares about city-planning meetings. Swear to God. I dream about signing papers. I dream about progress reports on freeway repairs. About digging through mile-high piles of office supplies for Post-its and paper clips. I'm a magician, an ex-gladiator, a killer, and now the Devil himself and my greatest night terrors revolve around lost memos and trying to remember the Hellion word for "incentivize."

Some nights I swear I'm tempted to sneak back to the arena and step in for a couple of fights, like a junkie looking for one more fix. It's sick, I know. Yeah, it's misery, but it's a familiar kind and sometimes that's as close to happy as I'll get down here.

No wonder Samael took a powder. For all his talk about going home to make up with the old man, he was really running away from eternal damnation as a salaryman. I didn't figure out until I was doing it that this is Lucifer's damnation. The Light Bringer reduced to riding herd on bank clerks. It was worse than any torture.

I get up and pour myself a drink. Throw the robe over the back of a chair and slip the black blade behind my back. I leave through the fake bookshelves and head downstairs to the kennels.

IT'S AFTERNOON and the senior planning staff is waiting in the palace meeting room. The place looks like Bring Your Clown to Work Day at a Masonic lodge. The slick suits and Hellion power dresses aren't the problem. It's everything else they're wearing. Ceremonial aprons covered with old runes. A morbid rainbow of colored scarves and gloves showing everyone's place in the food chain. Blinders. Gaggers. Masks.

They're all giving me the pig eye as I roll in. I take my time getting to the head of the table. The dirty looks aren't just because I'm late. I'll always be that sheep-killing dog Sandman Slim to most of them, and now, just to rub their ugly noses in it, I'm their boss. At least the armor is doing its job. No matter how much they hate me, they keep their hex holes shut with my devil armor shining like the mirrored belly of a chrome wasp.

There are twelve on the planning committee. With me there's thirteen. A cozy little coven. Buer is there. So are Marchosias and Obyzuth. Semyazah would be here but none of the generals will put up with this shit.

Technically I'm supposed to be in ritual drag too but I have a hard time picturing Samael dressed up like a Brooks Brothers Pied Piper, so I follow his example and skip the wardrobe call.

There's a silver circle in the center of the table. Lines radiate out to the edges, cutting the table into twelve sections. Each trick-or-treater steps up and sets down a different ceremonial object. The junk looks like leftovers from a Goth-club garage sale.

Obyzuth sets down a green rock, like a Templar meditation stone. The Hellion next to her sets down an athame knife that cuts through ignorance or butters magic toast or something. Buer drops a snake carved from the leg bone of a fallen Hellion warrior. It goes on and on like that. I'm supposed to light a red candle at the end of the ritual but things are going too slow. I fire it up now and light a Malediction off it.

"Don't take it personally, but if I have to sit through one more of these meetings, I'm going to gut every one of you like catfish, shit in your skulls, and mail them to your families. This isn't Hell. It's a PTA meeting. Maybe all we need to save Hell is a bake sale."

I flick my ashes over the candle.

"Here's how it is from now on. Do your projects any way you want. Fuck the budgets. Fuck the schedules. When it's done, you get one minute to tell me about it."

The room is silent. It's not like regular silence. More like the kind you get with a concussion.

"In case anyone thinks letting you off the leash is a license to steal or stab me in the back, let me introduce the newest member of our team."

I go to the doors and open them. A hellhound clanks in on its big metal claws and looks over the room. The hound is bigger than a dire wolf, a clockwork killing machine run by a Hellion brain suspended in a glass globe where its head should be. They're terrifying on a battlefield but in an enclosed space like this, the whirs and clicks of its mechanics, its razor teeth and pink, exposed brain, are enough to give a tyrannosaurus a heart attack.

The hound follows me around the table, folds up its legs, and settles down on the floor next to me. A dutiful guard dog.

"This is Ms. 45. The new head of HR. Any of you upstanding citizens that do less than your best work, conspire against me, or sell supplies to the black market can explain it to her. She works nights, weekends, and holidays, and if she's indisposed, Ms. 45 has a few hundred colleagues downstairs. In fact, the hounds now have the run of the palace, so watch your step. I hear stainless-steel turds stain bad."

No one says anything. Besides the hellhound, the only sound is people restlessly moving their feet.

"Now get to work and leave me the fuck alone."

All twelve of them file out, right into the other two hounds I stationed outside. It would have been a hoot programming them to eat each Council member as they left. A little counterproductive, though. I need them to do the work I'm sure not going to do. But if I can't have a little fun being the Devil, why bother?

Now I can get back to figuring out the rest of Lucifer's power so I can get the hell out of here.

I've made circuit after circuit of the empty parts of the hotel. I know Lucifer won't leave me hanging on half power forever. He likes games. I know there are clues for me around somewhere. But I don't know all the rules of the game, so I might be looking right at one without knowing it.

When he left he said he'd come back if I ever really needed him. I haven't heard a goddamn word since. I've tried to get a message through to Mr. Muninn. He's the one guy on Earth I *know* could come down here if he wanted. I guess he doesn't. I know why and we're going to have to have a long talk about it when I get home.

Saint James would have a plan but I'm just prowling relentless, hypnotic halls, floor by floor looking for clues. The windowless corridors could be anywhere. In space on a rocket circling the edge of the universe. Or Donald Trump's diamond-encrusted submarine at the bottom of the Marianas Trench.

Hellhounds glance up when they see me. I scratch the underside of their glassed-in brains and they growl contentedly. They're like temple dogs guarding a royal tomb, only here the altars are unused Jacuzzis and Hellion minibars. I don't even want to think about what's in those.

Fun as it was busting up the meeting, something real kicked in for me. Something I sort of already knew but couldn't put into words.

*They've gone insane down here. Every fucking Hellion has gone mad.*

They can't lay a finger on Heaven and they can't leave. They've been stuck in this hole for what? Thousands of years?

A million? Time doesn't move for angels like it moves for us. They've turned inward and created a rat-maze culture. All bureaucracy, schizo rituals, and murderous deadfalls.

Do you think God had a business plan when He created the universe? Did He worry about the invention of light or gravity running over budget?

Meetings and infighting. Made-up ceremonies and new religions and Noble Virtues. This is how you fill up eternity when all you have to look forward to is the clock running down and the universe collapsing in on itself and starting over.

There's something up ahead. I can't see it but I can feel it. There's a set of double doors leading to a meeting room. The opposite wall is blank but there's something funny about it. It isn't solid. To these Lucifer eyes, the plaster and paint are cheap sideshow effects. Change the light and you can see right through them. At least the wily bastard left me something useful.

Sooner or later even the nonstop rituals aren't going to hold and these assholes are going to turn on each other. The biggest baddest civil war ever, until none of them are left. What would Heaven think of that? Probably get a real chuckle out of it. A Hell without Hellions. A real-estate developer's wet dream. They can sell time-shares, "This two-and-a-half-bath beauty is close to schools, shopping, and on a clear day you can see the dismembered devil corpses floating in the lake of shit."

The ghost room reminds me of Vidocq's apartment in L.A. He put hoodoo on the place so no one can see it or remember it, so he hasn't paid rent in years. But whoever conjured up this blind isn't ducking bill collectors. This is a lot heavier magic than that.

"I've been looking for you, lord."

Fuck me harder, God. Seriously.

"I'm kind of busy now, Brimborion."

"I can see. Another busy day of wandering the halls. I hear there are some brick partitions on the third floor where if you stare just right you can see animals and fluffy clouds. Maybe you'd like to wander down there?"

"What do you want? Wait. How did you find me?"

"I stopped by your summer home in the library and had a peep at your peepers."

I make it to him in half a second, get my fingers around his throat, hoist him off his feet, and hold him against the wall.

"You went into the library without my permission?"

"It was unlocked," he croaks.

He starts turning blue. And he isn't lying. I can't remember setting a sealing spell on the place when I left. Besides, he probably could have walked in anyway with the opening talisman of his. I drop him to the floor and head back down the hall.

"What's so important you had to dog me down here?"

He gasps for air and waves a crumpled piece of vellum at me. He wants me to come down there and take it but that isn't going to happen. I wait until he can breathe again.

"It's the banquet tonight, my lord."

"What banquet?"

"To celebrate the laying of the City Hall cornerstone."

"Tell them I can't make it. I have the flu or the clap. Whatever it is you cloven-hoof types get."

"But, my lord. You have to bless the banquet."

More rituals.

"Get Merihim to do it."

"It's not his place, my lord."

"Okay. Then cancel it."

He scrambles to his feet. The vellum isn't crumpled anymore. He's holding on to it like a life preserver.

"You can't."

"Then don't cancel it. I'm putting you in charge. If Merihim can't do it, find someone who can. I'm busy."

I walk back in the direction of the fake wall.

I hear him come after me.

"You've been obstinate in the past, my lord. But refusing the banquet is beyond acceptable. And I heard that you dismissed the planning committee today."

He's right about one thing. I was having so much fun I forgot about politics. Lies and promises. It was goddamn stupid to let that slip.

I turn and he comes up short.

"And you know who Marchosias and a few others think put me up to it?"

"Who?"

"You."

He takes a step forward.

"Me?"

"Everyone knows you're paying off half the staff to spy for you. Let you know who's gaining power and losing power. I'm your power. You control my schedule and who gets to talk to me and see me. You must make a fortune selling my time. Of course, you can't go too far. If I'm too hard to get hold of people start thinking you're making a power play. A dangerous move for someone in your position."

I look at him. He wants to say, I'm not to blame. You're the one who doesn't want to do anything or see anyone.

I say, "Don't take it so hard. Marchosias has been yammering about you ever since I got here. She keeps bringing up people on her staff she says could replace you. Some of them have pretty good credentials. You didn't know any of that? Maybe you ought to run another background check on your staff."

He squints at me the same way the committee did when I came in late.

"With all due respect, my lord, I'm not sure I believe you."

"One, quit with the 'my lord' stuff. And two, I don't care."

He turns like he's going to walk away but he just stands there.

"You still here?"

"I was wondering what you're doing down at this end of the palace. Is it for something you've lost or something you've found?"

I go over to him, tear open his shirt, and rip the talisman off his neck. The chain leaves a nice red mark on his throat.

I get in close and whisper, "I cut off my own face once because it seemed like a good idea at the time. What do you think I'll cut off you?"

He gives me a tiny nod and steps back, rubbing the red mark where the chain broke.

"It's nice to see you with your energy back. I've been worried."

"What does that mean?"

He waves his hand up and down me.

"Just an observation. Since you replaced our other Lucifer, you've seemed so wan and . . . what? Weak? It would be awful if people thought your armor was the only thing keeping you alive."

How does this little shit know these things? I should snap his neck right now.

"I tell you what. Maybe you should keep this after all."

I hold out the talisman.

He hesitates.

I hold it by two fingers and waggle it at him.

When he reaches for it, I let it drop. His gaze follows it down. I slam my shoulder into him, pinning his right hand against the wall. Grab the blade from behind my back. One quick slash and I cut off his little finger. He howls and falls to his knees, cradling his mutilated hand against his chest. Black blood oozes down his shirt. I pull off the glove that covers my Kissi arm, pick the talisman up off the floor, and drop it in my pocket. I grab him by the hair so he gets a good look at my prosthetic.

"The next time you threaten me, I'll take your whole arm."

First rule of threats. Always threaten big. Second rule. Always mean it, even if you don't particularly want to do it.

He looks up at me.

"You pig. You human filth."

"What do you expect from the Devil? A note in your personnel file?"

He's wearing a collarless gray jacket. He manages to slip one arm out and wrap it around his bleeding hand. Leaning his good hand on the wall, he slowly gets to his feet, grimacing and cursing, and starts away down the hall.

I lean against the wall and light a Malediction.

I've got to remember not to drink anything I don't get myself, preferably from outside the palace. It might not be poisoned but it will definitely be pissed in.

I guess now there's another thing Candy doesn't get to know about. I should start keeping a list.

I stay put until I finish my cigarette and everything is quiet but the air-conditioning. Closing my eyes, I try to reach out. Feel if there's anything or anyone hiding nearby. I don't get anything.

I take a long look at the false wall. Sometimes objects can pick up residual magic when someone throws powerful hoodoo nearby. When that happens, a lamp, a chair, or that massager mom keeps in her bedside table that you're not supposed to know about can give off the same vibes as a genuinely enchanted object. That can happen to, say, a wall if someone was doing heavy spell work around here. There's no absolute way of knowing without going forensic and that was Vidocq's area, not mine. I wish he was here.

I step back and take a good look.

*You're not really there, are you?*

I charge at what I hope is a door and not a crossbeam. It's harder to menace people when you're gimping around with a broken nose.

I pass through the wall like it's air. And hit something hard. It cracks open. Wood splinters. Something heavy falls behind me. I think I found the door.

I'm in the middle of a dark, cluttered room. Behind me is the hoodoo wall, rippling like water on this side. The door is on the floor, in pieces. Someone isn't getting their deposit back.

Wherever the hell I am, it's dark. All I can see in the feeble pool of light through the wall is something that looks like a cluttered garage. Somewhere Dad keeps his tools for the weekend projects that help get him out of having to talk to the family.

Crates are piled all over the place. Scraps of cut and hammered metal on the floor. Tables with vises and C-clamps. Someone forgot their lunch. It stinks in here.

I feel along the wall. Find a light switch and flick it on.

Turns out it wasn't lunch after all.

Five body bags are stacked in the corner. A sixth body wrapped in plastic is strapped to what looks like an old wooden electric chair. There's a tear in the side of the shrink-wrapped shroud, leaking Hellion juice and exposing a black, bloated hand. It gets worse when I uncover the body. It's the kind of stink that would turn a buzzard vegan.

It's a woman. She's in a legion uniform but I can't read her name or tell what regiment she's from. The top of her skull is missing. It looks like someone was dissecting her brain. Clamps and sutures still cling to the rotten meat.

This is new. I never heard of Hellions vivisecting their own. They do it to some of the more heinous dead souls in the House of Knives, but not to each other.

Whatever this is, it doesn't look like torture. This was an experiment and this soldier was the lab rat. I bet if I checked the body bags I'd find more head-bone excavations. What kind of Dr. Moreau shit was going on in here? And who was doing it? Only one name comes to mind.

*Mason.*

What the fuck was he looking for?

You'd think with all the Hellions I've hacked up over the years, manhandling a dead one wouldn't be so disgusting. But I just killed them. I didn't stick around to watch them rot. Mason must have encased this room in heavy magic armor. Before I destroyed Tartarus, dead Hellions blipped out of existence like soap bubbles and ended up in the Hell below Hell. But Mason managed to keep these corpses intact even after they were dead. You have to admire the pure psycho will it took to pull off something like that. Admire it and then kill it. That last is the important part.

So what was he looking for?

I loosen the corpse's straps and let it fall forward onto its knees. The corpse leaves scraps of hair, rotten uniform, and skin on the back of the chair.

There's a long shallow divot cut into the wood where the soldier's head was held back. Whatever was in the shallow hole is gone now.

I undo the straps holding her arms. They're kind of glued to the chair with bodily fluids. I have to yank off each one, making sure to keep them wrapped in plastic so I don't have to touch them.

There are divots on each of the armrests where the dead woman's bare hands would rest on them. I pull her bare feet off the footrests. Divots there too.

I've wandered deep into the realm of What the Fuck.

Turn and scan the room for clues. Body bags. Rolling metal tables with drills, saws, and surgical instruments. A blackboard covered with what looks like machine schematics. A pile of empty bags. Rows of potions. Bet most are dope so the guinea pigs wouldn't squirm while Mason worked on them with a chisel. I keep scanning the room but stop when I see myself pinned to the wall.

The last twelve years of my life are spread across fake wood paneling.

Photos of the dozens of Hellions I murdered. There are notes about how and when they died. There are shots of dead people on Earth too. I didn't kill all of them. Everyone in the Magic Circle. Parker dead in a motel room with half his face missing. Doc Kinski. A shot of Josef the Kissi wearing his human übermensch face. A young vampire named Eleanor, her bitch of a mother, and her suicide father. Cabal Ash and his sister. Simon Ritchie, the movie producer. Snapshots of anonymous, well-groomed blue bloods, rich assholes that died during the New Year's Eve raid on Avila. Mug shots of bald young teenyboppers and worn-out middle-aged White Power morons who probably died when I torched a skinhead clubhouse a few months back. Like the Hellions, they have date and death notes.

There's a photo of Alice, the girl I left behind when I was dragged Downtown eleven years ago, off to the side by itself. I take it down and put it in my pocket. I'm not leaving her here in this madhouse.

There's a shot of another young girl. I'm ashamed that it takes me a minute to recognize her. Green hair and pretty eyes. She isn't wearing her uniform or ridiculous wire antennae in the shot. I like to think that's why I missed her, but the fucked-up thing is that she'd slipped my mind. She was a counter girl at Donut Universe. Two Kissi murdered her right in front of me. She hadn't done anything and wasn't a threat to anyone. She's dead for no other reason than that she happened to sell me coffee. And I forgot about her.

I take her photo and put it in my pocket with Alice's.

Near the photos of the dead are shots of people who so far have managed to stay out of pine boxes. Candy. Vidocq. Allegra. Mr. Muninn. Carlos. Even Kasabian and Wells.

What the hell is this? How do a stalker photo album and a bunch of mutilated soldiers go together? Was Mason stone-cold crazy by the end, staring at my life while slicing up the only victims who'd willingly come into Norman Bates's rec room?

I go over to the blackboard schematic. On a nearby table are wire cutters, soldering irons, a voltmeter, and other electronic hobby gear. Something like a computer or an elaborate radio lies gutted on the table, circuit boards and bits of fiber-optic cable scattered around it. It looks like someone was scavenging for parts. The device is vaguely familiar but I can't place it. I push one of the circuit boards out of the way and find something I was hoping I'd never see again.

A Golden Vigil logo. It fell off the device when it was pried open. Now I remember what it is. It's angelic tech—a psychic amplifier. I saw a few around the Vigil's L.A. warehouse. Their Shut Eye psychics used them to supercharge their powers for interrogations and remote viewing experiments. As much as I want to be surprised, I'm not. Mason was working with Aelita, the old head of the Vigil. Maybe she dropped this off with a basket of blueberry muffins as a housewarming present.

I pick up a curled metal shaving from the table. Turn it

over in my hands. It's a dull silver and dense. Not like something that would go into a machine as delicate as the amplifier. There are more shavings and half-melted ingots on the floor. I kick through them and there, lying by the toe of my god-awful, shiny dress shoe, is what I've been looking for.

I pick up the metal and go back to the chair with the dead soldier. The metal fits perfectly into the divot behind her head. The same thing for the holes in the hand- and footrests.

I weigh the key in my hand. It's heavy and solid and comforting. I never realized until now that I miss the weight of the key in my chest. This isn't like my key. It won't get anyone out of here but this possession key has its own charms, and with the psychic amplifier, I bet it's how Mason got the thing to work and let him ride people back on Earth like a voodoo Loa.

I thought Mason's workshop was upstairs, but the forge and tools were just for show. This is the real lab. And the dead soldiers were his first experiments as he tried to make the key work. These aren't Lucifer's clues and none of this gets me any closer to getting out of here, but it's still useful. Whoever has the key must also have a working psychic amplifier, the one Mason was scavenging parts for. That means I don't necessarily have to find the key. If I can find and smash the amplifier, it might kill the key's power. Better yet, if I can find the key and the amplifier, I might be able to talk to someone back in L.A.

This is good news. Not break-out-the-champagne-I'm-coming-home good news. More like open-a-six-pack-of-malt-liquor-I-didn't-drop-my-keys-down-the-toilet-at-work good news. But after the last three months, I'll take any good news I can get.

The dissected Hellion is really starting to stink up the place. I want to go back to my room and sandblast my skin off but there's one more thing.

By itself, in the corner of the room, is an ornate wooden table holding a black lacquered box. The box is perfectly square and featureless. When I touch the top, I can feel faint vibrations from inside.

I feel along the edges and find a subtle seam. Then others nearby. I push on one and nothing happens. Others move an inch or two. The damn thing is a puzzle box, but I'm not in a puzzle mood. I take out the black blade and bring it down hard, slicing off one side. No explosions or poison gas or snakes with machine guns. That's a good sign. I hack off the other side, get my hands inside, and push. A second later, the box rips apart in a shower of splinters and black velvet lining. It's kind of a pretty sight. Like an exploding ventriloquist dummy.

Something heavy and metal hits the floor. I try to pick it up, and rip the tip of my middle finger. Getting down on one knee, I slip the blade underneath it, raising it up like balancing an egg. In the light, I can't see any sharp edges. Carefully, I rest it in the palm of my hand. It's definitely a weapon but I've never seen one like it. When I turn it side to side, something weird happens.

As the light hits it from different angles, the thing changes shape. It's a spiked ball the size of a tangerine. It's a long silver dart with barbs at each end. It's a spinning cone of fire. It's ice knuckle-dusters. A parang. An elaborate Balisong, with six hinged joints that move at 180-degree angles to each other. Whatever kind of slice-and-dicer this is, it wasn't made for human hands.

Fighters liked to tell tall tales around the arena. Stories about ultimate weapons they'd heard about that would make them impossible to kill. Over a few jugs of bitter Hellion wine (our prize for having survived the day), we came to the consensus that the ultimate weapon would be the one that killed all your enemies and then flew you away to Heaven or Valhalla or anyplace where when you said the word Hell the locals would say, "What's that?"

One fighter from some Hellion backwater said that he'd seen the real ultimate weapon. Only archangels had them and only Gabriel was brave enough to use his.

"No rebel angel could defeat him because each time he used his weapon it was different. There was no way to attack or defend yourself against it. Before the battle was over, thousands of our rebel brothers and sisters lay dead at his feet. These other fools think it was God who defeated us, but the few of us who survived the battle know it was Gabriel."

I remember something Alice said before Samael took her back to Heaven. I'd left her alone with Neshamah, one of the five entities that have made up God since His nervous breakdown. Alice said that Aelita killed Neshamah with a weapon Alice had never seen before. I wonder if that's because what she saw was really a million different weapons. That would be pretty damn hard to describe at the best of times and even harder if it was only for a few seconds while someone gutted God in front of you.

Among the lacquered splinters is a kind of leather sheath that roughly corresponds to the shape of the weapon when it's configured like circular-saw blades. Carefully, I slip the thing into the case and lock the top flap closed.

I wonder if Aelita left the weapon for Mason to use on me or if he was just holding it for her while she hunted down the other four God brothers? Either way it's mine now. I drop it in my jacket pocket and get the hell out of Mason's butcher shop.

I HEAD TO THE BEDROOM but stop at the library to leave red "get your ass over here now" signal cards in front of a couple of peepers for Ipos and Merihim.

In the bedroom I strip off the suit and give it a sniff. The abattoir-fresh aroma all the kids love is deep inside the material. That's never coming out. I toss the suit over with the dead motorcycle jacket. It's sort of comforting seeing the growing pile of ruined clothes. I've killed off a lot of men's casual wear while getting shot and stabbed. Now all I have to do is decapitate someone and I'll feel like I'm home sweet home.

I grab an overcoat from the closet and toss it on the bed. I feel enough like me that I put on the leather bike pants and boots I wore when I came down here. They feel good. A little stiff with dried blood, most of it mine. I put on my hoodie. It's blood stiff too and one of the sleeves is missing from when the red legger relieved me of my left arm. I sliced him in half like a side of beef with my Gladius, my flaming angelic sword.

I keep the glove on, but leave my prosthetic arm bare since no one is going to see it under the coat.

Back in the library I smack the gyroscope like Merihim, making it spin backward. The monster-movie voice chitters like a groundhog that's burrowed into a meth lab. I check the peeper images on the movie screen. Brimborion is prowling his office, smiling at his staff. Trying to play it cool. He's almost pulling it off, but if you look hard enough you can see the wheels whirring in his head. Is one of these fuckers selling me out? Maybe better to kill them all and let God or the Devil or Oprah sort them out.

In other parts of the palace, people do funny little square dances when they come around a corner and find a hellhound. Maintenance guys on break in the basement check out my motorcycle. Staff witches sort through piles of dried bugs and plants. Outside, a couple of officers are kicking the shit out of a low-ranking Hellion while another officer uses his long leather sap to poke the dead bikers in the gibbets. Guess the book club let out early.

Ipos and Merihim show up a few minutes later. I tell them about the secret room while taking out my eye. I drop the other peepers into their saline storage jars so that mine is the only one showing on the screen. They watch the show like a couple at a drive-in movie. Bored during the dark part but starting a little when the lights flick on, giving them a full frontal of Ed Gein's rumpus room.

"Too bad you can only see the place and not smell it. It's memorable."

"You think this is Mason Faim's work?" says Merihim when we come to the first close-up of a dissected brain.

"Unless this is what Hellions call 'playing doctor.'"

He shoots me a look. I distract him by holding out the Magic 8 Ball.

"Ever seen one of these before?"

Merihim is too smart to grab things the Devil finds weird

but Ipos is more impulsive. He grabs the ball, turns it, and immediately gets his hand skewered by a barb.

He curses in lower-class street Hellion, which sounds even worse than regular Hellion. Like a shop vac sucking up sewer sludge.

On the screen I'm moving the soldier's body around while the pile of body bags forms a pastoral slaughterhouse tableau in the background.

Merihim bends to look at the ball in Ipos's bleeding hand but doesn't move to take it.

"Whatever this is, it reeks of unnatural power. You should let me take it and bury it deep in the Tabernacle vaults."

Everyone is on a power trip here, the church included.

"Thanks but no thanks. It stays with me."

"This isn't something to be left lying around."

"Which is why it stays with me and not buried somewhere I can't see it."

"And where will it end up if something happens to you?"

"I wouldn't worry about it. If whoever knows how to work this gets ahold of it again, my guess is that we'll all be dead by morning. Another good reason to keep me on the unkilled team."

On the screen I'm poking at the psychic amplifier. I watch them closely. Neither has ever seen one before. Neither reacts to the Vigil logo either. At least I don't have to worry about them working with whoever has the key.

"Either of you come up with any new information?"

Ipos nods and his church tattoos move like a flag promising salvation.

"I might have," he says. "The soldiers who attacked you were from Wormwood's legion. There are an unusual number of suicides and murders among his troops. Apparently it's been going on for some time, but since the dead no longer disappear into Tartarus he can't hide it anymore. My spies in other legions found that the same thing is starting to happen in other parts of the legion."

Merihim says, "Red leggers have been caught delivering bogus potions to physicians and hospitals. The real ones end up on the black market."

"Okay. Maybe bad drugs get them to kill themselves, but what do they have to do with killing me?"

Merihim shrugs.

"Well, no one likes you very much."

On the screen I'm examining the weird weapon. Ipos watches closely, safe from slicing himself open.

He says, "General Semyazah controls the distribution of vital goods. That gives him access to you and to a lot of power. There's a long list of generals who would like to replace him."

Damn.

"We're back to generals stabbing generals in the back? I thought that shit was over with when I killed Mason."

"In peace or war, there are always men who want power for its own sake."

Ipos has given up pretending to look at the peeper projection and has gone to my desk to fix the wobbly leg.

"You think Semyazah is letting his own trucks get ripped off?"

From under my desk Ipos says, "It's possible. Being smart doesn't exempt you from corruption."

He hammers a wooden spacer under one of the desk legs. Between taps with a small hammer he says, "Of course it could be another general earning some extra money while making Semyazah look bad."

"Why not just kill him? That seems to be a quick way to get promotions down here."

Merihim shakes his head.

"Murdering Semyazah risks an all-out war among the generals. Legion against legion. No one wants that."

Ipos says, "If someone could possess Semyazah and have him, say, attack you, then he could be killed and you would have to appoint another supreme general."

Merihim opens his hands in a weary gesture.

"We're back to speculating. We know more than we did but not enough to come to any reasonable conclusions."

I go to my eye and start the projection over again in case I missed something the first time through.

Ipos comes out from under the desk. He wipes dirt from his knees and says, "Even without war we're still trapped in chaos and fear. It reminds me of waking up here after the fall from Heaven."

He looks at Merihim.

"Do you remember? How many brothers and sisters cut their throats or threw themselves off the high mountains?"

"And the ones who turned on each other. I remember. It was a terrible thing to see."

Ipos looks at me.

"Lucifer saved us. The first one. Like you, he had us work building Pandemonium. It took our minds off those . . . other possibilities."

Richard Kadrey

Neither of them looks at each other or at me. Their eyes are glazed in an ex-soldier's thousand-yard stare.

I never thought of Hellions this way. They always seemed so full of Fuck You spirit when it came to the war in Heaven. It never occurred to me that being thrown here was as terrible for them as it was for me. When Heaven started shipping in damned souls, it must have been a nice distraction, but only for a while. Guarding passive, broken ghosts can't be that exciting. And maybe they reminded the fallen angels too much of themselves. The damned minding the damned. If Hellions hadn't tortured me for all those years, I might even feel sorry for them. But they did, so I don't.

I take a picture from my pocket and hand it to Merihim.

"While we're on the subject of lousy deaths, this is a girl from L.A. She had dyed green hair and worked at a donut shop on Hollywood Boulevard. She was murdered by two Kissi sometime between last Christmas and New Year's. I don't know if she's down here, but if she is, can one of you find her?"

Merihim hands the photo to Ipos. He wipes the blood from his hands before taking it. "There can't be that many pretty mortals killed by monsters in donut shops at Christmas. If she's here, we'll find her."

"When you do, get her a job. Something safe. Away from the craziness. I'd do it myself but being near me is what got her in trouble in the first place."

Ipos puts the photo in the breast pocket of his work overalls.

"She's a friend of yours?"

I shake my head.

64

"I don't even know her name."

On the screen I watch myself unwrapping the soldier's body.

Merihim cocks his head.

"I can't help but be curious: you want us to find a complete stranger to ease the burden of her damnation but you've never once asked about your mother or father."

"I don't have to. Believe it or not, I'm capable of doing a few things on my own. They're not here. It turns out being drunk and miserable are only venial sins after all. Lucky them."

Ipos says, "Didn't your father try to shoot you? Shouldn't he be here with us?"

"I suppose by Heaven's standards, killing an Abomination isn't the same as killing a regular human," says Merihim.

"I don't want to talk about it."

I look at the screen, not really watching it.

I say, "I think we're done here for now. Don't you?"

As they head for the fake bookcase, Merihim says, "Yesterday I said that I'd bring you a protective potion. That will have to wait until I can check that they're not bogus."

"Don't worry about it. I'm not sitting around waiting to get my brain cut open. I'm going to do something."

"What exactly?"

"I have no idea. Something, you know, subtle."

Merihim says, "Like when you burned Eden? I only ask because I'm still trying to gauge your definition of 'subtle.'"

I look at him and can't help but smile.

"That was a fun afternoon. Anyway, you'll know it when you see it."

"I have no doubt."

They go out and Ipos pulls the bookcase shut behind them.

I go over to the screen, put my eye back in, and set the others back on their projection stands.

I open the desk drawer and shove the Glock out of the way. That needs to go in the bedroom drawer with the Smith & Wesson. The Veritas is under some papers where I'd scrawled Hellion power charms. I found the originals stuck in an old notebook Samael tossed in the trash. I copied out all the charms and tossed off hoodoo for darkness and wind. I tried getting into the heads of the salarymen downstairs. Nothing. Maybe instead of trying to be Samael, acting like me again will make me better at this Lucifer thing.

I take out the Veritas and toss it, catch it, and slam it down on the table.

Should I go out or stay here?

There's an image of an open window and billowing curtains. In elegant Hellion script around the edges of the coin, it reads, DON'T WASTE MY TIME, ASSHOLE.

As always, the Veritas is right. I already have my coat on. If it said stay, I'd toss it in the trash and go out anyway.

I go into the false bookcase and head downstairs.

I GO DOWN BELOW street level to the garage. The door is locked but I touch the brass plate on the wall and it clicks open.

The place is full of the Council's limos, plus the legion's trucks, Unimogs, and Humvees. Why didn't I ever take any of these out for a late-night cruise? Do my own Dakar Rally through Hollywood. Play Vanishing Point with Hellion street security. Let them chase me all the way to Santa Monica. Hell's five rivers crash into each other there, churning the water into an endless storm of whitecaps, tidal waves, and whirlpools. At the edge of the sea I'd get out and show them who I am. We could have a drag race all the way back into town.

Tonight, though, I'll just have to settle for some moto-cross. Tomorrow, who knows? I could steal a Unimog and drive down the Glory Road to the gates of Heaven. Bring a bottle of Aqua Regia and toast Samael for the tricky, scheming motherfucker he is. I wonder if he'd drive me home or make me drive myself. Who's the designated driver when you have two Devils in the room?

I head up the ramp to where they keep my bike. Get on and kick it to life. The growling engine vibrates my body from my feet to my head, shaking the stench of Mason's chop shop out of my lungs. I whisper some hoodoo, and when I pull the hoodie up over my head, my face isn't my face anymore. The glamour makes me look like any other ugly Hellion.

I put the bike in gear and head up the ramp to one of the repair bays in back of the hotel. When I get the gate open and I'm sure the way is clear, I pop the clutch. The rear wheel screams and smokes and I blast off into the dark.

It takes my eyes a while to adjust to the night light. I hit the throttle and the bike tears over the city's broken streets, bouncing and flying high over sudden drops, fishtailing in the curves. By the time I can see right, Pandemonium is a super-highway of light, streaks of color bounded by the blood reek of sinkholes and the bruised Hellion sky. I cut in and out of traffic. Around troop transports and pedestrians. I'm up on the sidewalk, and in the few places that have working traffic lights, I run every red I can find. I'm a menace. I'm a monster. I'm a stooge and I don't care who knows it. I'm moving and for the first time in a long time everything is perfect. Hell can kiss my ass.

I HIDE THE HELLION HOG under the collapsed roof of an abandoned garage. On the way out I smooth over the dust to disguise my footprints and toss some cinder blocks inside to give the place an extra about-to-completely-collapse look.

I find Wild Bill smoking outside the Bamboo House of Dolls. When I walk over he shakes his head at me.

"Hop on by, froggy. You see this mark on my shirt?"

He shows me his sleeve. Lucifer's bloodred sigil. He blows out blue cigar smoke.

"I'm bought and paid for by Mr. Scratch himself and he doesn't appreciate simpletons manhandling his merchandise. It lowers the resale value."

"Is that what you tell people? That I own you? I suppose it's technically true, the way things work down here. I just never thought of it that way."

Bill leans forward and squints. Shakes his head and spits.

"I swear to God, boy. Warn a feller when you're going to come 'round looking like a goddamn hobgoblin. I was five seconds from tattooing your head with a shovel I leave out here for just that purpose."

He's telling the truth. There's a solid old shovel in a half-dug hole by the side of the building. I'll bet cash money that hole never gets any deeper or any more full.

"Next time I'll wear a rose in my lapel so you know it's

me. I can't stand another night locked in Gormenghast and thought I'd come by for a drink. Maybe let someone start a fight. It's one of those nights when I want to break things, bones especially. You know the feeling?"

Bill eyes me and tosses the stub of his cigar.

"I'm acquainted with it but you're not going to start any fights in my establishment. I don't want it to become known as somewhere bastards can pay for drinks with the heels of their boots. Also, there's some witches and other magical sorts from your palace inside. I don't know that they could see through your Halloween mask but it seems a foolish thing to chance."

I try to think of a good argument but nothing comes to mind.

"That's too bad. I really want a drink."

Bill shrugs.

"Speaking of drinking, did you get the trifle I sent your way? It's a bottle of a local swill I discovered that's not half bad by the standards of the Abyss. Tastes a bit like bourbon and turpentine. There's a note in there too."

"I haven't gotten anything from you in weeks."

Bill nods slowly.

"You might want to speak to your butlers or whatever kind of flunkies you have up there. Sounds like someone is pilfering your liquor cabinet."

I close in to whispering distance.

"How easy will it be for whoever stole the bottle to find the note?"

He waves his hand dismissively.

"It's sealed under the label. You'd have to look for it to find it, so I wouldn't worry. And any future bottles I send your way will be rotgut. Feeding your demon staff is not my job."

One more thing to worry about. One more reason to punch someone very hard.

"I'll go through the staff offices with hellhounds and a flamethrower. I bet that will turn up the bottle. Hell, maybe the Holy Grail and Amelia Earhart's bones too."

Bill looks past my shoulder as he lights another cigar. I half turn and see legionnaires staring at us. I slap the cigar from his mouth, grab him, and push him hard around the side of the building.

"Move, drytt!"

When we're in the dark, I let Bill go. He shoves me with his free hand and balls the other into a fist.

He yells, "What the hell are you playing at, boy?"

"We were being watched. Hellions and damned souls don't have heart-to-hearts in public."

He lowers his hand and uses it to rub the arm I grabbed, more out of annoyance than pain.

"I suppose you're right. Still, I don't care for being rough-housed."

"Would you rather *I* shoved you and stopped or that one of those other assholes who'd mean it did?"

"I suppose you have a point. But it don't make me any less aggravated."

"So what did the letter say?"

He leans his back against the bar and feels around for another cigar. Pulling one out, he lights it and glances back at the one I knocked to the ground. Cigars and cigarettes aren't easy things for the damned to come by. I'll send him a box in the morning.

"It wasn't much of anything," he says. "You're always concerned with how the local populace regards you. From what I've seen, the rabble takes you as the grand exalted master of the infernal hindquarters just fine. Though your boisterous days as Sandman Slim have left a deeper impression. You're credited with every cutthroat murder and cracked skull in town, of which there are more than a few."

"Lucky me. Most people don't get hated for one life. I'm hated for two. If I get a part-time gig as a meter maid, I can probably make it three."

I find Mason's lighter in my pocket but nothing to smoke.

"Do you have any cigarettes? I left mine back home."

Home. That's a bad habit. Stop thinking that way.

"Sorry. My last smoke went down the shitter when you knocked it out of my mouth."

"Liar."

He half smiles and pulls a pack from another pocket. Bill's been in enough saloons to know that a well-timed cigarette can calm an argument quicker than an ax handle.

"Was there anything else in the note?"

Bill takes a while tapping the Malediction out for me. At first I think it's just how a man who spent decades rolling his own smokes handles premade cigarettes. Then it hits me that he's stalling.

"No. I don't suppose there was anything else that mattered in there."

I check both ends of the alley for movement. Nothing.

More secrets. Just what I need. Is he changing sides? Bill isn't the happiest saloonkeeper in the universe. Taking orders and abuse from drunk Hellions isn't what he's built for.

Maybe someone made him a better offer. Is there anywhere in this fucking town I don't have to look over my shoulder? Do I have to fill the Bamboo House with peepers now?

I turn and start away.

"I shouldn't keep you from your bar, Bill. Thanks for the information."

"Where are you headed?"

"I'm thinking about getting drunk and seeing if I can pick a fight at the arena. I still want some carnage tonight."

"I'll walk with you."

I stop and look back at him.

"You can do that? Just walk around?"

He holds out Lucifer's mark.

"This keeps me out of all kinds of trouble. These pig fuckers might stab each other over a nickel's worth of beer, but they aren't about to break the Devil's toys."

"Come on, then."

"Give me a minute. I got saddled with a dim Hellion for help. Boy'd be a good thief if he ever actually took anything instead of losing it. He's too dumb to steal and too clumsy for the legions, so they made him a barman, which, sadly, in my experience is just about right."

I light the cigarette and watch Bill go inside. Johnny Cash singing "Ain't No Grave" drifts out when he opens the door.

I hate not trusting him. It's been nice being able to be human with him for a few minutes at a time. It's one of the few things that's kept me sane. If he leads me into another ambush, I'll know what side he's really on. If I'm on my own, that's just the way it is. It wouldn't be the first time.

Bill comes back to the side of the bar a minute later and cocks his head for me to follow him.

"Which way do you think is best?" I ask, giving him an opening to lead me down any blind alley he wants.

"Through the market, I reckon. There's a lot of traffic and people are looking at the goods and not at faces."

And crowds are good places to stick a knife in someone's back and disappear.

"Sounds good. Let's go."

We walk in silence. I can't hear his heart or his breathing, but I can see him fine and Bill's movements are definitely tense.

We pass the site where the new City Hall will go up. This Convergence L.A. is solid but there are small places where the real Hell peeks through. Like these Hellion cranes. The cabs are rounded and covered in heavy wired mesh and they have six or eight big portholes instead of windshields. They look a lot more like giant bugs grabbing food with long chitinous beaks than construction equipment.

Bill says, "You're quiet all of a sudden. Usually you're the chatterbox and I'm the one waiting to get a word in."

The market stalls cover the sidewalks and spill onto the roads where the original stores and businesses have burned or been abandoned. The big stalls sell anything a fine upstanding Hellion could want, most of it black market. Clean clothes. Jewelry. Health and hex potions. High-end Aqua Regia and wine.

"I was thinking about who I should flay alive for selling all of Hell's goods to these Harry Lime pricks."

"I see. Maybe you've got more of the devil in you than even I credited you with."

"Maybe it's time to see just how much."

There are ghosts in the crowd. Not damned souls. Ghosts. A few of them follow us.

Bill says, "Back there at the bar, you might have noticed I didn't want to say some things."

"I noticed that."

Bill looks at me.

"That's a cold tone. You peg me for a bushwhacker now too?"

"I'm tired of being surrounded by people with secrets. If you have something to say, just say it."

"All right. But I'll do it my way."

"Fine."

He puffs on his cigar. A red legger elbows Bill out of the way. Bill elbows him right back. The legger whirls around and grabs Bill's arm. I reach for my knife but the raider sees the mark on Bill's arm and backs away.

Bill turns and starts walking again like nothing happened.

"They tell me that back home I'm more notorious than John Wesley Hardin, which is a hoot, as he had more fights and killed at least twice as many men as I ever did. On the other hand, it pleases me no end that Broken Nose Charlie Utter, who so violently disrupted my final card game, is known to very few. Men with restless lives—and I'm including you in this—we don't seem to get much say in who's remembered and who's forgotten and with what amount of affection or derision."

"So I've heard."

"I'm sure you have, Sandman Slim."

Bill puffs his cigar and thinks.

"The point is, whatever you do, whether you'll turn out to be the Antichrist, the prince of killers, or perhaps nothing at all, it's time, not men, that will be the judge."

He stares off at nothing for a second.

"Sometimes I think that last one might be the most preferable state. To be nothing and erased from eternity strikes me as a fine thing some days. But, of course, that wasn't offered to me and it won't be offered to you.

"Where are you going with this, Bill?"

"Where I'm going is that neither of us is predisposed to backing down from a fight, so you need to pick and choose yours better than I did."

Ghosts trail us on both sides of the street. They're not threatening, but any more and they're going to start attracting attention.

"If I've learned one thing, it's that all shed blood, yours or your enemy's, stains Creation forever and there's no washing it away," says Bill. "That lesson came to me too late and I killed at least one good man, a Wichita deputy, because I was too free and easy with others' lives. If I'm in this wretched place for anything, it's that."

I flash on the pictures of dead faces tacked on the walls in Mason's hidden room. I glance at the ghosts. Dead Hellions used to go to Tartarus but I destroyed the place and released them. Now they have nothing better to do than wander Hell's streets until the end of time. I was proud of destroying Tartarus. Now I'm not sure I did anyone a favor.

"I'm not really in a position to turn pacifist at the moment. People want to kill me or take over my mind. I'm not going to lie down and let either of those things happen."

"That's not what I'm talking about. What I'm talking about is this. This moment right here. People are after you and you're off to the arena looking for trouble. There's more than a normal load of troubles on your back, son. You don't need to go adding to them with this sort of doltish behavior."

"Goddamn. Are you telling me to take the Middle Way, Buddha?"

"If that's a fancy way of saying not being a slave to your baser instincts, then yes. Or were you planning on returning here when you're dead and washing my dirty glasses until Judgment Day?"

I flick the Malediction butt into a puddle.

"If I have to choose between being the Devil and your bar back, I might choose bar back. There's free drinks and better hours. Besides, no one ever tips the Devil."

"I thought I just did," drawls Bill.

I look at him as he puffs his stogie.

"Maybe you did."

He stops and looks back the way we came.

"I should head back. That donkey of a helper will've given away half the liquor and probably set the bar on fire by now."

Bill puts out his hand. I shake it.

"Take care of yourself tonight, boy. Try not to be too stupid."

"Thanks, Bill. I'll see you around."

He turns and heads back to the bar, the ghosts trailing along behind him. After seeing a damned soul shove a Hellion and get away with it, I think he's their new hero.

Everything Bill said makes sense but I'm still in the mood to hightail it to the arena and draw blood. So that's what I don't do. I breathe. Count to ten and back down again. Over and over. I read about it in one of the Greek books. It's a kind of meditation to focus the mind, only mine is already focused. What I need is a good, strong unfocuser.

The Devil doesn't carry cash, so I make a deal to trade my practically new overcoat to one of the hawkers for a beat-up surplus trench coat and a bottle of good Aqua Regia. He looks a little suspicious when I agree to such an obvious rip-off but what do I care? I can have tailors run up a dozen more coats by lunch tomorrow.

It takes a few contortionist twists to get the overcoat off and the trench on without giving the market a full frontal of my prosthetic arm. Scaring monsters with scarier monster parts isn't the best way to keep a low profile.

When I'm done do-si-doing with myself, I toss the hawker my coat and take the Aqua Regia before he can change his mind. I open the bottle and take a couple of long swigs. I'm being good and I deserve a drink.

I kind of like what Bill said about picking and choosing fights but my fights always seem to have a habit of choosing me. Or is that just an excuse? I've been getting and giving scars for so long I don't know anymore. I need my own sur-veillance satellite to follow me around for a few months. Hire statisticians to count the punches, bullets, and blades and who blinked first. I don't want to be a cosmic shit magnet drawing trouble to me, but maybe that's how it is with nephilim.

In my new old coat and my fake face, I stroll down the long line of stalls checking out the goods. Is the market growing or is it that I never get out to see what's happening at street level? I take a couple of long pulls on the bottle.

If the market is growing, I know why. I try to count all bottles of black-market potions, ammo, and boxes of food. After a block, I give up and take another pull from the bottle.

Bill is right about one thing. I have plenty to deal with right now. I know his advice makes sense because it's what Alice would have said. She was always the smart one. Pick and choose the skulls you crack and when you do it. No skulls for me tonight, thank you very kindly. I'm as cool as a cat napping on a pint of Rocky Road. At the corner I'll head back for the bike.

I keep seeing red leggers in the crowd. That's new. No way raiders could be strolling around Pandemonium right out in the open without someone getting paid off. I should come down here more often. It's like a parade of the city's sins. Kind of like every boutique on Rodeo Drive.

I take another pull from the bottle. I've already killed half of it.

This bottle and no more. Cross my heart.

If Semyazah has turned into Scarface, that's bad news. I need him to keep a lid on things. And to help keep me alive. I have to find out who's trying to off me or I have to find a way out of here, and I have a bad feeling I'm going to have to do the first before I do the second. If Saint James was here, he'd know what was going on by now. He handles the Mike Hammer stuff and he's not bad at it. Me, I need crib notes and blueprints to make ice.

I go around the corner and head back for where I left the bike. All of a sudden I feel wobbly on my feet. That Aqua Regia was stronger than I thought. I'll have to order some for the palace.

I bounce off a hawker's table. Stepping back, I hold up my hands in apology as the guy calls me an asshole fifty different ways. Hellion might be a simple language, but it can be colorful.

The last thing I want tonight is trouble, so I toss the rest of the Aqua Regia at an oil drum full of trash. And miss. The next thing I hear is someone shouting.

I know that tone. I look over at him. If I stay, there's going to be boots and fists. If I run, I'm going to have six red leggers after me. Not exactly low profile. He and his buddies are headed this way. Basically, I have two options that add up to no options.

Sorry, Bill, but I wasn't the one who let you down. It was the Aqua Regia.

The offended legger is a head taller than me, built long and brawny. His friends are behind him. Dirty faces. Filthy clothes. Country boys who just rolled into town and are seeing the sights when a big-city drunk practically pees on their legs. No way they're going to be at all cool about this.

Still. I say, "Sorry. My fault. I can probably find someone to clean them for you."

If looks could kill, I'd be one grave over from Gabby Hayes right now.

The legger looks at his liquored boots and then at me.

He says, "Keep your money. Come over here and clean them yourself. With your tongue."

His friends laugh. I don't like leggers at the best of times, and this is not one of those.

Behind him is a squat legger with a soft fish face and eye patch.

"I would, but it would just make your girlfriend over there jealous."

Damn. Did I say that out loud? Maybe some of these fights are my fault after all.

The expression on Dirty Boots' face lets me know he's exactly dumb enough to get bent out of shape by such an obvious bait line. I know what's going to happen next but now I know that these are just infantry blockheads and not ninjas in disguise.

The trick in this kind of situation is to move first and keep moving no matter what. They'll think you're crazy and hold back maybe long enough for you to get away. But they're still six trained killers. Even in Lucifer's armor, they can kill me, but not before I take out a few of them first.

I sprint straight at them. Five of them peel off out of the way. The sixth, a bearded Hellion who's gone hungry long enough that his uniform is too big for him, pulls a KA-BAR from his boot and lunges at me.

Even drunk, I'm twice as fast as this backwoods benchwarmer. When he misses with the knife, he leaves himself wide open. I put my boot into his balls, and when he doubles over in pain, I bring my knee up to break his nose. He goes down spewing black blood, and right on cue, his five friends wake up and bum-rush me.

There's not much to do when you're on the bad end of this kind of pile-on except to keep punching and wait for an opening.

I duck, get my hands up in front of my face. Bob and weave. Throw the occasional jab just to remind them that I'm in here somewhere. Half the time they're smacking the armor, so the beating could be a lot worse. What I don't want is for them to get me on the ground, where they can take turns doing Olympic high dives onto my face.

The terrible truth is that I kind of like the beating. It's not like when I got ambushed on the bike. This I saw was coming. It's more like training in the arena. I'm not going to lie and say it doesn't hurt, but it's a familiar kind of pain and it's better than another quiet night in, just the Greeks and me.

*Don't fear God*
*Don't worry about death*
*What is good is easy to get, and*
*What is terrible is easy to endure*

Fuck you, Epicurus. You stand here with a bunch of inbred mouth breathers looking to cut some payback for their shitty existence out of your hide. Do that and then hit me with some cool, cool Hellenic logic. Convince me and I'll buy you all the ouzo and microwave moussaka in Athens.

This might actually be fun if Candy was here. By now she would have dropped her human face and let her inhuman Jade side out. Eyes like red slits in black ice. Claws and a shark-tooth smile. A gorgeous killing machine in ripped jeans and worn Chuck Taylors. The perfect girlfriend.

We've been dancing around for a couple of minutes and the beating slacks off just a bit. The brain trust is punching itself out. I'm supposed to be facedown getting kicked to death by now. The idiot with the KA-BAR is back on his feet but he's hurt and punching like his hands are packing peanuts in a bunny-fur muff. I've drawn blood from at least two others. Another is down on his face and isn't getting up.

The punching stops. Then everything stops. Everything. The leggers' cursing. The sounds of the hawkers. Catcalls from people betting on the fight.

The whole market is looking up the street. The smell of incense mixes with the smells of hot fry oil and garbage. Voices sing softly. Not quite a song. More of a chant. It's a lot prettier than most Hellion music, not that that's hard. Hellion music mostly sounds like a wood chipper falling down an elevator shaft.

Then they come into view. Everyone bows their head. It's a religious procession but not from Merihim's church. The march is almost all women. Obyzuth is up front in her mask and the other women all wear similar masks. The woman at the head of the procession isn't masked. Her face is scarred and battered, like she saw plenty of action in the war Upstairs. She wears her long black hair up, wrapped around a set of heavy, yellowed horns that stick out straight in front of her, the steel-wrapped tips pointing the way for her flock. She has to be Deumos.

Deumos is the head priestess of Hell's other church. From what I've heard around the palace, it's some kind of hard-ass goddess worship. Seems like Merihim and his boys got the giant tabernacle in the center of town and the girls got a piece-of-shit garage down by the railroad tracks. Everything is politics.

On the rare occasions her name comes up, the secret police and Merihim's Tabernacle representatives have a good laugh. Talking about Deumos and her bunch like an old Haight-Ashbury peace-and-love cult. A handful of harmless babes with love beads and delusions of hippie grandeur.

I'm not so sure they should write them off. The crowd seems to take them pretty seriously, including the men, so whatever Deumos is selling it isn't just to the women.

The chant turns quiet. Not quite a prayer. More like if you get close enough they'll tell you a secret. I can make out a few words here and there.

"The being and the becoming . . ."

". . . hand that sweeps clean the way . . ."

". . . cold that burns like black flame . . ."

I'm so caught up watching them that it takes me a minute to remember I'm in the middle of a fight. Then someone reminds me.

A gun goes off and it feels like a pickup truck just planted its front bumper in my right kidney. I fall to my knees, holding my side. Then it dawns on me that I'm not hurt. The only pain is where my knees hit the pavement. The bullet didn't even dent the armor.

The procession takes off at the sound of gunfire, with half the market right behind. The idiots sticking around probably have bets on the fight.

I get to my feet and turn to find Dirty Boots holding his Glock on me. He's surprised I'm standing and now he's waiting for me to fall over. Shooting a second time would spoil his gangster-movie moment. So will killing him in front of his friends but he doesn't know that yet.

When I reach into my pocket for my na'at, it finally dawns on him that I'm not going down. He raises the Glock to fire again. Too late. I whip the na'at out at his arm.

Only it isn't the na'at that hits him. And it doesn't hit his arm.

The Magic 8 Ball from the ghost room. It slams into Dirty

Boots and disappears inside him, leaving a gaping black hole in his chest. He leans forward a little but doesn't fall over. He shudders. And five metal spider legs burst from his back, skewering his friends.

The legs go through the men like a harpoon through Velveeta. The legs curl back and spear them again. And again. Curling and spearing over and over. When the barbed legs retract, his friends are ripped apart in a spray of bone and gristle like they were hit by chain saws fired from cannons.

The spider legs burst from the hole in Dirty Boots' chest and bend back on themselves, latching onto the edges of the hole. With a sudden jerk, the legs rip Dirty Boots' chest open like cracking a lobster. The legs don't stop pulling until they've bent back to touch themselves, practically turning him inside out.

Dirty Boots collapses in a wet heap and the spider legs disappear inside his body. A second later the 8 Ball rolls out and launches itself back into my hand.

The only Hellions that aren't already running are the ones who fell and are crawling under market stalls. I turn and walk the other way.

My hands are covered in Hellion blood. I wipe the 8 Ball and my hands on my coat. The 8 Ball I shove into the pocket of my hoodie. I throw the coat into an oil drum full of burning trash. I snatch a heavy peacoat off the hanger in a hawker's stall and get it on fast, moving the 8 Ball from the hoodie into the coat. I want a little more material between it and me.

There's no fast way back to the bike without going through the market, so I get lost in the crowd trailing the procession.

*Exactly what the fuck just happened?*

I swear I left the 8 Ball back at the palace. But I can't remember where. I'm sure I put the na'at in my pocket, but obviously I didn't. Did the 8 Ball trick me into taking it?

Exactly what the fuck just happened?

I'm glad I didn't let Merihim take the 8 Ball to the Tabernacle. I don't want anyone getting their hands on it. Even me. When I get back, it gets locked up. The damned Glock too.

My head is spinning with Aqua Regia and exploding bodies. I'm not going to figure out anything now. Best just to keep my head down and look for a chance to disappear.

The marchers bunch up a few blocks farther on. It's the women's church, if you can call it that. It's two stories tall. Not much more than one of the Holy Roller places you see scattered all over the poorer neighborhoods in L.A. Tiny congregations of true believers worshipping in what used to be nail salons or the Elks lodge.

Four banners hang in front of the church. The first three I recognize. Merihim's church gospels and the ceiling of Lucifer's library. The Thought. The Act. And the New World. But I don't recognize the fourth banner. There's a shape on it, but it's vague like a face lost in TV static. In between the banners is a wicker figure. I can't tell if it's a man, a woman, or André the Giant. The wicker whatever is as tall as the church.

I didn't know that Obyzuth was in Hell's rebel church or that she was such a big wheel in it. That makes it extra interesting that Lucifer recommended her for the Council.

She and the other higher-up churchwomen are holding burning torches. Women move through the crowd, handing out lit candles. Deumos is whipping up the crowd with a pretty good Elmer Gantry impression.

"The old must burn to make way for the new. Not because it is old, but because the ancient wounds it worshipped and that it believes define it have become diseased and the disease threatens to spread everywhere and to everyone and lay them low."

A murmur of agreement rolls through the crowd.

"You have to burn beliefs when they become convenient lies solely for the purpose of gaining and holding power. Isn't it interesting that when the entire city shook to its foundations and bled, the Tabernacle was barely scratched?"

More murmurs. She has a point.

"The city burned and they want to turn back the clock to the way it was. We will not permit that."

This time she gets cheers.

Deumos picks up a torch from the ground. Obyzuth brings over hers and lets Deumos light hers from it. She tosses the torch into the wicker figure as Obyzuth tosses hers. The other big-time churchwomen toss in theirs. The crowd tosses the candles and lurches forward. I go with it.

From this distance I can tell it's a man they're burning. God the Father blew it, so let's give Him a hotfoot and hope Mom will come down and set things right. I hope you ladies brought lunch because you've got a long wait ahead of you. Dad's broken into more pieces than Humpty Dumpty and Mom doesn't exist.

A young Hellion woman hands me a candle and automatically lights it.

"Are you part of the movement, brother?"

I look around at the crowd.

"I don't really know what it is. I just wanted to see."

She nods.

"That's all right. We all started from where you are. Throw a candle and take the next step."

I expect her to move on but she doesn't. She has candles in one hand and a cup in the other. There's a small pile of coins at the bottom.

"If you can help at all, brother."

She's a Hellion monster. But I'm a monster too. She was tossed over Heaven's walls like trash thousands of years ago but she looks and acts like a kid with her first summer job. Goddammit, for a second she reminds me of the Donut Universe girl and I'm digging in my pocket looking for something to give her. And come up with one big coin. The Veritas. I look at her one more time. No. She's never had green hair or dished up day-old apple fritters.

I drop the Veritas in her cup. You need advice more than I do right now, kid. Momentum and the power of Bible bullshit will carry me safely home to shore. Or not. Anyway, maybe you can trade the Veritas for some decent black-market food.

She doesn't see what I drop in her cup but nods her head in thanks.

"Don't forget your candle."

I follow the line of true believers up front. It seems the polite thing to do. Besides, I just paid for the candle. It might look funny if I dropped it and headed the other way.

People are laughing and singing like a high school pep rally up front by the flames. I should have a camera. Hellions laughing at a tower of fire. Now, this is the Hell I've been looking for. Flames. Mad cheers. And the tingling feeling of things right on the edge of getting out of control.

The fire is up over the wicker man's waist. I have to admit, he's staying upright better than I am. I toss the candle and watch as it tumbles into the flames.

Turning away, I duck deep into the crowd. And I can't help but laugh. This has got to be the strangest day of my whole damn strange life.

It's me in the barbecue pit. They're burning Lucifer.

I CIRCLE AROUND the market and back to where I left the Hellion hog. I tweak the glamour one more time, giving myself a new Hellion face. I don't toss off the glamour until I'm back in the palace heading up the secret stairs to the library.

I'm not in the mood to deal with assassins, Brimborion, or arsonist Joan of Arcs, so I use Vidocq's friend's trick of stacking furniture against the bedroom door.

In the morning I kick the bloody clothes I left at the end of the bed into the pile I want cleaned instead of burned.

I seriously don't like the idea of Brimborion being able to walk in here anytime he likes. Just because I took his passkey doesn't mean he doesn't already have a spare squirreled away somewhere.

My whole life is ruled by magic keys and the assholes who do or don't have them. I found a key in Mason's room, but unless I want to start prying open Hellion skulls, it's not going to do me any good.

Hell's carved enough meat off me that there's no way I'm touching the Magic 8 Ball with my real hand. I use my Kissi hand to move the ball from the pocket of the peacoat to the bottom dresser drawer with the revolver. Until someone can tell me what the thing is, I don't want it near me. Which means no one down here. Not after what I saw it do in the market.

My head pounds from all the Aqua Regia last night. I let the pulsing pain behind my eyes take over, an old arena trick. Dropping down into the center of the pain means I don't have to think, and not thinking means I don't have to find answers, and not needing answers means I might be able to get through the day without homicide.

I don't feel one bit bad about killing those leggers last night. But I don't know how it happened or how that thing got in my pocket. Down here in the pain, I don't have to know. I just note the question and move on. Answers are rare and come in their own time but hangovers are reliable and never in short supply.

After a while the pulse of the pain syncs with my heartbeat. Some old Greek philosopher said there's nothing but atoms and empty space. My head is one very big empty space right now. I take the bottle of Aqua Regia from the nightstand and swallow a short gulp. Hair of the dog. Got to balance the humors. Hippocrates said so. Blame him.

I open my eyes and look out the window. It's around four o'clock. Clouds tumbleweed across a bruised sky. A few fires have flared up again south of the city. The backlight looks like a slow-motion nuclear blast. My Golgotha L.A. has never looked more beautiful.

I don't hear from Brimborion all day. I wonder if he got someone to sew the finger back on. I don't even know if they do that kind of thing down here. Probably they think if you're dumb enough to lose a finger, you deserve for it to stay lost.

Vetis comes by to check on me later.

"You were burned in effigy in the market last night, lord."

"I heard. And don't call me 'lord.' "

"I've doubled your personal security and stationed more legion troops downstairs."

Ms. 45 pokes her head around the door. Vetis takes a step back. She waits a couple of beats and moves down the hall.

"Thanks. I'm feeling pretty well protected these days."

It's the middle of the night when the bedroom phone rings. It's never done that before. I've never used it. I pick up the receiver on the fourth ring.

"Hello?"

"Still alive and kicking, I see."

"Who is this?"

"Puddin' 'n' Tain. Ask me again and I'll tell you the same."

"Fuck you. I'm hanging up."

As I put down the receiver the voice comes again.

"You're always so serious. So linear. You've got to get into the spirit of things."

I almost recognize the voice but not quite.

"What spirit is that?"

"That you're nothing. You've been flailing at the universe your whole life, and where has it gotten you? You're not really the Devil. You're not Sandman Slim. You're not a man and you're not an angel. Some people live in gray areas but, friend, you are a gray area."

"Am I supposed to understand any of that?"

"You could always kill yourself now and save us the trouble."

"What would that solve? I'd just end up right back here. Did Brimborion put you up to this?"

"What do you think?"

"I think he's hiding somewhere nursing his hand with whiskey and a Valium chaser."

"There you are."

"Am I supposed to be spooked by this? You sound like someone's dad hard selling Girl Scout cookies."

"You're not the only one with peepers, you know. Don't think because you watch the world, the world doesn't watch you back."

"I'm going to find you, you know."

"I'm counting on it."

There's a click and the line goes dead.

Crank calls? Is this how things work from here? This isn't Hell. It's junior high.

I WAKE UP hurting. The hangover is gone and now I can feel every bit of the beating I took last night. My jaw aches and my ribs are bruised. Every time I move, the armor presses on them and makes me wince.

Something shatters down the hall. Glass and metal. Something heavy hits the floor, like a car falling through the ceiling. I grab my knife and run toward the sound.

Ms. 45 is lying on her side by one of the big picture windows in the front room. The glass dome holding her brain is smashed. Pink meat and spinal fluid leak onto the tile floor. I stand by the body listening. Ready for whoever got to her to come for me.

I don't hear a thing. It doesn't make sense that someone could get in here but they did. The peeper by the hall is gone, so I can't play back whatever happened.

Maybe I shouldn't have been so quick to ditch the Glock.

Making a pass through the rest of the penthouse, I don't see anything out of place. I need to get someone to clean up the hound before it stinks in here like Mason's lab. There's a phone in the bedroom. I get the Glock from the library and head there.

A shadow flickers across the bedroom.

Looks like Brimborion has a second passkey after all. Good. First I find out what he's looking for in my room and then I get to kill him.

But the moment the thought forms, I know it's wrong. Brimborion isn't the creeping-around-smashing-hellhounds type. Especially not when he just lost a finger. Whoever's in the bedroom has much bigger balls and a lot fewer brain cells than him. But he'll know who's after me and he's going to give me a name if I have to repaper the hallway with his skin.

With the Glock in a two-hand TV-cop grip, I shoulder open the bedroom door. No one in sight. I go inside, sweeping the room with the gun. The closet door is open, the space empty. If Mr. Soon to Be Dead is in toddler freak-out mode, he might be under the bed. More than likely he's in the bathroom trying to squeeze himself down the shower drain.

I start across the room but only make it to the end of the bed.

Behind me, the door creaks open the rest of the way.

"Here are your fucking messages."

No question about the voice. It's Brimborion.

I turn around. He sees the Glock in my hand and in an

inspiring display of self-preservation lurches back, cracks his head on the door, and falls onto his knees. I grab his shoulder and pull him to his feet.

"How did you get in here?"

He looks at me like I've gone insane and stupid all at the same time.

"The door was open."

"Not the goddamn bedroom. My apartment."

His eyes go to the gun and then back to me.

"I have another key. Are you going to kill me for doing my job?"

Glass breaks in the bathroom. Something hits the wall. Over and over. Someone is going nuts in there.

I shove Brimborion over to the corner of the room. He's not going anywhere until I know if contestant number two is someone he sent. If he's looking for some payback because of his finger, he's going to be disappointed.

The bathroom door swings open slowly and a Hellion walks out. You could mistake the guy for human if his arms and legs weren't half again as long as they should be. And if his skin wasn't the color of a dead fish on the ocean floor. He's wet too. I hear running water. Sounds like he ripped the sink out of the wall.

"Lahash?" says Brimborion. "What are you doing here?"

Lahash takes a couple of uncertain steps out of the bathroom. He looks up but barely registers us. I'm liking Lahash less and less. The guy is on some major drugs or some heavy hoodoo. The bedroom is huge by normal non–Lord of the Underworld standards, but if it was the size of a zeppelin hangar, I still wouldn't want to be in it with this guy.

"Lahash. I'm talking to you," says Brimborion. "How did you get in here?"

I shove Brimborion back against the wall.

"Shut up. There's something wrong with him."

Lahash stiffens. Turns his milky-white eyes in my direction. He recognizes my voice. No point in playing church mouse now.

"Who sent you here, Lahash? Are you looking for me or something in here?"

He swings his head to the other side of the room like he's trying to remember where he is. There's a brain working somewhere in his skull but it looks like the wiring is a little frayed.

Brimborion makes a break for the door. I sweep his feet, cutting him down at the ankles so he falls on his face. Lahash shrieks like a banshee in a blender and throws himself across the bed, crawling toward us.

There's a good twenty feet between Lahash and me. I shove Brimborion back in the corner with one hand and pull the Glock's trigger with the other. The bullet hits Lahash above his left eye. He freezes, arms stiff. Like I caught him in mid-push-up. A second later his eyes lock back on me and he's crawling again. Faster this time.

I put two more shots into his head. He doesn't slow. He stands on the bed, knees bent like he's going to jump. I put five shots into his chest dead center.

I should have stuck with head shots.

Lahash doesn't fall. He falls apart. His bones seem to crack and separate under his skin. Holes in his chest sag into slits and open like a plastic sandwich bag, only it's not egg salad on wheat inside. It's bugs. Lots and lots of bugs.

Behind me Brimborion alternates between hyperventilating and doing a passable impression of Little Richard's falsetto. I'm kind of at a loss myself. I never tried to beat up bugs before. Do you work the body or rope-a-dope them?

With nothing better to do, I fire off a few rounds into the writhing pile. No reaction from the bugs, but I'm pretty sure I murdered my bed.

The only thing that's kept Brimborion and me alive these few seconds is that when the bugs burst out of Lahash, they began eating him. Now the first wave is getting bored with his dead ass and wants fresh meat.

I throw some arena hoodoo at the swarm, a simple slam-down move that feels like someone driving a knee into your solar plexus. The middle of the swarm stops like it smacked into an invisible wall, but the other billon little bastards flood around it.

I could do an airburst and explode all the oxygen in the room. That would kill the bugs, but in an enclosed space like this, it would blow out my lungs and turn my organs into cat food. Some kind of fire is my best weapon but this is the wrong terrain. I go for the next best thing.

I crawl to the corner of the room with Brimborion. Bite down as hard as I can on my right hand until I draw blood, and splatter it on the floor between the bugs and me. The blood is like slop to pigs. They head right for it, lapping it up. I keep flicking my hand, throwing out as much blood as I can between the bugs and me. That sucks but it's the next part that's really going to hurt.

Whispering some bad black Hellion hoodoo, I punch through the wall above a wall socket. Feel for the wires with my bloody hand and grab the bare copper leads where they touch the wires going to the plug.

The average human body doesn't react well to having 120 volts blasted through it. In fact, it tries really hard to get away, so when you force it to do something as stupid as grab live wires and not let go, you get to experience the twin thrills of excruciating pain and a total revolt by your skin and bones because your body doesn't understand what your mind is making it do. It's pain on every level of your being. Nerves, muscles, and skin all trying to crawl away from each other. But you hold on because it's the only thing keeping you alive and your body can goddamn well cowboy up and deal with it.

The hoodoo kicks in just as I'm starting to black out. Blood kick-starts dark magic like nothing else, and when the hoodoo hits, my bedroom turns into the Fourth of goddamn July as the electricity flowing through my bloody hand explodes from the splattered patches of blood on the floor. Writhing drifts of bugs fry instantly. Thousands are blown into the air by the force of the blast. The bugs spin like pinwheels, each trailing a tiny lightning bolt from its head to the bloody floor. It's all skyrockets and flare guns in here. And when the bugs fall, they're as crisp and dead as autumn leaves.

I pull my hand out of the wall and fall flat on my back. My knees are vibrating. My jaw aches from being clenched so hard. I look down at my hand. Have you ever started cooking bacon, gotten a phone call, and forgotten about it until you smelled charred pig? That's me. I am bacon. Hear me roar. On the upside, the bite is nicely cauterized.

Behind me, I hear Brimborion push back the table he was

hiding behind. He crawls over to me. There's a neat, clean bandage wrapped around one of his hands.

"You saved me," he says.

I look up at him sitting above me.

"What?"

He sits back on his haunches. Rests his back against the wall.

Brimborion says, "I don't understand you. Yesterday you cut off my finger and today you save my life. What's wrong with you?"

"I'm just really tired."

"You could have thrown me to those things and gotten away."

"I'll have to remember it for next time."

He leans over me and makes a face like he smells spoiled milk.

"Your hand looks awful."

" 'Awful' is a kind of relative term. I mean, it looks better than Lahash."

Brimborion lifts his head to get a better look at the smear of bone and gristle on the bed.

"You knew him. Who was he?"

"An herbalist," Brimborion says. "He worked with the palace thaumaturgists. I used to buy . . . things from him."

"You mean he's your dealer."

"If you wish."

"Did he have access to the good stuff?"

"What do you mean?"

"Like maybe hypnotics. Something that would loosen him up enough for psychic control."

"Do you think that's what happened to him?"

"I don't know. What kind of persuading would it take for you to sit still while someone pumped you full of carnivorous bugs?"

Brimborion crosses his arms. Uncrosses them. Leans his head against the wall and looks at the ceiling.

I roll over onto my Kissi arm, the only part of me that doesn't hurt, and push myself into a sitting position. I try to move my burned fingers. When they flex, flakes of black skin drop off, revealing blistered red flesh underneath. At least there's enough good skin left to heal.

"Would you like me to get you something?" Brimborion asks.

"What?" I say, my brain and body not quite on speaking terms yet.

Brimborion points to my hand.

"Would you like me to get you something for that? The palace witches make some powerful healing potions."

"Yeah. Sure," I say. "And some cigarettes. I really need a cigarette."

"I'll be back."

He pushes himself to his feet.

"Don't tell anyone about this. Especially not Vetis. I don't want to be up to my eyeballs in security," I say. "Act like nothing happened. That should give whoever set this up something to think about."

"You don't even want the room cleaned?"

"Leave it just like it is."

"I understand."

He starts to leave.

"What did you say when you first came in?"

He goes to the end of the bed, picks up an envelope and a rectangular box from the floor, and brings them to me.

"I had your mail."

"That all came today?"

"The box yesterday. The notes before. I don't remember when."

"You wouldn't have given me any of this if we hadn't had our little talk in the hall last night."

"No."

"Why these particular letters?"

He shakes his head.

"They weren't the usual official correspondence. Holding them back would make sure you stayed isolated."

"People pay you off to hold back certain messages and to give me others."

Brimborion shrugs.

"Everyone in the palace has something on the side. It's the generals who get rich. Not civil servants."

"Who paid you to hold on to these?"

He looks at the bed.

"Lahash."

That's a nice way of covering your trail. Don't just kill the guy who knows too much. Turn him into a suicide bug bomb.

"If someone wants to assassinate you, there must be easier ways," says Brimborion.

"They tried easier. Now they tried this. Watch your ass. You work for me, so sooner or later you're going to be on the bug list too."

He touches his hand to his chest, about where Lahash

burst open. He turns and goes out, pulling the doors closed behind him.

I use my teeth to pull the glove off my Kissi hand. I'll be using it a lot the next few days.

I undo a couple of buttons on my shirt and slip my burned hand inside like it's a sling. The feeling is starting to come back, meaning it already hurts like hell. I growl Hellion hoodoo and the blackened skin on my hand lightens to its skin color. I've never been great at healing magic but at least I can make the hand look normal while it heals. I just won't be penning Candy any sonnets over the next few days.

I pull the black blade from my waistband. It feels weird doing it lefty. Prop the box between my knees and slice it open. It's what I thought. The bottle Bill sent me. I stick the point of the knife in the floor, twist the cap off the bottle, and take a long drink. Bill was right. It's not half bad by Hell standards.

I toss the box over by the dead bugs and look at the first envelope. Printed in a perfect, precise script on the first en-velope is the single word *Stark*. The envelope is made of something almost transparent. Like rice paper, only tougher. Barely visible angelic script is woven into the paper's fibers. I hold it in my teeth and, using the black blade like a letter opener, shake the envelope until the letter falls out.

*Dear James,*
*I know by now you must hate me and you have*
*every right to.*

I only have to read a sentence to know who sent it. Mr. Muninn.

*I should have been truthful with you from the moment you talked about returning to Hell. For that I'm sorry. You have my best wishes, my prayers, and my full confidence that you'll make a safe return home. I wish I could say more but time is short. By now I'm sure you know that my brother, Neshamah, is dead by Aelita's hand. She and my other brother, Ruach, the part of us that still rules in Heaven, seem to have come to some sort of vicious understanding. Aelita means to kill the rest of us and Ruach has agreed to let her, leaving him alone to rule. I should leave Los Angeles, in fact this world, but I've come to love it so. For now I'll lose myself in the tunnels where the dead once roamed under the city. I suppose it's a pathetic fate for a deity but one I probably deserve for deserting my brothers and not doing my part to stop this madness long ago.*

*Take care of yourself, my boy. I'm sure we'll meet again.*

*Protect the Singularity.*
*With warmest regards,*
*Muninn*

I guess it's nice that one of us thinks I'm getting out of this alive but it's annoying how wrong Muninn is. I don't hate him. I'm pissed. I want to strangle him, but only until he turns some funny colors. Not until he's dead. The guy is scared to death and I understand that. Plus, he apologized, which is more than I can say for Saint James.

There's nothing written on the second envelope. I turn it

over. It's closed with a red wax seal imprinted with twisted, angular lines like a piece of rusty bailing wire in an old barn. Samael's sigil is as crooked as he is.

*Dearest Jimmy. Or, if you prefer, your Infernal Majesty,*

*I bet you've had a few chuckles when you found out that all my plans and machinations designed to return me to Heaven returned me to one ruled by a bastard and a fool. I've laughed about it a few times myself, but only in private and very, very quietly.*

*Have assassins given you any interesting new scars? Murder is unsettling when you're on the receiving end, isn't it, Sandman Slim? Worst of all, it destroys your ability to trust, which is the point of this note. When you have no allies to go to for help, there's only one logical solution. Go to your enemies. When your back is against the wall, ask yourself this question: which bastard has the most to gain by helping me?*

*Here's hoping this note finds you as charming and unmurdered as ever.*

*Yours in Christ,*
*Samael*

I don't know whether to be madder at Samael or Brimbor-ion. It would have been really nice to know that someone out there was thinking about me, even if it was the asshole that stuck me here. And it would have been really goddamn helpful a few weeks back to get strategic advice from someone who has more reasons to want me alive than dead.

Squatting in the middle of a hundred pounds of dead bugs loses its charm fast. I put the knife in my waistband, shove the letters in my pocket, and tuck the bottle under my arm. With my good hand I close the bedroom door and head down the hall. Brimborion will know where to find me.

I'm sacked out on the library sofa when he knocks a half hour later. I open the door, and when he sees my bare Kissi arm, he doesn't try to come inside. He hands me a wide-mouthed clay jar sealed with an old cork stopper.

"I told the witches someone on my staff was hurt. I think they believed me. They said this will help but it might stain your sheets."

It's not really funny but I can't help but laugh a little.

"Keep it," I tell him. I hold up my apparently healed hand.

"We can't pretend nothing happened if I'm slathering that stuff all over me. I'm a pretty fast healer, and when the pain gets too bad, well, I'll probably be drunk a lot for the next few days, so you don't want to schedule me for any banquets or ballet lessons."

Brimborion nods.

"I can tell them you're working on the new sewage project."

"Good. That sounds so fucking boring no one is going to bother me wanting to help with that."

I get a piece of paper from the desk, write a note, and hold it out to him.

"I need you to do one more thing. Give this to Vetis."

Brimborion plucks the note from my hand with his fingertips, trying to keep his distance from the Kissi hand.

"Go ahead and read it. I know you're going to."

He unfolds the paper. I watch his eyes as he scans it a couple of times before putting it away.

"You want to arrest Deumos."

"And everyone who works with her."

"Do you think she had something to do with Lahash?"

"No."

"Then why?"

"It's like what that famous Greek philosopher Bugs Bunny once said: 'I don't ask questions. I just have fun.' "

He blinks at me like he's waiting for a translation. I nod good night and close the door.

Back on the sofa, I take a swig from Bill's bottle of Hellion moonshine. This stuff could grow on me. I'll have to get him to send more.

I look around for a Malediction and realize Brimborion didn't bring me any cigarettes.

See? One thing goes right and everything else falls apart.

Should I tell Vetis about the crank call? What am I going to say that isn't going to make me sound weak? Maybe I'll have him keep a closer eye on Brimborion.

Hell really blows.


I HAVE A PRETTY GOOD IDEA of what's coming the next day when Brimborion tells me Semyazah is on his way up. The only good thing is that it will be direct and contained. For now.

Semyazah bangs on the library door but he can't get in. After bug man's visit, I've laid even heavier hoodoo on the place. Sulfur and arsenic above the door. A line of iron filings across the entrance.

I get the door halfway open and Semyazah shoves his way into the room. Merihim and Marchosias come in behind him. Merihim has red patches on his face and arms where he's added some tattoos. More protection spells. Marchosias is dressed like Ilsa, She-Wolf of the SS's stunt double.

They notice my bare Kissi arm. They try not to make faces. None of them succeeds.

"Exactly what do you think you're doing?" says Semyazah.

I walk back to my desk, leaving them by the door. Let them follow me into my territory.

"I'm being Lucifer. I was ambushed. Someone with heavy magic possessed the idiots who attacked me. Last night I get a crank call telling me to kill myself or get murdered. It must have come from inside the palace, or are your people selling Satan's private number on Craigslist? On top of that, Deumos burns me in effigy. A trifecta of bullshit. So Lucifer is retaliating."

I pour myself a drink. Semyazah follows me back to the desk. If looks could kill.

"Retaliating against those pathetic witches? They couldn't have attacked you. Or called you. They're rabble with no re-sources. Deumos's followers are as lost as any damned mortal soul in Hell. By attacking them, you're making those fools more important than they have any right to be."

Merihim is just listening. He picks up random books and objects from the shelves. The same above-it-all bullshit he always pulls when he's trying to figure out who has the upper hand in a discussion. Sometimes he reminds me of Medea Bava, the head of Sub Rosa inquisition. Marchosias looks at me like I'm barbecue ribs and she's trying to decide between a Texas red sauce and Carolina mustard.

Merihim says, "I'm not so sure. Our lord's tone is boorish but he might be right to stop this false prophet with one short swift blow. Deumos wants to weaken our true church and divide the people."

"I agree," says Marchosias. "Are we going to stand around like those sheep in Heaven as she transforms herself into a new Lucifer and leads a rebellion against us?"

The general isn't happy his two compadres disagree with him. How far can I push him?

"Semyazah's just mad he missed raiding Deumos's church with Vetis. Don't worry. I'll wake you the next time so you can join the fun."

He takes a couple of steps in my direction.

"Don't you dare speak to me like that."

I push myself up off the desk.

"Like what? Your boss?"

"Like a fraud and a coward who plans to desert us the moment he finds a way out of Hell."

"Damn right. Your war landed you here. Me, I just slipped on a banana peel."

Marchosias taps a fingernail on the bookcase to get our attention.

"If it helps, we've identified the three soldiers who attacked you. They're from different companies within the legion. We're interrogating their comrades and senior officers. We're also interrogating the weapon masters and taking an inventory of the armory to see where they might have found their guns."

"Great. So you're going to chat up what, four hundred soldiers who are all going to lie and stick up for their buddies.

And how long is it going to take to count every pistol in the armory? How will you even know if you can trust the count? You'd be better off wandering the streets wearing a big sign that says 'Did You Do It?' "

Semyazah lowers his head and half smiles.

"This is the great and terrifying Sandman Slim, the monster who kills monsters? I never thought a feeble attack and a phone call would have you behaving like this. It's unbecoming for an assassin or the lord of Hell."

I sit down at the desk and sip my drink.

"Come on, boys and girls. We all know I'm a terrible Lucifer. I only got the job because I killed Mason."

"Don't be so modest," says Marchosias. "No one else could stop him. I mean no slight, General, but if it wasn't for Stark, Heaven would have laid waste to all of Hell and we'd be dead."

"So what? Killing Mason doesn't qualify me to run a muffin stand in a mall. You're all more qualified to be Lucifer than I am but none of you has the sand to step up and do it."

Merihim shakes his head.

"This is absurd and insulting. Come. Let's leave our lord to think his deep thoughts."

He starts for the door and Semyazah follows. Marchosias rolls her eyes and starts after them.

"Don't be so hasty," she says.

I shout some hoodoo and the door seals itself shut.

"We're having this out right now. Everyone agrees I'm no good. Let's do something about it. No one leaves until there's a new Lucifer."

They stare at me.

"You assholes love your rituals. Let's try this one on for size. Kill me and you get the job. Wound me and I'll give up. Trust me. I'm not going to fight hard to stay Lucifer."

I pull the black blade from behind my back with the Kissi arm. It feels awkward using my left hand, but the effect is worth it.

I hold out the knife to each of them.

"How about it? General? Merihim? Marchosias?"

I throw the blade so it sticks point first in the floor between them.

"Why don't you all do it together? I can't possibly take all three of you at once."

No one moves. Merihim's body language says he's somewhere between fainting and doing a Cowardly Lion dive out of the nearest window. Marchosias backs away behind a bust of Lucifer on a short marble pillar.

Semyazah's eyes narrow. I gave his ego a hotfoot. He looks like he might actually go for the blade.

The moment his shoulder twitches, I kick the desk chair in front of him. He's quick. The chair catches one of his legs but he still manages to get the knife. Rolling to his feet, he throws it at me. It's a pretty good shot for someone off balance on a hurt leg. But I've had a lot of knives heaved at me over the years. I know what good aim looks like and knife throwing isn't Semyazah's specialty. All I have to do is lean back and the knife sails past. Semyazah grabs a metal candle stand, holding it in front of him like a spear.

It's three fast steps to where he's planted himself. I drag the desk behind me as I go. Whip it around like a baseball bat, crashing through a bookshelf and catching him on the side.

There's a loud crack as I make contact and he half flies, half slides down the marble floor to the library doors.

Blood flows into my left eye. The crack when I hit Semyazah wasn't from him or the desk. It was a derringer he's pulled from his sleeve. The shot grazed the side of my head.

Merihim and Marchosias are backed up against shelves full of Hellion art books. Merihim has gone dead white. I throw each of them over a shoulder in a kind of half-assed fireman's carry, holding them low. Keeping their bodies between me and Semyazah. The general is flat on his back but he could be playing possum and he has at least one bullet left in the pocket gun. Merihim starts thrashing when he figures out he's a human shield. I pull my arm a little tighter and squeeze the air out of him.

When I'm over Semyazah, I step onto the arm holding the gun. The general's eyes are open but he doesn't move. I don't think he's broken. Just a little dazed. I toss Merihim and Marchosias down on either side of him, take the derringer, and drop the hammer so it won't go off in my pocket.

A minute later Semyazah sits up. I take the knife from a scabbard on his belt and slap it into his hand.

"We aren't done yet. It's still three against one and I'm not armed. You drew first blood, General. Take your shot. Kill me."

He doesn't move. I can't tell if his gaze is uncertain or unfocused.

"Afraid you'll miss?"

I grab him with the Kissi hand and press the tip of the blade into the base of my throat.

"Now you can't. Kill me. Become Lucifer."

When Semyazah doesn't budge, Merihim grabs his hand

and pushes. The blade goes in far enough to draw blood. I feel it run down my neck and under the armor. Semyazah twists and punches Merihim in the face. The preacher lets go of the knife when Semyazah elbows him in the throat. He looks at Marchosias like he's about to deck her. She holds up her hands, shaking her head.

Semyazah slides the knife back into its scabbard.

"This doesn't change anything. You're still a coward and a fraud."

"And you won't do anything about it 'cause you'd rather have a coward and a fraud on the throne than sit there yourself."

I find my knife where it's embedded in the wall and slip it into the waistband at my back. Walk back to where the last of Bill's bourbon fell. The bottle hit the floor but didn't break. Lucky me. My desk is cracked and splintered but still has four legs. I pull it upright and sit down, taking a couple of pulls from the bottle. The wound on my head throbs but is already scabbing over; my burned hand, though, got bounced around enough that it throbs and aches.

"You Hellions think you're so fucking special. What's that stuff on the ceiling? The Thought. The Act. The New World? You think God threw you out because you bravely stood up to Him? Bullshit. You started a fight and you lost and you've been whining about it ever since. Hell isn't righteous exile. With all your secret handshakes and horseshit rituals, you've made the place into one more members-only gated community. All you people need are Mercedes SUVs and illegals to clean your pools and you couldn't tell Hell from Brentwood.

That's why you hate Deumos and her heretic ducklings. It's not because they're crackpots, which they definitely are. What gets under your skin is that they want to move into the house down the street. Old money hates the nouveau riche. It's a sad, stupid story even down here in the stupidest place in the universe."

Merihim and Marchosias get to their feet. When Marchosias starts to help Semyazah, the general shakes her off.

"Are you going to open the door or are we your prisoners?" he asks.

I bark some Hellion and the library doors unlock.

"May I have my gun?"

I get the derringer, pop out the remaining bullet, and toss the pistol to him. He heads for the door without waiting for the other two. Merihim pulls a book from his robes and throws it on the floor.

"Here's the book you asked about, you ungrateful lout. Read it before you do anything else stupid. Pay particular attention to the final passage. It's more apt now than ever before."

When they're gone I go over and get the book I never asked Merihim about.

It's an old copy of Hellion psalms. Battered and annotated in the margins. Complete bargain-bin shit. The book doesn't matter. It's the note inside. I recognize Merihim's neat writing.

*Last night Ipos sent word that he found evidence of someone or possibly more than one person in maintenance uniforms using building plans to move*

*about the palace. This morning Ipos is dead. I'll
send updates when and if I can. Until then, do not
contact me.*

Looks like I just burned a few more bridges. Fuck 'em. I
was always the dog-faced boy to Semyazah. A sideshow freak
in a suit. Merihim might have been on Samael's side but he
knows I don't give two shits about his church. Marchosias,
well, she likes to be where the action is.

I feel bad about Ipos. One more face to go up on the wall
of the people who've died for me one way or another.

I check the peepers in the bedroom. It looks all clear. I go
in and grab everything I need. Clothes. Toothbrush. I toss the
na'at into the drawer with the Smith & Wesson, the singularity, and the Magic 8 Ball and carry it like a TV tray into the
library.

The front doors feel safe for now. I put down arsenic and
sulfur in front of the secret door that Ipos and Merihim used.
The truth is, I feel pretty good. I shook things up. I got to
break things. I got shot without dying. And I didn't even have
to go to the arena to do any of it.

The list of my enemies was the size of a phone book when
I got here and it'll be a whole set of encyclopedias by the time
I leave. If the enemy I'm counting on doesn't come through,
at least I'll have a lot more to choose from.

I've tried to avoid everyone, so I haven't used the hotel
phones much. The one in the library is like the others. Even
though the Beverly Wilshire is my demonic palace, it's still a
hotel and the phones are put together hotel-style. A regular
push-button model with a row of specialty buttons at the

top. Instead of direct lines to the concierge and front desk, this phone only has two buttons. They read VIAND and PISSANTS. I pick up the receiver and push PISSANTS. Brimborion picks up.

"Lucifer?"

"Do you know who's locked up in the dungeon?"

His voice drops to a whisper.

"Yes."

"I'm guessing you know discreet ways to get around the palace where no one's going to see you."

"Of course."

"I want you to get the leader out without anyone seeing. Especially the guards. Can you do that?"

"I'll have to distract them."

"Whatever you need."

"May I use a hellhound or two?"

"Use a zeppelin, for all I care. Just get her up here. I think we've come to an understanding, so I'll even give you your passkey back."

"Thank you," he says. There's a microsecond's hesitation.

"You have another stashed away, don't you?"

"I wouldn't be good at my job if I didn't plan ahead."

"Just get her up to the library. And be sure to knock. There was a little scuffle in here earlier and I've added new security."

"Is anyone interesting dead?"

"Soon."

I hang up and take out the black blade. Carve dark magic crosses and hexes on the floor up front and by the secret door. Shapes of ice, fire, and darkness. You can't be too careful, especially after you know at least one other person has the keys to the kingdom. Now I just have to not step in my own traps on the way out.

It's easy to lose track of time Downtown. I've been here one hundred days and a week. A week? More like three or four days since the first attack. In the next day or so I'll either have the assassins off my back or be dead. Either way I won't have a Dr. Caligari reject in the bedroom belching bugs on the duvet. On the other hand, there's no reason to think I'll destroy the possession key or the psychic amplifier anytime soon. So I'm still fucked, but finding out who's actually sending bug men and bikers after me and killing my killers should buy me enough time to figure out how to access the last of Lucifer's power.

I look at the hotel phone. If there are only two buttons and one is to a lackey, what's the second for? I push VIAND.

"My lord?"

"Is this the kitchen?"

"Yes, lord."

"Don't call me 'lord.' Did anyone down there watch the cable cooking shows I told you about?"

"Yes, lord. Lucifer. I did."

"Great. Let's keep things simple. How about you make me a burrito?"

"What kind of meat would you like?"

"What have you got?"

"Manticore. Greater and lesser sand jellyfish. Archaeopteryx. And white strangler fungi. It's called fungi but really it's a light-tasting parasite that grows in the bowels of—"

"I know what it is and I wouldn't eat that shit with God's

mouth. Make it manticore. And send up some Aqua Regia and a carton of Maledictions. Leave it all outside the library door."

"Will there be anything else, lord?"

"Yeah. Book me a first-class seat on the red-eye to Burbank."

"You want a book, lord? I thought you were in the library."

"Forget it. Just the food and smokes."

I know whatever they bring up will be horrible but at least it will look like something from home. And manticore meat isn't that bad. Sort of like a buffalo, a jalapeño, and a jar of vinegar had a baby.

Fuck me. I'm turning into a lifer. I'm calling the apartment mine and getting used to the food. I need to be dead or out of here fast.

THERE'S A SOFT KNOCK on the library door. I open it, careful not to step in any of my bear traps. Brimborion is in the hall with Deumos.

"No one saw us. Also, this was outside the door."

He holds up the food tray. I lift the metal top off the plate with the burrito. It looks like a giant maggot in a gray bathrobe. I put the top back on the plate and pull Deumos inside.

"Cool your jets for thirty minutes."

I take the Aqua Regia and cigarettes off the tray.

"Keep the burrito. I hope you like manticore."

Brimborian looks at the tray and back at me, surprised.

"Thank you."

"Thirty minutes," I say.

I close the door and look at Deumos. She looks very

human even if her skin is a little on the snaky side. She holds her head up high enough that it looks like she could use the horns wound in her hair as a weapon. She's in a floor-length robe that shades from a deep bloody red at her shoulders to a pink so pale it's almost white at her feet. I point to the floor.

"You're going to want to walk around those marks. Otherwise you'll end up boiled, blind, or a Popsicle, depending on which hex you step into."

She looks down, gathers up the bottom of her robe, and carefully steps over the marks. When she's clear she walks a few paces farther and turns and fixes me with her hard, bright eyes.

"Did you bring me here to kill me? You have quite a reputation for that sort of thing."

"I pretty much live in here. If I was going to kill you, I'd do it down the hall in the room with the dead guy and the bugs."

She looks around at the bookcases. When she looks at the fresco on the ceiling she smiles.

"I take it the first Lucifer made this."

"Yeah. I'm more the high-def TV man."

"I'm sure," she says. "If I'm not here to die, why am I here?"

"First to remind you that I'm not the first Lucifer. I didn't set up any deals with the Tabernacle and I'm not your enemy. Just because I'm the Devil doesn't mean I give a goddamn about religion."

"If you're not my enemy, then why are my sisters and I in a dungeon?"

"If you want to play it like that, how about you burned the goddamn king in effigy?"

"Ah. You know about that."

"I was there."

She clasps her hands in front of her.

"You shouldn't have been so shy. We would have welcomed you into the circle."

"Thanks, but I'm allergic to seeing myself executed."

She makes a *tsk* sound with her teeth.

"A symbolic burning is just that for us. Symbolic. We meant and we mean you no physical harm. Burning the symbol of authority is a signal that we must overturn completely the current order of Hell."

"Now you sound like a politician."

She shakes her head.

"I mean spiritual order. Though I suppose to Lucifer there's no difference between the two."

"You didn't have anything to do with the attacks on me, did you?"

"Don't be absurd. Assassination is the last thing we want. Hell has seen enough upheaval to last us a thousand years."

"But if someone else put a bullet in my head, you'd be happy to send flowers to my funeral."

"Asphodels and moon wort in a lovely arrangement."

"See? No one else admits they want me dead. That's why I don't trust them. You want a drink?"

I head down to the couch. Deumos follows, pausing to examine the broken bookcase and splinters from where I tossed the desk.

"What do you have?" she asks.

"Aqua Regia."

She makes a face.

"No thank you."

I find the bottle Wild Bill sent.

"This too. I've never heard of it before."

She looks the bottle over and nods.

"This I'll try."

I find a fairly clean glass behind the sofa and pour her a drink. I fill mine with Aqua Regia and raise it to her. She raises hers to me and takes a sip.

"You knew my church and I had nothing to do with the attacks on you and you arrested us anyway. Why?"

"You tell me."

She stares at her drink and doesn't say anything for a minute.

"To make a public spectacle. To make us look like more than we are and yourself less."

I hold up my glass like I'm toasting her.

"Give the people what they want. The ones who are after me. They want me weak and twitchy. I send a SWAT team to take out a storefront preacher and it comes off like a huge overreaction."

"You get your shadow play and we get to sit in prison. Forgive me if I don't applaud your cleverness."

"If I thought you'd applaud me, you'd still be locked up."

She sits on the sofa, relaxed but alert.

"Here we are. Two civilized beings having a drink. Tell me why you called me up here."

"You know why. To make a deal. A deal where you get released with a pardon and something else."

"What?"

"What do you want?"

"You know what we want. The old order controls the government and the brothers control the church. They treat us like drytts and chambermaids. We want the Tabernacle."

I shake my head and sit down on the other end of the sofa.

"I can't give you that. But I can give you your own church. We're rebuilding Pandemonium from the ground up. You can have a tabernacle as big and oppressive as Merihim and his boys'."

She sets her glass on the floor. Picks an invisible piece of lint from her robe.

"And what do I have to do for this indulgence?"

"You can get word out to your people from jail?"

"Of course."

"I'm going to need a few. Especially cops or soldiers. Anyone who won't get rattled when things get noisy. And a doctor or a nurse."

"What will you be needing them for?"

"They're going to help me get murdered."

I take her over to the peepers and show her the one on the far end. A deep bowl in the desert floor glowing red from exposed lava pits.

"That's where it's going to happen."

"What a fitting place for your demise."

"I thought you'd like it. And don't get too excited. I'm not aiming for supersized dead. More like a kid's-meal-with-an-action-figure dead. That's where you come in."

"Tell me."

"Let me pour you another drink."

And I do.

FIFTEEN MINUTES LATER we have a deal.

Deumos is a preacher, so she has her own damned ritual to perform. She holds up a mirror so both of our faces are framed in the glass.

She says, "As we're bound in the mirror, we're bound in the compact we make here tonight. If either breaks the pledge, may she or he shatter like the faces captured here."

Deumos lets go of the mirror and it falls, shattering into a million little pieces.

"Looks like we're married. Mazel tov," I say.

She squints and walks away from me.

"Don't even joke about that."

"Can you get your people together by tonight? I want to get this thing rolling."

"I'll need to start right away."

"Brimborion will get you whatever you need."

She looks at me when we get to the library doors.

"You agreed to the compact but don't believe in oaths, do you?"

"No. People do what they're going to do."

"Yet you're trusting me with your life."

"Believe me, if there was any other way to do it, I would. But you're smart enough to see an opportunity when it takes a dump on your lawn."

"For a chance to have our own tabernacle I'd make a deal with the Devil himself."

"You're a regular Phyllis goddamn Diller."

She doesn't look at me but I can tell she's pleased with herself.

Brimborion knocks a minute later.

I yell, "Hold on a minute," and look at Deumos.

"You're wrong. You know that? I don't think you mean to sell snake oil but your church is a New Age wet dream. There's no Hellion fairy godmother who's going to overthrow big bad Daddy and fix this mess."

When she smiles it's like she feels sorry for me.

"How is it you're so sure? Because you're the great and powerful Lucifer?"

"Because I've had drinks with God. The real one. He's broken into so many pieces He couldn't lead a high school field trip. And trust me, lady, He doesn't have a backup plan. We're on our own."

She pats me on the arm and angles around to get to the door.

"You let me worry about Hellion souls and you worry about your impending death. I have one more stipulation, by the way."

"What?"

"I want to be there tonight. I can supply you with fighters and medical help but I want to be there so that whatever happens there are no misunderstandings between the two of us."

"You got it."

I open the door and she steps out into the hall.

"Is there anything else?" Brimborion asks.

"Take her back downstairs and get her anything she wants. And keep a low profile yourself. Things are going to get weird in a little while."

"How weird?"

"Duck-and-cover weird. Take the lady downstairs. She can fill you in."

Brimborion wants to ask more questions. Deumos takes his arm and leads him away.

THE HELLION HOG rumbles to life. I slip out the back of the hotel and head north on Rodeo Drive. There's always a pang of nostalgia here. Once upon a time I got into a kaiju smackdown with Mason's attack dog, Parker, and almost burned the street to the ground. But that was almost a year ago and I've forgiven it for being so crowded with rich assholes. And for being so flammable.

I blow up Sunset heading north. My burned hand aches from working the throttle but that's just how it is.

Off the Boulevard, the road is a mess. Earthquakes tore up the asphalt. Fires melted what was left, and when it cooled it was like a lava bed, full of frozen waves and sudden dips. There aren't a lot of repairs going on up here. No percentage. There's nothing but scorpions and lost Tartarus ghosts out this way.

People don't go where I'm going for fun. It's not smart to take the direct route, so I turn off the main street onto winding two-lane roads that circle scorched hills and abandoned movie-mogul estates before dropping off into hidden canyons. It's midnight in a coal-mine dark out here except for the bike's headlight. I open up the throttle and the roadbed shakes and cracks under my wheels. Lines spread around me like thin bolts of black lightning. The edges of the road sag. Chunks break off and fall into the dark. Most roads north of Hollywood are suicide roads, streets so fucked up by underground blood tides and quakes that they could collapse into sinkholes at any minute. This is my way of keeping things interesting for whoever is following me.

I'm working from the idea that coming out to no-man's-land will encourage my assassin to make his or her move. And being in the boonies will give me a better chance of running the hell away without any freelance shooters or red leggers in town taking potshots at me when I go down. I might have spooked my assassins by not lying down and dying. If I give them a head start on the deed, let them get to me half dead, maybe it will encourage them to come out in the open to finish the job.

That's the idea. Truth is, I'm not even a hundred percent sure that I'm being followed. I hope I am. I better be. I don't want to have to do any of this again. I'll know soon enough.

There are lights ahead. I kill the bike's headlight and ease off the throttle.

Back home, Coldwater Canyon is a pretty green slice of Heaven where nice parents take their happy kids for weekend hikes to expose them to the joys of nature, rabid coyotes, and Lyme disease. In Hell, the canyon walls are hundreds of feet high and impossible to climb. Twisted spires of wind-smoothed granite are the only things that break up the bare landscape. Millions of shadows swarm across the valley and up the sides of the spires and walls. They beat, slash, shoot, and boil each other in open lava pools again and again and they'll do it until the end of time. Butcher Valley. This is where I found Wild Bill.

A couple of hundred yards around the valley is a guard station. We have these all over Hell. I have no idea why. No one has ever done a dine-and-dash out of any of Hell's punishment territories. My theory is that the stations are for the guards. You have to be a real fuckup to get dumped out here. The legions don't have brigs or courts-martial. They have babysitting dead assholes for ten thousand years with no days off. Worse, every year in Hell is a leap year.

Considering tonight's itinerary, I didn't bother putting on a shirt. Why throw good clothes after bad? I heel down the kickstand and cut the bike's engine before the lowlifes at the guard station notice me.

I'm wearing the leather jacket that prick Ukobach ruined with his sword. It seemed appropriate. I unzip it and toss it on the ground by the bike. All the way up the canyon I've been debating whether or not I should take off Lucifer's armor. It would make what happens next more dramatic. On the other hand, without my angel half, Hell's fetid air is like Kryptonite to my lungs and the armor is the only thing that lets me breathe. Without it I'll probably choke to death before anyone finds me. Which brings me to the other point I'm going over. In a life full of dumb stunts, am I hitting a new level of idiot behavior? I'm alone and trusting my life to people who had me in a barbecue pit a couple of days ago.

The burns on my right hand are just about healed but I've never tried invoking a Gladius with an injured hand. I take a half-empty bottle of Aqua Regia from one of the bike's saddlebags, have a long drink, and decide to keep my armor on. There's going to be drama galore even if I'm in my Tin Man zoot suit.

*I could use just a little help right now, Saint James. I swear to God if I live through this, we're going to have a frank and honest talk about our feelings while I cut the Key to the Room of Thirteen Doors out of your chest with a chop saw.*

I'm feeling light-headed. Fear will do that. I got it sometimes in the arena when I knew they were going to throw something special at me but I didn't know what. I pick up my leather jacket and bite down hard on the sleeve. It would be a shame to live through this having bitten off my tongue.

I don't know what to say, Candy. We only had a couple of days together but they were a hell of a couple of days. Sorry for letting myself get stuck here. Talk about a long-distance relationship. If I live through this, I'll tell you all about the new big stupid thing I did. If I die, just add it to the long list of bullshit you don't need to hear.

I always wondered what Lucifer felt when God hit him with the final thunderbolt. The one that scorched and dented his theoretically invulnerable angelic armor.

This should be interesting.

I manifest the Gladius. It burns my injured hand but not enough to stop. I hold it out and count to three. Then swing it.

Whatever it is I feel when the Gladius hits my chest, it's not pain. It's something so far beyond pain that my human brain can't register it. The only way I know I've made contact is that I'm knocked flat on my back with a heady bouquet of burning skin and seared metal in my nose. I don't think the Middle Way smells like this. Missed it again, Bill.

I'm done fighting and looking for answers. I got mine.

What did that last thunderbolt feel like?

Nothing at all.

Good night, moon.

I DRIFT FOR A MILLION YEARS. I'm in Mr. Muninn's cavern. Samael is with him. They're playing Operation. The buzzer goes off when Samael tries to take out the funny bone.

Muninn doesn't look surprised to see me.

"Would you like a drink, son?"

"Sure. Am I dead?"

He just smiles and wags a finger at me.

I look at Samael.

"No wonder you never went up against Aelita. You can't even work tweezers."

He nods and sips from a crystal champagne glass.

"Lovely to see you too, Jimmy. How's tricks?"

"Is this real? Am I here? Are you there?"

"Real is a relative thing for people like us. What's real? What's here? What's there? Things are as real and as where as you want them to be."

"I'm not like you or Muninn. My celestial half is gone. I'm just another human asshole."

Over my shoulder I hear Muninn laugh.

Samael sets down his glass and tries for the funny bone again. He misses.

"You're not a regular human any more than we are."

I look around the cavern piled high with junk from every earthly civilization that ever was. Everything from cave paintings to a Higgs boson trapped in a magnetic bottle.

I turn to Samael. He raises an eyebrow.

"I went to my enemies."

"And how did that work out?"

"I don't know yet."

"That's the downside of working with enemies. You seldom do."

Mr. Muninn brings me a glass of Jack Daniel's. He has to put it in my hand. I can't move it.

"Cheers," he says, and clinks his glass against mine.

"I think I'm just dreaming and all this is me talking to myself. Except it's a little like a phone call I got. It didn't make too much sense either."

Muninn shakes his head.

"I'm afraid we can't help you with those," he says.

"Let me at least ask Samael a question."

"Of course."

"All I've done down here is shuffle papers, try not to get killed, and now I've completely fucked myself up. When do I get to do the Devil stuff?"

He leans back in his chair.

"This is the Devil stuff."

"I was afraid of that. I need the rest of your power. Where is it?"

"Exactly where it should be."

"Don't riddle me, you bastard. Tell me where it is."

"East of the sun. West of the moon. Right in front of you. Stop looking. Sit down and you'll see."

"I can't stop. I have to get out of here."

"Then that's where it will be," says Muninn.

"Fuck you. Fuck you both."

I OPEN MY EYES. Standing over me is a girl with too much skin. It's in piles around her neck and hangs like dirty laundry from her arms. Her eyes are thin slits under a curtain of flesh.

She's dressed in a lizard-green Hellion EMT uniform. She adjusts an oxygen mask over my nose and mouth. I'm breathing, so I must be alive. Or this is another dream. But if it's a dream, why does it feel like Mike Tyson has been pounding on my chest with a bulldozer?

The EMT moves quickly. Her expression and gestures alternately resemble a cool medical professional and a nervous babysitter who just caught the cat's tail in the refrigerator door. Maybe she has a hot date waiting back in Pandemonium. Or she's never worked on the Lord of the Underworld before.

There are other people standing around. Some of them look worried. Others puzzled. A couple more EMTs. Some soldiers. From the guard station probably. Filthy Hellions in clothes like grimy rags. Some of the ones who lit out for the hinterlands. A few others I recognize from Deumos's procession through the marketplace.

It takes me another minute for my sluggish brain to put it all together. Someone besides my assassins saw me go down. None of them would imagine Lucifer would hurt himself. To them I'm the victim of an unsuccessful attack. Perfect. Word will get out that I'm vulnerable. If my killers are ever going to move, it's now.

The EMTs lift the gurney I'm on high enough to slide me into the back of an ambulance. I'd feel a lot better if it was a troop truck or Unimog. Hellion ambulances look a lot like garbage trucks. Not a comforting look.

I'm strapped to the gurney with heavy nylon across my waist and legs. My burned chest is covered with a heavy gauze dressing stained bloody orange with Betadine. There's a cool salve on my neck where the Gladius struck above the armor.

When the gurney is locked down, the EMT with the sagging shar-pei skin goes up front and starts the ambulance's engine. As we start to move, the other EMT, a big son of a bitch with crustacean eyestalks sticking out over a bushy Grizzly Adams beard, checks my pulse.

"Does this bus stop at the Sands?" I say. "I hear the Rat Pack is even funnier now that they're all in Hell."

Grizzly Lobster jumps a little. Guess I'm not supposed to be awake yet. But seriously, I'm Satan, asshole. Time is money. The Devil doesn't nap.

I push myself halfway up on my elbows. Grizzly shakes his head and puts his hands on my shoulders to hold me down. Message received. I relax and lie back down and wonder if he has a mouth under the beard.

The driver is running us through the hills at a nice clip. I crane my neck enough to see the glow of a GPS on the dashboard. Ipos told me they have them programmed with all the safe routes through the L.A. badlands. What he didn't say is how GPS works down here. Unless Hellions have their own satellites. That would mean they have their own space program and can I get a ride out of here on a sulfur-powered Saturn V? Do Hellion tots grow up and want to be demon cosmonauts? The old Greeks believed the stars and planets carouseled around the sky in celestial spheres. Megasize glass globes made of a mysterious something called Quintessence. It would be fun to go target shooting with Wild Bill and blow them to crystal kitty litter.

Plato and his pals are as full of shit as everyone else who ever thought they had it all figured out. Deumos especially.

The universe doesn't revolve around Earth. No goddess is going to come along with milk and cookies for Hell's lost lambs. We're so fucked.

The ambulance crunches and jerks hard to the right like we hit something. The rear end fishtails. Feels like it's skidding along the soft edges of the road. Then it catches again and we straighten out. I hear the engine rev as the driver punches the accelerator. But ambulances are built for stability. Not speed. A second later we're bouncing to the right again. This time we didn't hit anything. Something hit us.

Grizzly Lobster is on his feet, pressing his big hands against the ceiling to hold himself steady, and leans down to look out the rear window. There's a *pop* and Grizzly's head explodes. One eyestalk hits the wall and ricochets hard enough to knock bags of saline and bandages off the storage shelves. I unbuckle the gurney straps and haul myself to my feet, still wobbly and a little seasick.

Something hits us again and this time the driver can't hold it. She curses in a grunting Low Hellion growl while jerking the wheel one way as the wheels slide the other. We're tossed around like socks in a malfunctioning dryer. When we stop, the floor is the ceiling and the ceiling is the floor. We're upside down a few feet from a sheer drop off the road.

The engine sputters out and things go very quiet. The driver has fallen over onto the passenger side but her legs are moving. She's alive but pretty out of it. Voices come through the wall. Four? No. Three. A by-the-book Hellion hit team, just like back when Ukobach and his friends pile-drived me.

Grizzly Lobster's blood is everywhere. I slip on it and fall back, banging my head hard on the wall. The outside voices stop. A shot comes through the wall. More follow. I throw myself down on the ceiling, about knocking my teeth out on a light fixture.

The rear doors creak open, metal grating against metal. One falls onto the ground. Someone locks the other in place so it won't fall closed. All I can see are silhouettes framed in headlights. Two are way back from the ambulance. Lookouts. One hovers by the entrance for a minute then comes inside. He kicks Grizzly Lobster a couple of times, and when he's satisfied the big man is dead, he looks up front where the driver is starting to thrash around. He yells back to the two covering him.

"One of you get up front and pull her out. Keep her quiet. This is a private audience."

He turns back to me. Makes a big show of pulling a curved skinning knife from a sheath on his hip and waits for one of the grunts to get to work.

There's a lot of cursing and heavy breathing. The sound of feet slipping and someone being pulled to her feet against her will. The assassin in the ambulance pushes the driver to the assassin on top of the ambulance, who hauls her out the window.

The one running the show hasn't moved the whole time. He's the strong, silent type with his knife. I can see he's wearing standard-issue legion boots and pants. The pants are camo-colored, so he's not a red legger.

From outside someone yells, "All clear."

He kicks Grizzly's body out of the way and kneels with the knife right over my face. Light coming through the door outlines one side of his face.

"Do you know who I am? It's important that you know who I am. I know you're hurt. I can wait a minute while you work it out. We've got all night."

I can almost place the face but it's the voice that gives him away.

"Vetis. Look at you all grown up and slick as pig shit. You're finally doing your own dirty work. Of course you waited until I was in an ambulance. Am I supposed to be impressed?"

"Brave talk for a man covered in blood."

"The blood belongs to the dead ambulance guy. You can't get anything right, can you? You blew it bad with bug boy. And that phone call? What was that, you fuckwit Ghostface wannabe?"

He stares at me.

"So what's this all about? You and your crew want a raise? How about two weeks' vacation while I pull out your intestines with an oyster fork?"

He lowers the knife close to my eye and wiggles it around. The shiny blade glints in the headlights. It looks brand-new. I'm flattered.

"You mortals love to hear yourself talk, don't you?"

It's hard to shrug gracefully flat on my back.

"In Hell, I'm usually the most interesting person in the room, so it's kind of inevitable."

He glances away for a second like he's thinking and then jams the knife deep into my cheek, twisting the blade before pulling it out.

"Was that interesting enough for you?"

"Would it help if I said yes?"

He takes a breath and his mood changes. Tense lines of anger soften to something else. Not sadness. More like bone-deep exhaustion.

He says, "Why did you come back?"

"I ask myself that every day."

He pokes my cheek with the knife again.

"I came here to kill Mason Faim, you ungrateful mother-fucker. I saved your ass."

He lets his head sag for a second. Uses his sleeve to wipe my blood off the knife.

"That's the problem," he says. "If you'd just stayed away, we'd be gone."

I try to sit up. Vetis puts his forearm on my scorched armor and pushes me down. He doesn't have to push hard.

"Jesus fucking Christ. Are you stupid? Do you really think the legions could have taken on Heaven's armies and won?"

He looks out the back of the ambulance and then back at me.

"Of course not. They would have slaughtered us. And all of this"—he stretches out his arms to take in all of Hell—"would be over."

I'm so dumb sometimes I'm surprised I've never used dynamite for a toothbrush.

Now I know how Mason got so much of Hell and got so many generals and their troops working with him so fast. The war with Heaven wasn't a war. It was a suicide pact. Death by cop. Provoke the guy with the gun so he'll shoot. Storm the gates of Heaven until the golden army burns you in a rain of holy fire. Bye bye Hell. And they wouldn't have to worry about being sent to Tartarus because I destroyed that. A perfect setup for the biggest suicide cult of all time.

Semyazah was the only holdout. One of the few Hellions left that still believed in Lucifer's argument with Heaven. Semyazah isn't stupid. Of course he doesn't want to be Lucifer. How do you lead an entire civilization of wrist cutters?

No wonder Deumos and her shiny happy church popped up. She's the only one offering an alternative to dog-paddling around God's toilet forever. Even if it's New Age bullshit wrapped up in a Hellion wet dream.

Is this why God broke into a million little pieces? Before Aelita murdered him, Neshamah said Hell was never supposed to be like this. I thought he meant the fires and sinkholes and earthquakes. Now I know what he meant. He put the rebel angels in an eternal time-out and never came back. The Lord's just and wise punishment inspired millions of his children to mass suicide. No wonder the old man had a nervous breakdown.

"What happens now? You going to slit my throat? With no Lucifer, this place is going to get real interesting real fast. Maybe the whole thing will collapse into one big sinkhole. Won't that be fun, wading knee-deep in blood and shit for a trillion years, waiting for the universe to end?"

He taps the knife against my Kissi arm like he's trying to tell if a melon is ripe. He moves the blade to the gauze on my chest, trying to work the tip of the blade underneath so he can lift it and take a look.

"Don't worry about us. You need to be worried about yourself right now."

"Why? You're going to kill me and I'm too hurt to fight

back. I'd only worry if I thought there was something I could do and maybe I'd fuck it up."

"See? Talk. Talk. Talk. That's all you humans do."

"At least I don't get other people to do my killing for me. If I wanted to die, I'd do it myself and not trick Heaven into doing it for me."

He sighs.

"We must be such a disappointment to you, Lucifer."

He lays heavy sarcastic emphasis on "Lucifer."

"This whole dump is one big disappointment. Maybe that's why God forgot about you. You're so fucking boring."

Vetis presses the knife into the burn on my neck. I try not to wince.

He says, "Let me put you out of your misery."

"Give me the knife and I'll put you out of yours."

Outside someone yells, "Hey!" Someone else curses. There's the sound of running feet. A lot of them. More shouts. Guns go off and something hits the ambulance hard.

Vetis looks up as a dozen hands drag him out of the ambulance. One of them twists Vetis's wrist until it pops and he drops the knife. They drag him around the side of the ambulance and I lose sight of him. A moment later, a woman steps inside and looks around for somewhere to sit that isn't covered in blood. She finds a foam pillow pinned to the wall by the gurney and sets it on one of the cabinets.

"That worked out nicely, if I do say so myself," says Deumos.

"It would have worked out even better if you'd gotten up here five minutes ago."

She holds up her hands in a what-can-you-do gesture.

"Getting through the canyons without being seen took more time than we thought."

I sit up and lean back against the wall. Grizzly's blood soaks through my pants. I don't care.

"I wasn't sure you'd show at all."

"But here we are, keeping our part of the bargain."

"And I'll keep mine. Just one thing. Did you bring a doctor or nurse?"

"We have a doctor and a nurse. Why?"

"The EMT they pulled out of here is probably pretty out of it. Someone should have a look at her. Also, can someone come in here to dig around for painkillers? I want to lie in a kiddie pool full of OxyContin."

She pats me lightly on the shoulder.

"I'll see what I can do."

THERE'S NO OXY or Hellion Vicodin around, but Deumos comes back with someone's flask full of Aqua Regia. It'll do. We sit on the shoulder of the road looking back toward Pandemonium. Even falling apart, the place looks enough like L.A. to make me feel homesick.

The side of the hill where we sit crunches under our feet where the vegetation burned. But the place isn't entirely dead. Scrubs of ghost thistle and even a few asphodel flowers have made it up through the layer of ash.

"You don't look well," says Deumos.

"With a month's vacation, a face-lift, and a crate of Ecstasy, I might work my way up to feeling like shit."

"General Semyazah isn't going to be happy about any of

this. Running around the hinterlands with weapons. Attacking his troops. And especially you conspiring with me."

"He'll be fine. I'll send him a fruit basket."

We sit for a minute, neither of us saying anything. There's the kind of warm breeze that if you didn't know you were in Heaven's sewer you might find almost pleasant.

"So tell me, how does someone invent a new church in Hell? You run out of Sudoku?"

"I had a vision."

"Of course you did. All you prophets do is have visions. And burn heretics. That's like catnip to you people. Why don't you take a pottery class or learn Japanese?

She frowns.

"You don't believe in oaths or revelations. What *do* you believe in, Lord Lucifer?"

"I believe we're going to be dead a lot longer than we're alive, so anything you like you should do to excess. I believe America lost its soul when they took the big-block V-8 out of Mustangs. I believe Hollywood should stop remaking *A Star Is Born*."

She looks at me and slowly shakes her head.

"I have to apologize for burning you in effigy. I thought you were our enemy. Now I see that your greatest enemy is yourself."

"Don't get your panties in a twist, Mary Magdalen. Aside from a couple of paper cuts I'm doing fine."

"Of course."

She pulls a folded piece of paper and a pen from inside her robes and hands them to me.

"Before we left, I took the liberty of drawing up an agreement. There's nothing in here we didn't discuss earlier. My church gets its own Tabernacle and funding not less than but not exceeding that of the old church."

I sign the papers and hand them back to her.

"You're not going to read them first?"

"You saved my ass. I'm fine with whatever's in there."

She puts her hands on my shoulders and turns me toward her. Looks at my scorched armor and the wound on my neck.

"You did that to yourself? You're mad."

I shrug.

"I had to be out of it enough that the killers would make their move. It was either the Gladius or a bullet, and I've been shot enough for one lifetime, thanks." I say, "Tell me about your vision."

"No."

"Why not?"

"Because you don't believe in anything. To tell it to you would be to cheapen it."

"I just gave you a church."

"I just saved your life. And we both did what we did for the same reason. We wanted something from each other."

"You know I've only been Lucifer for like three months, right? I'm not the one that made you ride in the back of the bus all these years."

She waves to one of her men. He comes over and she hands him the agreement. He goes back to wait with the others. Smart woman. She wants the paper away from me in case I change my mind.

She says, "It suits you, you know. Armor for the man who is always armored."

"Visions and fashion tips? You do it all, sister."

She leans back like she's sizing up her kid for his first big-boy pants.

"I mean it. You look better in it than the other Lucifer. Look at the damage God's final thunderbolt did to the metal."

She touches the battered part of the armor.

"Even with the Lord's mark on him, Samael was so anxious to play the tragic warrior king that he added the thunderbolt crest."

She pats a blank spot in the center of the breastplate.

"I'm happy to see you removed it."

I touch the armor where she had her hand. There's a tiny divot where a bolt might have been removed. Suddenly I want to get back to the palace.

"I think I'm going to head out before someone realizes I'm gone. You can handle Grand Funk Railroad back there?"

"You'll release the rest of my people?"

"I'll make the call as soon as I get back."

"We'll drop off the prisoners when they're returned."

One of her crew, a tall silent woman with spiders branded into her arms and cheeks, drives me to the bike in the jeep Vetis took up here. She barely slows long enough for me to jump out before she's tearing back up the road. So much for Hail Satan.

I start the bike and head out, keeping the speed subsonic. Between the Gladius and the ambulance crash, I'm feeling a little rough. Deumos and her people are just about to leave when I catch up. When I slow the bike, I can feel tension ripple through the air. People holding guns thumb off the safeties. Ones without guns get theirs out. I wait, gunning the throttle and waiting for something to happen. Deumos comes over slowly. Stands an arm's length away, straight and defiant. I take the flask from my pocket and hand it to her.

"Tell the owner thanks."

She takes the flask and I pop the clutch, burning rubber out of there.

I TAKE THE SECRET STAIRS up from the garage straight into the library, careful to step around the hexes in the floor. I pick up the phone and hit PISSANTS. Brimborion picks up.

"It's me."

"You're alive."

"Surprise. Release Deumos's crew."

"Security isn't through questioning them."

"You mean torture? They're done. If any of them have a problem, tell them Lucifer said to put it in writing and shove it up their ass."

"I'll just say the order came from you."

"You're leaving out the best part but okay."

"How did you . . . ?"

"Got to go."

I hang up.

Samael knew I needed the armor to survive, so if I lived he knew I'd always have it with me. He was smart enough to hide the thunderbolt so that even if Mason won, he'd never have all of Samael's power. Not telling me any of this stinks like more of his "figure it out for yourself" Socratic horseshit. Or did he tell me something more? I have a vague impression of talking to him about it and him telling me something else. What was it?

The more immediate question is this: where would I hide if I was a missing piece of armor?

Samael told me to read the Greeks, so that seems like a good place to start, which is exactly why I'm not going to do it. I've pawed through every Greek book on the shelves. I liked one book I found, *Meditations* by Marcus Aurelius, but then I found out he was Roman and not Greek and that just pissed me off. For a while I thought that might mean something but probably someone just put it on the wrong shelf.

If the thunderbolt is anywhere, it will be anywhere but where Samael told me where to look. Aside from actuarial tables, Hellion tax law, and sports stats, what section would I be the least likely to look in? What other sections are there in libraries? I'm not exactly an expert on book jail, and when I walked around before, I didn't pay much attention to what books were where or how they were arranged. Time to get rigorous and organized.

I hate this already.

You know how when you drive somewhere new it always seems longer the first time? That's how it is the first time you walk through an entire library trying to figure out how it's put together. I could have done this when I first got here but I didn't give a fuck what was on the other shelves and mostly resented everything beyond my little pied-à-terre for not having more, meaning *any,* movies. If Samael really wanted me to pay attention, he'd have stuck Herodotus between piles of Howard Hawks and John Huston.

Twenty minutes of looking and my eyes are already glazing over. There are no section markers. No Dewey decimal system or card catalog. (Yes, I know about the Dewey decimal system. I didn't spend a lot of time in libraries but I'm aware of their existence.) Just rows of books with titles in Hellion script. And I was just in a crash. My neck hurt before. Now it's aching from holding it sideways to read the titles.

I should have brought a pencil and paper and been drawing a map as I go over the place. I find a general-history-of-the-universe section, including Heaven and Hell. There's a section on science, which is broken down into categories I've never heard of. What the hell is Quantum Melancholia?

There's politics, which is total bullshit. All Samael needs is one book with LIE AND CHEAT LIKE A SON OF A BITCH in neon on the cover.

There's also art. Instead of Sodom and Gomorrah cluster-fucking and Giger monsters, it looks like Samael has a thing for Rembrandt and mortal portrait painters. Probably looking for the right dead soul to put his mug on a Hellion dollar bill.

Military theory. Ha. I bet he wishes he had these books back in Heaven.

Law and economics. Was he studying for his goddamn SATs? I guess the Devil needs to know things like mortal rules and money. But still. I'm learning Samael's darkest secrets and they're really boring.

Philosophy. Okay. He gets some slack for this one. His argument with God seems legit. Is it the sin of pride not wanting to be a slave?

I'm about to start making my own sections. *Despair. Boredom. I Want a Nap.* And *Fuck This Shit Entirely.* I'll push them together in one big pile with a noose overhead.

This whole time I've been hoping to find a secret trove

of romances or westerns but the long shelves of true-crime books are probably Samael's pulp pop reading. He's exactly the kind of guy who flips to the end of every crime book looking for his name in the index. I wonder if I'm in one of these things. Which reminds me. I need to check the Sandman Slim entry on Wikipedia. I've tried killing it a couple of times but it's always back up the next day. If some psychic prick gets wind that I'm temping as Satan, I don't want it online. Satanists make junior high Goths look like NASA.

There's a reading area in the corner of the room. I drop down into the soft leather chair, mentally exhausted. There's a small table with a lamp and an ashtray with a few old butts. I forgot to pick up a pack of Maledictions before coming in, so I poke around the ashtray like a wino looking for one that might still be smokable. None of them are. I'm on a real winning streak tonight.

This is getting me nowhere. There must be a million or more books in here. I could wander the aisles for years and not find anything. Maybe I'm wrong about the missing armor piece. Even if he left it for me, it might not be in here. That means more wasted years wandering the whole palace, searching it one room at a time.

No.

Samael is a dick but he isn't that random or cruel, at least not to me. As much as he's fucked with me over the years, there was always a point and he's always given me something to work with. Saint James would have figured out this bullshit hours ago. It makes me want to hurt him even more.

First no cigarettes and now I realize I left my Aqua Regia

back at home base. My neck hurts. My chest burns. My right hand aches from picking up books. I'm sore and sweating like a fat man chasing a taco wagon across the Mojave.

Sitting here and closing my eyes feels good.

Then it comes back to me.

"Right in front of you. Stop looking. Sit down and you'll see."

I open my eyes and see I'm sitting in the middle of a huge section on magic. Samael takes the subject more seriously than I ever did. Because I was born a nephilim, I never learned much real magic. Even as a kid I had enough power to improvise my own hoodoo. The first and only real magic I ever learned was down here killing in the arena and later as Sandman Slim. There's probably a lot of useful information in these books. Too bad the whole reading thing is starting to give me hives.

A book lies facedown on the other side of a reading lamp. I didn't notice it before. It's a paperback with a bright yellow cover, the first paperback I've seen down here. I pick it up. The title is in big block letters.

ANGER MANAGEMENT FOR DUMMIES

Like I said, Samael always leaves me something to work with and a cheap joke is better than no clue at all.

I flip through the book looking for highlighted passages or dog-eared pages. I even read most of a chapter. It's all the usual straight-arrow self-help babble. No clues. No codes. Just sensible advice for sensible people, which leaves me out in the cold. I throw the book across the room. For all I know, Aelita brought it down so Mason could use it to mess with my brain.

I need a drink. Many drinks. And I need them now.

I kick over the chair as I get up, knocking over the table and sending the lamp flying.

There's something on a shelf that had been hidden behind the table. On a bottom shelf all the way at the back of the magic section is an old book whose cover is the same shade of yellow as *Anger Management for Dummies*. I kneel and pull it out.

It's musty and a little mildewed and the leather binding cracks when I touch it. The lettering and illustration of a kid on the front looks Victorian. Gold lettering reads *A Magic Primer for Little Gentlemen. Magnificent Feats and Rousing Conundrums for Boys of All Ages*. I open it. Inside, the pages have been hollowed out. Lying at the bottom of the empty book is something wrapped in purple linen. I unroll it. And find a golden thunderbolt. Bingo.

I stand up and clip it into place.

Nothing happens. Zero. Zip. Nada. I didn't think I was going to roll around the floor growling like Lyle Talbot sprouting Wolf Man whiskers but I was hoping for something. I'm so jacked up on adrenaline that all traces of exhaustion are gone, but that's still a letdown when you expect to feel like the second most powerful being in the universe.

Then something hits me like a baseball bat to the kidneys. My guts knot up and my body temperature shoots up a hundred degrees. Darkness spills out of me, rolling onto the floor and spreading like black Hellion blood. I'm spewing darkness from every pore of my body. The darkness isn't solid. It's a cold dead void like a drop into a bottomless pit. Things curl up from the nothingness, icy and sharp, like freezing rattlesnakes. Suddenly I'm a supercharged nitro-burning Hell beast with teeth the size of the Rockies and hands the size of Texas. If I bend down, I can lift all of Creation onto my back.

And then, like a supersonic orgasm, the feeling is gone. There's nothing left and I'm back on the floor gasping for air.

What the hell just happened? Does this mean I had Lucifer's power for a second but my human body couldn't contain it? Or did it just feel like it passed into me?

There are voices. They don't come through clearly. Whispers of Hellions all around me in the palace. Even though I can't hear individual words, the meaning still filters through. Most words are nothing. Empty compliments or straight-up information. Other things hang in the air. Faint wisps of vapor like steam coming off hot coffee. They're veiled threats and lies. The half-truths, evasions, and bullshit that's the blood in the arteries of this place. They float in through the walls like a ghost mist.

Okay. Right. This is new. It's not much more than a trick from one of those shitty amaze-your-friends-and-half-wit-relatives magic kits you buy off late-night TV but it's something. Maybe the superhero stuff will kick back in later. I like the darkness thing that just happened. I hope I didn't blow all my power in one big death-dive money shot. Maybe being Lucifer isn't about power but just being more aware of your Luciferness. That would be a hell of a letdown. I swear on every pointy little Hellion head if I start to grow bat wings and a tail, I'm going to cut them off and feed them to Samael through the wrong hole.

There's one supertrick I want more than anything, and even if I still have the power, I don't know how to get at it. How did Samael leave Hell? I never got a chance to ask. Maybe a hoodoo chant? Something you do in a Magic Circle? Walking through a waning arch? Maybe he just had a pair of ruby slippers like Dorothy.

I can't stand this. Get me out of here. Take me home.

The roar and the wind hit like a hurricane. Things shoot past me, shrieking like tracer rounds. All metal and leaving trails of lights. A blue-brown twilight sky hovers above gray clouds. I smell diesel fumes and scorched engine oil. A green sign trimmed in white catches my eye. It reads CRENSHAW BOULEVARD EXIT.

I recognize this. I'm on the I-10 freeway above where I did the Black Dahlia and splattered my brains and bones on a freeway support. I can't help it. I laugh and laugh like a lunatic way off his meds.

*This is L.A. I'm home.*

Mustang Sally, the beautiful sylph and goddess of the roads, is perched on the hood of a silver Mercedes 550 convertible in the breakdown lane, smoking like she's been waiting for me the whole time I've been gone. She smiles and crooks a finger to my right. I turn.

A sixteen-wheeler is bearing down on me going seventy. The driver is laying on the air horn as cars flash by all around me. Right. Cars. Fuck. Standing on freeways is bad even if you're magic.

There's nowhere to run. I close my eyes and try to come up with some clever hoodoo but all that's in my head is Oh shit. Oh shit. Oh shit.

Suddenly the roar is gone and the smells with it and the sudden gusts of wind as things whiz by. When I open my eyes, all that's left of L.A. is a faint afterimage of Mustang Sally's Cheshire-cat smile. I'm back in the library.

My brain is whirling like it's going to splatter itself all over the inside of my skull like carnival spin art. I was home and it wasn't any harder than walking from one room to another. Only I think I need to maybe get more specific about what room.

My legs are shaking too much to walk. I sit crossed-legged on the cool marble floor. Stare at it, making sure it's real.

My burned hand throbs and my chest itches and I couldn't give less of a goddamn. Suddenly every shitty, painful moment of the last three months has been worth it. I was home and I can do it again.

Every part of me wants to go back to L.A. right now and stay there and pretend none of this ever happened. But I know if I run off, there are things that will bite large chunks out of my ass later. Take care of business and get out clean. I'm half-way home. More than halfway. Getting away clean means making nice with people I never want to lay eyes on again. I've got to get Brimborion in gear and start making calls.

But that can wait a minute. Until I get off the floor, which will be any minute now. After my legs stop shaking and I catch my breath. Until then I'm just going to sit here in the cool quiet with my magic yellow book and think of how many ways this freak factory can kiss my ass on its way out the door.

I SPEND THE NEXT DAY tying up loose ends. I'm expecting a lot of ritual square dancing but it turns out blowing town might be easier than I thought. I decided to blow off the planning committee and their budgets. That leaves my inner council.

Merihim isn't returning my calls. A sore loser in a battle he hasn't even lost yet. But for the first time he and his church have to justify their existence and it's making him cranky. Boo-hoo. Take two altar boys and call me in the morning.

The other members of the Council are tied up. Buer is at the City Hall building site. There's no reason to get him off it since it's one of the few projects that's actually accomplishing something. Obyzuth is with Deumos, so she knows the score. There's Marchosias but she's not sending me any good-bye roses. She's busy wheeling and dealing with other Hellion politicos, giving them the good word that Lucifer is alive and well despite another ambush. The king is the land, the land is the king, and as long as Lucifer lives, the ground won't open and gobble the place down like a California roll.

The bedroom is still a broken little FUBAR island. What's-his-name the herbalist, just a pile of gristle and bones on the stained bed. Snowdrifts of Kentucky fried insects. Bullet holes in the wall. Burn marks around the electric outlet. Shards of porcelain from the broken bathroom sink. In all, a fitting monument to my stellar turn as Lucifer. Leave it just like this. Let the next Lucifer clean it up.

I toss my coat on the bed and give myself the once-over in the mirror. New scars on my face and hand. A left arm that looks like a tin-plated grasshopper. A livid burn on my chest above the armor. My eyes are stuck in a thousand-yard-arena death stare. I might even see some gray hairs. I look like old roadkill in new boots.

I can't go home looking like this. I take long, slow breaths and try to relax. I practice a smile but that just makes things worse. I'm not sure how wide to make it. How many teeth should I show? You're not supposed to think about smiling. You just do it. I curl up the ends of my lips and open my eyes. Not bad: if I want to look like a paint-huffing shark.

I call Brimborion and tell him to come up in an hour. Then dial the witches downstairs. Let them know I'll be paying them a visit. A couple of other short calls and then I head down to the kennels to feed the hellhounds.

Brimborion is a pain in the ass but he's a prompt pain in the ass. He knocks on the bedroom door in exactly one hour. I'm shoving clothes, Aqua Regia, and cigarettes into a duffel bag I found. With some silk stockings and chocolate, I could be one of Harry Lime's pals in *The Third Man*.

"The door's open."

Brimborion comes over to the bed where I'm packing.

"I'm taking off. We got Vetis but we don't know if we got his whole crew. You working with me makes you a target, so you should have this."

I toss him the Glock.

"You know how to use it?"

I'm stuffing a couple of last cartons of Maledictions into the duffel when Brimborion racks in a shell and presses the gun into the back of my head.

"That's not a Happy Meal, pal. No matter how hard you push, there aren't any prizes inside."

"Give me the weapon," he says.

"The 8 Ball? No. I need some souvenirs and the gift shop is closed."

"Lucifer's armor might give you power but I think five or six shots in the head from this range would kill even the Light Bringer."

"Before you carry out this brilliant plan, tell me this: Did Marchosias come to you or did you go to her?"

He hesitates.

"Why do you think she's involved? I'm the one with the gun to your head."

"First, she's the only one who might want the job. Second, you're the one with the gun to my head, meaning you're stupid and she's not. She'd never touch anything that might be traced back to her."

"Who cares? Vetis is going to be killed escaping. His confederates will commit suicide when they hear about it. You'll be dead and someone will have to step in to fill the vacuum."

I get the cigarettes in the duffel and zip it closed. Brimborion jumps at the sound and shoves the gun harder into my head.

"Is that the deal she offered you? You help Vetis. Get him and his boys maintenance uniforms so they can move around the palace. They get taken down but I'm killed by one of their vengeful stooges. Tragic but understandable."

"And I'm the only one who knows how you work," says Brimborion. "What you had planned. I'm the one to whom you came to for counsel. I don't have the rank or respectability to become Lucifer right away, but with no one else available, Marchosias will appoint me regent."

"And you'll do such a bang-up job everyone will grovel and beg you to become Lucifer 3.0."

"And I'll humbly accept."

"You know the only reason Marchosias brought you into the deal is because you hillbillies won't ever go for a woman Lucifer. So she needs a Muppet like you to be her beard."

I start to turn but he grabs my shoulder and holds me.

"It was worth a finger to get rid of you. No one in all of Hell will shed a tear when you're gone."

"I will."

I can hear his fiend's heart beating like a bar band doing a cover of "In-A-Gadda-Da-Vida." He stinks of Aqua Regia and some kind of Hellion speed I haven't smelled before.

"Did Vetis kill Ipos or did you? I'm guessing Vetis. Ipos would crack you open and play Jenga with your bones."

"Among the many reasons I hate you is that you only drank enough to be infuriating. Just a little more and the possession key might have worked and then none of this would have been necessary. You would have appointed me the new Lucifer and killed yourself on the palace steps. You don't even want to be Lucifer and it's impossible to stop you from doing it."

"But you won't be Lucifer. Marchosias will. Wise up, Tom Swift. She gets the power and all you're getting is a desk and new stationery."

I take Mason's lighter out of my pocket and pick up an unopened pack of Maledictions from the bed. Brimborion starts and takes a step back as I tear open the pack, tap out a smoke, and light up.

"How did you know Marchosias and I were working together?" he asks.

"It was the thing with Lahash. What a zany coincidence it was that your dope dealer attacked me. You and Marchosias got drugs from him to dose Ukobach. I'm guessing Marchosias got the idea from Mason when he was experimenting on those poor bastards in the hidden room. Vetis and his fake maintenance crew smuggled Lahash in using one of your passkeys. Lahash and I were supposed to kill each other but Vetis let him out early. I wonder why. If you died, Marchosias would need a new front guy. Vetis maybe? Think about it. A legionnaire is a lot better choice for Lucifer than a secretary. You're as dumb as a hat full of horseshit."

He cocks the pistol.

"You have ten seconds to tell me what you've done with the weapon."

"The weapon. You don't even know what it's called. I bet you about wet yourself when I upped the library security and you couldn't snoop around anymore. Too bad too. I was afraid of losing the 8 Ball, so I kept it close by. A few more hours and you would have had it."

"That's good enough. Better than talking to you any-more."

*Click*. He pulls the trigger again. Another *click*.

"Marchosias would never bet her life on a gun she wasn't sure worked. See what I mean about stupid?"

Semyazah and Wild Bill come out of the bathroom. Both are holding pistols. Brimborion stares at them. I put the lit end of the Malediction to the back of his hand and he drops the Glock on the bed. I backhand him with my Kissi hand and bounce him off the wall.

"What did I say would happen if you ever threatened me again?"

He stares dumbly, hugging his bandaged hand to his chest. I put my hand around his wrist.

"I said I'd take the whole arm."

I let the dark flow out of me. Twisting and growing, it expands like the corona of a black sun. The dark encircles us in a freezing void, leaving Brimborion and me the only two beings in a lonely, freezing universe.

Black tendrils like strangler vines flow down from overhead while tentacles whip up from deep below. Thorny, twitching things with circles of razor-sharp teeth that spin like drill bits. Brimborion backs away but the darkness wraps around him, pulling him deeper into the black tide. The drilling teeth brace themselves against his flesh, waiting for my signal.

I grab Brimborion's arm in my Kissi hand.

"Did Lahash steal from you or try to blackmail you or was he just a convenient fall guy? Do you think he could feel what was happening when they put the bugs into him? Or maybe later when they came out?"

Brimborion opens his mouth to scream but the dark flows in and he chokes on it.

I move my hand up to where his arm connects with his shoulder and say, "Here."

The teeth spin. The drilling starts. Brimborion tries to wriggle away but the tentacles have him and the black vines wrap around his head, stifling his screams.

When the drilling stops, he looks at the arm, expecting to see blood and bone. There's nothing. The skin isn't even broken. He rubs at a few faint scratches. The skin collapses under his fingers like papier-mâché. That's his cue to scream. He claws at the hollow arm, pulling dry dead flesh off brittle bones. Insects pour out of him. He's ripped his arm back all the way to the shoulder by the time he understands what's happening. He tries to shake off the insects but they're dug in too deep. Dry bones in his arm snap and it falls where it's snatched out of the air by a tentacle that draws it down into the void. He looks at me as the tentacles hold him, giving the hungry insects time to finish their work. It doesn't take long. When Brimborion falls, his body is as dry and empty as a locust husk.

I let the dark go and it flows back into me like it was never there.

"I hope I never have to see that again," says Semyazah.

"You could see that?"

He nods.

"Enough. Like through a fog."

Bill says, "Remind me not to get on your bad side."

"You still think I have a good side?"

"There's a search party out for it but I'm optimistic they'll turn up something."

Semyazah goes over to Brimborion's body. Touches it tentatively with his boot, like he's not sure its real.

"If only you took Lucifer's other duties as seriously as you take killing your enemies."

"Which duties? Leading spooky rituals or pretending I love pie charts? What I'm good at is killing sons of bitches who want to kill me. How long have you Hellions been trying it? Nearly twelve years now. What anniversary is that? Pewter? Shit? Napalm?"

Bill sits on the bed. Bounces up and down on his ass like a customer in a mattress outlet. He fingers the blanket and sheets. Semyazah gives Bill a look but he doesn't notice or doesn't care.

"And now you'll go home and leave us without a Lucifer and the city will burn. Hellions and damned souls will perish but you'll have what you want and isn't that all that matters?"

"I can't babysit you assholes forever. I have things to do. But I'm coming back. Samael used to leave all the time and he always came back."

"This was his home and we knew he'd always return. What incentive do you have to come back?"

"None, but I'm coming back anyway. Not to save you. Hell, most of you want to die anyway, so they don't care. But I'm coming back because there's souls down here I care about. I won't let Hell fall apart again."

"I expect we'll see."

He holsters his gun and I say a silent thanks. I don't want to get into a fight with the one general that can stand the sight of me. And I really don't want to go home with holes in my face.

"I'm taking the peepers with me. If there's an emergency or you just get lonely, leave a note on the desk in the library."

"That's very reassuring."

I motion for Bill to get up, reach between the mattress and the box spring, and pull out a full Glock clip. I eject the clip of blanks and slap in the real one. Out of habit I start to tuck the gun in the waistband of my pants but stop. I look at Semyazah.

"How much of this shit did you see coming and didn't let me in on?"

"Marchosias isn't a surprise but I didn't know it would happen so soon. As for Vetis, he was a surprise. And certainly not the rise of Deumos and her church. You've changed the very nature of Hell in the last couple of days, do you know that?"

"You're really worried about Hell's survival."

"This place is my home more than Heaven ever was."

"That's why I'm putting you in charge while I'm gone."

Semyazah's forehead creases and he shakes his head.

"Please don't."

"I don't trust you but you didn't join up with Mason, so you don't want to die right now. Besides you, I can't think of anyone else who actually cares about this place."

"My lord, please."

"Sorry, man. The thing is you're like David Coverdale and Hell is like Deep Purple without a singer. You don't know if you want the gig and the band isn't sure they want you up front, but you need each other to tour. So shut up. Tune up. Learn 'Smoke on the Water' and smile pretty for the fans."

I toss the Glock to Wild Bill.

"That's for you."

He turns the Glock over in his hands. Weighs in. Sights on Brimborion's body. Tosses it back to me.

"I don't trust a gun I can't see where the bullets go in."

He drops back onto the bed.

"But if you're in a generous mood, I'd take one of these. Without the dead man, of course."

"I'll have someone send one to the bar."

"And covers and such. These sheets are as soft as a widow's bottom."

"They'll send the works."

I tuck the Glock in the waistband behind my back. Semyazah has gone to the window to look over his temporary kingdom.

"When you were talking to Brimborion, I was impressed that you figured all that out."

"Half of it was guessing. After the Lahash thing it was just figuring out who could pull off a coup on short notice. Marchosias is the only one smart and ballsy enough and with the right connections."

He looks over his shoulder at Brimborion.

"I've never seen a man so cheerfully confess his crimes."

"You let a man hold a gun to your head long enough and he'll tell you all his secrets. Isn't that right, Bill?"

"I wouldn't know. Not having guns pressed against my head was among my utmost goals when I was among the living."

"Can you people trace phone calls, General? Vetis crank-called me, but when I asked him about it, I could tell he didn't know what I was talking about. I think he was possessed when he made the call. Where he called from could be a clue to who has the possession key."

Semyazah nods.

"I'll look into it."

"And keep an eye on the Bamboo House of Dolls. And Bill."

Bill throws down the pillow he's been fluffing and stands up straight.

"I don't need a goddamn demon looking over my shoulder."

"I bet that's what you said in Deadwood."

He sits back down.

"I suppose you're right but that's an unkind way to put it."

"I told you the search party would come back empty-handed. I don't have a good side to find."

Semyazah looks a little dazed. What I've done to Lucifer's beautiful room. How I let a damned soul talk back to me. Maybe imagination and rolling with the weirdness of the moment is what humans have over angels.

"Let people know if Bill or the bar get scratched, I'm going to cut so many throats they'll think I'm getting paid piecework."

"Always the diplomat."

"Oh. If you feel like overthrowing me while I'm gone, please do."

"Thank you for your permission but, no, I prefer soldiers to politicians and madmen."

I weigh the duffel bag in my hand. It's just a few pounds. Not much to show for three months as God's redheaded stepchild.

"If Deumos breaks her neck or chokes to death on a ham sandwich, you're going to have to do something about it."

"I won't send troops into the Tabernacle."

"Then make sure there's no reason to. You have spies in the church?"

"I'm a general. I have spies everywhere."

"Good. Give them a kick in the ass and tell them to keep their eyes on Merihim and his sky pilots. One more thing. I want someone to make a list of all the current punishments for damned souls. We're going to be making a few changes there."

"Is that all, Lucifer?"

I walk to him and put out my hand.

"Good luck, General."

Semyazah stares at it and then at me before putting out his own hand.

"I won't see you off, if you don't mind."

"Until we figure things out, the farther you stay away from me the better."

Semyazah nods curtly and goes off to polish bullets or give the troops a sponge bath, whatever it is generals do between wars.

Bill is on his feet. He has his hat in his hand and he's looking at the floor.

"What can I say, Bill? You're my Abilene Bodhisattva. I'm trying to pick and choose my fights better. All those people that got killed in the market, it wasn't me. It was the Magic 8 Ball. I swear on Lee Van Cleef's grave."

He shakes his head, smiling.

"I don't understand half of what you just said but that's all right. We never had royalty in the family before."

Bill isn't the hugging type, so we shake hands.

On his way out he says, "Don't forget the bed. I'll owe you a drink when you get back."

"If things go right, everyone in Creation is going to owe me a drink."

When I'm alone I go to the phone and push the PISSANTS button.

A female voice picks up.

"My lord?"

"Who is this?"

"Malabraxas. I'm assistant to Brimborion."

"He isn't coming to work for like forever, so you get to steal all his Post-its. But before that, I want you to call down and clear out the garage. I don't want anyone down there for an hour."

"Yes, my lord."

"Don't call me 'lord.'"

"Yes, Lucifer."

"You got it on the first try. Congratulations. You just got Brimborion's job. Let Semyazah know. Also, send a cleanup crew to my room. There's a couple of bodies. They can't miss them. But don't call them until after you clear out the garage."

"Yes, Lucifer."

I go to the closet and get out my bloody leather bike pants and hoodie. I found it in a cemetery when I first got back from Hell. Yeah, that's kind of disgusting but I'm the only one who knows where it came from and it doesn't smell any worse than anything else down here. After surviving the market, the Magic 8 Ball, being burned in effigy, and getting my arm cut off, it feels kind of like a good-luck charm.

I take a quick look around at the room. Nothing I need or want. I pick up the duffel, step over Brimborion's body, and head back to the library.

I step around the hexes in the floor. I should have told Semyazah about them but he's a smart guy. He'll send in another smart guy to check the place out first. With any luck, he'll be smart enough to look before he leaps. If not, it will be just one more Hellion watercooler story. Did you hear the one about Phil's head exploding in the library?

I open the false bookshelves, lock them from the inside, and go down the stairs.

THE GARAGE IS EMPTY. The sound of my boots echoes down to deep, deep sublevels. A B-movie Halloween spook show. I could make a fortune selling weekend Hell junkets to the movie biz. Nonmortal ones, of course. Vampire sound techs. Nahual film editors. Jade cinematographers. Give them the full tour. Where I first landed down here. The arena. The palace where I murdered my first Hellion. The field where the red legger cut off my arm. I wonder where it is now? I should check eBay.

I go to the bike, secure the duffel on the back, and do a quick walk around checking for oil leaks, a flat tire, or a broken chain. It looks fine. I swing my leg over the bike and kick it to life. It sounds good. Like it could crack the foundations of the palace.

I get a glove out of my coat pocket and put it on my Kissi hand. Better get used to it. I'll be hiding it a lot more soon. I hope.

Time to let go of a lot that happened over the last hundred days. I got ruthless and I got lucky. On the upside, I stayed alive this whole time. I found the 8 Ball. I even figured out Marchosias's game. On the downside, Samael tricked me into cleaning up his mess again. Creating the Council so I could put the right people in the right places and take the heat for everything that went wrong. Kick Buer's ass into building a City Hall that doesn't look like skinhead porn. Get Semyazah on board with keeping Lucifer, any Lucifer, alive at all costs. Draw Marchosias out and almost take the bullet that sooner or later would have been aimed at Samael's head. Obyzuth was the real ringer, though. She led me to Deumos and something that will change Hell forever. Whether or not that's a good thing we'll find out when the place becomes something new or blows itself apart. Samael handed me a leaf blower and left me to clear off the driveway, and for what?

So he could stay in Heaven? Or is he going to blow back into town looking like Steve McQueen driving the Batmobile? If he does, I'll shake his hand and thank him. Take the place back over. Pretend you fixed it all yourself and suck up the applause. Just let me go home and stay there.

I heel up the kickstand and wait, feeling the weight of the Hellion hog against my body. Letting it rattle my bones.

*Don't fear God*
*Don't worry about death*
*What is good is easy to get, and*
*What is terrible is easy to endure*

The only thing I'm sicker of than philosophy is philosophers. I bet Epicurus is living free and easy in Eleusis, the province of Hell reserved for righteous pagans. Next time I'll trade places with him and sip wine with the vestal virgins while Epicurus runs Bedlam's outhouse for a while. Then you tell me how easy it is to roll with the terrible, you goat-cheese-salad asshole.

I put the bike in gear and roll by the kennels before heading for the garage gate.

I'm leaving by the front door this time. No sneaking out the back. There's no reason to be subtle. In a palace, rumors are like flying monkeys. Annoying as vegan desserts and hard to stop once they're airborne. Besides Bill and Semyazah, no one is supposed to know when and where I'm leaving. But of course people do. Everyone in the fucking palace.

Troops from ten Hellion legions are spread out across the lawn when I roll up to street level. They're dead silent.

Dead still. They're not blocking Lucifer's way, but they're not happy to see me rolling out on my own. Someone is going to twitch first. It might as well be me.

I whistle. There's a low roar and the sound of razored steel on concrete. Shadows lumber up the driveway walls. When the hellhounds reach the surface, they spread out around me, pawing the ground impatiently. They scan the troops, pink brains sloshing in the bell jars where their heads should be. They settle around me in a protective semicircle.

The potion the palace witches whipped up for me we used to call a Sheol Sucker Punch. Technically, it's a kind of poison, but a very selective one.

When most people see hellhounds, all they see is the machine part. They forget about the brain, usually because when they're that close, it means a hound is gnawing off their leg. I don't know where hellhound brains come from, but I know that brains are brains and they need food to work. And any brain that needs food is a brain you can dose. A Sheol Sucker Punch burns out the parts of the brain that control memory but skates around smarts and motor functions. Mostly it resets a brain's emotional clock back to when it was a newborn. And like every good duckling, the newborns wake up looking for something to imprint on. I made sure it was me. I'm Mom now and the hounds, their gears whirring and pistons pounding, are a loyal pack.

The legions back off but stand their ground. They know not to run. Running makes you prey and no one wants to be prey to a hundred metal hounds.

Some of the troops want to cut my throat. Others stare at me like wounded children. Neither are good looks for crazed killers. I should probably say something, but what am I going to say? "Sometimes the Devil needs a little me time"?

The best I can come up with to say is, "Hell needs a Lucifer and Hell will always have one. Just not tonight."

The wind changes and brings new smells with it.

The gibbet holding Ukobach holds a bloated corpse. By the street, scalps and fresh skins are tied to the ornamental fence, flapping and drying in the breeze. Guess I know what happened to Vetis's men. I wonder if Vetis's hide is up there with them?

As the smell of rotting Hellion meat drifts across the lawn, whatever little guilt I've been nursing for running out on these poor slobs evaporates. Why did I ever think mass suicide for these murderous hellspawn hyenas was a bad idea? Let them all burn.

The lousy thing is maybe I deserve a seat in the frying pan right next to them. I dragged Ukobach behind my bike when I could have just snapped his neck. But Lucifer needs to put on a show and I never get tired of killing Hellions. Maybe I should send the hounds back to the kennels, go to my rooms, and die down here with these assholes. Maybe that's the real reason why Samael marooned me here. His way of teaching me one last lesson. The one he wouldn't tell me because I had to figure it out for myself. *That I don't deserve to go home.*

I thought I could skate and cheat and finesse my way around the worst parts of playing Lucifer but I was fooling myself. You can't play the Devil without becoming the Devil. That's why Saint James abandoned me. He knew what was coming and he didn't want to see it happen. He also didn't stick around to help me through it, so a few of those scalps belong to him.

I really was planning on coming back when I found some hoodoo that would let me stay in real L.A. while saving Hell from burning. Now I know I can't ever come back. If I do, I'll never leave. I won't grow horns or hooves, but if I come back, I'll never stop being Lucifer and it will prove what I've always secretly suspected. Hell didn't make me a monster. It just confirmed all my worst fears about myself.

I rev the bike, pop the clutch, and burn rubber down the driveway, past the gates, and onto the street. The hellhound pack sprints behind. After a couple of blocks, they catch up and fan out around me. We blitzkrieg traffic off the roads and pedestrians off the streets. We tear up the asphalt, burst store windows, and rip the bumpers from idling trucks. Unlike the troops at the palace, these haven't figured out I'm deserting their sorry asses. They scream and fire their weapons into the air like it's New Year's as we blow by.

I head to the 405 entrance at Wilshire. There's less than a mile of freeway left but that's plenty. I crank the throttle until the bike's engine glows cherry red. The hellhounds can't keep up. They begin to fall back. I hear them howling and baying above the noise of the engine. They'll be okay. They have the run of the palace now, and if no one feeds them, well, they'll just have to dine on whatever meat they can find.

This is it. The end of the road. A hundred yards ahead, the city spreads out below the thicket of jagged rebar that marks where the freeway has collapsed. I get low in the saddle. Every time we hit a pothole, Lucifer's armor collides with the gas tank and kicks sparks into my eyes. I'm blasting down a broken road toward the heart of a half-dead city with fireworks burning my face. Whatever happens next, it's a hell of a trip.

Jetting off the end of the freeway, the universe goes quiet and a ghost melody fills my head. "The Girlfriend of the Whirling Dervish" by Martin Denny. Carlos's favorite song on the jukebox at the real Bamboo House of Dolls. I picture home but I'm still in Hell. What am I doing wrong?

The front of the bike noses down toward the rubble.

Did I use up all the armor's power on Brimborion?

Wouldn't that be a hilarious goddamn end to everything?

The ground comes up fast. "The Girlfriend of the Whirling Dervish" mixes with the rising sound of the engine. What did I expect? Fucking up is my true home and I'm heading there fast.

I wish I had a cigarette.

Then there's nothing at all.

Then there's something.

The front wheel hits pavement. A rush of vertigo. Lights. Smeared and jittering. The nothing parts like heavy curtains. Or a trapdoor.

The rear wheel drops. The impact is like being rear-ended by a battleship. I can't hold the bike. So I lean it to the side. Lay it down and let it slide. Ten or twenty yards. The asphalt grinds against my legs but the leathers hold. I'm not so sure about the coat. Have I mentioned I'm hard on clothes?

When the bike finally stops, it's sliced a deep groove in the roadbed. I grab the handlebars, get my weight low, and tilt the bike upright. It's not even scratched.

*Welcome home.*

It feels good to say it and mean it. How do I know? The place doesn't smell like bad meat and misery. The sky is clear and full of stars. Clue number three: the bike's stopped right in front of the Hollywood Forever Cemetery. Tombstones never looked so good.

A big screen is set up by the columbarium. People sit and sprawl on blankets among the dead. Movie night at the cemetery. It's not as weird as it might sound. On Día de los Muertos, families offer food and eat meals with their dead. In Hollywood, we show up with offerings of cowboys and show tunes.

Tonight we're entertaining our favorite stiffs with a pristine print of *The Bad Seed*. Pigtailed moppet Patty McCormack just set Leroy the janitor on fire and her mother and best friend watch him burn from an upstairs window. How are you enjoying the movie so far, dead people? We could have shown *The Sound of Music* but we thought we'd scare the last few scraps of coffin jerky off your bones.

I'm back on the bike when I notice a kid by the cemetery gates. A girl in a frilly blue party dress. Maybe nine or ten years old and she's all alone. Who brings their kid to a murder movie in a graveyard drive-in and lets her run off alone? Hell, who brings their kid to one of these things at all? The place is half stoners and speed-freak hipsters. The moment the show is over the whole block will turn into one big bumper-car ride.

The kid doesn't move. Just stares at me until she realizes I'm staring back. Then she turns and runs through the cemetery gates. I can hear her laughing all the way across the street. With an attitude like that, she's going to grow up and start a mind-blowing band or become a serial killer. I flash on Candy: that could have been her years ago bouncing into Hollywood Forever, a tombstone Disneyland for kids too carnivorous for teacup rides and cotton candy.

I step on the kick-starter and the bike fires up on the first try.

First question. Where's Candy? No way she's at the Beat Hotel anymore. What's the second choice? L.A. is a lot to take in when it's not on fire. I can't get used to seeing the sky. I need to get my bearings and screw my head on straight.

I'm starting to feel just a little conspicuous on this Hellion hog, with a headlight that could blind the space shuttle, no driver's license, license plate, title, or insurance. Not that I ever had any of those things. But now I don't have them and I'm on an illegally imported foreign motorcycle. Back on Earth thirty seconds and I'm already a felon. Welcome home, shithead. I'll stick to the side streets for now.

I cross Hollywood Boulevard and pull the bike into the alley next to Maximum Overdrive video, the store where I lived with Kasabian. Kasabian used to be dead. I know because I cut off his head. It's where I've been staying since I got back from Hell the first time, which makes it the closest thing I've had to a home in eleven years.

A man and a woman walk by holding hands as I turn into the alley. It looks like they've been picnicking by a coal-mine fire. Their hands and faces—every exposed patch of skin—is smeared with gritty dirt, but their clothes are clean and pressed. I've never see two dirtier clean people in my life. They catch me looking at them and cross to the other side of the street.

Richard Kadrey

The alley by Max Overdrive is a snowdrift of junk. The Dumpster overflows with plastic trash bags and food cartons. There are enough broken bottles that the alley looks like a salt plain. I don't think the garbage has been picked up in weeks. I steer the bike and park in the Dumpster's shadow.

In the old days I'd use the Key to the Room of Thirteen Doors to walk into the store through a shadow but Saint James has that. I take the duffel off the bike, get out the black blade, and slip the tip into the door lock. One turn and it clicks open.

Inside, the place stinks of paint. The floors and display stands are covered with plastic drop cloths, but there's a fine layer of dust on them. No one's done any work in a long time.

There's a light on upstairs in the room I used to share with Kasabian. I go up the stairs quietly, knife out and ready. At the top I push open the door with the toe of my boot. It opens on a messy bedroom. There's a wooden desk where Kasabian used to keep his bootleg video setup. Now there's a computer surrounded by monitors. I push the door open more. Something is in the room with its back to me. A heavy mechanical body with a human head. It picks up a bag from Donut Universe in its mouth and heads for the desk on all fours like a dog. When it sees me, the head opens its mouth and drops the bag. It raises a paw and points at me.

"Don't say a goddamn word."

The last time I saw him, Kasabian was still just a chattering head without a body. Now he's something more, but I don't know if it's an improvement.

I come inside and drop the duffel. My armor is sticking out from under my shirt. Kasabian nods at it.

"Did the Wizard give you a heart, Tin Man?"

"Funny. Careful you don't pop a rivet, Old Yeller."

His face is like the couple in the street. Smeared with something dark and coarse, like black sand. He trots to the desk on all fours. Kasabian's head on a hellhound body isn't a pleasant sight.

When he gets to the desk chair, Kasabian pushes back with his hind legs until his ass is firmly on the seat. Then he leans the rest of his body back like half of a drawbridge rising. In a second he's gone from windup toy to Pinocchio on a good day, an almost real boy. He picks up the bag of donuts with his claws and drops it on the desk without offering me one.

"Is that the best Saint James could come up with? It's better than nothing but it doesn't exactly look finished."

Kasabian frowns for a second then gets it.

"Saint James? Yeah. That's about right. As for this"—he raps a fist against his chest—"your better half never paid off the charm maker reworking it, so he didn't finish the job."

"Why not?"

"The asshole disappeared."

"How did you know it was me and not him just now?"

"He looks like a bathing beauty and you're the Loch Ness Monster. Seeing you young like that was giving me the heebee-jeebies."

"You mean how I looked before you sent me Downtown."

"Something like that."

With the back of one metal hand, he pushes away an ashtray overflowing with Maledictions. Fidgety jailbird stuff, like now that I'm back he thinks I'm going to steal him blind. I lean in for a closer look at his body.

"So how does it feel?"

He flexes his arms and legs. Stands and starts picking up the beer bottles, pizza boxes, and crusted food containers that cover every flat surface.

"You remember that arcade game where you move a claw around to grab a shitty teddy bear out of a bin? It's kind of like I'm the claw."

He flexes his fingers and picks up a Chinese-food container. His hands are the hound's paws reworked and extended into clawlike hands.

"I know I'm ugly as a spider on a baby but it's nice to have hands again."

"Don't feel so bad. We're both in gimp club these days."

I take the glove off and push up my left sleeve.

Kasabian shakes his head in disgust.

"Is that Kissi?"

"Yeah. Josef's idea of a joke."

He shakes his head and goes back to picking up trash.

"I get Rin Tin Tin's gnawed-on bones and you get to look like Robocop. Story of my life."

I reach over and take the Donut Universe bag off the desk. Kasabian's eyes flicker over at me but he doesn't say anything. I take out an apple fritter and bite into it. Fuck me. People food. The day-old dried-out grease bomb is the best thing I've ever tasted.

"How'd you lose the arm?"

"In a fight."

"Did it hurt?"

"A lot. Does that make you feel better?"

He moves his head side to side like he's thinking.

"A little. Not enough. You can go out and pretend to be a person. Me? I'm still stuck in this room."

"Why? You've got arms and legs. Get yourself some clothes and some gloves and you'll be dancing in the rain."

He picks up a burger wrapper, sniffs it, and drops it in with the other trash.

"If only. The body works okay dicking around here but I can't go much further than the corner for beer. The legs won't hold. Like I said, the guy never finished the job."

"Take some of the Dark Eternal money and pay off the charm guy yourself."

After I snuffed all the zombies in L.A., one of the local vampire cohorts, the Dark Eternal, handed me a suitcase full of cash as a reward for saving the city, i.e., their snack supply.

"Saint James took it. Gave it all away."

"What?"

"Right before he disappeared. Got all pious about it being dirty Lurker money. That kind of bullshit."

I bite into the donut, talking with my mouth half full.

"I can't tell you how many ways I'm going to kill that prick."

Kasabian takes the bulging garbage bag, pushes open the alley window, and drops it into the pile on the Dumpster.

"That's why the trash is piling up and downstairs isn't finished."

"Smart boy. Now tell me what number I'm thinking."

He sits down at the desk and reaches past the overflowing ashtray to get a pack of Maledictions. Takes one for himself and holds out the pack to me. I take it and light our smokes with Mason's lighter.

"What are you watching?" I ask.

"*The Long Goodbye.*"

"Nice."

"The best movie ever made about L.A. Fuck *Chinatown*. And don't try to argue with me 'cause your opinion is going to be wrong."

We smoke and watch the movie for a couple of minutes. A gangster is starting to strip and he's telling Elliott Gould to do the same. I want to ask about Candy but the words won't come out. I had this fantasy that she would have moved in here, taken my place, and be waiting for me. Being alone makes you stupid.

"If the money's gone, why are the lights on? How do you pay for all this takeout?"

Kasabian blows smoke rings at the video screen.

"Not all the money's gone. Just what he knew about. I embezzled some. You tried to throw me out enough times, so I set myself up a trust fund."

"I know."

He turns and looks at me.

"When?"

"Always. You're a thief. You can't help stealing. And I probably gave you some cause to do it. How much did you get?"

"About two hundred grand."

I cough, almost choking on the cigarette.

"Two hundred grand and you're still hiding and living off delivery-boy donuts?"

He shakes his head.

"It sounds like a lot but it's not exactly the rest-of-your-life money. At least the store brought in a little cash but with that gone . . ."

A few months back, Samael gave Kasabian the power to see into the Daimonion Codex, Lucifer's Boy Scout handbook of clever awful things. Through it, Kasabian can also lurk behind the scenes watching parts of Hell like a surveillance cam.

"Did you ever look into the Codex? Did you see me Downtown?"

"Candy used to come by and ask me that."

"When was the last time you saw her?"

"Three weeks. Maybe a month ago."

"What did you say?"

He takes the Malediction out of his mouth with metal fingers stained yellow with nicotine.

"What I see is kind of erratic. I can't see everywhere. I could see you on and off for the first few days, then you went off the air."

"Maybe because of the Lucifer thing."

"Lucifer thing?"

"Never mind. I killed Mason, by the way."

"You sure?"

"There was a big hole in his head where his brains used to be."

"Oh man."

He leans an elbow on the desk and runs a metal hand over his head.

"That's the best news I've heard in a long time. I used to

dream about him coming back and finding me all crippled up and not able to run away."

I say it without giving myself time to think about it.

"Where's Candy these days?"

Elliott Gould is on a bus to Mexico. His suit is wrinkled and worn and his eyes are dark, like he hasn't slept in days. He looks like half the population of Hell and most of Hollywood, the half not working out in gyms so they look like lunch meat stretched over Beverly Hills mannequins.

"She didn't give me her fucking itinerary. The last number I have is for your friend's clinic."

He crushes out his cigarette and says, "You're not moving back in here, are you? I'm kind of used to having the place to myself."

I stand up, brushing the donut crumbs off my lap.

"Do you know who I am these days? I'm Lucifer, the lord high asshole of the Underworld. I'll sleep anywhere I want."

Kasabian tilts his eyes toward me without turning his head from the movie.

"You mean you're broke."

"Completely."

He opens one of the desk drawers and pulls out a carton of Maledictions. Instead of cigarettes, it's full of cash. He peels off two hundred-dollar bills and holds them out to me. I don't move to take them. After a minute he peels off a few more bills. I take them and stuff them in my pocket.

"Don't think I'm always going to let you be so stingy with my money."

"This is my money," he says. "You gave your money away."

I don't feel like arguing the point. I lift up the mattress and feel around for my guns.

"Don't bother. Saint James took them when he took the money."

"Even Wild Bill's Colt?"

"All of them."

The old Navy Colt wasn't Wild Bill's actual gun but it was as close as I'm ever going to get and now it's gone. That's cold.

I get the Glock and my na'at from the duffel bag. The na'at goes inside my coat while the Glock goes in my waistband at my back.

"I'm leaving the duffel here until I figure out where I'm staying."

Kasabian tosses me an unopened pack of Maledictions. That's quite a thing coming from him. He must think it's my birthday.

"Don't bother. Pope Joan still works nights at the Beat Hotel. Drop some gelt on her and I bet she'll give you our old room. I think I might have even hid some money in the air vent."

I pick up the bag and start out.

"Good to see you on your feet, Old Yeller."

"Happy hunting, Tin Man."

I catch a glimpse of Kasabian in the window by the desk. In the glass his face is normal and clean, but the guy sitting in the chair is a grimy mess. That's it, then. The Devil has special eyes. He can see sin. I wonder what Samael saw when he looked at me.

I get on the bike and drive at an entirely reasonable speed

through backstreets to Allegra's clinic. I use hand signals and everything. Look at me, Mom. A solid citizen at last.

WHAT USED TO BE Doc Kinski's clinic and is currently Allegra's is in a strip mall near where Sunset and Hollywood Boulevards meet. There's a fried chicken franchise on one end of the mall and a local pizza joint on the other, with a Vietnamese nail salon and the clinic in between. The parking lot smells like a high school lunchroom and is one of the top ten last places anyone hunting heavy angelic magic would look.

The blinds are drawn in all the clinic windows. It says EXISTENTIAL HEALING on the door in gold peel-and-stick letters. I take the handle and pull. It's locked. I raise my hand to knock and lower it. Seeing Kasabian is one thing—we're both the biggest freaks the other knows—but this will be different. There are normal people in here. Not normal normal people, but ones who act and feel like normal people.

I don't know what to say to Candy. Three months ago I told her I'd be back in three days. And Allegra. I didn't even say good-bye to Allegra before I left. She freaked out when I briefly worked as Samael's bodyguard and things haven't been right between us since. If Vidocq is inside, that's another whole complication. The old man is the closest thing I've ever had to a real father. But he's also French, and loud when he gets excited. Right now I don't know if I can handle either one, much less both. Still.

I knock on the door.

It opens a crack and a heavyset blonde with blue skin and horns peers out at me. She's a Ludere. A kind of Lurker. The whole tribe are compulsive gamblers. Probably the only

reason she works here is so she can run a line on which patients are going to recover and which are going to die.

"Do you have an appointment?"

"Everyone thinks I'm dead, so probably not."

She reaches out through the open door and shoves a business card into my hand.

"Call and Dr. Allegra will see you when she can."

She starts to close the door. I grab the edge.

"Is Candy inside?"

"Why do you want to know?"

"Does that mean she's in there?"

She points to the card.

"Call and make an appointment."

"Why don't I make one right now? My name is Stark and
in thirty seconds I'm coming inside. You have ten seconds to
write it in your book and twenty seconds to get out of the way
before I kick the door in."

She leans to one side so the light from the clinic lobby falls
across my face.

"Are you him or are you the boring one?"

"Do I know you?"

"I used to hang out at the Bamboo House of Dolls. Till he
came around."

"Princess, did the boring one go around kicking in doors?"

"It sounds like you. Wait here."

"Twenty seconds."

Twenty seconds come and go. Too bad. I always liked this
door with the gold letters flaking off. But never make a threat
you're not willing to go carry out. I step back a good kicking distance. The door doesn't look like much, so there's no

need to get dramatic. Just bring up a leg to kick out the lock. I draw it up and for a second I'm standing on the street like a leather flamingo. The door swings open and Candy is standing there. She looks at me on one leg, in dirty leather and a road-rash coat. I look at her. The same ripped jeans and Chuck Taylors. She has on a T-shirt covered with Japanese writing. Looks like it's for an all-girl band I never heard of. Then we're both looking at each other. Then it occurs to me to put my leg down.

"Hi," she says.

"Hi."

She looks at me like I'm a ghost or trick. Saint James must have done a number on these people if no one trusts their eyes. A minute later a grin spreads across her face. She comes out and throws her arms around my shoulders. Jumps and wraps her legs around my waist. She stays that way for a minute before climbing down. And John Wayne roundhouse punches me in the face. I put up my arms to rope-a-dope her in case she decides to punch again. She does, throwing haymakers to my body every couple of words.

"You asshole. You stupid goddamn dumb motherfucker. I fucking hate you and how fucking stupid you are."

There's a second of quiet and then a painful, "Ow."

She reaches inside my coat and pulls open my shirt. Looks at the armor and then at me.

"What the hell is that?"

"Protection from crazy girls who say hello with their fists."

"I have not yet begun to kick your ass. You run off for a weekend in Hell and don't come back and we don't hear anything. Then who shows up but some baby-face hippie version of you who'd rather save the whales than have a drink with me?"

"So you met the prodigal asshole."

"And then we figure it out. He's some kind of Hellion practical joke. A monster sent here to take your place. That's when we know you were dead."

I try to put my hands on her shoulders but she bats them away.

"I'm sorry about everything but this is me and I'm not dead."

"Well, fuck you and your good news. You're probably just a different stupid monster they sent up. What's your gimmick? You going to macramé us to world peace?"

"I'm my own monster and I sent myself up."

"Why?"

"To find you."

She looks away. Digs the toe of her Chuck Taylor into a squashed piece of gum by the door, trying to loosen it. Inside, the Ludere and a couple of patients watch us like a flesh-and-blood reality show.

She says, "I let Stark go because he was being all noble and I wanted to be noble too so he would remember me when he found Alice. Dumbest thing I ever did."

I get closer.

"How could I forget about you and you torturing me with those stupid robot sunglasses? If you think I was playing house with Alice all this time, you're wrong. I sent her home the day I found her. It's me here. Not that other guy. Alice and Hell and all the rest is over and done with."

She crosses her arms.

"How do I know it's you?"

"When I said I came back to find you? I lied. I came back for the knife I loaned you. Hand it over."

She looks at me and furrows her forehead. Her eyes get a little red. Not like "Oh, my God. Godzilla is going to step on me." More like tears red. But she doesn't actually cry. She's a monster and a killer like me. We sometimes tear up but leave the crying to the suckers we hit.

She comes over and puts her hand on my chest. Then slides it over to hug me. Through the armor I feel her body as she lays her head on my chest. She punches me in the side. Lightly this time, so it's barely a punch at all.

"You ever take off like that again, you take me with you."

"Deal."

She takes a step back, looking at the armor.

"What's the story with the Iron Man gear?"

Then she smiles.

"Oh my God. Stark. It all makes sense. You're really Tony Stark. You've been Iron Man all along."

"Oh God. I can see this joke isn't going to die anytime soon."

"You can count on that."

I put my arms around her and just hold her there.

"Things got weirder Downtown than I ever counted on. I got hurt pretty bad. The Pat Boone clone you met is a part of me that escaped. And he took some of my strength with him. The armor belongs to Lucifer and brings some of it back."

She looks up at me.

"Hurt like how?"

"If you're not sure which Stark you're talking to, ask him to show you his arm."

I push up my sleeve.

The Ludere and patients peeking over Candy's shoulder make little gasping sounds. Candy is the only one who doesn't look like she's going to be sick. She touches my robot bug hand and runs her fingers up the length of my sleek black arm until she gets to where it attaches to my shoulder.

"This is so fucking awesome."

If you ever need to confirm that a girl is worth coming back from Hell for, show her your monster arm and see what she says.

Allegra comes out of the treatment room with a bunch of purple plant bulbs in her hands. She smiles in a kind of rueful way when she sees me and comes over and gives me a hug. Unlike the others, she knows it's me right off.

"I'm sorry about that stuff that happened before. Please tell me there's no hard feelings. I'm just glad to see you alive."

"No hard feelings at all. I'm just happy to be back. You know, on the way over I was going to ask you to look at my jaw 'cause it hurt. Then I remembered I've been speaking nothing but Hellion for three months."

"You'll get plenty of practice at people talk when you tell us everything that happened."

I'm not talking to anyone about everything that happened, but that still leaves a lot to tell.

Candy turns and steps away from me. I hear her heart rate jump. Smell the faint beginning of tension sweat.

"Stark, this is Rinko."

Rinko is a couple of inches taller than Candy. Like her, Rinko is pretty, with dark almond eyes and black hair down to her waist. On her right shoulder is a tattoo of a rainbow-striped Oni. Lower down she has Astro Boy wearing a leather biker cap and chaps.

At least Candy hasn't been alone all this time.

Candy motions Rinko over and I shake her hand. There's a certain coolness to her skin.

"You're a Jade," I say.

Her eyes get hard.

"Something wrong with that?"

"No. I just never met any besides Candy. It's funny finally running into one."

"Hmm."

If Rinko could breathe fire I'd be crispy bacon by now. The girl can't stand the sight of me. It's probably how I would have been around some of Alice's exes.

Candy takes Rinko by the arm and walks her to the back of the waiting room. They have a fast, intense conversation. All stage whispers and hand waving.

Inside the clinic it's both familiar and not. There's the same cheap plastic chairs in the waiting room but the walls have been painted a pale blue. The same overflowing bookcase. The rickety old desk has been replaced with a shiny IKEA one.

Candy's conversation ends with Rinko throwing up her hands and stomping away into a back room, keeping her eyes down and away from me. Candy gets a jacket off the desk chair and says to Allegra, "I'm gone for the rest of the night. That cool?"

"Très cool," says Allegra. She gives us a little wave on the way out.

"Let's go," she says. "Are they still holding a room for you at the Beat Hotel?"

"I doubt it but cash is the magic anyone can do, and tonight I'm Houdini."

She stops when she sees the Hellion hog.

"Yours?"

"Yep. Like it?"

"It's almost as cool as the arm."

A girl to come back from Hell for.

Turns out Kasabian was right and Pope Joan is on duty. It takes $200 to get the old room but I'd rather get inside than haggle, so I give her the money and get the key.

Inside, Candy pushes me down on the bed and climbs on top.

"On the way over, I wasn't sure I was going to fuck you but then I thought that Rinko is going to be mad at me no matter what, so I'd rather get blamed for doing something than doing nothing."

She throws off her jacket and shirt and unzips my pants. I pull off my shirt, pants, and boots but not the armor.

"Um. You keeping that on?"

"I'm not sure what'll happen if I take it off. I know I'll just be a regular mortal and die if someone slips in here and shanks me while I'm asleep. Or I might choke to death from all the Hellion muck I've been eating and breathing."

She raps on the armor with her knuckles, takes my arms, and pins them down to the bed.

"That's cool. I'm into cosplay. Between the armor and the arm you can be both brothers in *Full Metal Alchemist*."

"So, we're having a three-way with only two people."

"Shut up and kiss me."

When Candy and I were alone together, we had a habit of wrecking rooms. Once upon a time we practically tore the walls down in here. Tonight isn't like that. It's slower and a lot more tentative, like Candy is still trying to convince herself I'm real.

Later, when we're lying around and the sweat is cooling under my armor, Candy says, "This is weird."

"Sleeping with a guy again?"

"Don't be stupid. I keep waiting for someone to yell 'April fool' and for you to vanish."

"The only joke in all this was me leaving. I'm not sorry about why I left but I'm sorry I didn't come back. Before I left, I should have thought of a way to let you know I was all right."

"There's that. So how was it down there?"

"Mean and sad and strange and it ends with me being crowned prom queen of Hell."

"Sure it does."

She leans up on one elbow and looks at the clock radio.

"Shit. I should get back. Rinko will be waiting up for me. You know how girls are."

"Don't keep her waiting. That doesn't turn out well for anyone."

She runs a hand through her messy hair.

"Listen, Rinko is an old friend . . ."

"You don't have to explain anything to me. Not now, not ever. Whatever you do is okay by me."

She smiles, gets up, and gets dressed. At the door she

tugs up her pants leg and slides my black bone knife out of a sheath on the side of her boot.

"You gave me this to hold for you. Now that you're home, I suppose you'll want it back."

"I stole Mason's. Why don't you go ahead and keep that one."

She smiles.

"For real? No take-backs?"

"No take-backs."

She slips the knife back into its sheath and pulls down her pants leg.

"I'll call you tomorrow."

"Talk to you then."

She blows me a quick kiss on the way out.

Once upon a time I saved the world and lost a girl. Then I saved Hell and lost another girl. This is getting to be a bad habit.

THE HOTEL PHONE RINGS.

"Candy?"

The line crackles.

"That was a hell of an exit, Lord Lucifer. I wasn't sure you were going to make it."

It's a man's voice.

"Were you relieved or disappointed?"

"Relieved. Thrilled even. The worlds below and above would be much more boring without you."

"Who is this?"

"Not Vetis. But you knew that."

"You're not speaking Hellion. You're either a possessed

mortal or a damned soul. I don't think a soul could call up here even with heavy hoodoo, so my guess is a mortal."

"Listen to you go, Deep Blue."

"Did the hounds make it back all right?"

"The ones that didn't follow you over the edge. More blood on your hands. You're like death on a bender."

"Your voice is familiar but so what? You'll be someone different next time."

"Chances are."

"Then what do we have to talk about? Fuck off."

I slam down the receiver and rip the plug out of the wall.

I should have known the moment I decided not to go back Downtown. I don't have to. Hell will follow me here.


IN THE MORNING, when I start to go out, I reach for a gun and remember that all I have is the Glock. A sleek manly gun. Guys who love Glocks love Corvettes because Dad had one and they're still trying to crawl out of the old man's shadow. Glocks: the only guns that come with a side of daddy issues. I hate Glocks. But I take it anyway.

I spend the day just walking around breathing in the perfume of car exhaust, dry air-conditioned air, and greasy Mexican food. I buy a fish taco from a van on the street. It looks like the *Mona Lisa* and tastes like God's own Lunchable.

I'm still getting used to a sky. And lost and frantic civilians piling up on the street corners, fidgeting, waiting for the green light. Running at the wrong time on the red and almost getting hit by a bus. They gasp like they're all gut-punched, never catching their breath from the endless running. If they knew they had a billion billion years of Heaven or Hell to look forward to after their measly eighty on Earth, would they slow down or would they get even more wired?

No one thinks of L.A. as ever being cold, but when it's winter and the clouds roll in and the temperature drops to sixty or below, it can feel downright chilly. But the armor doesn't notice. It has its own heat gauge set at body temperature. I could probably go to Antarctica and feed the penguins in nothing but flip-flops and a serape and not shiver once.

ON THE DYING edge of Hollywood Boulevard, another tourist trap is going out of business. I buy a couple of black button-down shirts with HOLLYWOOD spelled with palm trees over the breast pocket. They're loose enough that they hide the armor without making me look like the Michelin Man.

Back at the Beat Hotel, I take the one peeper I kept with me out of its saline-filled container, pop out my eye, and put the peeper in. Nothing happens. I can't see into Hell. Not the library, the grounds outside the palace, or through the peepers I put into the hellhounds. Lucifer is blind up here. Something else Samael kept to himself. I take the peeper out and put my eye back in.

Back when Samael was in L.A. and I was playing body-guard, he told me that he had very little power on Earth. That's probably why he gave Kasabian access to the Dai-monion Codex. Lucifer can't see it from here but half-dead Kasabian can.

I spend the rest of the afternoon playing around with the armor, seeing what Lucifer tricks I can pull up here. I find a few but nothing that'll get me a Nobel Prize. As usual I've timed things perfectly. I hang around Hell long enough to get all of Lucifer's power and then come home and lose most of it.

In the afternoon, Candy calls. She wants to meet at the Bamboo House of Dolls around ten. Why not? It's that or more *Brady Bunch* reruns, and that's goddamn depressing for the Lord of the Underworld, even when he's only operating at half speed.

Before I leave, I unscrew the air vent with a dime. What do you know? Kasabian wasn't just shining me on. There's a carny roll of twenty hundred-bills inside. The day just suddenly got brighter. What's ridiculous is how easy I am to buy off. Two grand out of two hundred and I want to kiss the sky? Don't let it get around but it turns out Lucifer is the cheapest date in Hell.

NOW, THIS IS SOMETHING solid and real. It smells like beer and whiskey and the sweat of the patrons and the cigarette smoke blown in through the doors by the trailing edge of a Santa Ana, which is just how it should be. It's a bar's job to be unambiguous. In a sea of troubles, you can hold on to a bar. The Bamboo House of Dolls is my Rock of Ages.

Everything is where it should be. Old Iggy and the Stooges and back-in-the-day L.A. punk-band posters. Behind the bar, it's all palm fronds, plastic hula girls, and coconut bowls for the peanuts. The jukebox chips and coos as Yma Sumac warbles through a spooky "Chuncho." Carlos the bartender is pouring shots of Jack for everyone bellied up at the bar and mine taste best because they're free. I hold up my glass to toast him for the third time tonight and he holds up his. It's that kind of night. I'm in my bar with my friends. Now I'm really home.

Vidocq has his arm around my shoulders. He's hardly taken it off since he got here, like if he lets go I'll blow away on the breeze.

"At least it wasn't eleven years this time. You're doing better," he says.

"Maybe you should try not going back at all," says Allegra.

"I signed up with Monsters Anonymous," I tell them. "Trying to kick the Hell habit one day at a time."

"I'll drink to that," says Vidocq. He holds up his empty glass and Carlos comes over and refills it.

Carlos says, "I wasn't sure if it was you when you walked in. Even with that fucked-up face, I'm still not a hundred percent."

He starts to pour me my sixth Jack of the night. I put my hand over the glass.

"Let's surprise everyone. Why don't you give me a cup of coffee?"

"See? I knew it wasn't you. Look at this place. It's like a wake for someone no one liked. Your *pendejo* brother just about drove me out of business."

He's right. The bar is maybe a third full. It used to be packed every night before I took off. Civilians and Lurkers like hanging around places with criminals, even if a few of them get chewed up, like the night a handful of zombies wandered in. What's funny is that's exactly why people come to places like this. They want to get close enough to death to smell the graveyard dust, as long as it's someone else's name that gets chiseled on the gravestone.

"I've been drinking almost nothing but Aqua Regia for

three months. I want something a human being might drink. And that little darling with my face is no brother of mine."

Carlos nods. Looks over the crowd.

"Maybe things will pick up when people hear the real you is back."

"If it helps, you can pour the coffee in six shot glasses."

"Great idea."

He goes away to get the coffee and glasses.

Candy comes in just as he sets them down. She takes one, throws it back, and makes a face.

"What the hell is this?"

"Coffee."

She slams the glass down.

"You're such a pussy."

"Yeah? Pick any random stranger and I'll punch them if you'll stay the night tonight."

Her posture changes. She tenses up. Looks over her shoulder to a table where Rinko sits alone.

"Don't. I can't. It's complicated."

"Sorry. That was stupid."

"No. It's all right."

Candy catches me looking at Rinko.

"She said she wanted to come."

"She wants to keep an eye on you."

"More like she wants to keep an eye on you. I guess I talked about you a lot. You know, when I thought you weren't coming back."

"You talked about me?"

Carlos brings Candy a shot.

"*De nada*," she says, and downs it. "I told her what an old fart you are and how you have rotten taste in music."

"Skull Valley Sheep Kill is the best band in L.A. these days."

"If you're an old fart. Anyone who doesn't drink Geritol for breakfast knows that Asaruto Gâruzu is the only band that matters."

She's wearing another shirt with the same band and Japanese characters.

"If I'm an old fart, you're a rice queen."

She puts on her robot sunglasses. The ones with pictures from some anime TV show I've never heard of on the frame. When she presses a button between the lenses, the glasses sing the show's theme song in a tinny voice.

"What makes you say that?"

The civilians all have dirty faces streaked with sin but the Lurkers are clean. I guess Lucifer isn't in charge of them. My friends aren't any exception when it comes to sin signs. Most of their faces are smeared, but not like Kasabian's. Allegra and Carlos aren't too bad. Vidocq is the dirtiest among my friends. His signs reach from his face to his hands, but I'm not surprised. I know he killed some guys in France a hundred years back. Like LAPD says, there's no statute of limitations on murder, even if someone deserves it. I checked my own face in the hotel mirror. No sin signs at all. Is that because I'm Lucifer or because I'm still not entirely human?

"I missed you, you know. I wrote you notes and left them around hoping Kasabian could see them and tell you."

She glances back at Rinko.

"Yeah. I missed you too. A quarter of a year's worth."

She's plenty pissed at me. Not as pissed as Rinko but pissed. I can't blame her. I promised her three days and gave her a hundred. This is going to take a time to pass. If it ever does, now that she's moved on to someone else. Still, she went to the hotel with me last night. Was that a welcome home or a good-bye fuck? I guess I'll find out. I'm so fucking good at being patient.

"I should go see how Rinko is doing," she says.

She takes her drinks and starts back to the table. She stops and turns.

"You were going to tell me something about Lucifer last night. What was it?" she asks.

"Nothing important. Go see Rinko before she eye snuffs both of us."

She goes and Allegra follows her over. Vidocq and Father Traven are together at the end of the bar, so I head down that way. When I get there, Vidocq drops his arm on my shoulders again. Damn French.

"Hey, Father. When did you get in?"

I put out my hand. When Traven shakes it, he lays his other hand on top like I'm the pope or Little Richard. Liam Traven is my favorite priest. Partly because he was excommunicated, which means he doesn't take corporate shit, and partly because he's nuts. He reads, writes, eats, and breathes ancient languages no one has ever heard of. He knows the names of more old gods than the Vatican and every Dungeons & Dragons player in the world.

"I just walked in," he says. "When Eugène called me, I wasn't sure whether or not to believe him. And here you are."

"If it's any consolation, I'm not sure if I'm here either. I feel like a bad Xerox someone put through the shredder."

"I'm sure that will pass."

"Sorry about your car. Did you get it back?"

On my way back to Hell, I had to abandon Traven's car on the street near the body of a dead cop. It was an ugly scene but it was Josef's fault not mine and there was nothing I could do about it.

"Eventually. The police held on to it for a few weeks. I feel awkward asking you this right away but I need to."

"No. I didn't kill that cop. But for what it's worth, I killed the guy who did it." And slept like a baby. But I don't tell him that part.

I say, "I'm glad I caught the two of you together. There's some stuff I want to talk to you about. Things that happened to me in Hell. Changes I'm still trying to get my head around."

"Is that what the glove is for?" asks Traven.

I look down, relieved I remembered to put it back on.

"This? No. I just lost my arm and the new one is kind of ugly."

"You lost your arm? My God."

"Don't sweat it, Father. Now I can get handicap plates."

"What do you mean ugly?" asks Vidocq.

I scan the room. No one is looking, so I slip off the glove and let them get a good look at my demon mitt. Immediately I realize that it was a mistake. Traven has gone white.

Vidocq says, "Allegra tried to describe it but didn't come close to capturing *la horreur exquise.*"

Traven stares at me. If eyes could scream, run home, and hide under the blankets, he'd be blind.

"Is that what Hell is like? What else did they do to you? I couldn't psychologically survive something like that."

Father Traven used to translate old books for the Church. Then he translated the wrong one. An evil Necronomicon thing. The Bible of the Angra Om Ya. The gods before God. He got excommunicated for his trouble, and in the priest game, excommunication is a one-way ticket to Hell. Traven is the dirtiest guy in the bar. His sin signs are deep and awful. Almost every bare inch of skin is black. His hands look like he dipped them in tar. They practically drip with sin. Then I remember. Traven's a sin eater, from a long line of sin eaters. He's swallowed more sins than a thousand of the worst killers and bastards you can think of. The weight of it must break his back. And he says he couldn't survive getting an arm like mine. I think he's selling himself short but we all define horror in our own way.

"Don't sweat it, Father. I met God. He isn't what you think He is. I know the Devil pretty well too. He isn't what you think either. Trust me, Heaven or Hell, consider yourself taken care of."

"I know that should reassure me but somehow it doesn't."

"Then let's have another drink," says Vidocq.

I call Carlos to bring over a round of drinks. We clink glasses and throw them back.

Vidocq raises an eyebrow at Traven.

"Have you told him about the Via Dolorosa?"

"Not yet."

"The Via Dolores? What is that?"

Traven shifts his weight. The subject makes him uncomfortable.

"Via Dolorosa," says Vidocq. " 'The Way of Sorrow.' It's something the father learned while you were gone."

"I suppose you inspired me," says Traven. "I've spent my whole life sitting by myself among books. I thought the work I was doing was important and that I was important. The sin of pride. Then I watched you march off to Hell by yourself and I knew that reading old books wasn't enough anymore."

"And that's what Dolores is?"

"You could say that."

"Is it a trick or something? Show me."

Traven shakes his head and looks at the sparse mix of civilians and Lurkers. He isn't used to seeing humans mixing with what he probably considers monsters. But he's dealing with it all right.

He says, "At the right time and place. When you tell me more about what happened in Hell, I'll tell you about the Dolorosa."

"Deal."

My legs shake so slightly it's barely noticeable.

"Did you feel something just now? A little earthquake?"

"No," says Vidocq. "Father?"

Traven shakes his head.

"Never mind. It's probably me. I'm still getting my land legs."

The bar doors open and standing there is my favorite professional zombie hunter, Brigitte Bardo. Ex-professional. It's not like she quit the business, but when there aren't any zombies left to hunt, it's hard to stay pro. She was also a porn star in Europe. Lots of civilians in occult work and Lurkers do sex work because the money is good and they can't deal with regular jobs. There's something else about Brigitte and it's not pretty and it comes to me every time I think about her. A zombie bit her while we were hunting together. We found a cure and Vidocq gave it to her but it was my sloppiness that almost turned her into maybe the worst thing in the world.

When Brigitte sees me, she smiles and comes over, every bit the legit starlet she is these days. We lost touch when she dumped me for a movie producer who could help her career and because I'm a shit magnet. It's nice to see she doesn't hold a grudge.

She gives me a quick hug and kisses my cheek.

"Hello, Jimmy," she says in her breathy Czech accent.

"What are you doing here?"

"I came by to say hello. That's all right, isn't it? I heard you've been off having adventures."

"Of course it's all right. It's great to see you. What I meant was how did you know I was here?"

"You are so wonderfully stupid. People are talking about you now that the other one is gone and you're back."

"I just got here. How do they know?"

"Oh my. How would they? Perhaps the huge motorcycle that fell from the sky by Hollywood Forever. Unlike you, normal people think that's unusual."

"Yeah. That. Well, at least Carlos's business will pick up."

She wraps her arm around mine and leads me to the bar. We lean in close so we can hear each other.

She says, "Tell me about yourself. What did you do on your summer vacation?"

"Can I tell you a secret? Something I haven't told anyone?

I have to tell someone and I think maybe it won't freak you out the way it would most people."

"Because I briefly joined the undead?"

"Because of who you are. It takes someone special to spend her whole life offing zombies. You can't be afraid of much."

"Only you and then just a little."

Her smile is all wolf.

"I never got to ask you. Do you remember anything after you were bit? Did it leave a scar?"

"I don't remember anything and the only change is that I eat more meat. Rare and bloody. People think of it as very European and eccentric. But I didn't come to talk about that. You have a secret and that's much more exciting. You must tell me."

I crane my head around, making sure no one is close enough to hear.

"I'm the Devil. Not metaphorically. I killed the other candidate and Lucifer took off back to Heaven and stuck me with running Hell. I'm the new Lucifer."

She takes a step back, a hand covering her mouth. She's laughing.

*"My o vlku, a vlk za dveřmi."*

"What?"

"Of course you are. Who else would run off to find his old love and come back the king of wolves? You're always an interesting boy, Jimmy."

"If only I was ten percent less dangerous, right? Isn't that what you said? Being Lucifer doesn't exactly put me on the safe list. Guess you were right to leave."

"I think so. Though some days I'm not so sure. Some days

I miss the hunt. The dead lying at my feet. Fucking you in this bathroom afterward."

"Aside from sex and murder dreams, how are you doing? Are you working much?"

She sighs at being dragged back to earth.

"I finished a couple of films. One large and one very large and artful. I costarred with a famous American actor, though I won't tell you who. I'll let it be a surprise when you come to the premiere. Will you bring a friend? That's my subtle way of asking if you're in love."

"That's it? That's all you have to say about me being Lucifer?"

"As you used to say, that and five dollars will get you a cup of coffee. I'm more interested in you than I am the Devil."

I point to where Candy and Rinko are sitting.

"The one with the short hair."

"She's adorable. Who's her friend?"

The girls notice us looking at them.

"That's Rinko. She hates me."

"She loathes you. It's obvious to anyone. Shall we make them jealous?"

She takes my face in her hands and kisses me hard. It takes me back a few months when she led me out behind the bar and taught me how a pro slaughters zombies—by ripping out their spines. Then I killed them all in one night and left her without a job. Except for being a movie star. It's nice to have something to fall back on.

The kiss goes on. She might just be going through the motions, but it's a hell of a kiss.

She whispers into my ear so quietly I can barely hear her.

"Now I will disappear. I have a car waiting to take me to a much more expensive bar full of expensive people with whom I'll talk about movies we'll never make together."

She glances at Candy and Rinko's table.

"Besides, there's nothing that interests a woman more than a mysterious stranger taking advantage of her lover and then vanishing. But not forever I hope. Please don't be a stranger, *Pán d'ábel*."

She winks, blows me a kiss from the door, and walks out. It's an Oscar performance. Ten more seconds the room would have given her a standing ovation.

When I turn back to the bar, Candy is standing next to me.

"I take back what I said earlier. I know who I want you to punch."

"Down, girl. Like you said about Rinko, Brigitte is an old friend."

"What's her story? She someone you rescued from a rabid lawn gnome?"

"I told you about her. She almost ended up a zombie because of me."

Candy's eyes go wide and she opens her mouth in exaggerated surprise.

"Oh my God. That was your porn star? I thought I recognized her. I take it back. Don't punch her. Get me one for Christmas."

"Forget it. The two of you together would be more dangerous than the Kissi."

Carlos comes over.

"You ready for another drink, little lady?"

"A shot of Jack, please."

"What about your friend?"

"Just water for her."

I look at Rinko. She waves to the Ludere from the clinic sitting at a table of other blue-skinned blondes.

"Is Rinko still into drinking people?"

"That's part of how we got together. Stopping her, I mean. I got her the same potion I take so she doesn't have to. She's trying to be good but it's not easy."

"I think she'd like to drink me."

"She'd like to cut off your head and shit down your neck."

"I see why you like her."

She pushes the button and makes her robot sunglasses sing.

"I'm a sucker for the dangerous ones," she says.

"Did you just feel that?"

"What?"

"Like a little earthquake."

"Maybe a tiny one-point-oh or something. So what?"

"Nothing. I've been feeling them all night."

"Maybe you were Downtown so long you're growing hooves."

"Where did she come from?"

Candy looks around.

"Who?"

I point to a tiny figure walking across the room. A little girl in a blue party dress.

"I know her. I saw her at the cemetery. Hey, kid. Hey, little girl."

I don't see the knife until she's already swinging it. It's a big brutal thing. Something you'd see in a slaughterhouse gutting cattle. She giggles and runs at a balding middle-aged Sub Rosa businessman in a gray suit that's seen better days. He's drinking a light beer and texting someone. She runs at him from behind. He doesn't stand a chance.

The little girl doesn't go for him all thumbs and awkward slashing like a civilian. She hits the guy like a tiny hurricane, driving the knife into his kidneys, then his spine, and finally his heart. Ten, fifteen times in a few seconds like she's done it all before. It's not even like she's mad. She laughs the whole time. And she knows how to use the blade. Not straight into him like an amateur shithead so the tip gets stuck on bone. She thrusts up so the blade slips between the ribs. Every shot is a kill shot.

I run at her but Mr. Businessman is already down, leaking like a waterbed in a razor factory. The girl turns on me, still smiling. Still laughing. I reach out to grab her and she swings the blade so fast I barely get my hand out of the way. That's all I need. Another prosthetic.

When I go in again, she grabs my human hand. Her grip is unbelievable. I haven't felt anything like it since the arena. She swings the knife and I grab her with my Kissi claw. She screams and pulls away. Not in fear. More like disgust. She isn't laughing anymore and the fierceness has gone out of her eyes. She's still holding up the knife but it's not threatening. It's like she can't let it go. Like the knife is an extension of her arm. She touches my Kissi hand again and shakes her head.

"You're not one of his," she says, and giggles like I just gave her a pony for her birthday.

I feel another little earthquake.

The door bangs open. Bodies go down hard. Four assholes

cluster by the jukebox in masks and body armor. They're supposed to be scary but they look like high-tech ninja scuba divers. They sweep the room with their rifles, looking for someone. I have a bad feeling who.

"You're just in time for the bake sale, boys. Who brought the cupcakes?"

All four of them have weapons, sleek rifles that conform to the shape of their arms and bodies. The business ends crackle with blue electric arcs. I've only ever seen those weapons one other place. In the Golden Vigil raid on Club Avila last New Year's Eve. Human weapons enhanced with angelic tech.

Laughing, the little girl runs behind them and out the door.

They raise their rifles and move in on me but don't get two steps before the first one goes down. Candy has gone full Jade. Red slit eyes. A mouth full of bone-white shark teeth and nails curled back into claws. A second later Rinko does the same and charges at the hit man Candy has pinned to the floor. Another hit man screams as a glass vial breaks against the side of his head, and then another. The first potion Vidocq threw didn't do anything. It's the second potion mixing with the first that has the hit man screaming as his mask and skin melt down the side of his face, burning into his neck.

One of the hit men gets a bead on me but the Incredible Melting Man falls on him, screaming for help. I grab the na'at from inside my coat and snap it out like a whip, hitting him in the eye. With a twist, spines open at the na'at's tip, digging into his skull. Twist the other way and his neck snaps. Unfortunately in all the fun I missed hit man four. He's off to my side. I know because his rifle crackles and the air feels like a thousand needles as the lightning comes at me.

There's another small earthquake. Something snaps and the next thing I know I'm flat on my back looking up at the ceiling from a hole in the floor. I get up covered in dirt and broken tiles and climb out.

Three of the four hit men are gone. The only one left is the dead loser Candy and Rinko worked over. The bar patrons are piling out the doors. I run over to Candy. She's wiping the blood off her face with her T-shirt and rubbing her nails on her pants leg to get out pieces of the hit man's bones. Rinko is licking blood from her fingers like a kid with an ice-cream cone.

It's not fun to look at but I'm grateful for the backup.

"Thanks for the help."

Rinko won't look at me.

"I didn't do it for you," she says.

Vidocq, Allegra, and Traven are behind the bar. Carlos is down. His shoulder and one arm are badly burned. He has a .44 Magnum in his other hand. He must have been trying to pop off a shot when he got hit. I pick up the gun.

"Who the fuck told you to turn Wyatt Earp?"

He smiles then winces as Allegra pulls scorched bits of his shirt from around the wound.

"It got boring watching you fight all the time. I thought I'd get in on it. I hope you don't mind if I never do it again. This shit hurts."

"You're lucky to be alive, you fucking idiot. Those fuckers were pros."

"At least now I know you're you and not your *cabrón* brother."

"I told you, he's not my brother."

Allegra says, "This is too severe to treat here. We need to get him to the clinic."

"Can you and Vidocq take him? I need to check out the dead man."

"Which one?" says Vidocq.

"Not the one the little girl got."

"Do you know who she was?" asks Traven.

"I don't care right now. I want to know who sent the boys in black."

"What should we do about the other dead man?"

"Leave him. Someone's probably already called 911. It's better to give the cops a body than have them asking why there isn't one."

"They'll be able to find his next of kin too," says Traven.

"Right. That too. You can't help being a good guy, can you?"

"I suppose not."

"Good. Someone needs to be."

While the three of them get Carlos into Traven's car, I go to the dead hit man. Rinko's carnivore tendencies have worked in our favor. She's gobbled up enough of the guy's blood that there's hardly any left on the floor. That means the cops won't be looking for two bodies and Carlos won't have to explain why he had a bunch of James Bond villains in his bar.

I carry the dead man into the bathroom and drop him on the dirty tile. He doesn't have any pockets, so I get out the black blade and slice off his shirt. No dog tags, gang burns, or tattoos. I pull off his gloves and find something even more interesting. He has no fingerprints. His fingertips are smooth as the *Venus de Milo*'s ass. Only hoodoo could take them off that cleanly. I check behind his ears and the inside of his arms and there it is. Barely visible. I probably would have missed it without the Lucifer eyes. It's a faint laser brand, and like his fingerprints, it's been removed using magic.

Candy comes in.

"What are you looking at?" she asks.

"A mark that's rare and even rarer on dead men."

"What is it?"

"Those shit sacks were Sub Rosa. A Sub Rosa SWAT team. I'm in town a day and my own people try to kill me."

"Lucky for you you went through the floor."

"That was lucky, wasn't it? I'm not usually that lucky."

I go to the hole and look inside. It's a pit maybe ten feet deep. The dirt around the edge is soft and fresh. It hasn't been here long. Almost like someone dug it right under my feet.

"What are you going to do now?" asks Candy.

"Me? I'm going to see a soon-to-be-dead man and tell him he missed."

"Cool. I'll drop Rinko off and we can go."

"No. Take her home. Give her the potion and keep an eye on her. The last thing I want is her hurt or strung out because of me."

"You bastard. You don't want me to go with you."

"Hell yes I don't want you to go. If I fuck this up, I'm counting on you and Vidocq to bust me out of whatever dungeon he throws me in."

"Who?"

"The Augur."

"Oh hell."

THE SUB ROSA love anonymity more than candy and puppies. If they're going to hit someone, they'll do it with poison so it looks like a heart attack or hoodoo so it looks like the luckless slob slips on a plutonium banana peel. There's only one person who can drop the cloak-and-dagger policy for a blanket shoot-on-sight order and that's Saragossa Blackburn. The Augur. The high exalted godfather of the California Sub Rosa.

In grand Sub Rosa tradition, Blackburn's mansion looks like a pathetic wreck. In this case, an abandoned residency hotel on South Main Street. The first floor is boarded up. The second and third have been gutted by fire and you can see the sky through the top-floor ceiling. Gang tags and spray-painted naked ladies are like outdoor cave paintings. Aeons of stapled ads and glued band flyers form a pale crust on the lower floors. Cut deep enough into those things and you'll find flyers for Babylonian death-metal shows printed in cuneiform on papyrus.

The mansion is protected by more hoodoo than King Tut's tomb. It can hold off the armies of Hell, a Bigfoot horde, and a Martian invasion all at the same time. In fact, Blackburn's place is so loaded with wards and mantrap spells that he doesn't have a single security guard. Not even a dog. The Augur is so high-and-mighty he thinks muscle is déclassé, which for him is sort of true but it's not polite to rub the world's nose in it. Someone should TP the place just to remind him he's human. I'd like it to be me but right now I don't know how to get close enough to even hit the place with a grenade launcher.

These Lucifer eyes can see the shimmering spells sur-
rounding the hotel. A series of crystal spheres set inside each
other like Russian nesting dolls. As far as I know, with the
armor on, I'm as hard to kill as ever, but that means I can still
snuff it or get hurt and I don't want to be known as the Gimp
Lucifer. I need to not fuck this up.

Most of my hoodoo is geared toward hurting people and
making things go boom. I'm pretty good at making up spells
on the spot but how many different ones will I have to wing if
I try to hex my way through Blackburn's defenses? Only one
thing makes sense if I want to get inside before Santa takes
a toy dump down everyone's chimney. It's really stupid but
stupid is sort of my specialty.

I take a few deep breaths and summon all the heinous bastard Luciferness I can and wrap myself in *Lord of the Flies*
drag. When it feels right, I go to the first layer of hoodoo and
lay my hand on it.

When I first got back to Earth, Samael strolled into my
bedroom above Max Overdrive. At the time I was so shocked
seeing the Devil at my door I didn't think about what it meant.
By then I'd laid out wards around the store and my own improvised protection spells. Lucifer walked right through
them. Is that one of the secrets the celestial types keep from
us? That most human protections don't work on angels? My
angel half is off somewhere sipping Shirley Temples and reading *Parade* magazine but I'm still Lucifer and wearing angelic
armor. Maybe that's angel enough to keep me from going up
like a refinery explosion.

I put my hand on the first layer of magic and press. Blue
flame engulfs me but it doesn't burn. Beyond the fire, the

layer feels thick and liquid. I'm not dead yet, so I keep pressing. Slowly and steadily, like stepping out of a warm glycerin bath, I pass through the first layer. I do the same thing on the next layer. This one is full of wind and grit. A sandstorm of razor blades. I press slow and steady, holding a "do not even begin to fuck with me" mantra in my mind. The layer cracks and splits just enough for me to pass through. Four more layers and I walk up to Blackburn's front door like the Avon lady. I reach out to test the door. The prick doesn't even bother locking it.

Inside, Blackburn's mansion is an old Victorian manor house with stained glass, potted palms, and a curiosity cabinet in every room. The kind of place where you wouldn't be surprised to see Sherlock Holmes shooting coke in the guest room.

On one side of a sweeping staircase is Blackburn's office. On the other side is what looks like a parlor. The sliding doors are open a crack. Inside are maybe twenty people listening to him ramble on about cost-benefit projections and which state political offices to keep and which corporate investments to kick loose. First someone tries to assassinate me and now another budget meeting. Where do I have to go to get away from this shit?

It looks like I walked in on a synod, a solstice meeting where Sub Rosa heavyweights get together to figure out what nefarious party games they're going to play in the New Year.

Blackburn is a scryer, a seer who gets glimpses of the future. The Sub Rosa Augur is always a scryer and Blackburn is supposed to be a good one. If he's predicted me coming, I'm in trouble. With any luck he's blind to Lucifer's tricks. Of course, this could be a trap and he wants me in close quarters where I can't run. Okay. I haven't killed any humans in months.

It's tradition at official meetings that the Sub Rosa sigil floats at the front of the room like the Super Bowl blimp. The sigil is a caduceus, snakes wrapped around each other in kind of a figure eight. A symbol of knowledge. In the first crossing, the top hole of the eight, is a circle surrounded by a square surrounded by a triangle. The squared circle. An alchemical symbol for the work. The work is magic and the secret things you can learn to expand your mind and perfect the world. The bottom crossing is a black circle with three lines radiating outside the snake like the sun. The alchemical symbol for gold. In the old days, gold stood for enlightenment. These days gold just stands for gold. I kick one of the doors out of the way, pull the Glock, and put a bullet through each end of the caduceus. The thing flares and drifts onto the carpet like ashes.

"Looks like a party. You busted in on mine, so I thought I'd return the favor."

Blackburn storms over, not the tiniest bit afraid. He's a good-looking guy with a primo Italian suit and a wide politician's face that looks like it should be on a hundred-dollar bill. His graying temples make him look like he's in his late forties but I know he's well over a hundred.

"How did you get in here? You've invaded my home and interrupted classified Sub Rosa business. If you weren't a wanted criminal before, you certainly are now, Stark."

Blackburn gestures past me at someone I can't see.

"Get some security . . ."

I swing the Glock behind me and fire without looking. Something hits the carpet. I put the still-hot muzzle under Blackburn's chin.

"If that sentence is headed where I think it is, you better say it pretty because it's going to be your last words."

"Pretty please, Mr. Blackburn. Let me do it. I've wanted to put the boot to this rude boy for a long time."

It's King Cairo's hoarse voice. Hoarse because screaming at the top of his lungs is as quiet as he ever fucking gets. He's head of a family specializing in freelance hoodoo muscle, stuff both on and off the books. He's a skinny Mohawked shirtless rat in a floor-length velvet coat trimmed with ostrich feathers. He thinks shrieking and jumping on furniture makes him a punk. Really it just makes him a Dixie Wishbone addict.

Wishbone is a kind of hoodoo meth. It makes you jittery and paranoid, but guys like Cairo get off on it because it doesn't fry them like regular meth. It burns out the people around them. A heavy Dixie Wishbone addict will end up surrounded by a pack of jaundiced, black-toothed psychopaths. Rumors are that's how Cairo's family got started down Alabama way.

He's standing on a heavy mahogany settee. Leaps off and tries to kick it at me. He almost makes it too, but it catches on the edge of Kyzer Navarro's chair and knocks him in his face. Navarro is head of the big South American Sub Rosa syndicate. Not someone you want to hit with a dining room set. Cairo's high-drama moment turns into Three Stooges dopefiend high jinks. He goes over to apologize to Navarro and a woman's voice quiets the room.

"Calm down, ladies and gentlemen. Mr. Stark might be guilty of many things but look closer and you'll see he's not who you think he is."

I recognize the voice. It belongs to one of two or three people I hate most on this planet. I pocket the Glock, grab my na'at and get ready for a hoodoo attack, but when I turn she's just sitting off by herself at Blackburn's desk looking at me like I'm the soggy banana at the bottom of her bag lunch.

"Shouldn't you be off somewhere playing Ragnarok?" I say and turn back to the room. "You know when she's not with you bastards Cruella de Vil here is hot to murder God. How's that for a grudge? Makes me seem downright reasonable."

Aelita is another goddamn angel. Not a fallen one like Lucifer but one of God's more recent rogues. Because God let a nephilim bastard like me live, Aelita's decided the old man has gone senile and needs to be put out of His misery. She used to run the Golden Vigil, God's earthbound Pinkertons, with a U.S. marshal named Wells. The Vigil is dead and I haven't heard anything new about Aelita until this minute.

Blackburn moves between Aelita and me.

"Stop this right now, Mr. Stark."

"Kill him. Fucking kill him, Blackburn," screams King Cairo.

I grab the cantaloupe-size crystal ball off Blackburn's desk and throw it at the ceiling. Shattered glass and smashed plaster rains down on Cairo.

"Fuck!" he screams, but he doesn't dare do anything without the Augur's permission.

I recognize a few faces in the crowd.

Tuatha Fortune, Blackburn's wife. She's a brontomancer. A thunder worker. A decent bronto can ride the storm clouds to find lost people and objects. A pro one can use lightning as a weapon. There must have been some heavy storms lately because Tuatha looks as green and worn as a civilian on chemotherapy. Some kinds of hoodoo take more out of you than others.

There's Nasrudin Hodja. He's a Cold Case. A soul merchant. From an old world Sub Rosa family. Like ante-fucking-diluvian old. His family might be oil and media barons these days, but buried in their vaults are ancient Sub Rosa relics traded along the Silk Road a thousand years ago.

L.A.'s Sub Rosa mayor lounges on a purple silk love seat surrounded by bodyguards. Richard William "Big Bill" Wheaton the Third. He dropped "the Third" for the last election but you always knew it was there, like he's the king of merry old England and everyone needs to know how many of him there are.

Near Big Bill a guy sits with his hands folded neatly in his lap. He's in a suit sharp enough to cut diamonds and has a manicure that would make the pope jealous. He's not Sub Rosa and he's on edge enough that I don't think he's ever seen so many in one place before. Or maybe he's spooked because a crazy guy just broke in firing a gun.

At the rear of the place is a girl with a shaved head and a lot of tattoos. I'd swear I know her from somewhere but I've known more than a couple of tattooed girls over the years. She has thick scars on her neck and the side of her face is like one of those women you hear about who get hit with acid by a psycho ex-lover. That means I don't know her. I'd remember those scars. You have to admire Sub Rosa who keeps their wounds. When you can go to a hoodoo clinic like Allegra's and have them healed in an hour, you know this girl loves her scars more than she loves being beautiful. Good for her.

I look at Blackburn and flick open the na'at.

"Why did you send goons after me tonight? They busted into a public place and started shooting. Civilians got hurt."

King Cairo laughs like I told a great knock-knock joke.

"Of course, Cairo. They're your assholes. Aren't they? I should have known by the Wishbone shakes. No wonder they couldn't hit anything they aimed at."

Aelita says, "They attacked you because they thought you were the other Stark. He didn't carry guns or use profanity. He was a refreshing change until he murdered the mayor's son."

"That ring-tailed choirboy? I don't believe it."

"Believe it. We have witnesses."

She folds her hands on the desk and gives me a cold smile.

"Maybe he got bored acting like a sane man and was trying to be more like you."

"Or maybe you just made the whole thing up to kill me piece by piece like you're doing with God."

"Your doppelgänger made a lot of enemies."

I take out a Malediction and light it. If you went by the gasp from the crowd you'd think I was skinning a deer on the Persian rug.

"I should have let Mason kill you."

She sips her tea and puts it down.

"What a strange thing to say. You saved us angels to keep the gates of Hell closed and now here you are. Hell itself. You saved this world from horror only to return as the embodiment of horror."

"Guess the God-killing business doesn't pay well if you have to wet-nurse these ankle biters."

"I go where I'm needed."

Cairo has inched his way closer behind me. I flick the na'at at his feet. He dances back a step. He looks like a prancing idiot but he's a dangerous son of a bitch.

"If the hit squad in the bar were legit Sub Rosa security, why did they take off their brands?"

Cairo clears his throat.

"New security policy. Some of the boys got God. Thou shalt not mark thy body or some such. Anyway, praying calms them, so I encourage it."

I shove Blackburn into a chair, say "Stay," and walk over to Aelita.

"Is that the idea? You resurrect the Golden Vigil with a bunch of inbred junkie berserkers? Kill 'em all and let God sort them out."

I turn to the room.

"Is that what the Sub Rosa is about these days?"

"Like God, the ways of the Sub Rosa are mysterious," says Aelita. "But in the end, they're for the good of all humanity, Sub Rosa and civilian alike."

Someone makes a break for the door. A woman wearing a blue fur coat. She looks like a plush toy. I snap out the na'at like a whip, grab one of her ankles, and lift her off the floor. Drop her down on a bunch of blue bloods still holding their teacups.

"Next person that runs, I take their head."

I retract the na'at and lean on the desk. Aelita rolls away from me a few inches.

"What about the freaky little girl with the knife? Is she part of your good works or are you running a thrill-kill day-care program?"

"Is the great Sandman Slim afraid of a ghost child?"

She makes a *tsk-tsk* sound.

"Don't concern yourself with the girl. We're dealing with her."

"Deal faster. She killed someone tonight. A Sub Rosa who stopped in for a drink. Not bothering anyone. Playing with his damn phone."

"If you're so frightened, why not come in under the synod's protection? Our psychics tell us that things aren't going well in Hell. We can protect you from your enemies in this world and the celestial realms."

"A two-for-one sale. How much?"

"Nothing you need. Burdens really. Give me the singularity and the Qomrama Om Ya and you'll officially be under the Sub Rosa's protection."

So that's what the Magic 8 Ball is called. It sounds like a Hellion sneezing.

"I survived Hell. I think I can survive Hollywood."

"Then just the Qomrama."

"Why don't you try possessing me again? Then I'd just hand it over."

"I don't know what you're talking about."

"Liar."

"I'll get it from him."

Cairo finally means business. He reaches into his velvet

coat and pulls out two gold knives. Long curved saw-tooth blades, the kind that hurt going in but hurt worse coming out.

"Hey, Chuck Norris, have you been listening to your boss? Tell him who I am these days."

She raises her eyebrows and speaks to Cairo.

"He's the Devil in the flesh. The vile thing that stands before you is the new Lucifer."

"Ha!" yells Cairo in that hoarse voice. It's hard to tell if he's really laughing or not. Everything out of his mouth sounds sarcastic.

"If he's Satan then I'm Spider-Man."

He charges. He's fast with the knives but I'm faster. I pull the na'at. I want him hand to hand. He slashes at my stomach. It's an easy parry. With the other hand he goes for my leg, trying to slice the femoral artery. I twist out of the way and rabbit-punch him. He goes down on one knee, and when I think he's going to fall, he slashes straight up with one hand. The blade scrapes sparks off my armor. I look down at my ruined shirt. Cairo is up and grinning. He looks puzzled when he sees the armor and I kick him in the chest. He goes ass over elbows across Blackburn's desk. Aelita is fast too. She rolls the office chair back out of the way and Cairo lands on the floor.

I go around the desk and get Cairo in a choke hold from behind, not because I need to but because I really want to choke this guy.

"First off, I'm not moron enough to carry the 8 Ball or the singularity with me. Second, I just bought this shirt. You owe me twelve dollars."

Cairo hangs onto my arm like a life raft in a storm, so it

takes him a minute to grasp the situation. He reaches into his pocket and pulls out some bills. They're all high denominations. I take the lowest.

"This is a twenty. I don't have any change. Is it okay if I go ahead and keep it?"

Cairo gurgles.

"I'll take that as a yes."

I throw him on the floor. He goes for a knife. I put the steel toe of my boot into his balls and he curls up like a kitten.

Heavy footsteps down the stars toward the parlor. Ten of Cairo's security punks fan out across the doorway. They're holding the same rifles as the bunch at Bamboo House. The parlor crowd doesn't like being between a kill squad and an armed loon. A few grumbles. A couple of cries. But no one is dumb enough to run.

I lower my arm and let Cairo go wild and free like a ferret returned to the wild. With him out of the way, everyone in the room can see Lucifer's armor. A few in the know recognize it and mutter personal protection hoodoo. Good timing.

I let the darkness flow out of me, across the floor, up the walls, and across the ceiling, making sure the hit men at the door are the first to be swaddled all comfortable in the nothingness. In a moment, thorn vines and tentacles wriggle up from the void. Wrap around people's legs. When the screaming gets good and loud, I raise my arm to manifest the Gladius and become the only bright thing in a universe of darkness. The Light Bringer.

"I didn't ask to be Lucifer but I am and that's the end of it. If any of you still doubts it and has the sand, you can come after me, but remember one thing. I run this particular horror show, and if anyone lays a hand on me, my friends, my bar, or my store, I'll drag you Downtown and make you into my own personal amusement park. It starts like this."

The dark snakes up and around Cairo's men. A couple actually have time to scream before black tentacles shoot down their throats, cutting off their breath. The room shrieks as all ten men are dragged down into the void.

That's my cue to exit stage right. I'm not going to get anything more out of this useless bunch. When I make it to the front door, I turn off the dark. No need to kill everyone. They know not to let their Chihuahuas piss on my lawn.

"Wait a minute. Hey."

I'm almost at the first of the house's protection spells when the woman's voice catches me by surprise. I turn and there's the scarred girl coming outside. She has her hands up in front of her.

"Don't hurt me. I'm just here to tell you something."

"Who are you? Why would you want to talk to me?"

"I'm Lula Hawks. I don't like Cairo or his thugs. I don't trust that Aelita woman either. And I don't like where the Sub Rosa are headed. I might be able to help you find your double. Maybe the crazy little girl too. Can you do something about her? She's hurt an awful lot of people."

"If the kid doesn't work for Aelita, then she's not my problem. If you know something about Saint James, tell me. If it pans out I'll owe you one."

She comes a couple of steps closer like she doesn't want anyone inside to hear her.

"Do you know a Tick Tock Man called Manimal Mike?"

"Never heard of him."

"He knows a lot of things. He might be able to help you."

"Why would he?"

"You own his soul."

Good reason. She writes something on a piece of paper. Hands it to me and I look it over. It's an address in Chatsworth.

"Don't tell him I sent you. Or that you know me at all. Good luck," she says, and goes back inside the abandoned hotel.

I put the paper in my pocket. Walk through the wards and into the street where the Augur's mansion is just another anonymous shit shack in a neighborhood full of them.

A block away a gray-haired homeless guy, not much more than a pile of rags with a face, puts out his hands for spare change. He smells like Four Roses and death. I'm the Devil. I don't save people or souls, my own included. I reach into my pocket, pull out Cairo's crumpled twenty, and drop it into his hands.

"You might buy a sandwich along with the jug," I say, knowing he'll never do it.

I walk on. I want out of this dead zone and back to the Beat Hotel. I've got no girl, no home, a gun I hate, and I have to beg a talking head on a dog's body for pocket money. Still, I wouldn't trade lives with anyone back at Blackburn's.

I RIDE THE HELLION HOG to the Beat Hotel to change shirts and pick up some gear. I made a mess tonight but I think I'm still following Wild Bill's advice. Pick and choose your fights. Carlos got shot by someone gunning for me, so this is the fight I pick. I hope the shooter was one of the sons of bitches I dragged Downtown tonight. Maybe I'll get Semyazeh to send their souls to Wild Bill's bar and make them lick his floors clean every night for the next thousand years.

Should I call Candy and tell her I'm okay? She's probably pissed that I sent her away. If I got us both locked up in the Sub Rosa Sing Sing, she'd be pissed about that. If I said forget about your girlfriend and run off with me she'd be pissed in a whole different way. I can't win. Maybe I should have stayed Downtown. At least people missed me when they thought I was dead. Punching Cairo and morons like him is a lot easier than being a person. I'll stick to that for a while.

KASABIAN HAS CONSPICUOUSLY NOT GIVEN me a key to Max Overdrive so I jimmy the back door with my knife. *Across 110th Street* is playing on the video monitor when I come in. Kasabian quickly closes the browser window on his laptop. Porn is my guess. Maybe something with Brigitte. He's a little obsessed ever since he found out I know her. He casually sips a beer when I come into the bedroom.

He says, "How's life back under the big black sun?"

"I almost got killed by a ninja hit squad and I crashed a Sub Rosa synod."

"So just another night in Wonderland for you."

"You didn't tell me Saint James murdered a kid."

"Oh. That."

He puts down the beer. Before getting the hellhound's body Kasabian was just a head. We stuck a bucket under him when he wanted to drink beer or eat. Now he has a hellhound stomach and that's both good and bad. It's less messy than emptying the bucket but it means I get to watch the skin sack swell as he fills it with beer and donuts. I don't want to know how he empties it.

"I didn't think you'd believe me. Who told you?"

"The four guys who shot up Bamboo House of Dolls and almost killed Carlos."

"Damn. That's verging on rude."

"Tell me you didn't know there were shooters looking for Saint James. I'll know if you're lying."

"Why the hell would I do something like that?"

"If I was dead, you'd have all the money."

"I already have all the money. Even I wouldn't do that shit to you. I might be a bastard but I'm not a complete asshole."

Kasabian is harder to read than live people. He doesn't breathe or have a heartbeat. But Lucifer's senses would catch him in a lie.

"I believe you. This would have been a lot easier if you were trying to get rid of me."

"I am trying to get rid of you, just not kill you. And thanks for the vote of confidence. You're back for a day and you're already starting with the hostile attitude. I'm starting to miss the choirboy."

I set the duffel bag on the floor.

"Look, I didn't think it was you but I had to ask. I've got something with me that might interest you. A peace offering because looking over my shoulder all the time is giving me cramps."

"What kind of peace offering?"

"A better look into Hell."

"And why would I want that exactly?"

"Because I'd pay you for the info."

"I think we've already established that I have all the money."

"And we both know I could take it back if I really wanted but I'd rather take money from uncool people."

"Like who?"

"King Cairo for one. I had to spank him in front of an audience tonight."

Kasabian shakes his head. Nervously taps one of his hellhound claws on the desk.

"I knew you freaks would go at it eventually. You two need to get a room and hug it out."

"Do you want a new superpower or not?"

"How does it work?"

"I'm not a hundred percent sure it will. But I'm guessing since you can already see into Hell this will be like souping up a Camaro with a nitrous injector."

"Do I have to do anything?"

"Just sit still."

"If you say 'trust me,' I'm climbing out the window."

"You don't have to trust me. You just have to not move."

He flinches when I set the jar of eyes on the desk and mumbles "Oh shit," when I take one out. He reaches for my arm. I pop out one of his eyes and he freezes. I put in the peeper. When I let go of him he wails like a scalded banshee.

"What did you do to me, you fucking freak? I'm fucking blind. Christ. For one second I let you get near me and this happens. Fuck!"

"Hey, don't forget who got you that body."

"And don't forget who made me need it."

"Quit whining and tell me what you see."

"Nothing. You took my eye, you crazy motherfucker."

"I just swapped it. If this doesn't work you can have it back. Relax and tell me if you see anything."

Kasabian sits rigid in his chair with his eyes closed, turning his head from side to side. He holds onto the seat with both hands. His legs pump nervously. Then they stop.

"Oh man."

"What do you see?"

"All kinds of stuff. It's like a bee's eye. Like there's a million little lenses and each one sees something different."

"Good. I left peepers all over. That means you can see through a bunch of them. Try to zoom in on one and tell me what you see."

"It's like a jail. There's cells and . . . No. Wait. It's pens. It's like a kennel. Oh shit, there are hellhounds."

"How nice. A family reunion."

"Shut up. I'm trying to concentrate. I'm in that library of yours. I can see all over inside. The big front doors are open a little and kind of burned. Like someone tried to slip you a hotfoot."

"Sounds like someone tried to get in after I left and stepped in one of the hexes. That'll keep busybodies out for a while."

"Man. I'm on a goddamn guided tour. There's soldiers and crowds and market stalls."

"Anything else?"

"I'm low. Like I'm a midget."

"I gave eyes to some of the hounds. You're probably seeing through those."

He nods, smiling for the first time since I got back.

"This is cool. What kind of information do you want? I can't hear anything."

"Learn to lip-read."

"Half these ugly fucks don't have lips. And they're probably all speaking Hellion."

"I forgot about that. Let me see what I can do about it."

"Okay. You've got a deal. How much are you going to pay me for information?"

"The going rate."

"You're not really going to pay me anything, are you?"

"No, but if I didn't lie you wouldn't have that nice new eye. It seems like a fair trade."

"I've made worse."

He takes a swig of his beer and discreetly closes the laptop.

"So what are you doing now? Mugging old ladies for pocket change yet?"

"They run too fast. I stick to Girl Scouts and nuns."

"I've got pizza coming if you want to hang around. After this I was maybe going to watch *Devil Girl from Mars*."

"I think I met her at Wild Bill's place. You have any coffee?"

"Are you kidding?"

"I'll have a beer."

He takes one from the mini-fridge under the desk and tosses it to me.

He turns the sound back up on *Across 110th Street* and says, "Shit's going to get weird again, isn't it? You running around killing people."

"It's already started."

He shakes his head and his half-full belly wobbles.

"You ever going to tell me about that armor, Tin Man?"

"Let me drink this, Old Yeller, and I'll tell you a weirder story than you ever dreamed."

"If it's about you I doubt it."

I'M BACK AT THE BEAT HOTEL when Candy calls around noon.

"Want to get some breakfast at our place?" she asks.

"We have a place?"

"Roscoe's Chicken and Waffles, stupid."

"How's Carlos? Can I see him?"

"Allegra worked him over pretty good last night. He's sleeping it off. You can see him this evening."

"Cool. Let's forget breakfast. Want to go with me and hassle people?"

"I thought you'd never ask."

THERE'S NO WAY I'm taking the Hellion bike out in broad daylight. I use the black blade to pop the lock and ignition on a Porsche Boxster Spyder and pick up Candy at the clinic. When I open up the car on the 101 North I can't help but smile. There's something about driving a pretty girl some-where potentially dangerous in a stolen car that just makes you feel good.

We drive to the address in Chatsworth that Lula Hawks gave me. It might be a waste of time but it's the only waste of time I have right now.

The address is a grease-caked car repair place that's such an obvious front they might as well put up a "Not a Real Garage" sign out front.

"Before we go in, there's something I've been wanting to tell you but it was never the right time."

"Let me guess. You're the Lindbergh baby."

"I'm the Devil. Lucifer went back to Heaven and stuck me with the job. I'm the new Lucifer. I just thought you might want to know who you're hanging around with."

She looks at me, her eyebrows slightly raised like she's waiting for me to say something else. She cocks her head when I don't.

"You thought I'd have a problem with you being devilish? Do you know me at all?"

"With things between us being complicated, I didn't know."

"Come here," she says, and gives me a good long kiss. "There's complicated and there's complicated. Wanting to kiss you isn't complicated."

"Just everything else?"

"Just everything else."

WE WALK OVER to the garage. When it's clear we're coming inside a couple of Lurkers drop their magazines and grab rubber mallets to start beating on the engine of a car that hasn't moved in a good ten years. The Lurkers are vucaris, Russian beast men. Mostly wolves. They're kind of like Nahuals, the local frat beasts. Like Manimal Mike's half-assed front job these two look don't look like much in the brains and ambition department.

"Is Mike around?"

"Who vants to know?" asks the taller of the two in a deep Boris Badenov accent.

"The Devil."

Ivan the Terrible considers this for a minute.

"He's busy."

"Tell him I might be willing to do a deal where he gets his soul back."

Ivan stares but the shorter vucari stands on tiptoe and whispers something in his ear.

"Vait here," says Ivan.

"That's okay. We'll come with you."

He weighs the rubber mallet in his hand but the little vucari says something else and Ivan backs down.

"This vay."

"Why don't you point to the door and we'll make our own introductions."

Ivan points to a grimy door with plastic "Cash Only" and "Protected by Smith & Wesson" signs tacked on the front. I open the door quietly and Candy and I go inside.

Manimal Mike is sprawled on a vinyl sofa with his back to the door. The sofa is patched with duct tape and smeared with enough grease to slick down the manes of all four presidents on Mount Rushmore. Across the room is a half-empty bottle of generic vodka on a worktable scattered with tools, gears, springs, and a sputtering half-finished mechanical python.

Mike has a little 9mm Kel-Tec in his hand and a shot glass on his head. I take Candy's arm and pull her over by a tire rack. It's lousy cover but it's better than nothing.

Manimal Mike takes aim and fires at a steel plate mounted on the far wall. The bullet ricochets and hits an identical plate on the wall behind him. It ricochets again and hits the back of the sofa. This isn't suicide. It's Billy Flinch. A solo William

Tell game where you try to shoot an apple off your head with a ricochet. I don't think Mike is very good at it but you have to give him points for perseverance. There are at least a hundred holes in the sofa's backside. Mike fires three more times without coming close to the shot glass on his brainless head. When the gun goes *click click*, Mike drops out the empty clip and reloads it from a box of bullets next to him.

I say, "Hi, Mike," and a handful of bullets go flying. The shot glass falls and shatters on the floor. He turns and looks at us with red hangover eyes, pointing the empty gun at us.

So this is what someone looks like when they've sold their soul. His face isn't streaked with dirty sin signs like other people. It's a thick liquid black like someone held him down and painted him with hot tar.

"Who the fuck are you?" he says in a high slurred voice.

"The friend of a friend who said you know things about things."

"What kind of things?"

"To start with, what happens to little boys who sell their soul? You've had a good run, Mike. Now it's time to collect."

I take off my glove and stick the Kissi index finger in the barrel of his 9mm. Lift it from his hand and drop it on the sofa. He falls onto his ass and crab-walks backward across the floor. It's an impressive sight considering how drunk he is.

"Twenty years! That was the deal! I'm just starting to break into the bigger markets."

Mike gets up and stumbles to his worktable. He picks up the mechanical python.

"See this? It's for Indrid Cold. A hot-shit demon wrangler. She came to me off a recommendation from another big shot. I'm starting to do for the high-and-mighties. You can't take me now."

Mike might be a drunk but the snake looks like good work. Mike is a Tick Tock Man, the modern equivalent of what medieval Sub Rosas would have called a Raven Maker. Tick Tock Men and Raven Makers create spirit familiars. Raven Makers out of flesh and bones. Tick Tock Men out of wood and metal. The kind of Sub Rosa that use familiars aren't usually the kind that has the money to have them built to spec. However, for rich witches and well-heeled Sub Rosa groupies, having multiple familiars is a status symbol. Like rich people owning summer and winter homes.

Seeing as how I already have Mike against the ropes, there's no reason to change my story.

"I know the deal was for twenty years, but if this is the best you've done with your time, I might have to call in your soul early on account of you pickling the thing like a county-fair gherkin."

"No. Please. What do you want? You want a cat? No. A lion for someone as powerful and glorious as you. And maybe a puppy for your lady friend?"

"A puppy?" says Candy. She picks up a wood chisel and points it at him like a knife. "How about I nail some wheels on you and ride you around like a toy horse. Would you like that, rummy?"

I gently put my hand on her arm and lower the chisel to her side.

"What my associate is getting at is that we're in the soul market, not the low-rent bribe market. Do you have anything else to offer?"

"You asked about information. What do you want to know? Lots of people want familiars who can't afford them. I trade them for info on bigwigs. Ask me anything. I bet I can help out."

I look at Candy. She smiles. I think she might like a puppy but she'd never admit it.

"I'm looking for an angel. He was in town until recently. People say he killed the mayor's son."

"Oh. That guy. Yeah, I heard about him. What do you want to know?"

"Where I can find him."

Mike shakes his head.

"If I tell you, I get my soul back?"

"No, Mike. It's not that easy. First, the information has to be real and worth my time. I won't know that until I check it out. Second, you're not going to get your soul for a lousy address. I got your address for nothing."

Mike takes a shop rag from his back pocket and nervously wipes his dirty hands.

"What else do you want from me?"

"Watch your tone, pony boy," says Candy.

Mike looks like he's about to keel over.

"Blue Heaven," he says.

"What's Blue Heaven?"

Mike shrugs and sits down behind the worktable. Picks up the bottle of vodka and takes a pull.

"I don't know a lot about it."

He starts to offer me the bottle but takes another look at the generic label stained with greasy fingerprints and changes his mind.

"All I know is it's a bitch to get into. Like the most exclusive after-party in the universe. You have to know someone."

"Sounds like a good place to hide from killers," says Candy.

"Or the girl," he says. "She's killed like a dozen Sub Rosa. She tried to cut your angel. That's when he disappeared. She's scarier than anything else around here."

He smiles at me hopefully.

"Except you, of course."

"Don't suck up, Mike. Not until you've had a shower. You say the ghost tried to kill Saint James?"

"If that's the angel, then yeah. Went for him on Sunset in front of a whole tour bus full of witnesses. She got a piece of him too. The girl isn't subtle."

"Why would she be? She's dead."

I turn my back on Mike and whisper in Candy's ear. Mike looks nervous. He takes big gulps from the bottle.

"I've heard of poltergeists that can toss cups and saucers around, but never one that hacks people up like Jason Voorhees. Have you?"

"No. I haven't."

"Remember when the girl came into Bamboo House?"

"Yeah."

"I tried to grab her and missed. She could have cut me but she didn't. She said something funny."

"What?"

" 'You're not one of his.' "

"Do you know what it means?"

"Not a clue. Maybe Saint James? Maybe Blackburn?"

"Maybe Colonel Sanders."

"Yeah. There's an annoying number of possibilities."

Mike is on his feet when I look back at him, the vodka cradled in his arms like a newborn baby.

"Let me get this straight. All you can tell me about Saint James is that he's someplace you don't know about and that you don't know how to get to. A dead girl tried to kill him but you don't know why or who the girl is or where she's from. Does that sum things up?"

"That's everything, man. I swear. Can I have my soul back now?"

"That's not even a postcard, Mike. That's not even a phone number scrawled on a cocktail napkin. Do you really think that's worth a soul?"

Mike shifts his weight from foot to foot like he has to go to the bathroom. By now he probably does.

"Yes?" he says.

"Wrong," says Candy.

"Wrong. It's worth shit. The closest thing you can get to nothing without being nothing."

Mike shrugs.

"Sorry. I mostly deal in gossip. Stuff like Blue Heaven isn't my specialty. Hell, I didn't even know how to get in touch with you to sell my soul."

No. A guy like Mike wouldn't, would he? He'd have to go to someone. A name pops into my head.

"Do you know Amanda Fischer?"

"That Hollywood devil-worshipping bitch?" says Mike. "I mean. Sorry."

"Forget it. So you know her."

"I built her a peacock and a Persian cat. One of her crowd did my soul conjuration. It cost me a wolf."

Mike takes an anxious sip from the bottle.

"I want to get in touch but I lost my address book. Do you have her number?"

Mike goes to a desk as filthy as the sofa and as crowded with junk as the worktable. It reminds me a little of Mr. Muninn's cavern, full of centuries of obsessive collecting. Mike finds an old gray metal Rolodex, pulls a card out of it, and brings it to me. It says FISCHER, AMANDA. Below that is a Beverly Hills phone number.

"Nice work, Mike. You pulled things out there at the last minute. I thought I was going to have to feed your bones to my associate but you came through."

"So now I can have my soul back?"

"Not a chance. But I'll tell you what you can do to get it back. I have a friend, really just sort of a yammering bastard. He's stuck on a mechanical body, only it's not finished. You finish him off and you're halfway home."

"What's the other half?"

"I need you to build something else. A Hellion-to-English translator. And it needs to read lips."

Mike sits on the sofa and sets the bottle between his feet.

"Is that all?"

"You do that and you can have your soul back."

235

He looks up at me. Big fat tears in his dumb, red eyes.

"You promise?"

I take out a pack of Maledictions and tap him out the last one.

"If you can't trust a man who gives you his last cigarette, who can you trust?"

He takes the smoke and I light it with Mason's lighter. Mike nods.

"What choice do I have?"

"None. I'll be in touch with the details."

Candy starts out. I follow but stop at the door to put on my glove.

"What's the story with the vucari out front?"

Mike shakes his head. Wipes the tears from his eyes with the heel of his hand.

"My cousins. From the old country. Fucking Cossacks."

"But you're not a Lurker."

"It was a mixed marriage," he says.

"I see why you made the deal. If I had to work with family, I'd prefer Hell too."

"Yeah. Maybe I'll sell you my soul back," he says. Then quickly, "I'm only kidding."

"I know, Mike. I know."

WE GO BACK to the Porsche. Mike's cousins beat on the dead car, smiling at us like they're tenderizing steaks for our dinner.

I get out my phone and dial Amanda Fischer's number. She answers on the fifth ring.

"I don't recognize your number. How did you get this one?"

"Don't you know me, Amanda?" I say in my spookiest Hail Satan voice. "It's Mr. Macheath."

The line goes quiet. I hear breathing, then, "This doesn't sound like Mr. Macheath. How do I know it's you?"

I try to remember what happened when I met her and her Devil toadies at the Chateau Marmont with Lucifer 1.0.

"I have the lovely pyx you gave me on the mantel in my library."

"Master!"

"New rule. Don't call me 'master.' Lucifer will do."

"Yes, Lucifer. What can I do for you, Master?"

This shit again. Why are all Hellions and devil worshippers bottoms?

"I'm sorry," she says.

"It's quite all right. Now I need you to do some things for me. I need some information."

"Yes, Lucifer. What kind of information?"

"I want everything you can find about a place called Blue Heaven. Where it is. How you get in."

"I didn't think anywhere was barred to you."

"You'll notice that part of the name includes the word 'Heaven.' All Heavens have a waiting list to get in and my name is at the bottom."

"Of course, Lucifer. Sorry."

Candy looks bored. She gets out of the car, goes back to the garage, and starts talking to the shorter vucari. By her body language she's flirting.

"What do you know about this ghost girl running around town?"

"Our mediums say she's a hungry ghost. A spirit that will

never be satisfied no matter how much she devours. She's killed a lot of people."

"I know. A lot of Sub Rosa."

"Not just Sub Rosa. Ordinary mortals too. In fact, she's killed members of our temple. When I knew it was you, I was hoping you'd returned to save us."

Now Candy is flirting with the taller vucari. She glances over her shoulder at the shorter one and she and Ivan laugh together. The short vucari isn't pounding on the car anymore.

"Of course I'm here to save my followers. But I have to know which of my flocks are worthy of saving. Yours isn't the only temple in California, Amanda."

"Of course. We'll prove ourselves worthy of you."

I doubt that.

"I'm sure you will. I'd like all information you can find as soon as possible. Let's say tomorrow."

"Tomorrow? That's hardly any time at all."

"Then you'd better get started."

Candy steps out of the garage, running her hand down Ivan's arm and holding his pinkie for a second. She blows the short vucari a kiss and comes back to the car.

I put my hand over the receiver when she gets in.

"What was that all about?" I whisper.

"Watch," she says.

In the garage, the vucari cousins are shouting. The little one pokes Ivan in the chest with the wooden handle of his mallet. Ivan swings and clocks the little guy. But he doesn't go down. He crouches and slams his shoulder into Ivan's belly.

Ivan falls on the shorter vucari and they end up in a pile of flailing fists and feet, rolling around the garage floor like a spider having a seizure.

I mouth, "You're evil."

Candy shrugs and mouths, "I was bored. And I love messing with dumb guys."

"One more thing, Amanda. I'm going to need guns. Pistols. I'm not sure what I'll be in the mood for, so bring an assortment. Like teacakes to a party. All right?"

"My pleasure, Lucifer. I live to serve you."

"Of course you do."

"Where shall I get in touch with you? The usual? The Chateau Marmont?"

Goddamn. I forgot about that place.

"Yes, the Chateau. My usual suite."

"I'll see you tomorrow evening, Lucifer."

"Ciao."

I put the phone away and Candy leans back like she's never seen me before.

"You have a suite somewhere? You've been holding out on me."

"I don't have one yet but I think I will when we get back to town."

"Is there room service? I like room service."

I put the black blade in the ignition and start the car.

"How does Rinko feel about you spending time with me? She knows about us, right?"

"She's not brain-dead, so yeah, she knows. I told you before, Rinko and I aren't married. She knows you and I have something and you know she and I have something. No one has to be here who doesn't want to be. I mean, there's nothing that's stopping you from seeing someone else."

"I'm not interested in anyone else."

"Really? Is that why Sasha Grey had her tongue down your throat last night?"

"Brigitte? That was nothing. Just a couple of old zombie slayers who haven't seen each other in a few months."

"Another month and you two would have been dry-humping on the bar."

"And spill our drinks? Against the bar maybe, but not on it."

"Keep talking and I won't go back to your suite with you."

"You started it."

"Did I? I don't remember. Home, Jeeves."

I pull a U-turn across four lanes of traffic and head for the freeway. When we pass the garage Ivan and his pal are still wrestling.

WE'VE BEEN ON THE FREEWAY maybe five minutes when I spot the pickup truck. It's not hard. It's been on our tail since we got on the road. It's white like a rental but the windows are tinted opaque black. There aren't many rental companies that do that, and by "not many," I mean none.

"We're being followed."

Candy turns and looks out the back window.

"Which one?"

"The white pickup."

"Are you sure?"

"Let's find out."

I stomp the accelerator and the Porsche tears a hole in the

traffic ahead. I squeeze between two SUVs as they're changing lanes and cut off a cable-company truck trying to pass
a wrecker on the shoulder. Candy turns and looks out the
back.

"The pickup is still there."

"Put on your seat belt."

"You always sound so serious when you think we're going
to die."

"I have an allergy to being dead."

"I didn't say I minded. I like it when you talk butch."

"Good. Shut up and keep an eye on the truck for me."

"Yes, sir."

Of course the truck can keep up with a Porsche. It'll be
some of King Cairo's crew in a pickup souped up with Aelita's
Golden Vigil tech. Outrunning the asshole isn't an option.
The only thing I can do is stay clear of it until one of us grows
wings or runs out of gas.

I let the wrecker pass and when the traffic thins for a
second I jerk the steering wheel, blasting the Porsche across
all six lanes to the far side of the road. A second later the
truck follows. I cut back a couple of lanes.

"They're still on us," says Candy.

There's no way they think I'm Saint James. The first attack
might have been a mistake but this is a straight-up hit.

I try to charge back over the way we came but we're
trapped between a lunch truck and a chop shop Camaro,
the body covered in primer and all the doors different
colors.

The pickup accelerates and rams us. I can't hold the wheel.
I sideswipe the lunch truck. We bounce off and tag the

Camaro before I get control again. I floor the Porsche and we shoot ahead to an open spot in the traffic.

"Still there," says Candy.

I aim the Porsche all over the road, changing lanes like I'm drunk, seasick, and snow-blind. The goddamn pickup stays on our tail.

I cut back to the slow lane and slide in between two sixteen-wheelers, drafting off the first. Bad idea. The pickup pulls alongside us and the front and rear windows roll down. I know what's coming and don't want to see it.

I jerk the wheel right, completely blind. Aiming for the shoulder of the road. Lucky for us there's no one there. It's shit news for the truckers though. The shooters in the pickup truck start firing their modified rifles. They miss us and hit the side of the rear truck. Rear and front tires blow. Shots hit the cab. I can't tell if the driver is hit or not. The truck starts drifting into the pickup's lane while its trailer slides in the opposite direction, pulling the rear of the truck around on the bad tires. It jackknifes, cutting off five of the six lanes. I hit the accelerator, trying to get ahead of the chaos. I do, but so does the pickup. It rams us again. And again. The little Porsche isn't made for this kind of abuse. There's a metallic grinding from the back like the rear axle is about to go.

There's an overpass ahead. I look at Candy.

"Do you trust me?"

"I hate that question."

"Do you trust me?"

"Yes."

"Then undo your seat belt and put your head down on your knees."

"I hate how this sounds."

"Don't worry. It gets worse."

The pickup moves up to ram us again. I stay ahead until just before the overpass. And stomp the brakes, pulling up on the handbrake at the same time. The pickup can't slow and hits us at full speed, driving up the rear of the car and over the top like we're a ramp. I throw myself on top of Candy. Wrap my arms around her. The car roof smashes down on my back but stops when it hits the armor. The weight of the truck is suddenly gone and we start to slow. From below I hear the sound of crashing metal and exploding glass. The Porsche slows and comes to a stop, grinding against the guardrail.

I slam my back against the roof a few times and manage to raise the crushed metal a few inches. When I have enough room to move my legs, I kick out the driver-side door, slide out, and run around to Candy's side. Her door is jammed so tight that I can't even get a good grip. I climb on top and drive the black blade through the roof, slicing it and prying it open like a sixty-thousand-dollar oyster. Candy looks up at me through the hole.

"This is what you mean by 'trust me'?"

"You're alive, aren't you?"

"Yeah, but I'm developing what are called trust issues."

"I'm sure Allegra knows some good shrinks. Reach up your hand and I'll get you out of there."

We get a ride into Hollywood in a station wagon with a family from Houston. I agree with them that we're damned lucky to walk away from an accident like that with just a few scratches. Luckier than the pickup that went off the overpass and crashed onto the street below. They drop us on Hollywood Boulevard near Allegra's clinic, and when I try to give the dad some money he waves it off.

"I'm sure you'd do the same for someone stranded. Just pass the good fortune along."

Candy and I look at each other and I know we're thinking the same thing.

Who knew people not playing angles or hustling something still existed. I thought they'd died out with the triceratops. I feel funny now. A little dirty. Like maybe I contaminated their car with bad luck. I wonder if they would have given us a ride if they knew I was the Lord of the Underworld. What's funny is I think they would have.

Nice people are fucking weird.

CARLOS IS SITTING UP in a plastic chair in the clinic reception area. His arm and shoulder are still bandaged and smell of aromatic oils and potions.

I sit down next to him.

"Hey, man. I'm really sorry to get you mixed up in my shit."

He laughs, patting his pockets.

"When haven't I been mixed up in your shit? I met you on the day you got back from Hell, remember?"

"I guess so."

"Yes so. I knew something like this could happen. It's called a calculated risk. And now it's happened and I'm walking away. It's like I got a measles shot. I'm immunized. Nothing bad will ever happen to me again."

"I'm not sure it works like that."

"Of course it does."

He gives up patting his pockets.

"You have any cigarettes? I'm dying for one. No pun intended."

"I thought you didn't smoke."

"Only after surgery."

"Sorry, but I gave my last one to a guy who sold his soul to the Devil."

He sits up in his chair.

"I guess there's some things worse than getting shot."

"Not many. Anyway, I hear the guy is such a fuckup he's getting his soul back. Even the Devil doesn't want it."

"I must have missed that day at Catholic school. The nuns never told us that being a dumb-ass was a weapon against the Devil."

"Now you know."

He leans forward, propping his good elbow on his knees.

"Don't apologize for any of this. Remember when you and your pretty squeeze killed all those zombies in the bar? Business doubled after that. With you back and ninjas going Wild West, I'm going to make a fortune."

"As long as no one shoots the jukebox."

"I'll kill any cocksucker that touches my jukebox."

"You've got someone to take you home?"

"My brother-in-law is going to give me a ride."

"You never told me you were married."

"I'm not. He's really my ex-brother-in-law but I like him a lot better than my ex-wife."

I get up and look around for Allegra.

"You take care yourself. Heal up before you reopen the bar."

"I'm going to make so much money I'll buy a Cadillac to drive me to my Lexus and drive that to my other Cadillac to drive to work."

"I'll catch you later, man."

"Later."

Candy disappeared into the back of the clinic right when we got here, but Allegra is putting things away in the treatment room.

"Welcome home. Candy says you two had an adventure today."

"The other guys had an adventure. We had a car wreck."

"And walked away with a couple of scratches. I'm jealous. Remember that time you took me with you to meet the dead man Johnny Thunders? I miss that kind of thing."

"Maybe you should train some people to take a few of your shifts."

"I am. You met Fairuza, the sweet Ludere, the other day. She's my chief apprentice."

"Cool. I'll drag you and Vidocq along when the right kind of craziness comes up."

She smiles and wraps two chunks of what look like pearly rocks in dark blue silk. Divine-light glass from the beginning of time. God broke a star and dropped the glass to Earth. One of his original fuckups. It wasn't all bad. It turns out it heals a lot of wounds. Doc Kinski once used it on Allegra.

"You don't know anything about the other Stark, do you? You're a doctor. Maybe he'd tell you something he wouldn't tell other people."

"No. Sorry. He never told me anything."

"Have you been getting some stabbings in here?"

"Are you talking about the girl? No. No stabbings. From what I hear, if she cuts you, you die. I heal people. She kills. There's no point in me treating the dead."

Candy comes in and crooks her thumb over her shoulder.

"Can I talk to you a minute?"

"Sure."

We walk outside into the cool, crisp L.A. afternoon. The sky looks a little strange. Clouds are rolling in fast and it's like the light is strobing behind them.

"I have to take a rain check on your suite. Rinko got a taste of blood last night and now she's kind of in withdrawal. I need to take her home."

"I understand."

"Sorry. I keep seeing you and running off."

I shrug.

"Maybe I deserve it. I ran out first. Anyway, you have to do the right thing by your friend."

"Doing the right thing usually sucks."

"Almost always."

She kisses me and goes back inside. Through the glass I see her giving Rinko a potion and leading her into the treatment room.

There's another reflection in the glass. A ghost.

I turn and the little girl is standing there. Frilly blue party dress and a knife as big as her leg. She stares at me like I'm a rat on her birthday cake.

"Who are you?" I ask.

She doesn't say anything.

"What the hell is wrong with you? Why are you killing people? You pissed off? Hungry?"

Richard Kadrey

Still nothing.

I take a step toward her. She takes one back. I take another. There's an earth tremor, like a small earthquake. I look down at my feet. When I look up again, the girl is gone. I walk out to where she was standing. Then to the far wall. I get on my knees to look under all the vehicles. The ground gives way and I land flat on my back. I was run over by a pickup truck about thirty minutes ago. It hurt. Falling six feet onto a sore back hurts more. I lie in the fresh dirt, trying to catch my breath.

"Hi, Stark."

The voice is breathy. Barely a whisper and hard to hear over the traffic.

I'm lying in a hole as deep as a grave. There's another hole like a tunnel leading off into the dark. The voice is coming from there.

"What is this?"

A desiccated corpse, gray parchment skin stretched like tissue paper over brittle bones, sticks its head out of the hole like a turtle and draws it back in when the light hits it.

"Don't you recognize me?" says the corpse.

"You're a fucking skeleton. How am I supposed to recognize you?"

"Once upon a time you wanted to kill me. Then you wanted to save me. You didn't do either. You let Parker murder me."

"Cherry? Is that you?"

Cherry Moon was a member of my old Magic Circle. One of the ones who stood by and let Mason send me to Hell. For staying out of the way, Mason gave her the gift of youth. Creepy youth. Candy is into Japanese cartoons but Cherry

248

Moon wanted to be a cartoon. A forever-prepubescent Sailor Moon love doll in a school uniform. Do you know what it's like to get hit on by a thirty-five-year-old woman who looks like she's twelve? No. You don't. It's strange and unpleasant on so many levels I can't begin to count them.

"Was that you who dropped me into a hole in Bamboo House?"

"Do you get followed around by a lot of tunneling dead girls?"

"You saved me from getting shot."

"Yes. You owe me. You didn't save me when I was alive. I want you to save me now."

"What do you want me to do?"

"Kill the little girl."

When I first saw her, I thought Cherry was a ghost cursed to stay on Earth and the hole was just a ghost projection from her mind. Seeing her skeleton crammed into the narrow tunnel, I see I was wrong. Cherry did this to herself.

"Is the girl hurting you?"

"She's killing us. All the other ghosts and spirits in L.A. When she isn't killing you, she hides with us in the Tenebrae. Kills us like she kills the living and we don't know why."

When Cherry died, she was so afraid of moving on that she made herself into a jabber. Jabbers are a kind of ghost so traumatized by death that they can't even haunt people or places like normal ghosts. They stick close to their bodies. Literally haunt their own corpses and tunnel in them from place to place. They won't come out of the ground because their bodies are fragile and they're afraid of being mistaken for zombies. Jabbers are about the most pathetic thing in the world.

"I don't know what you want me to do. I can't get near the kid."

"You travel between worlds. I saw you come here from Hell. Come into the Tenebrae and stop her."

"I don't know how."

"Find out."

I get nearer the hole. Cherry doesn't back away this time. I put out my hand. Slowly she creeps her hand forward until our fingertips are just touching. I was right. She's real. A ghost hiding in her own bones.

"Jesus, Cherry, all you have to do is let go. Get out of this body. Get out of the ghost realm. Go on to wherever it is you're supposed to go."

"No!" she says. "Do you think Heaven is waiting for me with open arms? We both know where I'm going, and as long as these bones hold together, I'm staying right here."

"I can help you when you get to Hell. Like you said, I couldn't save you when you were alive. Maybe I can help now that you're dead. But you have to let go."

She crawls closer to the tunnel opening. I can see her lipless smile and eye sockets full of dirt and dry plant roots. I want to look away but I don't.

"Where do you stay when you're not stalking me?"

"I moved into an old cemetery in a field of old cemeteries. It's the strangest place. Full of aetheric ghosts and physical ghosts like me."

She makes a sound that's almost like a laugh.

"There's practically a traffic jam with us tunnelers. We have to be careful digging or we can fall into each other's chambers."

"What do you mean by a field of cemeteries? What the hell is that?"

"It's like a cemetery for cemeteries. Or a garden where some kind soul has planted the dead and where we live. Go ask Teddy Osterberg. He's the one who collects the cemeteries. I'm just one of the flowers in his garden."

"So the little girl is killing Sub Rosas, civilians, and now ghosts. She tried to kill the other Stark, so she's tried to kill an angel. Do you know anything about him?"

"Other Stark? He's prettier than you. Like you in the olden days. Now you're a mess. A girl likes a few scars. They give a man character. But you don't have a shot with me anymore, darling."

"Does anyone call the Tenebrae Blue Heaven?"

"I'm afraid we're plain old Tenebrae. Tell me you'll help us."

I reach into my pockets for a Malediction and remember I gave my last one away. Anyway, Cherry wouldn't want me smoking. Dried-out corpses are perfect kindling.

"If Teddy Osterberg collects the dead, he could be connected to the girl and I know the girl is connected to Saint James. I'll check him out. Maybe I can help both of us."

"Thank you."

"Don't get too choked up. I'm mostly doing this for me. If I can get to King Cairo first, I'm going after him. I'm going to hurt him dead. I'm tired of people trying to kill me. Downtown. Up here. It's getting aggravating."

She makes the whispering sound that might be a laugh.

"You know what they say. All the birds come home to roost. The past catches up with us. And you have quite a past, Sandman Slim."

"Philosophy from a corpse. Are you sure you aren't Greek?"
She turtles her head back into the hole.

"I'll see you soon. Don't forget me."

"That's not likely."

Cherry disappears into the dark. There's a rustling and crackling of old bones as she turns around and crawls back the way she came. A homeless corpse living in a coffin squat. How desperate do you have to be to live like that?

I CATCH A CAB at Hollywood and Sunset and have it take me to the Chateau Marmont, the traditional crash pad for showbiz and well-heeled assholes from around the world. John Belushi OD'd there. Jim Morrison crabbed around the outside windows on acid. Hunter Thompson drank by the pool, and a few months back, I played bodyguard to the other Lucifer while he stayed in his secret suite upstairs. Now that I'm the black beast of the forest, the room is mine. I think.

The cabbie whines when I hand him a hundred but is all smiles when I let him keep an extra fifty. I don't answer when he asks if I want a receipt.

Inside, the desk clerk's face is streaked with plenty of sin but he's nothing special. He looks at me like I'm there to empty out the trash cans in the lobby. I still have the Glock in my pocket if things go wrong.

"Hi. I have a standing reservation. The name is Mr. Macheath. I'd like my special room."

He frowns and types something into the computer.

"We don't have a note saying you'd be stopping by, and according to the annotation you don't even look like Mr. Macheath."

I crook my finger at him. His name tag says CHARLES.

"Did you ever hear of the concept of low profile?"

He looks me over.

"That's extremely low profile."

I lean in closer. I'm so sick of dealing with pissants.

"You listen to me, you little fuck. The last time I was here, some people upset me. Like you're doing right now. I locked them in my suite with a horde of zombies. I don't know what the place looked like after I left—and it better be clean when I get up there—but I bet not good. Does that sound at all familiar, Chuck? Because if it doesn't we can role-play right here. I'll be the zombie pulling out your intestines while you watch. Then, and only then, when you've gotten a good look at your guts decorating the lobby like Christmas ornaments, only then will I kill you."

To seal the deal I take off my glove and put my Kissi hand over his. He yanks his hand away. I swear, this gimp arm is turning out to be the best party trick in history. Better than chasing girls around when you're five, trying to make them touch your scabs.

Charles edges over to the computer and types in something.

"Very good, Mr. Macheath. And how long will you be staying with us?"

"Until I leave."

"Of course. You remember the way to the room?"

"Second star to the right, then straight on till morning."

"Excuse me?"

"Top floor. Grandfather clock."

I take the elevator up. I'm a little surprised to see that the hall is exactly the way it was the first time I saw it. Since the night I locked Koralin Geistwald and her clan in here, I've always pictured the place as a Playboy Mansion slaughter-house. I hold my breath, open the front of the grandfather clock, and step through.

The suite is perfect. Like nothing ever happened. Clean and bright and full of brand-new *Architectural Digest* furniture. The kind that under any other circumstances would reject me like a dime-store kidney in a billionaire's back. I guess they gave up trying to clean brains and eyeballs out of the old furniture and brought in new stuff. And I have the place all to myself until Amanda and her demonic brown-nosers get here. Saying the place is a step up from the Beat Hotel is like saying Jean Seberg was pretty. I should take some phone shots and send them to Kasabian. THANKS FOR KICKING ME OUT. DON'T WORRY. I'VE LANDED ON MY FEET. But even I'm not that much of a bastard.

Samael was alone a lot when he was up here the last time. I don't know how he did it. The place is so huge it echoes when I walk around. I need to treat it like that library Down-town. Build myself a little vacation home in one part of the room and stay there. Over by the giant flat-screen. I'll bet my hooves and horns this place has every channel and every movie ever made on tap. With a little fixing up I could get used to the place. Maybe there are some earthly perks to being Lucifer after all.

I wonder if they miss me in Hell yet? And if enough people know about it to matter. Semyazah can hold things together, and if he has troops rounding up red leggers, it'll keep them too busy to think about offing themselves. Or me. I'd still like to know who made those crank calls. But I'm not worried. There'll be more. Maybe the hotel can tap my phone so I can trace them. I'll have to remember to ask.

Watching my back has left me exhausted. I want to find Saint James and I want to kill King Cairo and Aelita. Not necessarily in that order. After shooting Carlos and spilling good whiskey and the stunt on the freeway this afternoon, I want to put the hurt of all time on someone. Saint James included. Throw Blackburn in too in case he switched the hit from Saint James to me.

I take a couple of pictures with my phone and e-mail them to Candy. Let her see what she's missing. So much for not being a bastard.

I DIAL TRAVEN.

"Hey, Father, with all the diabolical stuff you studied, have you ever met real-life, honest-to-God devil worshippers?"

"No. I don't think I have."

"You should come over. I have some stopping by. You'll see how lame the Devil's minions are. Maybe it'll make you feel better about Hell and things."

"I'm not sure about that but it would be good to talk about what you showed me in the bar. Your hand, I mean."

"I'll send a cab for you. When you get to the hotel, call me from the lobby and take the elevator to the top floor. I'll come out and get you."

"All right."

I pick up the house phone and dial room service.

"Yes, Mr. Macheath?"

"Hi. I'd like some food sent up."

"Certainly, sir. What would you like?"

"I don't know. What do you have?"

"Our steaks are very good. And we have a chef's special salmon today. It's grilled and rubbed with a—"

"That sounds good. I tell you what. I don't know what my guests will want, so send up a little bit of everything. Whatever you think is good. And not too many frilly dishes with mango-chutney goddamn glaze or diarrhea chilis. You don't have to tart up meat to make it good. Make sure there are some ribs and a porterhouse steak medium. And desserts. Send a bunch of those. And black coffee."

"Will there be anything else?"

Drunk on power, I say, "Yeah, a bottle of Aqua Regia."

"Just one?"

I move the phone to the other ear to make sure I heard him right.

"You have Aqua Regia?"

"We have several bottles left from the case in your private stock."

Goddamn Samael was smart. I have a lot to learn about the evil game.

"Just one bottle for now but stand by for a possible drinking binge."

"Yes, sir. The first dishes will start arriving in thirty to forty minutes."

"You're my hero."

Hell yes, it's good to be king.

FATHER TRAVEN and the first round of food arrive around the same time. All he says as I take him through the grandfather clock is, "Oh." Then, "Oh my" on the other side.

"Welcome to the dark side, Father."

Waiters wheel in cart after cart of food and line them up neatly against the wall like a satanic buffet.

I pick up a pork rib in Texas red sauce and take a big bite. It isn't Carlos's tamales but it'll do.

"Eat up. The Christians said this much food is gluttony and the Greeks said it's a sign of a small mind. Might as well dive in because we're already fucked."

He smiles but approaches the food cautiously, like there might be a tiramisu-shaped pipe bomb somewhere. Traven picks up some red grapes and puts one in his mouth. Smiles and nods.

"Weak, Father. Very weak."

He walks over and sits on the arm of a plush light blue sofa. He's a little like Merihim. Out of his own space, all he can do is wander and perch.

"Have you ever heard of Blue Heaven?" I ask.

"It's an old song."

"Aside from that."

"I'm afraid not. Are you sure, whatever, it is that's its real name?"

"You're right. Blue Heaven does sound a little carefree for an extra-dimensional power spot."

"I'll look into it if you'd like."

"Thanks."

He picks a couple of grapes off the stem, sets them on his plate, but doesn't eat them.

He says, "I wanted to ask you a favor."

"I've got plenty of everything. What do you need?"

"I reacted badly when you showed me your hand last night. I was wondering if you'd show it to me again."

"Sure."

I take off the glove and roll up my sleeve. I sit beside him on the sofa so he can get a good look.

"It's just an arm, you know. Kind of an ugly one but it's still just an arm."

"How did you lose your real one?"

"In a fight. I used to be a gladiator but I'm a little out of practice. The Hellion I was fighting took it off in one clean shot."

"My God."

"I killed him, so the story has a happy ending."

"I'm glad for you."

He drops his grapes into an ashtray and sits on the sofa looking shaken.

"Listen, man, I keep telling you that I'm not sure the excommunication thing matters anymore. When I say I have an in with God, I'm not kidding. I know the guy and at least one part of Him likes me."

"What do you mean one part?"

"Didn't I tell you? God had a nervous breakdown and split into five little Gods. But like I said, I'm pretty well acquainted with one of them."

"You are?"

He shakes his head. Holds up his hands and drops them into his lap.

"If any of this is supposed to comfort me, I'm afraid it's not working."

I go to the buffet and get the Aqua Regia bottle and two glasses.

"Ask me whatever's on your mind."

He takes a breath.

"Let's say that I really am going to Hell with no hope of salvation. You said you could help me. That means you know someone in power? I guess what I mean is . . . have you ever seen Lucifer and does he hate the clergy as much as I've heard he does?"

I set the bottle and glasses on the table between us.

"Father, I am Lucifer."

He looks at me, waiting for the punch line. When I don't give him one, he leans back on the sofa and laughs his weary old-soldier laugh.

"And here I thought you were my friend. The prince of lies is right."

"I am your friend and I didn't lie to you. I wasn't always Lucifer. Trust me. I didn't ask for the job. The previous Lucifer forced it on me. That's how I know if you end up in Hell you'll be taken care of. I run the goddamn place."

He gets up and goes to the buffet. Shovels fruit and cheese onto a plate and brings it back.

"God is in pieces and you're the Devil. You're right. I might as well eat."

"That's the spirit."

I go back over and spoon black caviar and sour cream onto a plate.

"You know, if anyone should be freaked out here, it's me. You're like the third person I've told about the Lucifer thing and everyone is taking it really well. I mean, I'd like just a little polite shock and horror when I tell people I'm the king of evil."

Traven spreads Brie on a cracker with the care and attention of a sculptor.

"If people don't seem shocked, maybe it's because it's a bit much to process all at once. And you do have a colorful history."

"So that's what people say behind my back. That I'm colorful."

"Would you rather be boring?"

"Sign me up."

THERE'S NOTHING SADDER in this word than a true-blue Satanist. I don't mean the ones who dress in black, listen to Ronnie Dio, and use the Devil as an excuse to throw graveyard key parties. I mean the ones who've bought the gaff that if they pray to the baddest of the bad, he'll drop doubloons, luck, and hotties in their laps all the livelong day and then, when they die, they'll get their own castles and pitchforks and get to join the endless torture party. They're the ones I feel sorry for. Haven't they figured out that Lucifer cares even less about his flock than God cares about His? Some of these nitwits have actually met Lucifer and he treated them like expired meat.

Career devil worshippers are Dungeons & Dragons freaks that never grew up and still believe that if they had just one superpower they'd be the belles of the ball or prom king. On the one hand, I want to FedEx them hot cocoa and a pile of self-help books. And on the other hand, I want to use them ruthlessly for whatever I can squeeze out of their service bottom carcasses. Maybe when I have more time, I can play Dr. Phil and get them to do an honest inventory of their collective psychoses. Right now, though, I'm on a timetable and I don't have time for tea and sympathy. Maybe the best thing I can do is show them what Hell is really like. Make them copy the entire *Oxford English Dictionary* onto three-by-five cards. Stamp them. Date them. Put each word in a separate folder and file it. Then take all the words out, burn them, and start over. Do it until I say stop and of course I never will. They'll use up all the ink in the world and all the paper in the western hemisphere. Some will slit their wrists with a thousand paper cuts. Others will get cancer from the ink fumes or go snow-blind from the scanner. Welcome to Hell. It's just like high school but with more boredom and entrails.

I DON'T KNOW if Samael put them there, or the hotel, but the bedroom closet is full of suits and expensive shirts and shoes. I toss my ripped shirt on the bed and pick out a purple one so dark it's almost black. Samael wore shirts like this because the color hid the blood seeping from an old wound. The Greeks and Romans considered it the color of royalty and that wouldn't appeal to Samael's vanity. No. Not one bit.

Someone is knocking on the grandfather clock. Traven sets his plate down on the table. He looks like he's waiting for the seven plagues to stroll out of the clock.

Three people come in. A trinity. Pray for us sinners now and at the hour of our boredom.

There's Amanda Fischer, a high-society babe with a young woman's face and a crone's hands. Plastic surgery or hoodoo? Your guess is as good as mine.

With her is a man about her age carrying a briefcase. He's balding and seems to be compensating for it by growing bushy muttonchops. He looks like her husband. Maybe muscle or an over-the-hill skinhead. The third one is a dark-haired young guy with a bland pretty-boy face and dressed so perfectly in Hugo Boss he can probably recite back issues of *GQ* by heart. All three of them are caked black with sin signs, like they crawled here through one of Cherry Moon's tunnels.

The disappointment on their faces is spectacular. Samael is Rudolph Valentino handsome. When they see my scarred mug, they wonder if they're in the right room. Maybe they stepped through the wrong magic clock.

"Hello," says Amanda. "We're here to see our master, Lucifer."

"You're looking at him, Brenda Starr."

"I've seen you before. You're his bodyguard."

I take a bite of a rib and suck the barbecue sauce off my fingers.

"Do you think Lucifer has access to only one body? Look into my eyes. Can't you sense my power and glory and all the other shit that makes your crowd moist?"

"Do you know who you're talking to? Watch your mouth," says Muttonchops. He has a high-toned British accent. The kind that says, "I've never opened a door for myself my whole life."

"Why do I care who she is if she doesn't know who I am? Doesn't the fact I'm in here with many tasty snacks tell you something?"

"Yes," Muttonchops says. "That you're a clever enough impostor to fool the hotel. But you can't fool us."

"What's he doing here?" squawks the pretty boy.

He points at Traven.

"He has the stink of God all over him."

"He's a colleague. If that's a problem, you can all ride down the elevator shaft headfirst."

Muttonchops says "There's the proof, eh, Amanda?"

She nods.

"A crude threat not worthy of our lord. We're leaving."

They're headed for the door when Traven says, "Which one of them carries the least sin?"

All three stop and look back like questioning their dedication to sin is an insult.

I look them over.

"The kid."

Traven walks to him and puts his hand on the boy's shoulder.

"What's your name, son?"

The kid leans back away from him.

"Luke."

"Do you want to go to Hell, Luke?"

Luke looks at the others for help. Muttonchops takes a couple of steps in their direction but stops when the knife I throw at his feet embeds itself in the tile floor with a metallic *twang*.

"Do you want to go to Hell?" Traven asks.

Luke puts his hands in his jacket pockets. Stands up straight, trying to look defiant.

"To be with Lord Lucifer forever? Yes. Of course."

"I can help you with that right now."

Traven shoves Luke against the wall so hard his head bounces off the marble. When the kid opens his mouth to yell, Traven holds it open and leans in like he's going to kiss him. Luke pulls back but there's nowhere to go.

Black vapor drifts from Traven's mouth into Luke's. A breeze of dust. A wet, oily stream of fluid. Buzzing things like microscopic wasps. It smells like burning feathers and rancid onions. The kid's face darkens with sin until he's as black as Manimal Mike. When Traven steps back, Luke collapses on the floor, coughing and drooling on his designer lapels. Amanda and Muttonchops rush to him.

Traven looks down at Luke and says, "Did you think damnation would be easy?"

Amanda screams, "What have you done to my son?"

"I damned him for all eternity. Isn't that right, Lucifer?"

"The father here gave him a black karma enema. Luke is stuffed with more sin than the entire NBA."

I kneel down and push up Luke's eyelids to have a look at his pupils. They're pinpoints. Barely visible.

"You understand that there are traditions and procedures Downtown. My guess is that bloated with this much sin, there isn't much I can do for him. He'll end up on a paddleboat on the river of fire. Or in the Cave of the Despised, with razor crystals and flesh-eating spiders. Which do you think he'd prefer, Mom?"

Muttonchops looks at the kid. Takes out a silver coin and puts it on the kid's tongue. Black tarnish creeps over its face. In a few seconds it looks a hundred years old. He looks at Amanda.

"He's telling the truth. I've never seen so much sin in one body."

He turns to me and bows his head.

"Forgive us, Lucifer. We were blinded by your outward appearance and couldn't see the real you."

"You'll have plenty of time to nose-polish my ass Downtown. Right now I want the answers to my questions."

"And my son?" says Amanda.

"Answer my questions and I'll see what I can do for Little Lord Fuckitall."

"Praise to you, my lord."

"He wishes to only be addressed as Lucifer," Amanda says to Muttonchops.

"Forgive me."

Luke opens his eyes and tries to push Amanda away but he's too weak. She and Muttonchops help him to the sofa and leave him slumped like a jellyfish on a rocking chair.

"You asked about Blue Heaven," says Muttonchops.

He takes a piece of paper from an inside pocket of his jacket.

"It has many names but its real name translates roughly as 'the Dayward.' It doesn't exist in any one location. It exists in time. It's said that in 1582, when Pope Gregory switched from the old Julian to the Christian calendar, fifteen days were lost. Those fifteen days, existing outside of our space and time, are the Dayward. Blue Heaven."

"And how do you get there?"

"I haven't been able to find that out, Lucifer."

"Not a good start, Lemmy. What about the little girl?"

Amanda touches the back of her hand to Luke's forehead. Brushes back some hair that's fallen over his face.

"We don't have her true name but we believe that her living form was a child known as the Imp of Madrid. She actually lived in Sangre de Sant Joan, a trading village outside of the city. The story is that she killed and mutilated travelers along the nearby road. When people stopped traveling there, she killed the inhabitants of a nearby town. When they called in priests and wolf hunters for protection, she killed them and turned on her own people. After she murdered and mutilated half the village, the men managed to corner her in a barn and lock her in. They burned her alive. When they found her body, a priest dismembered her corpse, down to the individual bones. They believed that if you left bodies inhabited by evil spirits intact, they could reanimate. By separating the bones, she couldn't revive. A child's body has two hundred and eight bones. They buried each one in a separate grave. The Imp of Madrid's body takes up an entire cemetery. No one else has ever been buried there and the ground remains unconsecrated."

"So, a typical Valley girl."

No laughs. Even Traven won't give me a polite smile. Bunch of stiffs.

"Have you ever heard of something called the Qomrama Om Ya?"

"No," says Amanda.

"What about you, Wolverine?"

Muttonchops shakes his head.

"I'm sorry, Lucifer."

I go to the buffet and pick up a piece of *rumaki*. Hold it up for the room.

"Dig in. There's plenty for everyone."

Amanda glances at Luke.

"Thank you, no."

I bite the *rumaki* and talk with a full mouth.

"How about you, Father? You just had a workout."

Traven comes over, pours himself some mineral water, and goes to sit by the window.

"You ever hear of a guy named Teddy Osterberg?" I say.

Amanda brightens.

"Yes. Teddy is part of the family. That is, he's part of your temple in Los Angeles. He's not terribly observant but his family has honored you for three generations."

"What about King Cairo? Any of you know him?"

Luke rolls over in his chair and kicks his feet, trying to get them flat on the ground.

"Cairo," he says. Of course the little shit knows him. Rich kids like him love hanging around criminals. Slumming to the rich is like NASCAR to tobacco chewers.

"Write down his address and phone number."

Luke gets his phone from inside his coat. Fumbles and drops the thing. He sits up and pats himself down for a pen and paper. I grab the phone from his hand and type KING CAIRO in the address book. A phone number and address come up. I copy them down on hotel stationery. Toss the phone into Luke's lap. He's coming around. Still obsidian black. Still silted up with sin.

"Amanda, does Teddy know who Mr. Macheath is?"

"I don't believe so, Lucifer."

"Good. I want you to tell Teddy that Mr. Macheath, a bigwig from an out-of-town temple, is coming to see him but don't tell him anything more about me."

"You should know that Teddy has always been a bit of a recluse and even more so since he was mugged a few months ago. He hardly sees anybody."

"I promise not to touch his toys. Will you call him for me, Amanda?"

"Yes, Lucifer."

She smiles. Finally something she can do without a roomful of minions.

"Swell. Okay. I think we're done here for now."

"Lucifer, what about Luke?" says Amanda.

"What about him? He'll be fine."

"What about his soul? After all he's done in your name, it's unfair that he should be tortured in Hell and not standing at your side."

"What part of my CV gave you the idea that I'm fair?"

"Please," pleads Amanda. She puts her hands over her mouth for daring to ask Lucifer a favor.

I nod at the attaché case Muttonchops brought in.

"Are those the guns?"

"Yes," he says.

"You brought ammo too?"

"Of course."

I go to the table and pour two glasses of Aqua Regia. Set one down on the table and give a small one to Luke. He sips and spits it out like I gave him a mouthful of hot coals. He's not happy but he can stand and his pupils have expanded to something like normal size.

"Tell you what," I say. "You leave the guns, see what you can find out about the Qomrama Om Ya, and fuck off out of here. I'll see what I can do to keep Richie Rich here out of the meat grinder Downtown."

"Thank you," says Amanda, grabbing my hand. I pull it away when she pulls it to her mouth like she's going to kiss it. She helps Luke to the back of the clock.

Muttonchops makes several small bows on his way out.

"Praise you, Lucifer."

I shut the door behind them and take the attaché case to where Traven is sitting. Pop the locks.

"Are those what you were hoping for?" Traven asks.

"Oh yeah."

What's in the case is a bit like the buffet. A smorgasbord of firepower. It's good stuff too. Not as flashy as I was afraid it might be. There's a silver Sig Sauer .45 and a little .38 Special derringer. A nice pistol to have in your pocket for when you're feeling not so fresh. There's also a Desert Eagle .50, a gun I hate even more than the Glock. It's a pistol you see in movies because it's as big as a turkey leg and shiny as a silver dollar polishing a mirror. When we see it we're supposed to admire the guy who has it because he can handle something so manly and powerful. What we should be thinking is that unless he's whale-hunting, the only reason anyone has a gun that size is because he can't aim worth a damn, so he has to blow garbage-can-size holes everywhere hoping he hits something important. I set the Desert Eagle aside.

There's a completely impractical but heartwarming .40 mare's-leg pistol. It's like a short rifle with a lever action to chamber each shot. I don't know if I'll carry it but I'll definitely keep it around. The last gun is a Swiss 9mm folding pistol. It's the flashiest piece in the case but still semipractical. When it's closed, the folder looks like a black lunch box, but hit a switch and it springs open into a 9mm pistol with a rifle stock. Candy would die and go to Heaven and Houston and back if I gave it to her. I might do it but I'm not sure I'm going to give her any bullets. She might like the bang-bang sound too much to be trusted. I'll take her shooting and see how it goes.

I get the Glock out of the duffel and put it on the table with the pistols.

"Want a gun, Father? These are troubled times."

"We're always living in troubled times. It's why we have religion."

"Is that why? I thought it was so I could get rid of all the change people gave me that week."

"You have a very practical view of the divine."

"I've seen how the sausage is made."

Traven picks up the Sig, weighs it in his hand, and sets it down gently.

"Is that boy really going to be tortured in Hell?"

I shrug.

"I was just giving them something to think about. I can send anyone anywhere I want. And don't get too weepy about the kid. Everyone has a lousy time Downtown. Even Lucifer. I'll tell you about my recurring lost-toner-cartridge nightmare sometime."

Traven sips his mineral water. I probably shouldn't have said that last part. I spooked the poor guy again.

"I guess I finally saw the famous Via Dolorosa."

"Yes. After you returned to Hell, I decided I couldn't just

read about all this arcane knowledge and do nothing with it. I had to act. I had to learn to make use of it. How do you think I did?"

"You freaked out the Devil groupies pretty well, so good choice of ways to be scary. Just don't try it on crackheads knocking over a gas station. It's a little slow for that."

Traven smiles his tired smile.

"I'll remember that."

"Where does a nice academic like you pick up tips about something like the Dolorosa?"

He hesitates. He runs a hand through his hair.

"I found it in a sixteenth-century book of Baleful magic."

I nod.

"You know that's illegal, right? You're an outlaw. Jesse James with a dog collar."

"Thank you," he says. "What are you going to do now?"

I wish I had a Veritas. It would help me answer the question. Muttonchops left his tarnished silver coin on a coffee table. I pick it up with my Kissi hand.

"You're going to help me decide. Kill King Cairo or talk to Teddy Osterberg about the girl and Saint James?"

I flip the coin high in the air.

"Call it, Father."

"Heads," he says.

"Always an optimist."

The coin hits the floor and I put my boot down on it.

It's heads.

"You win. Which is it?"

"Go talk to Teddy Osterberg."

I go back to the buffet.

"You didn't care what the second choice was, did you? You just don't want to make it easy for me to kill Cairo?"

He shrugs.

"Damned as I am, murder is still a hard thing for me to condone."

"Like I said, you can't help being a good guy."

"Not yet."

I wonder if Samael left any Maledictions downstairs.

"You don't happen to have a cigarette on you, do you?"

Traven shakes his head.

"I don't smoke."

"I was hoping you'd started."

I go back to the food and pick up the Aqua Regia. Set it down and pour myself some black coffee.

"Seeing your world. It's frightening but exciting," Traven says.

"Thanks, but the truth is I'd rather you cracked the books. I need information from someone I can trust. Is there a way into Blue Heaven? And what's the Qomrama Om Ya? I know it's a weapon and Aelita wants it. But that's all. Maybe you can find out why."

"If you think that's how I can be of the most help."

I go to the window and look out in the direction of the Hollywood sign. It's going to take some time to get used to being home.

"Hey, Father. Is it me or did the sky turn green?"

Traven comes to the window.

"When did that happen?"

"I don't know. What kind of fucked-up poison is this city spewing to turn the whole sky a different color?"

"I heard a strange story on the radio on the way over. They say that Catalina Island has disappeared. There was no earthquake, so it didn't sink. It's simply gone. And everyone on it. Almost four thousand souls are missing."

Killer ghosts and missing islands. That sounds an awful lot like Aelita but where's the percentage in killing off tourists? It's not going to get her any closer to offing God. Unless He's vacationing off the coast of L.A. under an assumed name. Does God have a secret yacht full of bathing beauties?

It's a fun thought but I don't think Mr. Muninn is the sunbathing type.

I RIDE THE HELLION HOG along the Pacific Coast Highway into the hills above Malibu. I figure that with a Gumby-colored sky and radio tall tales about Catalina as the new Atlantis, no one is going to pay attention to the bike. Manimal Mike has a garage. I'll ask him if he can set me up with a set of plates. These cardboard-and-Sharpie ones are only convincing if you don't actually look at them.

As I hit the crest of the hill, my phone rings. I park the bike and answer. It's Candy.

"Holy hell. Where are those pictures from?"

"My new digs," I say. "I decided that if I'm stuck being Lucifer, I should live like him."

"Can I come over and see them?"

"Later. Right now I'm in Malibu seeing a guy who collects corpses like other people collect comics."

"You know the most interesting people, Mr. Macheath. Call me when you get back. I want to come over and break some of your new stuff."

"I think I can squeeze you in. Don't eat before you come over. I have enough food to feed the Crusades."

"Later, Bruce Wayne."

"Later, Major Kusanagi."

Teddy Osterberg's place is a rolling green estate at the highest point of the Malibu hills. This area likes to dry out in the summer and burn even when it doesn't go brown. You can tell Teddy's place hasn't had so much as a campfire in a century. It takes a lot of money and manpower to keep a spread this big green all year. A lot of company for a recluse.

The house is a turn-of-the-century Gothic hulk. More like a bank than a house but with a view to West L.A. one way and practically to Japan the other. There's a white Rolls-Royce Phantom convertible in the circular driveway. I knock on the door. A few seconds later, I hear footsteps and the door swings opens.

I recognize him immediately. Teddy is the civilian at the synod with the nice suit and the Michelangelo manicure. He's dark with sin signs but he comes from old money, so he was probably born prestained and has been piling it on ever since.

I turn and point up.

"Mr. Osterberg, does that sky look green to you?"

"Hmm," he says like a guy who's seen much stranger things. "It certainly does. You must be Mr. Macheath. Please call me Teddy."

He puts out his hand and I shake it. The door is only open wide enough for him to stand in, so I push past him and go inside. I've gone from annoyed to pissed that Traven sent me up here instead of going after King Cairo and I'm prepared to take it out on Teddy.

He doesn't say anything as I go in. Just stands by the door for a minute and then closes it, locking us in a big foyer as silent as a tomb and as clean as an operating room.

"I was surprised to see you open your own door. Malibu people usually have out-of-work B-actors standing at attention all day hoping someone comes up the drive."

"I'm sure some do but I don't keep a staff. It's just me up here, so door opening is a skill I've had to master all on my own."

The foyer is dark but there are dim lights on in the other rooms. I'm going to need night-vision goggles if I want to see anything interesting without starting a bonfire. What I can see in the dimness is an unlit chandelier over an oval space. A sweeping staircase to the second floor. A slice of a dining room and living room off to my left. Tables around the edges of the foyer are dotted with sculptures made from bones. Birds. Dogs. Flowers. Teddy is sort of an abattoir Tick Tock Man. It's good to see he has something to while away the long days and nights all by his lonesome.

Teddy says, "I don't usually have guests in the house."

"So I hear."

"What I mean is, it's a bit rude of you to barge in, even if you are one of Amanda's friends."

"I'm not Amanda's friend. She's way too low on the totem pole for that. This isn't where I want to be today, so I really don't care if you're put out. I also don't see any tributes or signs that you're part of Amanda's world. Where are the sacrificial virgins and inverted pentagrams?"

I caught Teddy off guard. He laughs nervously and keeps his hand on the doorknob.

"You won't find any virgins around here, and as for tribute to Lord Lucifer, I keep those in my private rooms. They sometimes upset the few guests I have over."

"Any I can see?"

"Nary a one."

"Nary? And you called me rude."

I walk around the room taking a closer look at the sculptures. They're strange little things. Intricate and crude at the same time. I think some of the bones might be human.

"Who maintains the grounds if you don't have a staff?"

"People come and go. I find if you keep any crew around too long, they get bored and the work gets sloppy. A steady flow of new faces coming through keeps everyone on their toes."

That's the first thing he's said that sounds like the rich asshole I was expecting. He doesn't like me inside his castle. It's more than me being rude. His heartbeat is up and his pupils are constricting under the strain of maintaining his calm.

He says, "The truth is, I value my privacy more than I value a pristine lawn. Now, how can I help you, Mr. Macheath? Amanda said you were visiting temples around California and had some questions about my collection."

Good work, Amanda. Maybe I'll keep your kid out of the fire after all.

"I do. First off, what exactly is it?"

"Ah, definitions. Always a good place to start. Most people who know about the estate say I—meaning the family—collect cemeteries. That is wrong. In fact, it's backward. We collect ghosts. We're a ghost sanctuary in much the same way that there are sanctuaries for wolves, tigers, and other endangered creatures. The cemeteries are the outward part of the work. Ghosts need someplace to live and most enjoy familiar places."

"They don't haunt the house?"

"A few try. I have a service for that. A team of Guatemalan witches comes by once a month and touches up the spirit barriers. They've been dealing with Mayan ghosts for five hundred years, so I think they know what they're doing. I love my ghosts, but like the family cats, they're outside, not inside friends."

"How many dead friends live here with you?"

"I have no idea. Would you like a tour?"

"Why not?"

He looks relieved that he can finally get me back outside.

We walk around the front of the house to where a pristine golf cart is parked in the shade. I slide in next to Teddy and we head out into the wilds of his estate. I'm wearing the same shirt I had on when Amanda was over. I hope it's dark enough to keep light from glinting off the armor. I don't want to have to explain it to Teddy. Though I shouldn't have to explain anything to a guy who uses skeletons like model kits. It's a funny hobby for someone who comes off so reverential when talking about the dead.

"Amanda tells me you're a high roller in the local temple. How's that working out for you?"

Teddy shakes his head.

"Dear Amanda. She has all these fantasies about getting my little clan involved in the day-to-day drudgery of it all again."

He turns to me quickly.

"I hope I'm not being offensive, you being from a temple yourself."

"No. God's a drag. The Devil's a bore. The only people worse are the ones who run the temples. They think everyone should be on their hands and knees scrubbing the floors right along with them."

"Well put," says Teddy.

I wonder how Deumos is doing. Has anyone murdered her yet? I don't know how long it will take Buer to design and build her temple but I bet it won't be fast. Merihim and his crew will sabotage the project. Someone might blow the whole thing up the day it opens. That's all Hell needs. Another martyr. I wonder if Deumos is counting on her fairy goddess godmother to protect her. That's not a bet I'd take but then I'm surprised she and her church have lasted this long. Maybe they've got some angels on their side that don't have horns and tails.

There's a crowded subdivision of stone minimansions up ahead. A metal gate out front just says PARISH. Which parish it is fell off a long time ago. It's an old New Orleans cemetery with its aboveground tombs hauled all the way up this hill like Fitzcarraldo hauled his boat.

"So you didn't spend your summers at Satan sleepaway camp burning Bibles and pissing on crucifixes?"

Now that we're on his turf, Teddy seems more relaxed. He takes out a black Sobranie cigarette, puts it in his mouth, then takes it out again without lighting it.

"I spent my summers here or with my father or grandfather scouting new haunted places in need of protecting. I'm polite to Amanda and her crowd but I haven't been to one of their meetings in years. No one in the family has taken them all that seriously since Grandfather."

Teddy gestures toward graveyards in the distance, using the cigarette like a pointer.

"He collected our first cemeteries around the same time he struck it rich in silver mining. He believed these two events were inextricably linked, so he saw it as his duty to create a haven for ghosts. He joined Lucifer's temple because the political connections made it easier for him to shave the taxes on the silver income and to bring in foreign graves."

"A lot of ghosts seem to stay here. You don't try to keep them earthbound?"

Teddy shakes his head.

"My charges stay or go as they please. Perhaps if God presented Himself more readily, they wouldn't be so afraid of what awaited them when they finally crossed over."

"I can't argue with that."

Teddy's unlit cigarette is driving me crazy. I still don't have any Maledictions.

"Mind if I have one of those?"

"Not at all."

He holds out the pack to me. I take one, break off the filter, and toss it on his lawn. Teddy doesn't flinch but he saw the butt fall and knows exactly where it is. He'll be out here with tweezers and bleach later to clean up my mess.

I light the cigarette with Mason's lighter. Without the filter, the smoke is rough and rich, like a three-hundred-pound nurse giving me CPR.

There are acres of land below us carved up and divided between several graveyards. It's a whole housing development for the dead.

"Speak of the Devil, to your right is a foreign sanctuary. A small one from the Cannes region of France."

It's a pretty collection of stone monuments and phone-booth-size tombs filled with cats. Cats seem to love dead Frenchmen. I'll have to ask Vidocq about that sometime.

"Over here is our first import from Asia."

Miniature candy-colored pagodas and ornate stone barges fill a very old, very crowded Thai graveyard. Beyond it is a re-creation of an improvised Civil War graveyard, complete with crumbling wooden markers.

"How the hell do you do all this?"

Teddy beams, delighted that I'm impressed.

"We keep a group of necromantic engineers on retainer. They survey the cemetery proper, caskets, tombs, and bodies. Whatever's appropriate. Then chart the exact depth and position of each burial against the stars. The cemetery is then dismantled and rebuilt here, reproducing the original alignments down to the millimeter."

Teddy bats away a fly, the first I've seen here. Maybe an ungrateful jabber left a hole open nearby like an oversize groundhog.

"If need be, we can transport native soil back with the disinterred remains."

What's funny is that Teddy is as unimpressive as the estate is impressive. I'm even forgetting to treat him like shit. For all his eccentricity, Teddy is one of the beige people. They want to fade into the woodwork and disappear. It's not depression. It's more like a desperate desire to become invisible. He's only tolerating me because he doesn't want to piss off the other Devil freaks enough to shun him. Plus, it's a chance to show off. If I sat next to him at the synod, I guarantee he wouldn't have said a word to me all night. He's cold oatmeal in thousand-dollar loafers. Dad and Granddad must have done some serious damage before leaving him alone on a hill with nothing but dead playmates.

"Have you heard about the little girl?"

He finally lights the damn cigarette and takes a puff.

"Everyone's heard about her. If you're implying that she's one of mine, she's not. Like most ghosts, mine are completely nonaggressive."

"You've never had any trouble with any ghosts?"

He shrugs. Turns the wheel and runs alongside a long stone burial mound.

"They have their moods just like anyone but they don't go around stabbing people."

I keep thinking about Amanda's story about the Imp of Madrid. She'd be right at home here.

"Pull over."

Teddy stops the cart under a towering stone angel.

"I don't buy any of what you're selling, Teddy. This funfair for ghosts and they're all tame little bunnies? I don't believe it. You're connected to the girl. I don't know how but you are. And, you see, she went after Saint James."

"Who?"

"Shut up. Coming after him means she came after me."

I take out the .45 and push it into his ribs.

"Do you know what happens to people who try to kill me or mine?"

Teddy has gone as white as his Rolls. He tries to swallow but chokes on his spit.

"Please. I don't know what you want. The girl isn't one of mine."

I say, "Liar," to double-check, but the moment has passed. I can read it in his heartbeat and his breath. The microtremors in his voice. The fucker is telling the truth. I keep the gun out anyway.

"Who could do that? Summon and control a spirit that powerful?"

"I don't know. Maybe someone from the temple. For all I know, it could be Amanda."

"Please. She can't even keep her kid in line. What's she going to do with a little Lizzie Borden?"

"Please don't shoot me."

"Are you sure? You can stay here forever with your drinking buddies."

"What can I say to make you believe me?"

I lower the gun, resting it in my lap.

"Nothing. You already have."

There's no way the girl is one of his. At least if she is, he doesn't know.

If she isn't connected to Osterberg, then I'm back to nothing and this whole trip has been pointless. Traven ought to appreciate that. At least one of us will be happy. I should shoot Teddy just for getting in the way of me getting King Cairo.

"Let's head back to the homestead, Teddy. All this fresh air is giving me hives."

On the way back, we pass what looks like a pretty ordinary cemetery. There's only one thing wrong.

"What's the story with that patch of graves?"

"What do you mean?"

"American tombstones point east at the rising sun. Those face west. I think your necro-Teamsters blew the gig."

He shakes his head.

"You have a good eye for someone so . . . excitable."

"I'm an asshole. I'm not blind."

"To answer your question, it's an English Gnostic plot. They were contrarians to their very core, rejecting the reality of this world. When they died they were buried and marked in the wrong direction to display their disdain for this world for all time."

"You'd make a billion dollars on *Jeopardy!* if all the categories were 'creepy facts about the dead.'"

"Would you mind putting your gun away, Mr. Macheath? I think you can see that I'm no threat."

"Yeah, but I'm a nervous passenger and it's kind of like my security blanket."

Teddy brings us back to the front of the house. He parks the cart back in the shade. Gets out and waits for me like an obedient kid.

"I hope there's no hard feelings, Ted. After the ghost went after Saint James, you understand I had to check you out."

"Of course. May I go now?"

"Sure. Run along, you scamp."

He doesn't move until I put the gun back in my waistband.

"Thank you for stopping by."

"My pleasure. See you around the afterlife."

Teddy heads for the house fast. He doesn't run even though he wants to. Yeah, someone did a real number on him if he thanked me after what I put him through.

I take it all back, everything I've ever said about the rich. I love the loud rich. I want the rich to be coked up, ugly, flashy, and decked in blood diamonds. Teddy's kind of mousy Emily Dickinson rich is so much worse. Trying to hate Teddy is like trying to hate wallpaper paste. When I get home, I'm going to write a love letter to the loathsome rich letting them know how much I appreciate them. Their glorious excess gives me something substantial to despise and I love them for it.

It takes twenty minutes to get down the hill. The sky is blue again when I climb on the bike but the clouds have turned a dull gray. I swear I can see rivets along their sides like they're floating islands of steel.

I'm about to kick-start the bike when my phone rings. Candy is as bad at patience as I am. But it's not her.

"Are you settling into your new home all right? Good water pressure? Is it clean under the bed? I hear the Chateau is close to all the hot spots."

It's a different voice this time. A woman's voice but I know who it really is. This isn't going to stop.

"You again. I know you're speaking through a mortal. Why don't you come over to the Chateau and we'll talk things over like a couple of friendly, reasonable monsters?"

"What would Alice say about you settling into Satan's residence so quickly and easily? Good thing she went back to Heaven when she did. Who knows what would have happened to her if she'd stayed with you."

"Don't talk about Alice, you Hellion puke. I know what you're trying to do. You want me back down there."

"Can you see her now? Her pretty face on the wall with all the other dead you have to account for."

"You think you want me back but trust me, you don't."

"Speaking of the dead, we're knee-deep in them down here. No one thinks you're coming back. Least of all me. Every burble and bubble in every sinkhole sounds like doom to the rabble."

"If I came back, I figure the best way to find you is to kill every Hellion down there. I don't know how long that would take but we've got all eternity to try. I hope you have a good call plan."

"If you think things were falling apart before, wait until you see what happens this time. Those poor lost souls without you to protect them."

"Just because I'm not coming back doesn't mean I don't have plans. They'll be fine long after you're drytt food."

"It's such a comfort hearing your voice."

"Yeah. You're my evil past. All the birds come home and shit on your head. A dead girl told me all about it. As far as I'm concerned, Hell can burn to the ground this time. Tell everyone down there I said it."

"No matter how far or fast you run, it won't be enough. I'll always be with you."

I hang up. Immediately, the phone rings but I ignore it. It keeps ringing all the way through Malibu.

I look for Catalina on the ride back but I can't find it. Sometimes the weather hides it. That's probably what it is.

CANDY IS IN THE TOP-FLOOR HALL at the Chateau Marmont when I open the grandfather clock.

"You've got to be kidding me."

"Are you going to stay out there or come in and see for yourself?"

She comes through and stands just inside the entrance trying to absorb it all. I've been here and I've lived in Lucifer's palace Downtown but I'm not sure she's ever been in such a conspicuous consumption situation before.

She puts her hands on my shoulders and turns me back and forth.

"Nice shirt. You going for your real-estate license?"

"Baby, the only real estate that counts is the pretty grave the other guy goes in."

"I love it when you talk dirty."

She walks around the main room, running her fingers over the expensive furniture and paintings.

I say, "Rinko's doing better?"

"She's apprenticing with Allegra. Why don't you let me worry about Rinko."

"Okay."

She circles the room to the area I've settled into near the chocolate-brown leather sofa, low coffee table, and a couple of overstuffed chairs near the TV.

"This is all yours?"

"I guess so. They keep it for Mr. Macheath. As far as I know, Lucifer is the only Macheath around."

"So you can do anything you want."

"Yeah. But I can't decide between a gun range or a macramé studio."

Candy jumps onto the sofa and bounces up and down like a kid on a bed, her short hair flapping around her face, her Chuck Taylors leaving soft footprints in the sofa cushions.

"You having fun up there?"

"This is really well built. They usually collapse by now."

As she jumps she takes off her jacket and throws it at me. Then her shirt. Then her sneakers and her pants.

Still jumping, she says, "Come on. Let's break it."

I catch her on a jump and drop her flat on her back. Climb on the sofa and kneel over her. She unbuckles my pants while I take off my shirt.

This time it's more like when we first stayed at the Beat Hotel together. We smash the coffee table when I flip her over on top of it. We knock over potted bamboos and splinter chairs. But we never make a dent in the sofa.

Later, my phone rings.

"Answer that and you're a dead man," Candy says.

"Since when do you ever not answer your phone?"

"That's not what I mean. I just don't want a bunch of monsters or demons coming over so I have to get dressed."

"There are robes in the bedroom."

"Really? I love robes."

She disappears down the hall. The phone stops ringing.

She comes out in a maroon terrycloth bathrobe as thick as the Lawrence, Kansas, white pages.

"Is 'robegasm' a word?" she asks. "Because if it is, I just had one."

My phone pings. There's a text from Kasabian. Someone broke into Max Overdrive.

I pick up the hotel phone and call the front desk.

"I need a car right now."

"Of course, Mr. Macheath."

I put down the phone and start pulling on my clothes.

"If you want to come along, you need to get dressed."

"I am dressed."

"No, you're not," I say, and hand her the folder pistol.

"What's this?"

"Push the button on top of the grip."

The folder snaps open from the bottom, like bomb-bay doors opening on the jet. Candy puts the rifle stock to her shoulder, sights around the room, and pulls the pistol's trigger making *Pow!* noises.

"That's exactly why I didn't load it."

"No fair."

"Them's the rules."

"Killjoy."

"You can always give it back if you don't like it."

"Are you kidding? This is my new bedtime teddy bear. You and Rinko can move over. I'm snuggling with this cuddly puppy every night."

I don't bother pointing out that she hasn't spent more than a few hours at a time with me, much less an entire night.

WE RIDE IN THE HOTEL LIMO to Max Overdrive. The driver doesn't talk to us. Doesn't even look at the rearview mirror. He must have heard about Lucifer's last driver. The one who ended up with his lips sewn together.

The side door at Max Overdrive looks like an angry drunk beat it to death with a sledgehammer. The store area on the first floor is as trashed as an empty room can be. Every rack and piece of shelving has been tossed around and smashed. That answers one question. It would have taken at least a half hour for one person to do this much damage. So, there was more than one. How many are left? I take out the Sig and start upstairs.

The door is half open. I push it the rest of the way with the toe of my boot.

Kasabian sits on the floor sipping a beer, his back to the minifridge. The bedroom is trashed but in better shape than the store. Nothing looks particularly broken. Just turned over and dumped on the floor. When Kasabian moves, one of his leg's gears scrape and crunch together. His left leg is bent to the side just below the knee. Hellhounds aren't dainty devices. It took a lot of strength to do that kind of damage.

"Goddamn," I say.

"Careful in case one of them is still around. They were very picky about blasphemy," says Kasabian.

"Hey, Kas," says Candy. "Does your leg hurt?"

"Only when I breathe or think."

Candy and I sit on the bed. Kasabian holds out a beer. We shake our heads.

"This wouldn't have anything to do with you and your beef with King Cairo, would it?"

"I don't know. Did they say what they wanted?" I ask.

"There wasn't a lot of chitchat. Mostly it was crashing and throwing and then a couple of them that bounced up and down on my leg asking where it was."

"Did they say what 'it' was?"

"I thought they meant the money. I told them where it was, and when they found it, they left it and took off. Two hundred grand in cash and they just walked away."

A pack of Maledictions lies next to the overturned desk. I get the smokes and light a couple, passing one to him.

"They're good Christian boys. Thou shall not steal and all that Ten Commandments hoodoo. The new Golden Vigil. Smashing the place and fucking up your leg is for the greater good but taking a nickel is a mortal sin."

Kasabian sets down his beer and tries to stand. The leg collapses the moment he puts weight on it. He lies down on his back.

"Look at me. I should have stayed on my skateboard."

"It's okay. I met a guy and he owes me a favor. He'll finish your body."

Kasabian props himself up on his elbows.

"And then what? I wait around for the next Curious George to come through the door and break my other leg? Everything was quiet and boring and fine until you came back, and now it's all shit again."

"That's pretty harsh and it's not even true," says Candy.

"So says the pretty girl with two working legs. If it wasn't for you, he would have been here to kick those guys' asses."

I say, "Don't go blaming her. You're the one who wanted me gone, Old Yeller."

"And you're the one who should've ignored me like you used to. What do I know? I'm a head on a stick. I get emotional."

The Magic 8 Ball and the singularity are still in the duffel at the Beat Hotel. I need to move them to the Chateau.

Kasabian tosses the beer can into a small pile across the room. He opens the fridge and takes out another.

"I've been watching Hell on your peeper, by the way. Without sound I can't understand everything, so maybe you can help me. Are burning churches a good thing or a bad thing?"

Shit. Merihim works fast. Deumos isn't going to take an attack lying down. I wonder if Semyazah let it happen to lure me back. That's not going to happen.

"Anything else?"

"Lots. I keep wondering about the uglies in uniform kicking the shit out of other uglies in red pants. Are red pants like a no-white-after-Labor-Day thing down there?"

"I need to get some things from the hotel to a safe place. If you don't want to stay here, you can come with us."

"And be crippled and a third wheel in your little love nest? No thanks. Cairo's Muppets know there's nothing here. They won't come back."

"I hope you're right. I'm going to put the side door up and lay down some hexes there and in the alley. You want to leave, you do it through the front door. I'll lay down some lighter hexes there."

"I hope I remember all that when I go to meet the cool kids at the Viper Room."

"Is there any Spiritus Dei around here?"

"There's a small bottle in the medicine cabinet."

On the way back to the Chateau, we make a quick stop at the Beat Hotel. I feel bad about Kasabian. If I'm a shit magnet, he's a getting-stomped magnet. Maybe I should've forced him to come with us. He would've loved that. One more thing to complain about.

At the Chateau, Candy and I break more furniture and afterward I try to figure out what to do next. The sofa won't budge. It sits like an iceberg surrounded by a sinking Titanic of broken furniture.

I go to the window to have a smoke. Something that might be an iceberg slides down Sunset Boulevard, tearing up the road, smashing windows in the buildings across the street, and crushing cars. Then it slips silently out of sight. The stars overhead blink on and off like colored Christmas-tree lights. In the distance, there's the glow of fire and sound of sirens. What's that line from *The Outlaw Josie Wales*? "Get ready, little lady. Hell is coming for breakfast."

IT COMES TO ME sometime around dawn. Fuck Saint James. I don't need him. I want the Key to the Room of Thirteen Doors but I'm doing fine without it. It's sure not enough to put up with this carousel of bullshit. An apple-cheeked ghost that has everyone jumpy as a chicken on an electric fence. A pushy skeleton whining like the clingiest girlfriend since Ophelia. A fruit bat in Malibu who has high tea with skeletons. Downtown is turning to shit again and L.A. is on fire. And I know things are only going to get worse. If Semyazah can't handle Hell, how am I supposed to? I don't need any of it. Fuck Saint James. Aelita and King Cairo are the ones I need to worry about and by "worry about," I mean kill.

WE'RE SITTING in a stolen Ford soccer-mom SUV between a hipster art gallery and a costume store.

"So this is your idea of a double date," says Allegra.

"You wanted back in the field. Welcome to the exciting world of trench warfare."

"We're just sitting here."

"We're waiting for the order to advance. Then we run straight into the enemy's machine guns and barbed wire."

"But until then, we have teriyaki, *gyoza,* and miso soup," says Candy, passing around Styrofoam cartons.

"And sake," says Vidocq. "I will light a candle for the lovely goddess Matsuo to honor every bottle she has given to us over the years."

Candy says, "That's going to be a fire hazard."

"What's life without risk?" says Vidocq.

"Long," says Allegra. "And with a lot of time to be grateful for the stupid things you didn't do. Like staking out a killer's apartment."

"We're not staking out Cairo's apartment. I think he owns the whole building."

"I feel better knowing we're after a man with real estate. It makes the whole thing seem friendlier," says Candy.

Allegra dunks a *gyoza* in soy sauce with her chopstick and feeds it to Vidocq. He smiles and kisses her lightly on the lips.

He says, "The good father tells me that you witnessed the Via Dolorosa yesterday."

I nod, keeping my eye on a doorway across the street.

"That I did. Traven's turning into a real bruiser. He's done that to other people? After Amanda stopped by, he wanted to come with me to meet Teddy Osterberg. That would have been a lot of laughs."

Vidocq shakes his head. Sips more sake.

"The father is a good and serious man. He would never abuse his power."

"If you say so. I just hope he isn't a kid with a loaded gun."

Candy stops eating for a second.

"Is that crack aimed at me?"

"Your gun is unloaded. I checked."

She turns to Allegra.

"Stark is going to take me shooting. You and Eugène should come with us."

"That sounds like fun."

Candy frowns.

"Father Traven isn't Sub Rosa, is he?"

"No."

"Then how can he do the Dolorosa?"

I shrug and take a bite of teriyaki chicken.

"Allegra isn't Sub Rosa and I taught her to make fire with her hands."

Allegra waves her chopsticks like shaking her head.

"You didn't teach me that magic. You gave it to me."

"Fair enough. But there are some kinds of old hoodoo that even civilians can do if they learn the right spells and make the right sacrifices. Which is the problem. They didn't grow up around real magic and they don't understand the power they're playing with."

Vidocq says, "Plus, much of the most common old magic is Baleful. That's what Father Traven used."

"What's Baleful magic?" says Candy.

"It's what Sub Rosas call black magic," I say.

Vidocq says, "The Sub Rosa believe in four systems of

DEVIL SAID BANG

magic. The Aethereal, which describes psychic abilities, scrying, telekinesis, and the like."

"In other words, standing-there magic," I say.

"There's Corporeal magic. Physical magic."

"Touchy-feely magic."

"Magic with the hands," says Vidocq. "Potions. Healing. Charm making. The reading of objects. And there's Baleful."

"Which is the most popular. Especially with kids. That's why even owning most of the old Baleful books is illegal and Traven has piles of them."

"What's the fourth kind of magic?" asks Candy.

Vidocq says, "Theoretical magic."

"What's theoretical?"

"God," I say. "The angels. The stuff that holds the universe together and makes it run. It might not even be magic the way we understand it. That's why it's theoretical."

Candy punches me lightly on the arm.

"Why don't you tell me these things?"

"I don't think about them. Why should I bug you? If you want to know more, talk to the Frenchman or borrow one of his books."

Vidocq makes a small bow, his mouth full of chicken. He swallows and says, "I'd be honored to loan you one or two."

"Just history. Nothing practical," I say.

Allegra laughs like she just got something over on her little sister.

"You can learn some magic after you learn to shoot," I say.

"Thanks, Daddy. You going to get me that two-wheeler for my birthday?"

"For that, I thought I'd teach you how to steal cars."

"I'm glad to see that this relationship is keeping you both out of trouble," says Allegra.

Candy puts her hand on Allegra's arm.

"Did he tell you where he's crashing?"

"Later. I'll tell her about it myself."

"Lucifer's private suite in the Chateau Marmont," Candy says.

Allegra looks at her food, moving it around the container with her chopsticks.

"You two must still be tight if he's loaning you his apartment."

Allegra had a tsunami-size freak-out when I was Samael's bodyguard while he was in town working on a movie. We barely spoke for a while. I didn't even say good-bye when I went back to Hell.

"I don't know how they'd be tighter," says Candy. She laughs.

"Shut up."

Candy looks at me, then at Allegra.

"Oh. Shit. I'm sorry."

She puts down her food.

"That's why I wanted to tell her," I say.

"Tell me what?" Allegra says.

I sit there like an idiot. My mouth won't open. I know what will happen when it does.

Vidocq says, "Darling, things have changed a great deal while Stark was in Hell."

Allegra's hand moves halfway to her mouth. A gesture of fear or concern or maybe she's just stifling a burp.

"My God. You didn't sell him your soul to get out, did you?"

"No," I say.

I keep looking across the street at Cairo's place.

"I am Lucifer."

I turn and Allegra is looking at me like I answered her in Urdu.

I say, "I didn't ask for it and I don't want it. Lucifer, the one you know about, dumped the job on me. I had to protect Alice and the other souls down there. I didn't have a choice."

She sets down her chopsticks.

"So now you take souls and lead people into sin."

"Mostly I just handle paperwork."

She looks at Vidocq.

"You knew about this?"

He nods.

"It wasn't my place. He wanted to tell you himself."

She looks at Candy.

"You know too. So I'm the only ignorant one here. Why is that?"

"Because of how you're acting now," I say. "You said that all that stuff that happened between us before was over and forgotten, but it's not. You liked it when I showed you how there was real magic in the world. But you couldn't handle it when it got down to the hard stuff. Magic and Lurkers were fun and sexy, but Heaven and Hell? You never even tried to deal with them and they're part of everything that's happening."

Allegra is quiet for a minute. She looks out the van's window at the sky.

"Is that why the sky keeps changing colors? Or the sink-holes?"

"I hadn't heard about sinkholes. And I don't know any-thing about the sky. I was talking about my current employ-ment situation. I'm half a person with half the universe on my back, and if you think that makes me a monster, then you can go to Hell yourself, princess. The door handle's there and there's a bus stop at the corner."

She sits for a minute looking at the floor, then slides the van's side door open hard enough that it almost comes back on her. She gets out and walks away.

Vidocq gives me a look he's never given me before. Like he actually wants to hit me.

"Well handled, boy. As graceful as always."

"You better hurry. Make sure she doesn't fall and crack her halo."

Vidocq gets out and slams the door closed.

Candy and I sit in silence for a minute.

"Well, that just happened," she says. "I have a big mouth. I'm sorry I said anything."

"Forget it. It was going to happen sooner or later. Wait here."

Lula Hawks, tattoos and scarred face, is walking our way. I get out and go around to her.

"Are you stalking me? You could have just asked for an autograph."

She takes a startled step back.

"What are you doing here?" she says.

"I asked first."

She nods toward Cairo's place.

"You know King lives over there, right?"

"Yeah. When he comes back, I'm going to kill him."

She pushes her hands deep into the pockets of her leather jacket. Takes a breath. That wasn't what she wanted to hear.

"How is it you know him and want to sell him out to a bad person like me?"

"We went out for a while," she says. Shakes her head. "I don't like what he's become since Aelita arrived. He's out of control."

"He's always been out of control."

"Not like nowadays."

"Why did you send me to that stiff, Manimal Mike? He was pretty much useless."

"What does 'pretty much' mean?"

"It means I have important questions and he didn't know shit."

"What did he say?"

"He said the girl tried to cut Saint James and that he ran off somewhere called Blue Heaven but he didn't know where it was."

"Anything else?"

"Nothing. I had to twist his greasy arm to do some Tick Tock work for a guy I know. That's all."

She nods like she's deep in thought. "So, he told you where this Saint James is and his motives for going there. And that the ghost girl attacked him specifically, not randomly. He also agreed to do tens of thousands of dollars of Tick Tock work for, I'm guessing, free. You call that nothing?"

"When you put it like that, it sounds like something, but I'm telling you, the way it came out of his whiskey hole, it sure seemed like a lot of nothing."

"I'm glad I could help you take a second look. Now I'd like to go before anybody sees me talking to you."

"What happened to your face? Did Cairo do that to you?"

"That's none of your business."

"I know but I'm uncouth, so I thought I'd ask."

"And I answered."

There's something about her.

"Have we met before? I mean before Blackburn's."

"Why did I even bother talking to you? You're as bad as King. Leave me alone."

She takes a couple of steps back and detours around me, heading the way she'd been walking when I stopped her.

I'm making all kinds of friends today.

When I get back to the van, Candy says, "Who was that? Another one of your porn stars?"

"Someone who tried to help me but then I asked a dick-headed question."

"She's the one who told you about Cairo?"

"Yeah."

"Looks like she told you the truth. There he is. Who's that with him?"

"No idea."

Cairo is walking on the other side of the street screaming and waving his arm like a windup gorilla. A few feet in front of him is a pretty dark-haired girl in a long sweater and boots over a tiger-print dress. He gets up right behind her, shouting loud enough that people turn to look. He curses at them too. Tiger Stripe Girl keeps walking, trying hard to ignore him. The leather bag on her shoulder slips and slides down her arm. Cairo puts a hand out and grabs the strap. Tiger Girl turns and shoves him hard with both hands. He grabs her arms and shouts in her face. Tiger Girl's face switches from disgust to fear. She bends back at the waist to keep some distance between her and Cairo.

I get out of the van and start across the street.

Horns honk. Growling engines pass behind me. Most cars stop. I squeeze between them and wave on the rest.

Cairo turns to check out the noise and sees me. He smiles. Gives me the finger. Tiger Girl tries to pull away but he has her tight and he's dragging her to his door. She swings one of her heavy boots out and roundhouses Cairo in the shin. He screams a stream of cryptic 'Bama curses and drops her arm, holding his leg. He lunges at Tiger Girl but pulls up short. Now it's his turn to look scared. He backs away and fumbles keys from his pocket. Opens the steel door to his building and slams it shut.

Tiger Girl stands there with the strap in her hand and her bag on the ground, having no idea what just happened. I do. The little ghost girl is behind her. Maybe twenty feet away and walking fast. She's laughing that high childish tinkling laugh. Finally Tiger Girl hears her and turns around. She just stands there. She knows who the girl is, and like most normal people when confronted with flat-out evil, her brain vapor locks and she freezes in place. Me, I pull the Sig and start shooting.

Cars skid. People scream and dive for cover.

All the noise snaps Tiger Girl out of her trance. She dives for cover and I keep firing. When I reach the sidewalk, I get between her and the ghost. The Spiritus Dei–covered bullets punch holes in the little girl. She stretches like warm taffy every time one hits but the hole snaps back and closes by the time the next bullet reaches her. She doesn't come any closer but she sure as hell doesn't leave.

Out of the corner of my eye, I see Candy jump from between two cars.

I yell "No!" but it's too late.

Candy heads straight for the girl, probably thinking she's wounded. She's not. The little girl turns, and even though Candy is moving Jade fast, the girl's knife blurs the air and she slashes Candy across the stomach. Candy falls. The momentum carries her a few feet away, where she lies on the pavement tucked up in a little ball. Ghost Girl gets over her with the knife held in both hands. I'm wearing a long, deep-pocketed coat I found in Samael's closet. I reach into a pocket and whistle. The girl looks at me. I do a Dizzy Dean windup and throw the Magic 8 Ball at her as hard as I can.

She screams when she sees it, a long, high-pitched wail like a giant's fingernails scraping over miles of blackboard. She shrieks louder when the 8 Ball hits her, tearing a hole in her side. There's no blood or bone. It looks like someone ripped a piece out of a photo in a magazine. The girl's face turns dark like she's about to start crying. She disappears.

I run to Candy. Pick her up in my arms and lean down to grab the 8 Ball. When I turn to get Tiger Girl, the little girl is there. She slashes at Candy again. I pivot away fast enough to protect Candy but the girl slices my arm. I hold the 8 Ball like a rock and slam it into her face. She turns dark again and this time her scream is loud enough to crack the glass in nearby cars. When she disappears, I grab Tiger Girl's arm.

"Come on. She might come back."

"That was the ghost."

"No shit."

I slide open the van's side door and put her and Candy in the back. Grab the big Chateau towel we were using as a tablecloth and have Tiger Girl hold it to Candy's stomach. Candy moans and tries to curl into an even tighter ball.

"What the hell . . . ?" she says.

"It's okay," I say. "I'm taking you to the clinic."

Cairo lives in Silver Lake and Allegra's clinic is right on the edge of the neighborhood. It's a short drive and even shorter through three red lights. Each one explodes when I throw hard, fast hoodoo to turn it back to green. Not having the Key to the Room of Thirteen Doors was a pain in the ass before, but now this is Candy's life. I never really thought about killing Saint James, but if Candy doesn't come through this, I might have to.

Someone inside must hear the van screech to a stop in the parking lot. Fairuza, the Ludere girl, opens the door and she and Rinko come out. Candy is awake and wobbly, but on her feet. Rinko guides her inside without even looking at me and Fairuza closes and locks the door.

Candy's blood is all over me and the back of the van. I pour the last of the sake on my hands and the knife slash on my arm. The burning feels good. I get back in the van and wrap Candy's towel around my arm. Toss the other towel to Tiger Girl.

"Your dress is messed up."

She looks down and sees streaks of blood. There really isn't that much but she lets out a panicked moan.

"No. Shit. Goddamn."

I'm tempted to tell her that even if God cared, He isn't in a position to do anything about it, but I keep my mouth shut. It's done enough damage today.

"Calm down," I say. "None of it's your blood."

Tiger Girl pats herself down enough to see that I'm right.

The sky shifts between blue, pistachio green, and the kind of deep purple I remember from when Downtown was on fire. Clouds turn to metal and burst into flame before going white and puffy again.

"We can't stay here and I can't drive this van across town."

I dial the Chateau.

"Can you send a limo for me right now?"

"Certainly, Mr. Macheath."

I give the clerk the address.

"Make it fast. Tell the driver I'll keep his or her ass out of the fire forever if they get here in ten minutes."

"I'll drive it myself."

"I don't care who. Just drive fast."

Tiger Girl's breathing is almost back to normal but her heart is still going Mach 5. Mild shock. She'll be fine. My adrenaline is off the charts. I want to kick the clinic door in and find Candy but I don't want to slow Allegra working on her.

My goddamn arm won't stop bleeding.

"What's your name?" I ask Tiger Girl.

"Patty Templeton."

I wrap the towel around my arm and hold it out to her.

I say, "Tie the ends together, Patty."

She takes the ends of the towel and pulls them tight.

"I'm Stark. You can ride with me unless you want to get out and walk home."

"No fucking way."

"Good. Now we're friends and we're going to talk to each other, and no bullshit, right?"

I fire up the van and pull it into a corner space behind some delivery vans. I'll come back after dark and ditch it somewhere.

"Yeah. Okay. Just keep her away from me."

"No problem. I know somewhere she'll never find us."

The limo pulls up with thirty seconds to spare.

"What about your friend inside?" Patty asks.

"She's in good hands."

Patty and I get in the limo.

"Looks like you got yourself a ticket to damnation paradise," I say to the driver.

He turns the big car around.

"What if I'm not damned?" he says. I recognize the voice from the phone.

"Trust me, pal. If you weren't before, you are now."

As we pull into traffic, I glance back at the lot. The hole Cherry dug yesterday is closed up good as new. Cherry works harder dead than she ever did when she was alive.

IF YOU EVER NEED to pull a girl into a secret room through a grandfather clock and not have her make a big deal about it make sure she's attacked by a knife-wielding ghost first.

I leave Patty on the couch and go to the bathroom for a new towel. This one is soaked through. When I come out, she's sniffing the open bottle of Aqua Regia.

"You might want to skip that. There's regular wine with the food."

She sniffs again and pours herself a little in a wineglass. Tosses it back and makes a face.

"I told you."

She pours more. I sit down across from where she was. She shrugs and brings the glass over. Yesterday's food is gone and there's a fresh spread laid out buffet-style.

"I've had worse," she says. "Some kind of akvavit?"

"Some kind."

"I've never seen it red before."

"It's pretty rare." I don't want to tell her that the red is semipoisonous Hellion herbs and a few drops of angel's blood. She's had a rough enough day.

"Was Cairo trying to kidnap you back there?"

She sips and rolls her eyes. Just holding a glass in her hand relaxes her.

"Don't be stupid. I'm King's girlfriend. If you can call it that. When he's not playing Gene Simmons and trying to fuck every other girl in the room. I think he's doing that Aelita bitch."

I wasn't expecting that. Her face is smudged with a moderate amount of sin signs but nothing special. A lot less than I'd expect from someone involved with Cairo.

"What were you arguing about?"

She shakes her head. Stabs the air with one finger.

"Fuck him and all his coked-up crew. They're disgusting. Have you met them? They're like animals."

"They can't help it. He's taking a drug that drives them insane. What were you and Cairo arguing about?"

"My job. What drug?"

"It's called Dixie Wishbone. Try to concentrate."

She finishes the glass and gives a little shiver.

"Sorry. I might be in some kind of shock, you know? Post-traumatic stress. That prick saved his own skinny ass and left me hanging, didn't he? Fuck that guy. Okay. Ask me anything you want. If it'll hurt that feather-wearing pussy dickbag, I'll tell you. You know, he has the tiniest balls of any guy I ever dated. Isn't that weird? Tiny balls."

"That's not really the information I was looking for. What were you arguing about?"

"I told you. My job."

"What's your job?"

"I'm a dreamer."

"What is that?"

She looks at me.

"You're that Sandman Slim guy, aren't you? I've seen you at Bamboo House of Dolls."

Blood trickles down my arm. I rewrap the towel and lean on the wound. It really should have started healing by now. Goddamn ghost wounds.

"You've been to Bamboo House? Do you like the jukebox?"

"Yeah."

"Who do you like better, Martin Denny or Arthur Lyman?"

"Martin Denny."

"Yeah. I'm Sandman Slim. What's a dreamer?"

"I thought you were supposed to be some hot-shit rock-star superhero. How is it you don't know about us?"

"Just because you know my name doesn't mean I'm on the Sub Rosa clubhouse mailing list. I spent my whole life running from that world."

"Looks like it did you a lot of good. You're bleeding and you don't have a clue how anything works."

"Figuring out Hell was easier than figuring out L.A. What's a dreamer?"

She waves her hand. Picks up her glass and goes back for more Aqua Regia. It's impressive.

"Stuck-up old people call us a real, real old name. Surgeons of the Night Sky. You know what we call ourselves?"

"Tell me."

She flops down on the couch, grinning. The Aqua Regia is hitting her hard.

"The Mile High Club."

"That's great, but I still don't know what you do."

"We dream. We make reality with our dreams."

Outside, smoke is blackening the sky from what I swear is the cone of a small volcano. Ash falls from the sky like dirty snow.

She raps her knuckles on the table. She pats the couch.

"See this? And this? We did this. There wouldn't be anything here without us."

"You're telling me you're God."

"Don't be stupid. Okay. We don't actually make reality. We just dream the forms and give them substance so they don't blow away."

A jet turns from the volcanic plume, heading out to sea, trailing thick smoke from one engine.

"You're telling me that the world is run by a bunch of cat-napping party girls and club boys?"

She sets down the glass and lets her head loll back.

"Not all reality. And some of the dreamers are old. There's

houses all over the world. But ours is the biggest. Duh. Hollywood. The big dream machine. This is where the world's imagination lives. The power spot for collective unconscious. All that crap. Anyway we're here and it works, so why fuck with it, you know?"

"I've never heard of you. Does everybody know?"

"Of course not. Just the right ones."

"How long have you been around?"

"How many birds on a wire? That long."

I hate these grade school history lessons. They're embarrassing and they're my fault. I didn't want to know how the world worked when I was young. Didn't want to know about the Sub Rosa or anything they cared about. Then, when I wanted to know, it was too late and I was busy just trying to stay alive Downtown. I've been playing catch-up ever since. Probably always will be.

"Okay. You're a dreamer and there's other dreamers and the whole nondreamer world will lose its Rice Krispies if you stop dreaming. Why were you arguing with Cairo about the job?"

"'Cause we're dying. That crazy little ghost bitch has something against us."

"The Sub Rosas being killed are all dreamers?"

"Mostly."

"You're why the sky is like a broken kaleidoscope and Catalina went AWOL."

She rolls her eyes, trying to be sarcastic, but she just looks drunk and scared.

"Now you get it. Murder is a downer and people get scared. Sometimes there aren't enough of us in any one place to hold reality together right."

Richard Kadrey

"Does Cairo blame you for reality breaking down? Is that what the fight was about?"

"No."

She gets up and goes for more Aqua Regia. I cut her off and pour regular wine into her glass.

"Ooh. A gentleman."

"I don't want you to melt your brain too soon."

"Whatever, dude."

She drops onto the couch.

"King wants me to quit or leave town. I tried telling him what I do isn't a job. It's like a vocation. It's what I am. I dream. That's it. But he says he's working for people who want to get rid of us regulars. Take over and put in their own dreamers. I thought he was just talking big. He does that sometimes."

What do you know? Cairo isn't a complete monster after all. Just a coward.

"Maybe he was trying to protect you by telling you to get out of town. If someone is using a ghost to kill dreamers, when the little girl appeared, he probably knew he couldn't fight her."

"He knew she was going to kill me and he left me to that little bitch? That fucker."

"Who runs the dreamers?"

"Big wheels in the Sub Rosa. Who else?"

"What happens if you stopped dreaming? If all of you in L.A. stopped completely."

"If we go down, the dominoes start falling. Ping. Ping. Ping."

She flicks her fingers, knocking over imaginary dominoes in the air.

"I don't know that the other houses can keep the whole world together without us. Next thing you know, nothing is what it used to be and then I don't know. Maybe we all just disappear. No one knows because it's never happened."

"Who in the Sub Rosa is in charge? Blackburn?"

"Do I look like Google? Go buy a fucking laptop."

My arm is starting to hurt. I get my own glass of Aqua Regia and walk around until I find some Maledictions. I take the pack back to the table, tap one out, and try to light it one-handed. Patty snickers at me. Takes the cigarette, puts it in my mouth, lights it, and hands it back to me.

"Thanks."

"No worries. I'd've done it for a dog."

My head is spinning a little. Not with pain or liquor but with all that's going on. Not to mention worrying about Candy. I check the time. Too soon to call the clinic, god-dammit.

"So someone is trying to replace the current dreamers or kill them off. Cairo is working with them but he can't use his muscle because that would bring down the heat and whoever is running him knows he'd squeal like a piglet. That means whoever is behind all this also controls the girl. You can't arrest or kill a crazy ghost. She's a good cover. And maybe you kill a few nondreamers to make the killings look random. It's all for the greater good, right?"

"If you say so."

"I say so because I'm pretty sure I know who's behind this. The question is why does an angel care about our reality? Tell me this. If you're walking around with your boyfriend, then dreamers must work in shifts, right?"

"Yeah. Two days on and three days off so we get our heads back together."

"Where do you do your dreaming?"

She sits up, almost spilling her wine. She points to what she thinks is north. It's not.

"There's a place in Universal City. Near the movie studio. It looks like a regular office building. Really boring on the outside. Like camouflage, you know? The tour buses go right by it. We're in there."

"Has anyone been attacked around there?"

"No."

Good. That means the building has good protection against spirits.

"You should go there and stay and get the others to do the same. As long as you're inside, the girl can't get you or she would have done it already."

"Anything you say, Sir Galahad."

"Goddamn arm."

I need both hands to tie the towel tighter, but if I hold the cigarette between my lips, the smoke goes straight up my nose and I can't set it down now because the towel will come off completely.

Patty comes around the table.

"Let me help you. Goddamn men. They can tie you to a bed but you can't do up your own shoes."

"Thanks. I'm usually a fast healer. It should have stopped bleeding by now."

"Shoulda woulda coulda," she says. "Since like you said we're all BFFs now and I can ask things I always wanted to know, what the hell kind of name is Sandman Slim?"

"Well, I'm not fat."

"I grasped that."

She gets the knot good and tight. Then sits back to admire her handiwork.

"They used to watch a lot of old movies in Hell before the cable went out. A *Sandman* is an old B-movie word for 'hit man.'"

"Oh. Okay. Wait. They have cable in Hell?"

"Now they do. It was out but we got it working again."

Patty doesn't hear or has lost interest in what we've been talking about.

She says, "This looks like a nice hotel. Don't they have a doctor or something?"

That's what happens to you when you spend eleven years in the arena tending your own wounds. When you're hurt, you look around for rags and string to hold whatever part of you is falling out on that particular day. A doctor is way down on the list of things you think about when you're a gladiator slave. Lucifer, on the other hand, wants a whole team of neurosurgeons flown in from Switzerland and he wants them now.

I dial the hotel phone.

"Yes, Mr. Macheath."

"I need the hotel doctor. Do you have one?"

"Not one to tend your, um, special needs."

"I'll take a seamstress and a nurse right now. Send up whatever you've got. Tell them to keep their eyes closed. I'll bring them in the clock."

"Very good, sir."

I'm bleeding all over the nice furniture and Candy is hurt

and L.A. is being buried in volcanic ash. I wonder what's going on in the rest of the world. I'm formulating a new mantra. WWWBD. What Would Wild Bill Do? I can't burn down Cairo like I did when I set Josef and the skinheads on fire. I'll have to kill him later. And I don't know where Aelita is. The little girl is the only clear line to anything I've got, and if she isn't out slicing and dicing, I know where she'll be. That's what Bill would do. If he couldn't find the head of the bad guys, he'd find the arms and break them. It's time to say *hola* to the Imp of Madrid.

"When the doctor leaves, we'll get you to the dreamer safe house."

"Okay. Is it all right if I take a nap while we're waiting?"

"I'll get you some aspirin. You're going to need them."

AFTER THE HOTEL DOC STITCHES ME UP, I take Patty downstairs and we catch a cab just like regular schmucks. No limos today. I don't want anyone at the hotel knowing where we're going. All the cabbie will see is me taking my half-tanked squeeze to Universal to throw up on the big plastic shark.

The hotel is practically empty. Even in L.A., the Apocalypse is bad for business.

The freeway north is a joke. Angelinos and tourists are fleeing the city, locking traffic in a snarl of bumper-to-bumper traffic like a university experiment demonstrating just how impossible it is to flee L.A. And it's not like the sky is any closer to normal up here. Clouds shoot overhead at double speed, like the whole sky is on fast-forward. The volcano and ash have disappeared as cleanly and thoroughly as Catalina but it seems to have made an impression on the unwashed. If that wasn't enough, the cabbie's radio explains how as part of its clever plan to panic even the nonpanicked population, the powers that be have shut down both LAX and the Burbank Airport.

I have the cabbie drop us off by the office buildings at the edge of Universal City. Instead of heading back in to town, the cab gets on the freeway north with the other abandon-the-ship types.

Patty leads us into the heart of Universal City, past huge glass buildings and to a squat four-floor building hidden behind a row of trees, just off the regular tourist route. There's a guard station but it's empty. I get the feeling the big office towers are deserted too.

Patty takes a pass card from her purse and lets us in. She seems perfectly sober now. The girl can hold her liquor. I've never seen anyone mix Hellion and civilian booze before. I hope she doesn't explode and destroy the rest of the world.

The first floor of the dreamers' building looks like any un-finished office space. A big open area with cable for DSL and phones. A couple of offices roughed in at the back. Walls a neutral shade of suicide beige. How could you work in one of these places and not seriously consider going apeshit postal at least once? An optional murder-suicide pact ought to be part of the hiring agreement right next to the 401(k) plan.

The stairway to the second floor is locked. Patty waves her card again and the door clicks open.

It's dark inside and smells faintly of asphodel and bella-donna. Forgetting and stimulation. Sounds like a party to me.

A cobweb brushes my face. I start to push it away but Patty says, "Don't touch it. Don't touch any of them."

Through the dark I see more of the webs. They grow thicker the higher we climb. As my eyes adjust to the dark, I see that they're not webs. They're long, almost invisible filaments, like fishing line. Only they seem to hum and whisper.

"It sounds like they're talking to each other."

Patty glances back over her shoulder.

"Good ears. They're alive. When we're asleep, our nervous systems merge with the Big Collective and these nerves broadcast our dreams."

The second floor is a neural obstacle course. Most of the nerves are bundled along the walls like computer cords but the densest bunch run out from a twelve-sided wood-and-brass enclosure in the middle of the room.

A room off this one is a small but comfortable-looking rest area with a fridge, a massage table, and big overstuffed chairs.

The floor around the wooden enclosure is inlaid with the images of silver arches. The twelve vaults of Heaven. Patty touches each door as she walks around the big toy box. And stops by one. She pulls it open.

"Someone isn't here today. Johnny Zed is supposed to be in here. I hope he's all right."

Inside the chamber is a fleshy pitcher-shaped pod of clear fluid. Nerve filaments drift inside like pale seaweed.

"This is it," says Patty. "Dreamer central."

"You get in there?"

"Strip down for a two-day skinny-dip. It's not bad. It's warm and you don't feel a thing. You just float there. A womb with a view."

"What do you dream about?"

"It's hard to describe. It's not things so much as the places between them. I wouldn't dream of a table or you. I dream about big empty spaces. The hollow parts inside things. The atoms and molecules. I don't dream about how fucked up things are out here but how perfect things are when you go deep down inside them."

"Sounds nice."

"Want to strip down and try it? You're a little tightly wound, you know. It would probably do you some good."

"What's the dreamer safeword?"

She does a mock sigh.

"You've been to Hell but won't even give Heaven a try. Silly boy."

She closes the door and crosses her arms, looking serious for the first time since I got her away from the ghost.

"What happens now?"

"What happens is you stay here. Go inside the Silly Putty and try to calm down the sky a little or just hang around the lounge. I'll see what I can do about the little girl. Don't leave until you hear from me."

I start back down the stairs, stepping carefully around the dreamers' nerves.

"Hey, Sandman," says Patty from the top of the stairs. "Thanks for today. You didn't have to do all that."

"No problem. I'd have done it for a dog."

She smiles and goes into the lounge.

I TAKE A CAB to Max Overdrive. Thank God for cabbies. People joke that when the world ends, all that'll be left are the roaches. They forget about the cabbies. As long as the roaches have money to pay or something to trade, the cabbies will be there to drive them from their roach motels to their roach offices and out to the roach suburbs, slamming on the brakes, cursing out the window, and overcharging them all the way.

The freeway into the city is almost empty, so we make good time. I go into the store through the front door, careful to step around the hexes.

Kasabian must have heard me come in because he isn't surprised to see me.

"Come to check if the Glory Stompers came back and finished me off?"

"Remember when you said I should have been unreasonable and ignored you the other night?"

"Yeah?" he says, looking more nervous than I've seen him since I cut off his head.

"You got your wish. Get your gear together. You're coming with me."

"Where?"

"Somewhere safe. Those guys who broke in here are trying to change the entire fabric of reality and they're using hit squads and a crazy little ghost with a great big fucking knife. You want out of harm's way, you come with me right now."

"I didn't know you cared."

"Of course I care. You know where my money is."

"It's my money. Does this hovel have cable, because if I have to stay with you I'll need a lot of distraction."

"It's nice as hovels go. There's indoor toilets and everything."

Kasabian doesn't want to go with me but he doesn't want to stay in the store on his own anymore. He slowly closes his laptop. He's trying to figure out a way to get me to stay so he doesn't have to leave, especially on a gimp leg. He drums his fingers on the desk and gives up.

"There's a tracksuit on the floor next to the bed."

He has to struggle into the suit because of his leg. I don't offer to help because I'm not in the mood to get barked at. It takes him a few minutes and he's sweating but he finally gets the clothes on.

"You look like you're in the Russian Mob."

"Yeah? Then carry my crap, Comrade. I'm a cripple."

We take the same cab back to the Chateau. When I take Kasabian through the clock, he just stands there looking the place over. The celebrity-magazine furniture. The trays of food and booze. The thick robe Candy tossed over the arm of a chair. The epic bedroom with a closet full of clothes.

He limps back into the main room. Holds out his arms and drops them in exasperation.

Finally he says, "Fuck you."

"*Mi casa es su casa* blah blah blah."

"Fuck you."

"There's food over there."

He goes to the spread, balancing himself on furniture on the way over. He looks at it and turns.

I say, "I know. Fuck me. Quit whining. It's your lucky night. You're going to help me commit suicide."

"Goody."

MY NEW CHEST scar itches at the thought of me hurting myself again but I don't have a lot of choices.

Before I off myself, I dial the clinic to check on Candy. No answer. Are they busy or screening my calls? I let it ring and then call back. Still nothing. Not a problem.

I leave Kasabian sucking down a plate of filet mignon and onion rings the size of horseshoes while *Django the Bastard* plays on the big screen. I forgot how movies look better when they're not on a laptop screen. It's a nice change. I don't bother saying good-bye. Between the movie and the food, Kasabian wouldn't hear me anyway. I go to the garage, steal a Volvo (every crook's go-to car when they don't want to be noticed) and drive to the clinic.

Traffic isn't bad. Everyone who isn't running for the hills must be bugging in. I only have to run a couple of red lights to get across town. When I get there, I beach the Volvo across three spaces in the parking lot, get out, and give the clinic door a copper knock. That authoritative knuckle rap cops have to master before they get to make the donut run solo.

The door opens and Allegra comes out, pulling it closed behind her.

"You thought if you didn't answer the phone, I'd just go away?"

"Sorry. I thought the answering machine was on."

" 'Course you did. I want to see Candy."

I start for the door but Allegra puts her hand on my chest. Then pulls it away when she touches the armor.

"She's all right. It was just a slash and didn't go too deep. I closed her up and gave her something to sleep. She'll be out for a few hours. Rinko's taking care of her."

"Speak of the Devil."

Rinko hits Allegra's shoulder when she pushes open the clinic door. She comes right up to me. I'm ready for the slap

I know is coming. I got her girlfriend hurt. I won't even try to stop her.

Rinko's hand flashes up. The shirt rips. Sparks kick off the armor. She slashes down again with the scalpel, this time at my throat. I step back and catch her hand, shoving her hard enough into the clinic door to rattle the glass.

"Don't hurt her!" yells Allegra.

I won't. I can see it in her eyes. She's possessed. Someone is having fun Downtown. Rinko already hates my guts, so it probably wasn't hard getting in her head and tweaking her to come at me. I was hoping that with Aelita up here, the possession games would stop for a while. Maybe I should have burned Hell on my way out of town. Maybe I should have hung more skins on the fences. Was I too awful a Lucifer or too nice? Neither. I was just lousy. Am just lousy. I should have seen this coming.

The clinic door opens again and Vidocq comes out. He has another scalpel and the same dead-fish possessed look in his eyes. When he raises his hand to slash me, I pop him once in the jaw. Not hard enough to hurt him. Just hard enough to lay him out.

Allegra gets between us, dragging poor dazed Rinko with her.

"Eugène. Stark. What's wrong with you? Stop it."

"He can't hear you. He's possessed. So was Rinko."

Rinko is starting to come around. Allegra kneels by Vidocq and checks his eyes. Looks back at me.

"Why are you looking at me like that?" she says.

"These days, when one possessed person goes down, another pops up. I thought you were going to go off with the scalpel next but maybe you're immune because of the angel hoodoo you work with all day. Lucky for both of us."

Rinko comes over and helps Allegra get Vidocq back on his feet. She looks at me funny. She has no idea how she got outside or why my shirt is ripped or why I'm dressed like an extra in a Hercules movie.

"Vidocq will be fine. When his head clears, he won't remember a thing."

I get around them and open the door. Allegra looks like she might slash me without being possessed.

"We don't need your help."

She waits until I step away from the door before taking Vidocq inside.

"I'm not the villain here. I'm the one who got knifed."

"This time," says Allegra, pulling the door behind her. I grab it before it closes.

"Take care of Candy. And don't let either of these two near her."

"I know how to run my own clinic."

"Really? Does your staff settle all its arguments with a knife fight?"

Allegra doesn't say anything. She tries to pull the door closed. I don't let her.

"When I've done what I have to do, I'm coming back and I'm going to see Candy whether any of you like it or not."

I let go of the door. She pulls it closed and locks it.

"It's nice to see you've still got the magic touch with people."

The voice is behind me. I recognize it because it's mine. I turn around and look at me.

Saint James is dressed in tan khakis and a blue pullover
with an off-brand logo over the pocket. He looks like me if
I was eleven years younger and a Mormon kid on my mis-
sionary work. I'd never admit it but I feel strange and it even
hurts a little seeing myself without all the scars. The guy I
was before I went Downtown has been gone so long I don't
even remember him but I'm looking at him and that's bad
enough. What's worse is that Saint James, patron saint of
traitors, cowards, and general pricks, knows it.

"How's Heaven, pal? I mean Blue Heaven. What the hell
is that? Some kind of time-share hideout with D. B. Cooper
and Ambrose Bierce?"

"I was about to pull you out of Vidocq's way but as usual
you solved the problem with your fist. You're punching friends
these days. It's good to see a man broaden his interests."

"The only reason you'd save me is because half my skin is
yours."

"True enough, but you didn't have a shred of common sense
up here, and Hell hasn't helped you gain any perspective."

I take out a Malediction. Sit on the hood of the Volvo and
light it. I don't offer Saint James one. No way this milque-
toast smokes.

"You're wrong. I have plenty of common sense. I've hardly
killed anyone since I've been back. Okay, maybe those ten
guys at Blackburn's. But I'm the injured party here. Everyone's gunning for me because of something you did."

He shakes his head. Clamps his jaw angrily before
speaking.

"I didn't kill the mayor's son and you know it. It was the

ghost. I was trying to stop her just like I tried to stop her before. I was there when the boy was killed, so it was easy to pin it on me. I think someone is protecting the girl."

"If I'm supposed to be impressed with your detective skill, you're going to have to try harder. I know all that and I know who's doing it." It's a lie but I'm not about to let this asshole in on how in the dark I am. "All I need to figure out is why. You know, even if you showed up with all the pieces of the puzzle and a carton of Carlos's tamales, it doesn't change the fact that you left me to clean up Mason's shit. Now I have to clean up yours and I'm supposed to swoon over a happy reunion because you finally stepped up?"

"Right. Like you never left me holding the bag. Running wild up here and down below. Getting us backed into corners so that I had to figure a way out."

I puff the Malediction and blow smoke in his direction but the wind carries it away.

"All that's what's changed. Being on my own Downtown, I learned to think more before I break things. I did some bad things as Lucifer but not nearly as many as I could have. I saved the place from imploding and taking a whole lot of souls down with it."

Saint James smirks. He isn't buying it.

"I saw you playing cowboy with Great-Granddad. How is Wild Bill?"

"You were there spying on me?"

"Checking up on you. Believe it or not, I was concerned."

"I bet you were. You found out it's lonely out here on your own and you want back in my head. That's why you're here.

Forget it. I'm done with the *Three Faces of Eve* routine. I don't need you."

He looks me over. Another shirt ruined. I need a tailor or at least a clothes fairy. I wonder if Manimal Mike can make one for me.

"Are you going to wear that armor forever?" says Saint James. "You'll never be more than half a person without me."

"I read books when I was Downtown. I learned about the Greeks. 'Loss is nothing but change and change is Nature's delight.' Marcus Aurelius said that."

"Marcus Aurelius was Roman."

"I know. Ain't that a bitch?"

This time, when I blow smoke, I get him. He steps away, waving his hand at the cloud.

"This armor is why I don't need you. I have all the power I had when we were together and even a few new tricks."

"The armor hasn't improved your thinking."

"The only thing you have on me is the Thirteen Doors Key and I can live without that."

"Really? How much longer can you ride that beast of a motorcycle before the police catch up to you? How many more cars can you steal? The police aren't fools. Julie Sola told me they have a whole task force looking for the car-theft ring. You're a whole criminal conspiracy."

"A task force just for me? I'm flattered as hell. I've never been a gang before."

"You realize that if you're captured, they'll take the armor. And since you don't have the key, you'll be stuck in jail. Just another mortal fool in a sea of monsters."

I flick the cigarette butt at him and burn a small hole in his pullover before he flinches out of the way.

"You left me to the monsters when you blew Hell. Let me change what I said before. It's not that I don't need you. I don't want you. Have fun in Blue Heaven."

I get off the Volvo hood and start around to the driver's side.

"You mean it, don't you? This isn't just the anger talking. You really intend to give up half of yourself forever."

I pull up my shirtsleeve and show him the Kissi arm.

"Remember this? I lost part of me already and I learned to get along without it. I can do it again."

"Can you honestly say you don't miss the Room of Thirteen Doors? The quiet. The perfection. Knowing you're at the still silent heart of the universe and that no one can touch you."

"I miss it like a junkie misses the needle. But it's like Herodotus said—and that guy I know is Greek: 'Very few things happen at the right time and the rest do not happen at all.'"

"How does that even apply?"

"'Cause you're a day late and a dollar short, so fuck off."

He leans on the top of the Volvo.

"Without the Key you can't get to Blue Heaven and you'll never see me again."

"You can travel with the Key but I have people who watch my back. What do you have besides frequent flier miles?"

"Everyone who watches your back gets shot, stabbed, or punched. How long will they put up with that?"

I get in the car. Talk to him through the open window.

"Good-bye. Say hi to Amelia Earhart for me."

Saint James steps into a shadow and is gone.

"YOU KNOW, I had to kill myself a little in Hell a few days back."

"Maybe you'll get it right this time," says Kasabian.

When someone asked Willie Sutton, the safecracker, why he broke into so many banks, he said, "Because that's where the money is." When you want to find a ghost who tried to kill your girl (okay, not technically mine but I like her a lot), you go to the Tenebrae because that's where the ghosts are.

I stick the tip of black blade into my arm until the blood flows.

"This is the funniest thing you're going to see all day."

Kasabian looks at me and turns abruptly away.

"Jesus. Give a guy some warning. Why are you doing that? You don't have enough pain in your life?"

"It's not the cutting that's funny. It's that I'm cutting the nice clean stitches the hotel doctor just put in. I need some blood."

"What for?"

Don't think for a second that just because I'm hard to kill, getting hit or burned or cut doesn't hurt. It feels the same to me as it does to anybody else. It's just that I get over it faster. When it's happening, though, I feel every little twitch and twinge of pain. Cutting into a recent wound is an especially interesting experience. There's a lot of internal "What the hell are you doing?" screaming.

"Remember when you tried to shoot me with that booby-trapped weapon? The Devil's Daisy that Mason gave you?"

"Yeah," says Kasabian. "Damn thing ruined a perfectly good surrogate body."

"Remember that I talked to you in the deadlands when you were gone but not in Heaven or Hell yet?"

"Yeah? Is that what that's about?"

I nod. Grimace when I dig down too deep and hit bone.

"Shit. I'm going back to the same neighborhood to talk to another ghost. She gave me this little paper cut, so I figure blood from the wound will get me close to her."

"You cut yourself up when you came to see me?"

"Worse than this. Usually you have to slit your wrists and be at death's door for this trick. I'm hoping I can get away with a little less blood this time."

He takes a chance and sneaks a look in my direction. The blood is flowing and I'm dripping it around a Magic Circle I've carved in the tile floor. Thirteen interlocking circles and lines meeting at seventy-two points. Metatron's Cube. The Flower of Life.

"The really funny part is that I shouldn't even have to do this. Lucifer can hop from Hell to Earth. I bet he can get to ghost central too but I still haven't figured out ninety-nine percent of his power."

The circle is nearly closed with blood.

"When you see me come back, it would be swell if you helped me out by breaking the circle. Just wipe up a little blood."

"I was just sitting here thinking that what I'd love to do after a nice lunch is wipe up your body fluids."

I toss off my sliced shirt and strip naked except for the armor.

"The Tin Man comes out of the closet at last."

I toss him the ripped shirt.

"Shut up, and when you see me twitch, you can use that to break the circle."

"You're not going anywhere, are you? This is just some kind of frat hazing where I have to stare at your sack while standing on one leg and reciting the alphabet backward."

He picks up a chair, limps over, and sets it down a few feet from me.

"Don't get lost over there. Candy will find me and break my other leg."

"That's the trick. Anyone can go over. It's the smart ones who come back."

"I never thought of you as one of the smart ones."

"Me neither. That's why there's Plan B."

"What's that?"

"I'll let you know when I think of it. Hand me that bottle of Aqua Regia."

He does and I take a big swig.

"One for the road."

I put the bloody blade between my teeth. Normally I'd use a crow or raven feather for something like this but the wet knife will have to do.

Bleeding myself has left me light-headed. I lie down and wait for a little touch of death. I drift and sink and it swallows me up.

I OPEN MY EYES underground in a subway tunnel. L.A.'s subway system isn't a system so much as a miniature golf course spread over a few miles and connected with trains.

New Yorkers laugh when they see our puny line but it's ours and we love it and mostly ignore it. This is L.A. Sitting in traffic in your own car is much more chic than actually getting anywhere. Only squares want to be places.

The tunnel looks clean but unused. There's a layer of dust on walls and platform. I climb down to the tracks and walk toward a light maybe a quarter of a mile ahead. I bounce off the walls a couple of times and trip on the damned rails. I'm still woozy from the trip down, but when I reach the platform, it's worth it. The sign above the tracks reads TENEBRAE STATION.

The escalator has come completely off its track, so I take the worn stone stairs up to the street.

Travelers only ever go to the open deadlands. No one except necromancers and fetishists ever goes to the populated areas. Now I see why.

I'm still in L.A. The Tenebrae might be another Convergence. Whatever it is, it looks like all the landfills west of the Mississippi have been dumping their trash here since the beginning of time. I stumble through debris like an arctic explorer in a snowstorm. Garbage drifts down the long boulevards of abandoned buildings and forms loose drifts of newspapers, parking tickets, menus, and shopping lists. Swarms of flies move through the streets like flights of migrating birds. I'm on Broadway near the old Chinatown gate. Burned-out cars lie everywhere in heaps like a giant kid got bored and dropped them here. If I can't save a few of the dreamers, L.A. is going to look like this place soon. If we don't fall into the Twilight Zone like Catalina.

Ghosts are funny. They have a lot of self-esteem issues.

The Tenebrae place looks like some of the shittier neighborhoods in Hell, which is ironic since most ghosts are here because they're afraid of crossing over.

It doesn't take long before I'm noticed. Ghosts lying curled up on benches or sitting in windowless coffee shops stare at me. Some take a few tentative steps in my direction before losing strength or interest or both. Most look as windblown and worn out as the empty buildings. Most but not all.

I recognize Cherry Moon from all the way across Chinatown Plaza. Her spirit is still strong enough to look better than the other ragged ghosts. Closer to her ideal form, which for her is a walking, talking anime schoolgirl complete with loose socks and pigtails. That kind of thing was creepy enough when she was alive, but it looks worse now that she's dead. Her skin is a pale gray and her eyes are bloodshot. She looks like Sailor Moon's evil twin. Cherry comes over and looks up at me coquettishly like she's practiced the move a thousand times in front of a mirror. At least she doesn't smell as bad as she looks.

"You came. I can hardly believe it. My slightly smudged white knight."

"Hi, Cherry. It's nice to see you with a face."

"Are my eyes still the mirrors of my soul?"

"Sadly, yes. Having skin must be nice. I love what you've done with the place."

"God's little acre."

"Of shit."

She touches my nose with the tip of her index finger.

"Don't be mean, James."

She loops her arm in mine and we walk through the end-less garbage dump.

"This isn't the afterlife. This isn't anywhere. You can leave anytime you like."

"Is that how it works? How kind of you to explain."

"If I'm inconveniencing you, I can go."

She tightens her arm around mine.

"Please, James. Play nice. You don't know what it's like here. We all died once and now we have to do it again because of that little bitch. It looks like it hurts even more the second time around."

"I'm not killing the Imp until I talk to her, so don't get your pigtails knotted up if I don't go in like Bruce Lee."

We turn out of the plaza and head downtown.

"She's a monster. She kills us. Hurt her for me, James."

"You know that back in the world I'm lying in a pool of my own blood. I'd really like to get things rolling before I muss my hair."

"Cool your jets, jet boy. We're almost there."

A mob is following us. I must be the most interesting thing that's happened here since the girl. How sad for these dopes. How terrified do you have to be to put up with this dismal trailer-park universe? If I had time, I'd make every one of these assholes a deal. Let go. Come to Hell. You can camp out in Eleusis, the town God built for righteous pre-Jesus pagans. It's still the nicest place down south. Crap parking but no torture and other reasonable souls to pal around with. I'd do it just to clear out this shit sink. But none of them would do it. They're too chewed up by the demons in their own brains. I want to blame God for these losers. For not making Himself known and available to humans, but I wonder if it would make a difference to this crowd. There's something willful about this kind of self-punishment. Without realizing it, they've made their own second-rate sitcom Hell.

Cherry says, "I hear you killed Mason."

"Nope. He killed himself."

"But you helped."

"Russian roulette is a hell of a game. Second place sucks as much as, well, there isn't anything worse than second."

"You cheated, didn't you?"

"I'm not stupid enough to play Russian roulette with Mason for real."

Up ahead, it looks like a small nuke went off. A deep crater is spread over four square blocks. Buildings and the remains of cars and street signs lie in heaps on the edge of the blast zone.

"What's Hell like?"

"It's not as bad as this. Normal people would rather be inconvenienced by Hellions than be this bored for the next billion years."

"They don't have any imagination. We make our own fun. Did you ever lie on your back, look up at the sky, and make garbage angels? It's very cathartic."

"You tunnel in the dirt and play in garbage. You've come a long way since the Lollipop Dolls."

"I miss the old gang. I wonder how they are."

"I'm dating someone with an anime and manga fetish. I'll ask her."

The crowd behind us keeps growing. It's officially a throng

on its way to becoming a mob. Off to the side are groups of kids in dirty rags—eight, nine, and ten years old—standing off by themselves.

"Who are they?"

Cherry doesn't even look at them.

"They're lost kids. Ones that all died badly."

I think she's telling the truth. The kids look worse than I do. They're crisscrossed with knife slashes. Long straight cuts along their throats. More slashed and crescent-moon marks on their arms and faces.

"Does anyone do anything for them?"

"They're not exactly chatty. Little savages. They keep to themselves and we leave them alone."

Cherry stops and points down into the crater.

"There she is."

Our ghost escort backs away from the hole and keeps going to the end of the block.

The only things in the bottom of the crater are the Imp and the burned and rusted chassis of a school bus. She sits on the bumper in her blue party dress, idly stabbing the ground with the knife.

I start down the steep crater wall, walking sideways to keep from sliding. Pieces of broken pavement and loose dirt tumble down around me. The Imp looks up and screams. A full-on animal scream, nothing held back. She raises the knife and rushes me. I get down to level ground as fast as I can and pull the 8 Ball from my coat.

She freezes in her tracks. Takes a couple of steps back. I stay frozen. In a few minutes, she decides I'm not going to charge her, so she goes back to the bus bumper and stabs the ground harder than before, digging up fist-size clods of packed dirt.

When I get close enough to hear her, she says, "Are you here to kill me?"

"You think that because of the 8 Ball. The 8 Ball kills you?"

She looks at me.

"Qomrama Om Ya."

"What is it?"

"It's not yours."

"I know. It's Aelita's."

"No. She had it but it's not hers either."

"Is it yours?"

She shakes her head.

"You're not one of his. Who are you?"

"One of who's?"

"The cruel one."

"King Cairo?"

She jams the knife angrily into the ground. It goes in up to the hilt. I forgot how strong she is.

"I'm not allowed to say."

"You can tell me. I'll make sure the cruel one doesn't hurt you."

"I can't."

"Tell me which who and I'll stop it."

"The old one. He watches through the dark."

"Lucifer? Is it the old Lucifer's?"

She gets up and walks away. I follow her.

"If it's not Lucifer who watches you through the dark . . . Another ghost? God?"

The crowd of spirits spreads out around the rim of the crater. They back away from whichever direction the girl faces like she's a four-foot-tall icebreaker.

"It's God, isn't it? I'm Lucifer, so I'm not one of His. That's what you meant. That's why you didn't hurt me."

"Why would I?"

"Is that who you kill? Anyone who isn't damned? Kid, even in L.A. that's a lot of people."

She shrugs.

"Them first. Then the others."

A rotten telephone pole lies lengthwise, half buried in dirt. She swings the knife, knocking out a chunk of wood the size of a basketball.

"Mostly I do what I'm told. Mostly that's all I do."

"Someone sends you to kill the dreamers."

She nods, digging into the pole and prying the metal rungs out of the side.

"And sometimes other bad people."

"Who tells you to kill them?"

"He does."

Talking to ghosts is like pulling eels out of a tank of motor oil. Pointless. And anything firm you grab onto is hard to hold. Most aren't as direct as Cherry. Most have brains dustier and more barren than the shittiest parts of Death Valley.

"He? Okay. What man tells you to kill?"

She stares at the ground for a minute.

"The one with the flowers."

I'm looking for a homicidal florist. Sure. Why not? Getting stuck with rose thorns all day. And the height of your day is sticking a Mylar balloon on a basketful of daisies. That will make you moody. Then it hits me. Not a florist. A gardener. Cherry said it. She's just one of the "pretty flowers in his garden." Teddy Osterberg. My favorite freak. Color me shocked. But there's a problem.

"You're not his ghost. I know that for a fact. How can he tell you what to do?"

She stands up. Hair has fallen across her face. She brushes it off with the back of her hand, leaving a dirty smear across her cheek.

"He just does."

"Did he tell you why?"

"Should he? I don't know."

"You're killing the whole world, you know."

She nods. Giggles.

"It's fun. I like the funny skies."

Talking about destroying the world has changed her mood completely. She comes over, takes my hand, and leads me to another school bus buried on its side. Hands claw at the windows. Faces scream silently. Ghosts that weren't able to get out when she did whatever she did to blow open this crater. If I was a betting man, I'd say she fell from the sky and landed here like a meteor.

"My name is Stark. What's yours?"

She leads me past the bus and lets go of my hand. She kicks up clods of dirt with the heel of her Mary Janes. Picks up a stone and throws it. It looks like she's thinking.

"Lamia."

"Hi, Lamia. What kind of name is that?"

"Mine."

"I mean where is it from? Where are you from?"

"I'm not really me. I used to be but I'm not. I lived here."

"Do you mean Spain? Or here in the Tenebrae?"

"No!" she yells. She's angry now. "It was a long time ago. It was dark and there wasn't anywhere to stand."

"Were the streets broken? Was there an earthquake?"

"I don't remember any streets. I floated."

She puts out her arms and twirls around like she's a toy balloon.

"Sounds like fun. Were you on a boat?"

She stops. Gets on her knees and stabs the windows along the side of the bus. The ghosts inside shriek and crowd to the other side.

"All I remember is the cold and the wind and stars twinkling."

She's really worked up now. She turns to the ghosts at the edge of the crater. Screams and charges at them. She's only run a few yards and they've all disappeared. She turns on the first bus, stabbing the metal. Kicking it. Crushing the roof and sides. This kid is pure power stuck in a broken mind. I don't know whether to feel sorry for her or to run like hell.

She turns and looks at me like she forgot I was there.

"Are you here to kill me?"

"You already asked me that."

"You'll kill me later."

"Only if I have to."

"Mostly I do things because I have to."

"Does someone tell you to kill other ghosts?"

"No. They're mostly his and don't run too fast, so I just do it. But the people. I like killing them. The ones that deserve it."

"How do you know they deserve it?"

"I just do. I feel it inside when the man gives me their names."

"Teddy?"

"The cruel one tried to kill me, you know. You're not going to kill me now?"

"Not now."

"I'll only kill you if I have to."

"Thanks. You know, cruel ones tried to control me and make me do bad things. Maybe I can help you get free and you can stop killing."

She holds out her hands and spins.

"I'm Lamia. I breathe death and spit vengeance."

She drops her arms and sits in the dirt. She rubs her eyes, suddenly a tired, dirty little girl.

"I'm sleepy. I don't want to talk anymore."

"Are you going to kill more people?"

She curls up on the ground in her party dress.

"Oh yes. Lots. The sky will be all sorts of funny colors."

Along the edge of the crater are the gangs of murdered kids. They're cut up but they're not scared of Lamia. Whatever happened to them, she didn't do it.

Cherry is waiting when I climb back up to the street. She runs over and grabs my arm. I keep walking.

"You didn't kill her. Why not?"

"I'm not ready. I know a part of what's going on but not enough. Until I do, I'm not killing the only thing that might be able to give me answers."

"And what about us? What happens when she comes for us?"

"Has she ever attacked you personally?"

"No."

"Then you're safe."

"How do you know?"

" 'Cause ghosts like you aren't on her hit list and it'll be a while before you are. Long enough for you to wise up and move on."

"How do you know?"

"Drop it."

Cherry gets in my way.

"How do you know?"

"Because you're not one of His, which means you're one of mine. That means you're definitely damned. And she's not after the damned yet."

Cherry takes a couple of steps back. Puts a hand over her mouth.

"You bastard."

"You don't have to wait around for her. Get out of here and save yourself."

She leans against the ruins of the Chinatown arch, resting her ridiculous cartoon face in her hands.

"Go away, James. You let me down again. You're no better than Parker."

"Take care of yourself. Think about what I said."

I head back to Tenebrae Station. The crowd follows me to the stairs but none of them follows me down.

"Any of you can leave too. You don't have to live like this."

I climb down into the tunnel and walk back into the dark.

And open my eyes, flat on my back in my room in the Chateau. Kasabian limps away from the circle with my shirt in his hand. There's a smeared spot on the tile where he broke the bloody circle.

I sit up. There are clots of blood on my arms and in my hair. I stink from sweat. But there's one nice surprise. The wound the Imp gave me is completely closed. There isn't even a scar.

"I'm going to take a shower."

"Best news I've heard all day," he says. "Now here's some for you. The rope and poison industries are way up in Hell. Suicide looks like the new thing with the cool kids. Those demonic sad sacks don't need back into Heaven. They need a teddy bear, a warm glass of milk, and some Prozac."

I TAKE A HOT SHOWER and go back to the living room. Kasabian has the news on with the sound turned down. The shots are fast and jittery, like whoever has the camera is running.

"Do you know about the Mile High Club?"

He doesn't look up from the big plate of fried shrimp he's shoving into his face.

"Sure. Mason talked about them sometimes."

I'm so out of the goddamn loop.

He points to the flat-screen with a shrimp in one of his metal doggie hands.

"Did you see when you came in? Big Bill Wheaton is dead. Laid low by the crazy little ghost not five minutes ago at a press conference he called to—you'll love this—announce a special serial-killer task force. Is that fucking funny or what?"

He eats half the shrimp in one bite.

"They sure it wasn't a volcano or dinosaur?"

"Nah. That stuff seems to have calmed down some."

If that's your doing, Patty, thanks.

"If you know something about that stuff, keep it to yourself. I'm working on some serious denial over here," says Kasabian.

I button another of Samael's dark shirts over the armor.

"A while back you said that spending all that time alone at Max Overdrive, you'd developed some nefarious computer skills."

"Yeah. You looking for missile-launch codes now?"

"No. Child murders. Maybe ritual killings. Not beaten or abused, just cut up. See if you can find anything."

He frowns.

"What, the mayor getting murdered by a ghost isn't interesting enough for you?"

Big Bill's bloody mug fills the TV screen. One clean slash across his throat. A long defensive wound across both arms. The cuts are deep red valleys in his skin. They almost look fake, the way violent death often does. The camera stays on Bill for a long time. Somewhere in L.A., a news director thinks he's going to win an Emmy but all he's really going to get are bad dreams.

"You think the dead kids have something to do with the Spirograph sky and the girl?"

"Look for possessed children too. The village murdered the Imp because she was a monster. Maybe there are other monster tots."

"This shit's depressing, man."

"Try to squeeze it in between looking for Brigitte's videos. Pretty please with shut-the-fuck-up on top."

Ain't this the funniest thing since corn beef hash? Here

I am looking for big bad King Cairo and scary Aelita, and Captain Beige has been running the girl all along. I'm still going to kill the other two but now I have to pay Teddy a visit and make him tell me his deepest darkest secrets. It's great timing. I really need to hit someone.

Hell looks better and better the longer I'm here. I knew there was no one to trust and no one I could count on besides Wild Bill. One guy in a land of billions. I bragged to Saint James about people who'd watch my back in L.A. but who's that now? Allegra and Vidocq won't be inviting me over for whist anytime soon. Candy is Switzerland. Neutral territory between hostile nations. Kasabian is a half-broken whiner. Maybe I should have sucked up my pride and merged or whatever it is I was supposed to do with Saint James. At least I'd have the Key. Then I'd be able to walk away from this veil of shit. But I had to shoot my mouth off. And Saint James is right. I'm usually the one backing us into corners. He was the smart one who got us out. I got us out too sometimes but mostly by shooting out the windows, jumping, and hoping there was something besides dead air on the other side. If he shows up again and doesn't want me to grovel, maybe I'll give merging a shot. What I'm doing now isn't doing me any good.

My phone rings. This time I check the caller ID.

"Father. Nice to hear from you but this is a bad time. Can we talk after I beat the holy hell out of someone?"

"We really should talk now. I think what's happening is bigger than a ghost and a few murders."

"A lot of murders. The girl. The Imp. She's the center of it. Someone is controlling her."

"How do you know?"

343

"I went to the land of the dead and asked her."

"You can't stay away from dark places, can you? Please. We really need to talk."

"I'm on my way to Malibu."

"Good. I'll drive you. We can talk in the car."

"Okay. Come to the Chateau Marmont and call me from out front. If anyone gives you trouble, tell them you're here for Mr. Macheath."

"Like Mack the Knife Macheath?"

"Yeah. If you're good, I'll do my Bobby Darin for you. Call me when you get here."

I'm checking my guns when someone pounds on the other side of the grandfather clock. Suddenly I'm in Grand Central fucking Station. The knocking gets louder.

"Hey, Old Yeller, can you get off your fat ass and let whoever that is in? I'm trying to get dangerous."

I hear Kasabian grumbling and thumping across the living room and opening the door. He says a few words to someone and thumps back.

"Hey, you."

I swing around.

"Candy? What are you doing here?"

She looks a little pale and worn. She still has on her torn shirt. Underneath it are fresh bandages stained with Beta-dine. She has a *Cowboy Bebop* backpack slung over one shoulder. Comes into the bedroom, where I have all my guns laid out. She drops the backpack on the floor. Winces as she sits down.

"Do you mind if I crash here for like ever? Allegra just fired me. And I think Rinko and I just broke up. It was hard to tell with all the screaming and her throwing things. Did something happen with you two?"

"She just wanted to unstitch my seams is all. I already have a roomie," I say, nodding to Kasabian. "But it's a big place. I think we can squeeze you in."

She smiles and lies back next to the guns.

"This is a big bed. Think maybe I could stay in here with you? I promise to be good."

"Good people end up on the couch. Only the bad ones get an all-access pass."

"I'll do my evil best to stay off the couch, sir."

I lie down next to her. She slides against me.

Someone knocks on the bedroom doorframe.

"We're out of beer," says Kasabian. Then, when he sees us, "Oh Christ. Is this turning into a domestic bliss situation? I can't stand that *It's a Wonderful Life* crap. Take me back and let me die at Max Overdrive."

"Be nice, Kas, and I'll loan you my *hentai* discs," says Candy.

Kasabian frowns.

"Schoolgirls and tentacles? No thanks. I prefer my porn mammal-only."

"Hot cow-on-cow action. I like it," Candy says.

Kasabian puts his hands up in an "I've had enough" gesture.

"I'll leave you degenerates to work out whatever it is you're working out. Just remember that I claim the bedroom at the far end of the place. It has the second biggest TV."

I look at Candy.

"As much as I'd like to give you a proper naked welcome,

345

I have to go and see a man about a ghost. You know where the food is. Please make Kasabian watch whatever you think will annoy him most."

"Where are you going? Can I come along?"

"You got knifed a few hours ago, so no."

"She just got skin. She didn't even hit muscle."

I put on my boots and check my ammo.

"No."

She sits up.

"Seriously, we talked about this. When you run off somewhere you might not come back from, I go with you. No more stoic monosyllabic bullshit."

I set aside the Glock and put the .45, the knife, and na'at in my coat. I hate that Candy is right. We made a deal and I don't want to be an overprotective liar right off the bat. There's plenty of time for that later.

"Okay. But you stay behind me if the things heat up. No going Jade and eating people. It's my circus and I'm the ring-master. Got it?"

"What does that make me?"

"You're the head clown. You get out of the little car first while the others are still crushed inside."

"And when they're out, you know what we're doing?"

"What?"

"Clown-car sex."

I hope Traven gets here soon.

TRAVEN CALLS TWENTY MINUTES LATER. Candy and I go down and meet him out front.

She brings the folding pistol with her. She's already covered the case with *InuYasha* and *Samurai Champloo* stickers. I'm not sure if that's technically low profile but the case looks more like an eighth grader's lunch box than a gun tote, so I guess it works.

Traven is in the car when we get there. He's uncomfortable in the presence of the last few beautiful people fleeing the hotel. Their opulence and generic decadence must be like seeing Martians to a cloistered brainiac like him.

"Thanks for the ride, Father."

"I'm glad to help. You picked a good day to go to the ocean. Most sensible people—"

"Let me guess. Are hunkering down because the sky is plaid and Godzilla is fighting with Paul Bunyan in the Scientology building parking lot."

"I'll drive and you'll see."

"Hi, Father," says Candy.

He smiles to her in the rearview mirror.

"It's good to see you."

Traven drives west on Sunset and I do see. The sky isn't a bad color but the light pulses like a slow strobe. It's the kind of thing that could give you a migraine if you stared at it long enough. Farther down Sunset, it gets more interesting. Sometime during the night, cars, mailboxes, stoplights, and telephone poles sank a foot into the roadbed like someone turned on a hot plate below the street. Traven's Geo Metro bounces over asphalt frozen into low waves. Cop cars block side streets that have collapsed into sinkholes. A few look like they're floating several feet in the air. The PTSD Hell flashbacks are coming on strong. At least there's not much traffic.

"Do you still want to go all the way to Malibu?"

"I have to but you don't," I say. "Drop us off and I can steal something."

He shakes his head.

"No. I want to tell you a story and I'd like to tell it now. It has to do with the Qomrama Om Ya and it ties into all this madness."

"The ghost girl too. She's scared to death of it."

"You showed it to her?"

"I hit her with it. It's the only thing that stopped her. And she has a name. Lamia."

"Are you absolutely sure about that?"

Traven sounds about like someone just read him the winning Lotto numbers and he thinks he hit the Mega Millions.

"It's two syllables. Even I can remember that."

"So what is the Qomrama?" asks Candy.

Traven looks at me out of the corner of his eye.

"Remember you once asked me where I thought the old gods, the Angra Om Ya, had gone?"

"Yeah. You said you thought they hadn't left but you didn't say what that meant."

"Well, I was wrong. They are gone. But not for much longer."

"How soon is longer? I mean the world is coming apart."

Traven picks up a book from the dashboard. It's an old one I once saw in his apartment. There are rust-colored stains on the front that are probably blood.

"Lamia is the name of an avatar of one of the Angra Om Ya."

"I pistol-whipped a goddess?"

He shakes his head.

"I think what you encountered was a kind of demon. An incomplete piece of one of the Angra."

"But she's the ghost of a real little girl. She was born in Spain."

"How will lost deities enter our universe from the outside? They're creatures without form. Maybe they have to do it through the mortal bodies to gain substance. What kind of a girl was she? Was she considered holy? Did she perform miracles?"

"She was a monster. Her own village killed her and buried her in an unconsecrated cemetery."

Traven is quiet for a minute.

"I wonder if she brought the Qomrama Om Ya with her or came to retrieve it?"

"Forget the girl. What's the Qomrama?"

Traven slows and steers us around a sinkhole that's swallowed part of a sandwich shop and auto-parts store. Cops on the side streets look worn and shell-shocked.

"In the first language, 'Om Ya' simply means 'God.' 'Angra,' depending on how you say it, means 'great' or 'grievous.' 'Qomrama' is a bit murkier but it means something like 'devourer.' The Qomrama Om Ya is the Godeater. A weapon designed by gods to kill other gods."

I check the side mirror.

"Father, did you come straight to the Chateau from your place?"

"Yes. Why?"

Candy looks out the rear window. I keep an eye on the mirror.

"There's only one car back there and it's been with us for several blocks. Speed up."

The car falls back for a few seconds then speeds up and stays on our tail. It's a Charger, not that that matters. In a flat-out chase, a skateboarder with a broken ankle can outrun a Geo Metro. The Charger is overkill. It accelerates and comes up behind us.

"Take it up to forty and keep it there."

"The car will shake apart on this uneven pavement."

"Yeah, but it'll make it harder for them to shoot at us."

"Oh," says Traven. He hits the gas.

The Charger doesn't even notice. It pulls up alongside and King Cairo rolls down the front passenger window.

"Switch places with me," I say to Candy.

I squeeze into the backseat and she gets in the front.

Flame hits the side of the Metro.

"Don't slow down."

Traven nods. Steers around the bumps the best he can.

Cairo is hanging out the window of the other car. Rolling his eyes and making faces. He tosses another fire hex at the Metro. It hits hard enough to shake the little car.

Candy is turned around in the front seat looking at me.

"Remember when I told you I was going to take you shooting?"

"Yeah."

"Congratulations. Consider this your first lesson."

I take a 9mm clip from my pocket and hand it to her. She grins like a wolf. Hits the release and the gun case opens like a metal flower. She shoulders the gun, slides in the clip, and chambers a round.

"Don't get too excited. You don't shoot until I say to and you only shoot at what I tell you to. Got it?"

She nods. With the gun in her hands, she can't stop smiling. Traven isn't. Flames are hitting his car, blistering the paint and turning the driver-side window black. And now there's an armed amateur in the seat next to him.

"Aren't you glad you came along, Father?"

"I wanted to do more than read books. I guess this is it."

"Welcome to *le merdier*. Does this back window roll down?"

"I'm afraid not."

"Too bad."

I put my fist through it. It catches around my wrist like a big glass bracelet. I pull it off and throw it at Cairo just as he's about to toss more fire our way. The glass shatters in Cairo's face. He slides back into the car, covering his eyes. The Charger slows down.

"Is it over?" asks Traven. "Did we win?"

"No and I doubt it."

The Charger cuts right and gets behind us again.

"Keep talking, Father. I like hearing stories when I'm killing people. Lamia is a demon of an Angra. How did she get here? What does she want?"

Traven's voice quivers a little. I can't tell if it's fear or the uneven road.

"The weapon is your answer. She, and we can assume the rest of the Angra, will return to take back what's theirs."

"The Qomrama?"

"If the books are right, they'll want everything. The entire universe."

The Charger moves up on us again. I can see Cairo shouting at the driver.

"Candy, shoot that son of a bitch."

"Which one?"

"Any of them. Just pop a couple of shots at them and see what they do. Keep talking, Father."

Candy leans out the window and shoots twice. One shot misses and the other takes out one of the Charger's headlights. Not a bad start. It gets them to put a little more distance between us.

"Father?"

"We once talked about the idea that the being we call God is merely the Demiurge."

"More like the universe's janitor than an all-powerful creator. Got it."

"The book you saw in my office when we first met. The one you called the Angra Om Ya Bible has an alternate Creation story. It's entirely possible that the entity that we call God didn't create this universe. The Angra Om Ya did. God merely usurped it."

The Charger pulls up right on our bumper and Cairo climbs out of the sunroof.

"Slow down," I shout.

Traven backs off the accelerator.

Behind us, the Charger lurches, trying to keep from hitting our bumper. Cairo slams into the side of the sunroof and falls back inside.

"Keep going."

"Talking or driving?" says Traven.

"Both. See if you can hit the windshield, Candy."

"In math there's something called M-theory. It says that we live in a universe with many parallel dimensions and many universes all separated by infinitely large membranes."

Candy pulls the trigger just as we hit a bump and the shot goes high. The second shot hits the Charger's windshield.

"Nice work, Calamity Jane. Get back inside the car and wait for me."

Traven says, "I believe that the Angra are in one of the parallel universes and that the changes in reality we're experiencing have been going on longer than we think but have only become noticeable now."

"With all the dreamers dying, I'm not surprised."

"The breakdown of reality caused a crack in one of the membranes and a tiny piece of Lamia leaked back into this universe."

"How did the Angra end up in another universe?"

"According to the alternate history, God tricked them. The Angra were already here when our God manifested Himself. When He made Himself known, He gave the Angra an offering."

"What kind?"

"The books don't say. But it was a trick, and exiled them beyond the edge of our universe."

"And now they want back in to take what's theirs. Which is everything."

"I'm afraid so."

We hit a deep gulley that rattles everyone's teeth.

"And they'll kill God to do it," Traven says.

"That old man has more enemies than Stalin."

The Charger accelerates. It comes around parallel to us.

The road is getting worse. It rattles my bones and balls but it forces the heavy Charger to slow down.

"What happens to us if they come back?"

"The book doesn't say. But there are other texts that talk about battles between Gods in other dimensions."

"And?"

"In every one, the winner scours the universe clean and starts over."

"Scouring sounds bad," says Candy.

"Can we stop them?"

"I have no idea," Traven says.

The Charger pulls up parallel again. Cairo climbs out the sunroof on top of the car.

"Look at the bright side, Father. When the Angra destroy everything, there won't be a Hell for you to go to."

"Every Apocalypse has a silver lining," says Candy.

"That's my girl."

"Can I shoot some more?"

"Almost. When I get out, you come back here. If anyone in the Charger shoots at us or tries to get out, you shoot them. Don't waste ammo. Unless Cairo looks like he's going to win. Then spray the fucking car and kill as many of them as you can."

"Neat," she says.

I put my hand on Traven's shoulder.

"When you hear me stomp on the roof, hit the brakes. Don't worry about me."

He nods.

I pop the sunroof and crawl out on top. The cheap plastic hinges snap and the sunroof flies off the car and into the street behind us. Cairo opens his arms in greeting. I give him the finger.

He's fast. He crouches and throws a shower of fire my way underhanded, like a softball pitcher.

I drop back halfway down into the sunroof and the fire passes over me.

"Shoot," I say to Candy. She does, whooping like she's at the rodeo. Glass explodes out of the Charger's side windows.

I toss some arena hoodoo Cairo's way. It's an old crushing hex. Supposed to break an enemy's bones. Cairo dodges the hex but I didn't throw it at him. I hit the car's engine.

There's a horrible grinding and snap as the Charger's engine drops and hits the street, gouging deep ruts in the road. Cairo flies off the roof, bounces off the hood, and falls in front of the Charger. I stomp my boot and Traven stops the Geo. I jump off the back, throwing protection hoodoo around me as I hit and roll. Cairo lands on the street in front of his car. From where I'm lying, I'm at just the right angle to see the Charger roll right over him.

Candy blows the rest of her clip into the side of Cairo's car. His boys duck out the passenger side and take off down a side street.

Traven backs up. I climb into the car.

"Turn us around. I'll hurt Teddy later. We're going to Blackburn's."

Candy blows across the tip of her gun barrel like a cowgirl, leans between the seats, and gives me a kiss. She uses her thumb to wipe lip gloss off my lips.

"Why Blackburn's?" she asks.

"Cairo was using hoodoo in the open right in front of God

and Joe SixPack. Either he's nuts or they're not after Saint James anymore but me instead. Permission could only come from Blackburn or Aelita and I know where Blackburn is."

We drive past Cairo's car. The engine steams and spits. Spills gas all over the street. There's blood on the bumper and a long wet streak on the asphalt like something was dragged but Cairo's body is gone.

I give Traven Blackburn's address and we head over.

"I hate to point out something to you," he says.

"If it isn't 'Great job. I'm thrilled to be on your side,' I don't want to hear it."

"We're on a major thoroughfare. Half the streets we just passed had traffic cameras. Tomorrow LAPD will have the entire fight on tape."

Shit.

"No worries, Father. With the street fucked up, the cameras are probably out and half the police force will be hunkered down at home. By the time someone looks over the tapes, we'll either be dead or heroes."

"Or dead heroes," says Candy.

Traven thinks for a long minute.

"At times of crisis, my mother used to recite an old Hungarian saying. 'The strength of the serpent and the peace of the dove.' "

"I don't know the last time I saw a dove," Candy says.

"Then let's do some slithering."

TRAVEN PARKS ACROSS THE STREET from Blackburn's abandoned hotel mansion.

"Here's what's going to happen. I'm going inside to talk to

people and hurt them. Not necessarily in that order. You two are going to stay out here and watch my back."

"I want to come with you," says Candy.

"You can't. I have to get through layers of heavy protective hoodoo. I don't know if I can take anyone with me and this isn't a great time to start experimenting."

It takes her a minute but finally Candy nods.

I give her the Sig pistol.

"This is a .45. The bullets are bigger, so there aren't as many as your nine-millimeter and the kick is a lot harder. If you have to shoot, do it slowly and carefully."

"I still want to go with you."

"I know."

When I'm outside the car, my cell rings. I'm not in the mood for a chat but my blood's up, so I'll give the crank caller a friendly "fuck you."

"Hello."

A voice breaks up then repeats itself.

"Stark? Where the hell are you? I've been waiting."

It's Patty Templeton.

"I told you I'd call you. Wait for me in the lounge."

"What are you talking about? I'm outside. On the corner by the freeway. You called and said you were coming by to pick me up."

The anger turns to a sick feeling in my stomach.

"Listen, it's a trick. Go back to the dreamers' building now. Run!"

"Oh God."

She forgets to hang up. I listen to hear her running. Panting. She excuses herself and then curses, pushing through crowds.

Over the tops of the nearby buildings, black plumes rise like twisters into the sky. Somewhere, the city is burning.

Patty screams, her voice distorting into an animal wail through the tiny phone speaker. Then the crowd screams. What follows is a sound I recognize from the arena. A blade cutting through the air. Little girl's laughs drift from the phone with the bloody, drowning gurgle of someone choking on their own blood.

The ground shakes beneath my feet. I expect to see Cherry but the shaking goes on. Windows up and down the street shatter and fall. The sound is like another thousand knives going into a girl's throat. I brace myself against the Metro until the shaking stops. It takes a few seconds, and when it stops, I know that Patty Templeton is dead.

I don't know how many people, Hellions, and hell beasts I've seen die over the years. The ones in the arena or the streets all went down the same way. In front of me. The worst times in the arena were when the games were going while I waited in my cell. All I could do was listen to the fighting and dying. Listening was so much worse than seeing. It was like dying by whispers. You were never sure if that other fighter was dead, paralyzed, or being eaten alive by a scaly beast. Dying by phone is no way to go. Not for anyone. Not for anyone I know.

Candy puts her head out the window.

"Are you okay?"

"Great. Peachy."

"Who was that on the phone?"

I shake my head.

"No one. Wrong number."

I start across the street.

Getting through Blackburn's wards is just like last time. Slow and steady wins the race. He's added two more layers since I was here but I move through them just like the others. It's all about concentration and channeling Lucifer's hate through the armor so it radiates like hellfire. No earthly magic is going to stand up to that.

No one is in the front of the house, so I head straight into the parlor. Blackburn is sitting at his desk like he's waiting for me. Tuatha, his wife, is in a chair across the room. She looks worse than last time. Like she gave up martinis for formaldehyde. Perched on the end of Blackburn's desk is Brigitte.

"Hello, Jimmy," she says. "I was hoping you wouldn't come back here."

She shifts her eyes from me to her right then back to me. I take a step into the parlor and snap out the na'at to where she looked. One of Cairo's men drops to the floor.

I go over to Brigitte.

"What are you doing here? Tell me you're not part of this shitstorm."

She puts her hand on Blackburn's arm.

"Saragossa is a friend. That's all."

Blackburn just sits there. Useless and staring at his wife. He puts his hand over Brigitte's. It the gesture of an old man trying to find something to hold on to while his ship is sinking.

I pull Brigitte off the desk and push her into a chair. Drag my arm across Blackburn's desk, knocking everything to the floor.

"What the fuck is wrong with you? Killing dreamers?

Playing with reality? Do you have any goddamn idea what you're doing?"

"Please. My wife."

He holds out his hand to Tuatha.

"Fuck you and your wife. You're not just turning the sky the wrong color. You just killed a girl whose only sins were having an asshole for a boyfriend and wanting to keep the world from falling apart."

Blackburn's hand falls on a pen that was still on the desk. He delicately straightens it and then clasps his hands together.

"I'm sorry. It started well. We would replace the dreamers with our people and mold the world into our own image. A better place for Sub Rosa and civilians. No one was supposed to die."

"That's what every amateur killer says when they're up to their elbows in blood. Not only did you kill all those people but you poked a hole in the universe. Opened us up to angry Godeating motherfuckers who want you and me and Brigitte and your precious wife flushed down the cosmic toilet."

He shakes his head.

"I had no choice," he says. "You see, they took her soul."

"Who?"

Brigitte raises her eyes to something behind me.

He catches me with the first bullet before I can turn around. It shouldn't go through the armor but it does. He must have used my Spiritus Dei trick. My back burns and my chest aches. It feels like a rib is cracked. When I turn to face him, Cairo empties the rest of a 9mm clip. Fourteen quick shots. I throw myself onto the floor and roll toward him. Even hurt, I'm fast and he's hurt worse, so most of the shots miss. Still, he tags me three more times. It's bad but not enough for this punk to kill me. When I'm close to him, I extend the na'at, knocking the gun out of his hand. Very suave, but when I try to sit up, the bullets grind in my chest, taking my breath away. I spit and there's blood in it.

The next thing I'm looking at is the ceiling. Then Cairo's grinning face. It's covered in blood and road rash. There's a nice chunk of radius bone sticking out of his right arm. One of his knees is ripped open but he's still walking on it. That's not healing magic. That's Dixie Wishbone. He's higher than the Goodyear blimp. He pushes a finger into each of the bullet holes in the armor when he talks. It feels exactly what you think having a junkie's bony fingers in your chest feels like.

"Funnyman. You look awfully funny down there, funnyman."

Cairo pats me down. Feels the Qomrama Om Ya in my coat pocket. He's so pleased with himself that when he reaches for it, he doesn't see me shake the glove off my hand. I don't have a lot of strength but I have enough to pull him down on top of me and hold him while I stab my oh-so-pointy Kissi arm up between his ribs and into his heart. I feel him twitch and die and enjoy every second of it.

A light flares in the hall. Aelita manifests her Gladius and comes at me.

I get my legs under Cairo and kick his body up at her. She slashes down with the Gladius, cutting him in two. Blood and bile spray in all directions, ruining Blackburn's pretty rugs and wallpaper.

The move bought me just enough time to pull the Qomrama and throw it at her. Which turns out to be exactly what Aelita wanted. She kills the Gladius and lets the Qomrama sail past. When it starts back, she catches it in an iron box studded with Angra runes.

She throws the catch and says, "Thank you for bringing it to me. You're the most helpful Abomination of them all."

She manifests her Gladius again and heads for me. Five shots hit her in the chest. She drops the box and falls to her knees.

I look back and see Brigitte holding the gun of the guy I killed when I came in.

She kneels down next to me and helps me up.

"Thanks," I say. "Get the box."

When she reaches for it, Aelita twists and kicks her in the face. Grabs the box and runs out of the room. I pull myself to my feet and help Brigitte up.

"What the hell are you really doing here?" I ask.

Brigitte goes back to Blackburn and I drop into the chair she'd been sitting in. My chest is on fire but I can breathe. At least a couple of the bullets are still inside me but the armor is holding me together.

"I've been seeing Saragossa," says Brigitte. "Tuatha has been, as he said, unwell for some time. He was so depressed. And my career was not going as well as I might have led you to believe. He introduced me to people."

"What was that about his wife's soul?"

"Nasrudin Hodja, the soul merchant, took it," says Blackburn. "But I know it was on Aelita's orders. I made her head of security. It kept her close by."

"Where is it?"

He shrugs.

"Where do you hide a soul?"

"So you assholes have been killing off dreamers to control reality and you use the Imp to do it. Was that Aelita too?"

Blackburn nods.

"And who controls the Imp?"

"Osterberg."

"And who controls him?"

"Aelita."

"Are you sure?"

"Fairly," says Blackburn.

Brigitte says, "Teddy's family had power and lost it. He isn't Sub Rosa but he thinks like one. The world is all status with him. He had a vicious little ghost in his collection and he let her loose for Aelita so he could remain in the synod."

"That's not true. The ghost isn't his. I'm sure of it."

"I know he controls the girl. That's all that matters," says Blackburn.

"It makes a sick kind of sense. Someone gave him power over the ghost but didn't give him the ghost itself. That way when I asked if she was his, he could say no and I wouldn't detect a lie."

"That sounds like Aelita's way of thinking."

Blackburn pats his pockets in a way I recognize. I toss him the Maledictions. He looks at the pack. Doesn't like that he doesn't recognize the brand. But beggars take what they can get. He takes one and tosses the pack back.

"People tell me that the Imp killed people who weren't dreamers. Did you or Aelita order that?"

He shakes his head and lights the cigarette. Coughs and

starts to put it out. Brigitte takes it from him and puffs gently like she's teaching him how it's done.

"I never ordered her to kill."

"Jimmy, I was Blackburn's friend but I didn't know about any of this until today. Please believe me."

I have to think for a minute.

Blackburn goes to where his wife is sitting, takes her hand, and holds it in both of his.

"I do."

She says, "I think I know why other people were killed."

"Go on."

"If I'd known about Teddy, I swear I would have told you myself. I thought he was dead."

"Why?"

"Because I stabbed him almost three months ago. I didn't know he was alive until Saragossa told me he'd been at the synod."

"Why did you stab him?"

Brigitte looks away. I've never seen her uncomfortable like this before.

"He wanted to eat me," she says, shrugging. "Teddy is a ghoul. He eats the dead but he'd never eaten a revenant. Though I wasn't a real zombie, I was as close as was left in the world and he wanted me. I thought I killed him."

"Amanda said Teddy had been mugged. It's what he must have told people. Does anyone else know about this?"

"I don't think so."

I flash on the ragged kids in the Tenebrae. So scared they form gangs and avoid other ghosts. I see their knife slashes and crescent-moon wounds. *Bite marks*.

I get up and feel my ribs. The armor saved me but something wet inside is sloshing against something else and it's hard to breathe. That's okay. Teddy doesn't look like a sprinter. If he runs, I'll take his little golf cart and chase him around the graveyards until his heart explodes.

"I'll come with you," says Brigitte. "I've felt dead inside and I thought it was the bite. It wasn't. It was losing the hunt. When you killed off all the undead, my life lost meaning. Now, fighting again, I feel alive. Let me come with you and we'll kill Teddy together."

Sure. Candy wouldn't mind the woman who kissed me in the bar tagging along. Maybe they can have some girl talk about shoes on the way to Malibu.

"If you want back in the game, that's fine by me. But Teddy I can handle. I need you to get these idiots somewhere safe. If Aelita comes back, I don't want her taking the royal assholes hostage."

She nods.

"Just makes sure Teddy dies this time."

"That I can promise. I'm cutting him into little pieces and burying him with the Imp. Let's see how they enjoy each other in the Tenebrae."

I look back at Blackburn.

"I'm sorry about your wife's soul. I don't know what to do about it, but if I come up with anything, I'll let you know."

He nods and puts his arm around her shoulders.

Pain is pain and even the rich and powerful get shafted sometimes. I want to hate Blackburn but I can't. He's too pathetic and his wife is too fucked up for that. But a part of me still wants to take his head. He let all those people die. He let Patty die. The Sandman Slim part of me that killed dozens of high families wants to cut a piece of revenge out of his hide. But this isn't Hell and I'm not Sandman Slim full-time any more than I'm full-time Lucifer. I'll stick to the Teddys of the world. The sure-thing monsters. That's a judgment call I can make. A monster knows another monster and a real monster knows which ones need to die.

CANDY GETS OUT OF THE CAR when she sees me. I'm breathing better but walking slow.

"What happened in there?"

"I forgot to tip the maid and she short-sheeted the bed."

"You realize you're covered in blood?"

I look down at my shirt and armor. I'm a mess. If I wasn't me, I'd probably be alarmed.

"Don't worry. It's mostly Cairo's."

"You're holding your side."

"I got nipped a couple of times but I'm fine. Just sore."

She opens the Metro's door.

"Get in the damn car. We're going to the clinic."

I shake my head.

"I'm going to Teddy Osterberg's. I'm not letting that corpse fucker kill one more person. If you're going to be part of what I do, you have to understand this is how things are sometimes. I'm used to bleeding and being hurt and they don't have a damn thing to do with finishing the job."

She stalks away, spins, and walks back again.

"You're such a fucking guy. I bet you never stop and ask for directions."

"If I stopped and asked for directions, I wouldn't end up in Hell so much and where's the fun in that?"

Candy gets in the car, which is a good thing because the ground trembles and opens where she was standing. I go to the edge of the hole.

"Not now, Cherry."

"The girl is on a rampage. You have to save us."

"Up here too. She's not going to stop until I get Teddy, so crawl back into your box and hide."

"If you don't kill her, I'll never leave you alone. I'll pull the floor out from under you and drop you so low you'll be a cripple . . ."

I get in the Metro while Cherry is still talking. Traven looks a little alarmed.

"You were talking to a hole. Why?"

"Sometimes you need to remind the dead to stay dead. Maybe I hurt her feelings. She'll get over it."

"Who?"

"After we deal with Teddy, I'll tell you all about it. Now please, can we just fucking go?"

Traven starts the car and pulls away from Blackburn's, aiming us at Malibu.

"Why do we hate Teddy so much that we have to go there now instead of patching you up?"

"Teddy kills people and eats them and I don't know if he does it in that order. And if he keeps killing dreamers, the world is over."

Traven nods.

"I understand. But maybe we could stop and at least get you some bandages?"

"Also, Teddy seems to have a real taste for kids."

Traven stops the car.

"Drive, Father."

"I'm sorry. I can't just leave you bleeding. I have towels in the trunk. You can at least staunch your wounds."

"Fine."

Traven pops the trunk and Candy grabs a couple of towels. I stuff them under the armor. The pressure feels good but I can't help wondering a little if Traven doesn't want me leaking all over the back of his car.

While Traven drives, Candy reaches between the seats and squeezes my bloody hand. I squeeze hers back.

WHAT AM I SUPPOSED TO THINK about someone like Teddy Osterberg? I want to kill him but I want to understand him. Maybe that makes me weak. Maybe it's just self-serving. Teddy is a stone-cold son-of-a-bitch killer. I want to look into his eyes and cross my fingers and hope I don't see myself looking back. Which me would it be? Stark? Sandman Slim? Lucifer?

As much as I hate this guy, I can't get rid of the image of those Hellion skins hanging loose and limp around the palace in Pandemonium. Maybe that's the joke and has been all along. I go after a ghoul with all kinds of righteous fury, but looking back at all the things I've done, what if I'm there too, gnawing on skulls right along with Teddy? Just another ghoul in love with the dead.

I hid a lot of myself from Alice and I've hidden what I did in Hell from Candy. I know the monster part of myself. I love it and I hate it. Sometimes I'm ashamed of it. I don't want to be Teddy, sitting on a hill by himself with only his ghosts and corpses for company. Being a real monster is easy enough on your own but not so much when you have something to lose. When this is over, I'm taking Candy back to the Chateau Marmont and get good and drunk and tell her a long story about how I spent my summer vacation in Hell. I should have done it earlier. It's one thing to congratulate yourself for saving Wild Bill and maybe a couple of other souls from torture but it's another to let someone who thinks they know you in on your dirty secrets about the bodies in gibbets and wet skins flapping like flags on the Fourth of July. That's how you don't become Teddy. You lay it all out and let others decide if they want to hang around the graveyard with you or catch the bus back to town.

Thank God for whiskey or the world would be so full of secrets the weight would spin us into the sun.

THE FRONT DOOR is open when we reach Teddy's Malibu mansion. The sky has stopped pulsing. Now clouds spin like airborne tornados, coming together in a single funnel cloud as big as the sky and then falling apart into islands of mini-twisters that skim along the top of the ocean. A rain of fish, birds, and smooth ocean stones falls like hail when we reach the door. We don't have any choice but to run inside or be brained.

Like the first time I was here, it's mausoleum dark inside. We leave the door open for a little light but there's not much to see besides the spindly foyer tables and Teddy's bone sculptures. I take out the .45 and head into one of the side rooms to look for Teddy.

I left the towels in the car. It's hard intimidating people with fluffy white towel corners sticking out from under your

Richard Kadrey

shirt. I feel a little liquid in my chest when I take deep breaths. Maybe a bullet sliced into my lung. The armor is holding me together, but whenever I cough there's blood in it. Besides Teddy, my biggest worry is not letting Candy see it. I wish I had some Aqua Regia. That stuff is better than a swimming pool full of penicillin.

Something small shoots past my ear. A hand grabs my shoulder and slides down my back. When I turn, Candy is lying on the polished marble floor.

"Wow. She really is a Jade. I wasn't sure."

I kneel by Candy. Hold my fingers to her throat. She's still breathing and her heart is beating.

I look around for the voice.

"This stuff doesn't do anything to regular people but it's like curare to Jades. Completely paralyzing. Amazing stuff."

I turn slowly while Teddy talks, listening for where he might be. I hear him reloading the tranq gun but the foyer echoes, making him hard to pinpoint.

"Are you going to play with your gun all day or do something?"

"Come for me," he says.

Traven leans down beside me and says, "There."

In the dark, I can make out someone at the foot of the sweeping staircase with his hands up like a bank robber surrendering in a movie.

I charge him. Fish and rocks smash and splat outside and in my head I see Teddy hitting the ground and splitting open with them. Maybe I'll toss him off the roof.

I fall. But it's not really a fall. More like I'm a piece of iron sucked down by a magnet the size of Arizona. I land

370

on my injured side on a big square of canvas, coughing up an impressive fountain of blood. Something is holding me to the floor like two-ton shackles. Lying here isn't so bad. It's hard to catch my breath, so I doubt I could stand right now anyway.

Traven moves from Candy to kneel beside me. He tries pulling me up but I don't budge.

Teddy flicks a switch and a crystal chandelier lights up the foyer. There's someone with him. She's on the stairs above him, so even though she's smaller, she towers over him. She has a pistol in her hand.

"You. Priest. Get away from them. Over by the wall."

She moves the barrel of the gun to indicate where she wants Traven to stand.

Teddy opens his hands wide.

"Two-for-two. I've never been so lucky. You're a gem. Do you know that? Poison for the Jade and a binding circle to trap the Devil."

He looks at Traven and frowns.

"We didn't expect a civilian. All there is for you is the gun. How boring."

I can move just enough to crane my head around and see the woman. I'm low and from this angle can only see her upside down but I know those scars. It's Lula Hawks.

Teddy comes over from the stairs. I haven't seen him like this before. Happy and animated. The crazy fuck is practically skipping like a little kid to dinner. He walks right past me to Candy. I try to turn my head but I'm stuck.

"I'm keeping this one alive," he says. "She'll go into one of the Gnostic graves until she's ripe. I won't eat her all at once. How often does one get to eat a Jade? I have to make her last."

All I can see are his calfskin loafers as he circles in front of me. He bends at the waist and looks down so we're eye to eye.

"Cat got your tongue?" he says.

He looks at Lula and brightens.

"Can I have his tongue? You can have the rest. I just want one little taste."

"No," she says. "The deal was you get the girl and I get the monster."

She comes around next to Teddy, one hand on Traven's arm and the other holding the gun.

"You know me now but do you remember me from before King's place? Before Blackburn's? Before I got these scars?"

"Didn't I scrape you off my boots at a Fresno dairy farm?"

Teddy laughs. All worked up like this, he sounds creepily like the little girl.

"You killed Josef right in front of me. I loved him and you cut off his head and handed it to me like it was a big joke."

All the birds do come home to roost. Cherry was right. The past catches up with us in Hell and in L.A.

I remember a girl. It was right before New Year's at a skin-head clubhouse where Josef the Kissi had set up shop. His pretty-boy Aryan face and dominant personality made him a perfect White Power leader. He used the skinheads for muscle and cover. Lula was there but I didn't know her name back then. She was just a pretty tattooed girl with a shaved head. It was right after I escaped from Hell the first time. I hadn't been back on Earth very long and was still getting used to mortal women. I fell in love with her for the ten seconds I saw her in her white wife beater. A day or two later I burned the skinhead clubhouse to the ground. Probably killed a lot of them. Burned the hell out of others. I cut off Josef's head that night. Of course, all I did was kill Josef's human body. The Kissi part of him was fine but Eva Braun here never got the joke because she never copped to the fact that Josef wasn't human. I'm going to die because a dumb little Nazi bitch had a crush on another monster. Maybe God has a sense of humor after all.

"Why?" I say. It's all I can get out.

"Why didn't I kill you when I met you at Blackburn's? Why didn't I feed you to King or send you straight to Teddy to die? Because I knew all I had to do was give you a little push and you'd find your way up the hill on your own. And it would hurt a lot more along the way. I hope it did. But not as much as what's going to happen."

"Mr. Osterberg," says Traven. "When God threw Satan out of Eden, he said, 'Thou art cursed above all cattle, and above every beast of the field. Upon thy belly shalt thou go, and dust shalt thou eat all the days of thy life.' Do you know how much lower than that you are?"

Good for you, Father.

Teddy raises his eyebrows in mock innocence.

"None of this is my fault. I was just hungry and King Cairo told Lula here my secret. All the men in my family have the hunger. If you want to blame someone, blame Great-Grandfather. He made a deal with . . ." Teddy leans down into my face and yells, "The Devil. Yes, Great-Grandfather made a deal for wealth and power and volunteered to become something abominable—an eater of the dead—to prove his loyalty to Satan."

Samael must have laughed his ass off at that. He would have been happy with the idiot's soul, but when the nitwit offered to eat corpses for the next fifty years, how could he say no to that? Some people are too stupid to even damn themselves properly.

"None of you will be as tasty as the kids but I'm forced to go on a child-free diet for a while. The Imp hasn't killed all the parents of the ones I've already taken and until then I'm forced to subsist on dreary adults."

I was right. He used the girl to kill for Aelita, then for himself when Aelita didn't need her. A sweet deal for a guy like Teddy. I wonder if he used her to kill new food for his pantry? How could he resist? I think I finally know what Aelita wanted out of all this. Not that it matters down here on the floor.

I take a deep breath and cough up blood on Teddy's shoes.

His face turns red and he kicks me in the teeth. Lula slaps him hard enough to leave a mark.

"You don't touch this one."

Traven says, "How do you control something as powerful as the girl? You barely seem to be able to control yourself."

Lula hits him in the back of the neck with the gun butt.

Teddy goes to a table where a child's skull sits under a bell jar.

"Isn't she beautiful? The angel bought me the Imp's cemetery for safekeeping. As payment, she gave me the skull. There was hardly any flesh left on her and it was as dry as paper. I soaked it in toddler fat and fried it brown and crispy. The Imp was exquisite. And after I said the words the angel gave me, her ghost was mine to command."

"That's it," says Lula. "They've heard enough to know they've been fucked all along. Especially this one."

She kicks me in my injured side. Teddy laughs.

"He pulled a gun on me, you know."

Lula rolls her eyes.

"Yes, I know. You've told me at least twenty times."

"I was being polite and he pulled a gun."

She nods.

"Go play with yours and leave mine alone."

"I want to watch," he says.

"Then get out of my way."

Lula disappears and comes back with a big jerry can. I can smell the gasoline from here. She kicks Traven.

"Turn him over on his back and drag him outside on the canvas. We don't want to break the circle. I want plenty of room to see him squirm while he burns."

Teddy smiles down at me.

"Burn yours if you want. I'm eating mine raw."

Fish and stones fall outside. Traven looks scared. He doesn't want to help Lula kill me or go out into the supernatural rain. I know the look on his face. He's vapor-locked. His brain can't process the choices. He's a good man and good men shouldn't be in places like this having to do these things.

I feel a tiny earthquake. Teddy screams and drops the Imp's skull. Tries to turn and falls backward into a hole.

All I can see is the top of the hole. Teddy's hands scrabble around the edges trying to pull himself out while Cherry's bony arms pull him back down. Lula points the gun at Traven and sidles up to the hole.

"What the fuck?"

She's disgusted. The dead are misbehaving. You have no idea, lady.

Lula points the pistol into the hole and fires shot after shot. She doesn't see Traven. He picks up the Imp's skull and hits Lula from behind. She drops the pistol into the hole and falls to her knees. Traven hits her again and knocks her against the wall. He pushes Lula upright and pins her arms.

"Do you want to go to Hell, young lady?"

"Fuck you."

She spits at him. Traven leans in like he's going to kiss her. Black vapor and dust stream from his mouth into hers. I watch with Lucifer's eyes, as her skin, already stained black with sin signs, turns wet and sloppy like she's been dipped in hot tar. Her body sags. Traven has to hold her up to continue the Dolorosa.

"Enough" is all I can get out. Traven stops. I've never seen that look of fury on his face before. It's happened. He wanted to do more and he walked into the belly of the beast. Ghouls. Jabbers. Murderers and hit men. All in a day. The good man that came in the house is gone. The man I'm looking at is still good but in an angry, wounded way that matches Traven's lined soldier's face.

Traven looks to where Lula slid down the wall into a sitting position. She's unconscious and twitching. Eyes rolled back and breathing hoarse as her body tries to absorb the Dolorosa poison.

I whisper, "Help me."

That wakes Traven up. He looks at me in a dazed way. Recognizes what's happened and flips through all the books in his head. He takes the knife from inside my coat and slits the canvas, ripping out a piece to break the circle. Suddenly I can take a decent breath. I can even stand. Slowly. I spit blood and go to where Traven is bent over Candy.

I collapse onto my knees next to her body.

"She's alive," Traven says. "But the other woman. I think I might have killed her."

"Who cares? Dead now or dead later. Either way she's hellbound."

He looks at me with a mixture of sorrow and shame. The preacher inside is still hanging on by his fingernails. Traven understands damning someone but not being an executioner. Maybe later I'll tell him that the first one is always the hardest. Maybe not.

"Do you know how to do mouth-to-mouth?"

"Yes," he says. "The Red Cross came to the seminary."

"Get her to the car and do what you can. She's just paralyzed now but we don't want any brain damage, do we?"

"No."

"Get her out of here."

Traven nods. Picks Candy up in his arms and runs with her through the cursed rain.

I go to the hole and look inside. Lula plugged Teddy five or six times. There are lots of bone fragments in the dirt. She hit Cherry too.

I shouldn't do what I'm doing but I'm still doing it. I pick up the Imp's skull and throw it on the floor as hard as I can. The marble cracks and the skull explodes into a thousand pieces, destroying Lamia's connection to this world. I don't have to kill her. She was never really responsible for what she did. She was a slave killing for a sick bastard. I did plenty of that in Hell. With any luck, she'll be just another ghost in the Tenebrae now. Maybe she'll be strong enough to squeeze out whatever hole she came through and go home to the Angra. Who knows, maybe freeing her will buy humanity some brownie points when the Angra come back to eat our lunch. They can keep us around like sea monkeys and teach us tricks. Why not? One God fucked with us at the beginning of time. What's one more?

I pick up the jerry can and spread gasoline all over the floor. Before I light it, I find the kitchen and rip all the gas hoses out of the walls. I go outside and light a Malediction, letting the house fill with fumes. When I'm halfway through the smoke, I open the front door and toss it inside. The house catches. Windows blow out, sending burning debris onto the perfect lawn. Traven starts the car. The flames light our way down the long hill.

Good-bye, Teddy. So long, Lula. I hope Lamia and the ghosts of those kids don't let your souls get to the afterlife too quick. I hope they give you a good long tour of the Tenebrae. Welcome to the Hell you made, assholes.

BY THE TIME WE HIT HOLLYWOOD, the sky has stopped puking ocean down on our heads. The streets are choked with dying fish and colorful stones. I don't think there's a car windshield or store window left intact anywhere in Southern California. Traven steers around the worst of it as well as he can with a cracked windshield, heading for Allegra's clinic.

"I thought you had a falling-out with the woman who runs the clinic."

"Allegra might be pissed but she won't let anything happen to Candy."

Traven carries her out of the car while I pound on the clinic door until they open it. Fairuza looks out and lets Traven inside. I stay in the parking lot.

Traven comes out a few minutes later.

"They say it's a common drug. She'll be fine," he says.

"Thanks."

"What happens now?"

"You mean what does a person do after car chases, arson, and their first kill?"

Traven looks out into the street. Some of the fish are still alive, gasping for breath on the sidewalk. He'd like to save every one of them.

"Even if you're in the right, how do you cope with it?"

I shrug. It hurts.

"Drinking helps."

He looks at himself in the clinic windows. I know the move. He's checking to see if he's still him.

"You jumped on a flying saucer today, Father. You're on a whole other planet now."

"That's exactly how it feels."

"There's no going back. You know that, don't you? You can't unsee or unknow any of this."

"I wouldn't if I could. I didn't just translate books because I had an aptitude for it. I did it hoping that one or two might reveal some deeper truth. That somehow my work would benefit people. These last few days . . ."

"I know. Truth can kick your ass. You know the Greek word for 'revelation,' right?"

"*Apokálypsis.*"

"Apocalypse. The truth shall set you free, but not before blowing your brain to Rice Krispie Treats."

"Would you like to get a drink?"

"Yeah. But tomorrow. I have one more stop to make before this thing is over."

"Are you going after Aelita?"

"No. She'll be long gone with the 8 Ball. I'm seeing someone who owes me a favor."

"Do you want some company?"

"This one I have to do on my own. But I'd be grateful for a ride back to the Chateau."

The Metro's windshield is too far gone. Traven and I kick it out of the frame and throw it in a Dumpster at the back of the lot. We don't talk on the ride across town. My chest hurts like I was hit by a cruise missile, but I'm not spitting up blood. Kasabian is asleep on the couch when I get back. A big metal dog curled up and surrounded by beer cans. I lie down and nap in bed for a couple of hours. When I wake up, I change clothes, get on the Hellion hog, and head downtown.

THE BRADBURY BUILDING is an Art Deco beauty in one of the amnesic parts of town that can't remember whether it wanted to be a neighborhood or a tourist wasteland and now isn't quite either. Once upon a time I killed a vampire named Eleanor near here. Her family was the one I locked in the Chateau Marmont with a roomful of zombies. Now I'm back here again, not starting trouble but trying to end it.

I park the bike on a pile of dead fish. The sky flickers like a lightning storm but there's no thunder.

The Bradbury Building is closed up tight but I jimmy the lock with the black blade. Silent motion-sensor alarms will go off the moment I'm inside. I'm sure the cops will rush right over after they dig out their squad cars from under all the rocks and carp. Even if they come, they'll never find me where I'm going.

I get in one of the ornate wrought-iron elevators and press the buttons for the first and third floors simultaneously. The elevator rises to the thirteenth floor in a building that only has five.

I get out and walk to Mr. Muninn's antiques shop. The door is unlocked. Go through the store, out the back exit, and down hundreds of feet of bare stone steps into a cavern below the city.

"Mr. Muninn!" I yell. "Olly olly oxen free."

Mr. Muninn comes out from behind a Russian icon-style portrait of a king from a country that hasn't existed for two ice ages.

"I didn't expect you to come in that way. I'm so used to you appearing out of the shadows."

"That's Saint James's trick these days. I just break into buildings and ride the Wonkavator to places that aren't there."

"It sounds like more fun when you say it."

Muninn's cavern is maybe the biggest antiques shop, curiosity cabinet, and junkyard in the universe. Shelves and tables sag under his crazy trinkets. Helmets and ancient weapons enough to take on Hannibal. Acres of old coins and endless galleries of paintings, jewelry, potions, *karakuri,* and old books. Piles of what look like dinosaur bones beside a moored zeppelin. Like a raven, he's been plucking shiny pieces of this and that and hiding them in his lair for aeons. Maybe that's why he goes by a raven's name.

"I thought you might come to see me before this."

"That was the plan but there was this ancient god and a whole Apocalypse thing happening. Maybe you heard about it."

"I wouldn't worry. You saved the dreamers. In a few days, they'll take control of reality from the safety of their slumber and the sky will be blue and the world will be made beautiful again."

"Make that brown skies, panhandlers, and things getting back to passable and I'll believe you."

"Always the optimist."

I lean on a table and knock over piles of Confederate money.

"Sorry." Then, "You lied to me, Mr. Muninn. This whole time. And I trusted you."

"I know. And I have no excuses, just an explanation. I was afraid. To break down from one mind to five is troubling enough but then my own brother, Ruach, let Aelita kill brother Neshamah to save himself. It was too much to take. I don't even know where my other two brothers are."

He picks up a pile of gold Minoan coins and tosses them through the eye socket of a pterodactyl skull. A nervous tic.

"I've been down here and away from family squabbles since the world was young and I had hoped to stay here for eternity. But that's not going to happen, is it?"

I shrug.

"That all depends on you. You asked me to take the singularity to one of your brothers in Hell. You said you'd owe me a favor. I made the delivery and now I'm calling in the favor. That's if you're willing to keep your part of the bargain."

"Do you have the singularity with you?"

"No. It's somewhere safe. I'll keep it for now. If I get bored, maybe I'll start a new universe, just like the Angra Om Ya."

"I know Father Traven told you the story. Would you like to hear my side of it?"

"Yes. But not right this minute. I took some bullets today, and don't tell anyone, but they still hurt."

"Would you like me to take them out for you?"

"Sure. Later. Right now I want to get the other thing settled. Are you willing to do me the favor you promised?"

"Yes."

"I think you know what it is."

"I suspect so."

I walk over to him, passing a table piled with old Hollywood head shots and shattered pieces of the Druj Ammun seal.

"I don't care if you didn't really create the universe. You still made the souls. There are a lot of them Downtown that could use someone to keep an eye on them better than Hellions can. The Hellions aren't doing all that well themselves. They're killing each other when they aren't killing themselves. Hellions are your children too, right? They can both use the kind of help a half-assed Lucifer like me can't give them."

"And you think I have the right experience to be Lucifer? I'm not sure if I should be flattered or hurt."

"You're a deity. At least you have something to work from. I was just playing free jazz. You really need to take the job. If I go back to Hell, I'll never leave and Hell will burn without a Lucifer."

He looks away and throws the last of the coins in the air. They hang there before falling on the table in a neat stack.

"Of course I'll go. A bargain is a bargain. But you must do something for me first."

"What?"

"Forgive the part of you you call Saint James."

"Forget it. He's a useless Pat Boone twerp with a bad case of poor poor pitiful me. I'm always the bad guy and he's always the victim. Forget it. He left. He can stay left."

"Are you sure that's how you want it?"

"I have the armor. I don't need him."

"But you just appointed me Lucifer. The armor is mine."

I hadn't thought of that.

"He left. I don't beg favors."

"You don't have to. Just tell me, would you like to be whole and complete again?"

"Are you God or Dear Abby?"

"You're avoiding the question because the answer is yes and you're too proud and hurt to say it."

"Bullshit."

"You can't lie to me, James. I'm God."

"Fine. Sure. I'd like to be one big slice of apple pie but I'm not kissing Saint James's ass."

"You don't have to. While you were talking I reintegrated you."

I look at my hands.

"Bullshit. If he was back in my head, he'd be screaming. I don't feel any different."

"Which is exactly as it should be. When you're whole, it's not necessary to think about yourself as whole. You simply are."

"Cool it with the koans. Wild Bill is my Buddhism adviser."

I look at myself in an old mirrored shield.

"I don't know how I feel about this."

"Of course you do. You're angry. You're always angry with me. God tricked you again. But let me remind you of something. I still am God and there are certain things I can and will do for the good of my children, including you. You're whole because it's necessary for you to be whole and there's nothing you or Lucifer or Sandman Slim can do about it."

"See? You do have the right attitude to be a good Lucifer."

Mr. Muninn walks to an old L.A. Red Car and steps inside.

"I'll miss my collection."

"It's not going anywhere."

"I'll miss my solitude."

"I got very big on delegating Lucifer's duties at the end. Keep the same policy and have all the solitude you want. Trust me. You don't want to sit around working out budget projections for the next thousand years."

He steps out of the Red Car and perches on a Persian hoodoo carpet hovering three feet off the ground.

"One last thing before I go. Do you forgive me for deceiving you all this time?"

"Sure. Do you forgive me for being a loudmouth asshole Abomination?"

He holds up a hand. Shakes his head.

"You're only an Abomination to Aelita and her ilk. You're simply James Stark to me. Not nephilim or monster. Just Stark."

"Your brother Neshamah told me his name. What's yours?"

"Can't we stick with Muninn? It's the name I prefer."

"Muninn it is."

"I suppose it's time for me to be going."

I touch my chest. Lucifer's armor is gone. I look at Mr. Muninn and he's wearing it. It looks funny strapped to his round body.

"That's a good look for you," I lie.

He raps his knuckles on the metal.

"I haven't worn armor since the war with Lucifer. Now here I am wearing his, preparing to become him. Even I couldn't have predicted that."

"It'll get the groundlings' attention when you walk in like that."

He looks strange. Like he's made of dense smoke.

"Will you come and visit?"

I feel a familiar weight inside my chest. The Key is back inside me.

"I'll come down. Take care of yourself and Wild Bill for me. One last thing. If you were going to hide a stolen soul, where would you put it?"

He thinks for a few seconds.

"The Guff. The hall of souls. Where new souls wait to be born into bodies."

"Someone stole Tuatha Fortune's. Normally I wouldn't care about the Augur's family troubles but that seems kind of harsh even for rich bastards. If you happen to find Tuatha's soul under the sofa cushions, maybe you could send it home."

"I'll see what I can do. Take care, James."

"You too, Mr. Muninn."

The smoke drifts apart like parting fog and Mr. Muninn is gone. There's something in my hand. Three deformed bullets. I open my shirt. No holes. No pain.

I step through a shadow and into the Room of Thirteen Doors. It's as cool and silent and perfect as I remember. I go through the Door of Ice, the portal to neutral places, and out into the street. I push the Hellion hog into Muninn's cavern for safekeeping. I don't know if I can ride it once reality gets back to normal. If I can't, I think Mr. Muninn would like it in his collection.

I step back into a shadow, feeling at home again. I can't hear Saint James in my head, but with luck, he feels it too.

I COME OUT OF A SHADOW in the hallway in the Chateau with the grandfather clock. I step through. Kasabian is watching *Major Dundee* on the big screen. He glances over his shoulder when I come in then turns back to the screen.

"I think we'll have to clear out of here soon."

"When?"

"Not until they figure out I'm not Macheath anymore. A few days. Maybe a week. I don't know."

He nods, not taking his eyes off the screen.

"I had a feeling this was too good to be true. Okay. They haven't sent up any food for a while. Tell them to bring a few carts. Start stockpiling so we can take it with us when we get the bum's rush."

I sit on the arm of the leather sofa, suddenly very tired.

"I can't keep doing this. Saving the world and ending up broke and homeless."

Kasabian crushes a beer can in one of his hellhound hands and opens another one-handed. Neat trick.

"Speak for yourself," he says. "I've got my future locked. Between the Codex, your magic eyeball, and the Hellion translator you said you're getting, I'm going to become the biggest medium on the Web. I can actually see into Hell, which is where most people's asshole relatives are going to be. Isn't that something? I'll be the only honest online psychic in the world. I'll make a fortune."

"Yeah. Telling people their loved ones are burning in eternal hellfire will have the money rolling in."

He nods his head from side to side.

"Well, I might have to leave out a few details. Shave the truth a bit. I already know how to do that."

"Good. Then I'll move back in; we'll use the rest of the money to fix up the store and reopen."

"Slow down, Seabiscuit. I don't even have a site yet."

"We'll fix the store or you can give me my money back."

"It's my money."

"We'll see."

I get a bottle of Aqua Regia. Light a Malediction and dial the clinic to check on Candy. No one answers. I dial again.

BAMBOO HOUSE OF DOLLS is crowded. Packed in like cavity-search close. Just like the old days. I don't know why I'm surprised. It always works this way. A little mayhem. A touch of homicide without too many casualties. Just enough to give you a good story. And the Bamboo House is on the map again. Home sweet home.

"Here's to two weeks under the radar," says Candy, holding up a glass of Jack Daniel's.

I clink my glass against hers.

"They haven't tossed your asses out of the Marmont yet?" says Carlos.

His arm is still in a sling but it's not his pouring arm, so who cares?

"Not yet," Candy says.

"I have a feeling Mr. Muninn has something to do with it. I don't know how long the ride will last but I'm ready to go till the wheels come off."

Candy brightens.

"You ought to take a night off and come over," she says to Carlos. "I'll make dinner. And by 'make dinner,' I mean I'll call down for enough food to sink the Titanic."

"It's a date," says Carlos, and he pours us another round of Jack.

Father Traven pushes his way inside. He looks a little overwhelmed. I wonder if he thinks every bar is like Bamboo House. Will he be disappointed the first time he goes to a civilian one?

"Hey, Father. Damned anyone today?"

He smiles.

"Not a single soul."

"The night is young. How are you holding up?"

He shrugs. Takes a sip of red wine.

"Fine. Still processing it all. The newspapers are saying that the Osterberg family had investments in the defense industry and that his death is being investigated as a possible instance of domestic terrorism. Apparently Homeland Security is involved."

I put my Kissi arm around his shoulders. I have long sleeves and a glove on so he doesn't have to look.

"Don't sweat it. I used to do jobs for them. They're looking for guys in ski masks, not a priest and some monsters. We're not even on their radar."

"I hope you're right."

He turns and looks over the crowd.

Blue-skinned Luderes are gambling at a table near the jukebox. Manimal Mike and his vucari cousins sit with a bunch of Nahuals trading shots of expensive tequila and cheap vodka. Shape-shifters, gloomy necromancers, and club kids dressed like electric peacocks slow-dance to Bob Wills and the Texas Playboys doing "Blues for Dixie."

"What if someone got my license-plate number coming down the hill?"

"When would they do that? When they were being knocked stupid by rocks or buried under flying sharks? Relax and have a drink."

He takes another sip of wine.

"So your angel, Aelita, seems to be behind everything that's happened. How tragic that she chose that particular vengeful ghost."

"I don't see it that way."

Carlos looks as happy as I've seen him in a long time. His brother-in-law is helping out while he's healing. He seems to like having a partner.

"There's nothing tragic or bad luck about it. Aelita doesn't make mistakes like that. She knew who the Imp was."

"She deliberately let loose a piece of the Angra Om Ya in this world? Why?"

"To help her kill God. I figure that she can't do it on her own. Why else would she leave the Qomrama in Hell? She got lucky when she killed Neshamah, but she doesn't really know how to use it. The Angra do."

Traven picks up a single peanut from the coconut bowls full of them.

"Why would she invite entities that can destroy the universe? Presumably, she'd be destroyed too."

"You said it yourself. God made an offering that tricked the Angra into another dimension. Maybe she has that or knows how to do it. She brings the Angra in, uses them, and sends them on their merry way. It's exactly how she likes to work."

"How do you know all this?"

I shrug. I don't want to tell him that Saint James and I are dating again and that he's probably the one who figured it out and I'm just taking credit.

"It's the only logical thing."

"So this isn't over."

"This is just getting started."

Brigitte wobbles by. She's more than a little drunk. She opens her mouth in exaggerated silent-movie surprise when she sees me. "I couldn't find you in this madhouse. I heard that you took care of Teddy once and for all."

I nod.

"He's dead, burned, and gone. Hallelujah."

"Thank you," she says.

She looks at Traven.

"Who is your friend? You haven't introduced us."

"This is Father Traven. He saved my ass when we were at Teddy's. Father Traven, this is Brigitte Bardo."

He puts out his hand. She smiles at his politeness and how he obviously has no idea who she is.

"Very nice to meet you. Please call me Liam."

"A father, eh, Liam? I've played nuns in many of my movies."

"Really? You're an actress. Can I find your movies in stores? I've just started watching movies."

I shake my head at him.

"Stick to musicals and John Wayne for a while. You're not ready for Brigitte."

I whisper in Brigitte's ear.

"Be nice. He was for real. Not one of your Hollywood hoodoo Holy Rollers."

She touches his arm.

"A past-tense priest? What happened? Did you fall in love with a beautiful woman? A handsome boy?"

"He fell for giant-tentacle bastards from another dimension who want to eat us."

"They sound charming. You must tell me all about them."

The father's eyes shift back and forth between us. I've revealed his darkest secret and he's still standing.

"It's okay, Father. She's one of us. She's probably taken out more monsters than you and me put together."

I nod at Brigitte.

"Ask him about the Via Dolorosa."

She smiles brightly.

"The Stations of the Cross? I did a movie about that too."

"Please tell me about it."

She loops her arm in his and leads him away.

Vidocq is coming my way. Allegra isn't with him. When he reaches me, he clamps me in a big bear hug.

"I hear that I have you to thank for this sore jaw."

"You came at me with a knife and I had to defend my new shirt."

"I don't remember any of it."

At a table, a couple of civilian card sharks are going broke trying to hustle psychics at poker.

"And you won't. That's how it's set up. Bastards get in your head. Play around and pop out and you never have a clue. They tried doing it to me."

"Did it work?"

I shake my head.

"The tinfoil hat I had installed saved me."

He raises a glass of whiskey.

"To the madness we choose. Not the madness others choose for us."

"Is Allegra with you?"

He pats me on the shoulder.

"Give her some time."

"I'm drunk enough to apologize sincerely."

"I'm sure she'd appreciate that. But give her some time."

A succubus slaps a vampire when he bites her throat and makes a face at the taste of her blood. The Bewlay twins are loaded enough that they're transforming other pretty boys into clones of themselves. There's going to be a very confusing orgy somewhere tonight.

"I'm not Lucifer anymore. I did to some poor slob what Samael did to me. Backed him into a corner so he had to take the job."

"And who was this innocent youth?"

"God."

He nods.

"May He learn well how the rest of us feel."

"I need to go out and grab a smoke."

Candy is talking to Brigitte and Traven. I kiss her as I go by and head out the door.

The street is crowded with civilians and Lurkers. I go around the side of the building far enough that there's no streetlight and fire up a Malediction. I feel a little earthquake under my feet. A hole opens in the concrete a few feet away.

"Hi, Cherry," I say. "Thanks for helping out with Teddy."

I go to the edge of the hole and look down. Cherry is a mess. She's lost an arm and a lot of teeth. There are a couple of bullet holes in her skull.

"Thanks for whatever you did to the Imp. She's gone."

"I didn't do anything to her. I set her free and let her make her own choice. My guess is she went home."

"As long as she's gone."

"Agreed."

"Are you fishing for compliments?"

"No. Just thinking about things. Back in Hell, Great-Great-Great-Granddad told me to pick and choose my fights. I agree with him but sometimes it's hard to pick which fights because you don't know what they are until you start. I thought I was Elvis on Ice when I stopped Mason's war with Heaven. But I left all those Hellions worse off because they thought they were going to get free from Hell. Then I come back to L.A. to find Candy off with someone else, Aelita is back, there's a murdering ghost on the loose, and a scar-faced skinhead's looking to kill me all because I cut off a Kissi's head a year ago. He deserved it but that doesn't matter in the big picture. What matters is everything down the line that killing him triggered. But how do you know what bad juju you're shaking loose before you start shaking things up?"

Cherry turns her hollow eye sockets up at me.

"And the point of your eloquent speech?"

"I don't exactly know. Maybe we need to be more careful about the messes we leave behind. Try to tidy things up a bit when the bullets stop flying."

"Maybe you could cut off fewer heads."

"That too. Muninn told me to forgive part of myself, and as much as I hate that healing-your-inner-child yammer, I'm trying. You need to let go and move on. Look at you. You were a sad sight when you were in one piece. Now you're not even a skeleton. Just a sack of random bones. Come out of there. Even if you don't want to pass on entirely, have a little dignity. Be a ghost and not a burrowing bug."

"I am a ghost."

"I mean a real ghost. Ditch the skeleton and do a regular haunting. How about the Lollipop Dolls store? Think of it. A high-end J-pop place with its own ghost. It'll be like *Kwaidan* with pigtails."

She's quiet for a minute. If she had a face, she'd look lost in thought.

"I couldn't just move in. I'd have to ask the girls."

"I hardly know anything about that anime stuff but Candy has a Ph.D. I bet she'd talk to them for you."

"Why are you going out of your way to help me?"

"Because you and me have a past too. You thought I could save you when you were alive and I didn't. I figure getting you out of that hole might make up for that a little."

"Maybe it will," she says. "Have your friend talk to the girls."

"I will. See you around, Cherry."

But she's already gone.

I throw the rest of the cigarette into the hole and start back inside when my phone rings. It's a blocked number. Sure, why not?

It's a man voice this time.

"I haven't seen it myself but I hear you ruined Lucifer's armor."

"God dinged it with a thunderbolt. I put a few bullet holes in it. It gives it character. Like scars."

"From what I hear, you must have some new ones. Did striking yourself with the Gladius leave a mark? Did King Cairo shoot you in the face? Are you terribly disfigured?"

"I'm not Lucifer anymore. I thought that would get me off the hook with your bullshit."

"You hurt me. You're not on the hook. These are fireside chats while I bring you news from far away."

"Thanks, but you can shove your news. I'm done with Hell. I don't care anymore."

"I hear you broke the priest. Poor thing. They're so delicate, aren't they? So confident in your world but they come apart so quickly down here. Still, it's nothing for you to worry about. A mad priest. It's like a gothic romance. Add his to the list of lives you've ruined. But the priest is still walking the Earth, isn't he? So he's only half a demerit. God must be very proud of you. You keep filling our houses with new playmates."

"Here's my final thought to you. Kill yourself. All of you Hellions should kill yourselves. Or murder each other. You're Muninn's problem now."

"How long will it take you to break your new girlfriend? What's her name? Something sweet and simpleminded. Does she know how gruesome you can be?"

"I told her all about what happened in Hell."

"And she's still with you? She must be an exceptional woman."

"She is."

"So was Alice, I suppose. You do seem to go through a lot of them. Exceptional women. Murder isn't your greatest sin. It's being as careless with others' lives as you are with your own. You need to watch that or sooner or later all that will be left are women who'll run from the very sight of a monster like you."

"If you're calling to threaten me, hurry up. I'm going inside and I won't be able to hear you being scary."

"I'm getting better with bodies in your world. I can do more than talk now. Soon I'll walk and drive and look just like anyone else and I can pay you a visit."

"You better get to it, Merihim. When the Angra come back, you're as fucked as the rest of us."

"Clever guess."

"That's exactly what it was. Don't make me tattle on you to Muninn."

I hang up and head back inside.

Candy is dancing to Les Baxter's "Balloon Waltz" with Vidocq. I cut in and he graciously takes a powder just like a real Frenchman. I have no idea how to waltz but I can count to three and I can rock back and forth, and with the bar so packed, that's pretty much what everyone else is doing too.

It's been raining on and off for the last couple of weeks. Not fish rain. The regular stuff. Between the storms, the sky is even blue sometimes. Catalina is back and no one has reported any floating streets or volcanoes in days.

Sometimes I step back and look over everything and wonder how the hell I got here. According to Uriel, my real father, I was always destined for this land of bloody laughs. I'm not human or angel or Lurker or demon. I'm just a natural-born killer. What I don't know is if I'm attracted to places where the worst things are happening or if I bring the shitstorm with me. Until I know, all that matters is that I'm still breathing and I'm dancing with a pretty girl.

The world is going to end when the Angra Om Ya come back. They'll eat the planets and stars. When they hit L.A., they'll get a movie deal with points and a percentage of the merchandising. They'll learn to surf and practice Transcendental Meditation. One of them will OD in the bathroom at the Whisky a Go Go and another will be on the cover of *People,* caught having an affair with the new mayor. The others will develop depression and go home to their gloomy universe. One more set of suckers. One more one-hit wonder. It's a nice little universe you built but what have you done lately? Leave your head shots and our people will call your people. This is L.A. There are so many Apocalypses around here that most don't even make the paper, so be happy yours got any press at all. By the way, Strawberry Alarm Clock is a cool name. Angra Om Ya sounds like a brand of Chinese dog food.

With luck, the Angra won't pass through these parts for another million years. I don't usually get that lucky but I've got Candy, a place to crash, food, and the Key. L.A. might be a tourist-trap province on the outskirts of Hell, but that's okay. At least in this Hell, I'm not alone.